Chaotically
Inappropriate
Magic

Books by Clayton Taylor Wood:

The Runic Series
Runic Awakening
Runic Revelation
Runic Vengeance
Runic Revolt
Runic War

The Fate of Legends Series
Hunter of Legends
Seeker of Legends
Destroyer of Legends
Avenger of Legends

Magic of Havenwood Series
The Magic Collector
The Lost Gemini
The Magic Redeemer

The Magic of Magic Series
Inappropriate Magic
Ridiculously Inappropriate Magic
Ludicrously Inappropriate Magic
Absurdly Inappropriate Magic
Insanely Inappropriate Magic
Chaotically Inappropriate Magic
Furiously Inappropriate Magic
Epically Inappropriate Magic

The Masks of Eternity Series
Elazar the Magician

Chaotically Inappropriate Magic

Book VI of the Magic of Magic Series

Clayton Taylor Wood

Published by Clayton T. Wood.

ISBN: 978-1-948497-28-2

Cover designed by James T. Egan, Bookfly Design, LLC

Printed in the United States of America.

Special thanks to Howie and Nancy, who have a kind of inappropriate magic all their own. And to the hidden magic within each of us, waiting patiently to be found.

DISCLAIMER:

This book contains (chaotically) inappropriate depictions of (chaotically) inappropriate people doing (chaotically) inappropriate things. Including, but certainly not limited to, inappropriate language and very thinly-veiled connotations of the naughty variety.

And of course, (chaotically) inappropriate magic.

Table of Contents

Chaotically Inappropriate Magic

Prologue

When destiny knocked on his son Chaos's door, Chauncy Little decided he'd better answer it for the boy.

He happened to be busy slaving over a hot stovetop at the time, cooking a hearty breakfast for Chaos. The boy was thirteen, technically old enough to cook his own meals without setting himself on fire. But after over a decade of cooking the ol' sausage and eggs for his family, Chauncy had grown quite fond of doing so. And besides, given that Chaos had a habit of being rather spectacularly unpredictable – and having ignited the occasional international incident as a result of said habit – Chauncy had made it one of his life's missions to protect the boy from everything. Especially himself.

For the most part, that meant keeping the boy close, while Chauncy was wearing the Chaos Ring. A magical ring from the Cave of Wonder whose power was to buffer Chaos's magic. Which was to create chaos, naturally. A gift and a curse, as it turned out. For while it made Chaos incredibly powerful, it also made him dangerous to be around, as the great wizard Imperius Fanning could certainly attest to. The last time Chaos's magic went awry, poor Imperius had been struck by an errant meteorite. Which had made home-schooling the boy seem like the responsible choice, all things considered.

Chauncy heard the telltale *thump, thump* of heavy feet coming down the stairs and into the foyer, and looked up from the sizzling sausage to see Chaos shambling into the kitchen, rubbing his eyes wearily. In the nine years since their last adventure together, the boy had shot up considerably, and was at Chauncy's chest-level now. With a shock of messy brown hair that was a bit too long, and a wrinkled orange shirt and pink shorts, he looked true to his name.

"Gah!" Chauncy play-blurted out, flinching away from Chaos. "Oh, whew," he added with a smile. "Thought you were a zombie."

"Ughhnnn," Chaos moaned, not at all playing. He slumped into his chair as usual, not so much as looking Chauncy in the eye. But Chauncy was hardly hurt by this, knowing full-well that Chaos was much like his father, in that he was a little bitch when he was hungry. And – quite *un*like his father – just about every other time as well.

Whump-a-thump, thump-BANG!

Chauncy ignored the awful cacophony coming from the stairs, attending to his sausage and eggs instead. A moment later, another member of the family shambled into the kitchen, looking for all the world like a zombie. Because it was, in fact, a zombie. An utterly gorgeous one, slender and fit, with long, flowing golden-brown hair and perfectly arched eyebrows. And large eyes that would've been awfully pretty if they hadn't been dull and glazed over and such. Even her lips were lovely, save for the bit of zombie-drool dribbling from one side.

"Grarrrrghh," Zora greeted.

"Hey Mrs. Little," Chauncy replied. For she was, in fact, his second wife. Not that he'd ever left his first. Valtora and Zora were both quite happily – if illegally, in Zora's case – married to him. "Still suck at stairs, eh?"

The zombie, of course, didn't reply.

"Not the only thing she sucks at," Chauncy joked rather inappropriately, waggling his eyebrows at Chaos, hoping to get an appropriately disgusted reaction from the boy. He was in the very throes of puberty, after all, and found discussing the subject rather horrifying. But Chaos just sat there, glaring at him. "Here we go," he added, making a plate for the boy, then putting it on the table. Chaos just stared at it glumly. "Eat up," Chauncy prompted. Then he paused. "Wash your hands first," he added. For Chaos had spent a fair amount of time in the bathtub this morning, which for a teenage boy, could only mean one thing.

"I did," Chaos muttered, eyeing his food. Or rather, the steam still rising from it. "Too hot," he complained.

"Blow on it," Chauncy replied. He went to turn back to his sizzling pan…and *shrieked.*

For there, standing before him, was none other than Epic, his youngest son.

"Holy…!" Chauncy blurted out, taking a step back. Epic just stared at him with startlingly silver eyes, which contrasted quite powerfully with his jet-black eyebrows and meticulously slicked-back, jet-black hair. Which, in turn, contrasted with his pale skin. Awfully pale. *Unnaturally* pale.

"Good morning father," he greeted. Which was awfully – and unnaturally – formal for a nine-year-old boy. But that was how Epic was, in addition to being disturbingly stealthy. "Give me breakfast," he ordered, holding out his hands.

"Ask nicely," Chauncy reminded the boy.

"Give me breakfast please," Epic corrected. Which was about as good as Chauncy was going to get. He complied, supplying his somber son with a plate. "Thank you father," Epic stated, going to the table and having a seat. And promptly ate the steaming food without a care about the heat. He was quite a serious boy, Epic was. And formal not just in his speech, but also in the way he dressed. For, starting two years ago, he'd chosen to wear a three-piece gray suit. Every single day.

BAM! BAM! BAM!

Chauncy flinched, turning toward the source of the sound. And saw a nine-year-old girl bounding loudly down the stairs, flinging her wavy hair from side-to-side. She turned the corner, skipping into the kitchen with a huge smile on her face.

"Daddy!" she exclaimed jubilantly, rushing at him.

"Fury!" he cried, kneeling and opening his arms for a hug. She leapt into his arms, giving him the most adorable, heart-melting-est hug a girl could give. "How's my sweet little baby-girl?"

"Sweet and little," she answered, beaming him another smile, her purple eyes twinkling.

"Would my sweet little girl like some breakfast?"

Her eyes went to the sausage and eggs, and she made an instantaneous "ew" face.

"Ew," she replied, confirming the sentiment of said expression.

"Yogurt then?" Chauncy guessed. Her expression brightened instantly.

"Yay!" she exclaimed, for exclaiming was her usual mode of communication. And "yay" was her relationship with pretty much everything, which made her an absolute joy to be around. This made her his absolute favorite child, though he would never admit it to Chaos and Epic. Chauncy had never met someone quite so effervescent, except for his wife Valtora, of course. Who, as fate would have it, came down the stairs and into the kitchen, stifling a yawn with one glittering diamond hand.

"Hey poopy-dooz," Chauncy greeted, puckering up for a kiss.

3

"Hey Chauncy-poo," Valtora replied, providing said kiss. The kind of kiss a respectable couple would never have in front of their impressionable children. The kind of kiss that got a rise out of Chauncy, in fact. But as you're fully aware by now, dearest reader, this was no respectable couple. And therefore they disrespected their children's eyeballs – and peace of mind – with unfettered glee.

"Gross," Chaos muttered, blowing his sausage irritably.

"Aww," Fury exclaimed, clutching her cute little hands to her cute little heart. All while Epic merely ate, not paying his parents any mind. Or rather, his father and stepmom-ish. For while Epic was technically a product of Valtora's original body's loins, he was also technically Zora's son. Which was the least odd thing about the boy, really.

"Hey pop-pop," Valtora greeted Chaos.

"Hmph," Chaos hmphed, glaring at his breakfast. For when he was in a bad mood, he wasn't hungry…and when he was hungry, he was in a bad mood. An unsolvable problem that they'd been forced to face every morning since he'd turned five.

"Mommy!" Fury gasp-exclaimed, rushing to give Valtora some love.

"Good morning mother," Epic piped in dutifully, finishing his meal, then cleaning up, also dutifully. "I followed your destructions," he added. "I want chocolate."

"*In*structions," Chauncy corrected.

"That's what I said," Epic replied. Which was technically a lie. But Epic truly believed it, not being able to tell the difference between the two.

"Oh," Chauncy mumbled, knowing well enough not to fight this fight.

"I want chocolate," Epic repeated. Chauncy considered asking the boy to ask nicely, but decided against it, grabbing a piece and handing it over. Epic went back to the table, sitting down and eating the treat as if it was his grim duty to do so. Which to be fair, was how he did pretty much everything.

It was at this very moment that destiny did its thing, announcing its presence with a fateful knocking at the front door.

"I'll get it," Valtora offered. Which would have changed the course of this particular tale considerably, and almost certainly for the better. But as it was, chivalry got in the way.

4

"Nonsense," Chauncy declared. Chivalrously. "You go eat, my sweet, and let your husband get it."

"My *hero*," Valtora gushed, batting her eyes at him and giving him a kiss.

"Aww," Fury cooed, clutching her hands to her heart for the second time that morning.

Chauncy did his husbandly thing, walking to the door and opening it up. And then stopped dead in his tracks, his eyes widening in surprise.

For there, standing at his doorstep, was a man. An uncomfortably *old* man, slender and stooped, with big knobby hands and a face so wrinkly it was frankly hard to look at. A man with a long white beard and long white hair, carrying a long wooden staff topped with a sparkling blue crystal. He was dressed in an equally blue robe and a blue pointed hat, and had blue eyes that regarded Chauncy rather regally. Which made perfect sense, for the man was a regal person indeed, none other than Imperius Fanning, Arch Wizard of the Order of Mundus...and bestower of wizardly destinies.

"Chauncy Little," Imperius stated in a stately fashion, looking Chauncy up and down. Chauncy blinked, then looked at himself, and realized he was quite nude, save for his chef's apron. A fact that would have made him terribly ashamed nine years ago. But he was a different sort of wizard now, having cast his shame aside. Mostly.

"Imperius," he replied. "Um...are you here for business or pleasure?"

"My business *is* my pleasure," Imperius replied. "Otherwise I wouldn't be in the business of doing it."

"Ah," Chauncy said. "So...destiny's calling I take it?"

"Indeed," Imperius confirmed.

Chauncy took a deep breath in, then nodded, squaring his shoulders and giving Imperius a steely-eyed, slightly squinty look. The kind of gaze a badass hero gave. And also Chauncy.

"Right," he declared heroically. "I'll get dressed."

"No need," Imperius stated. Chauncy blinked.

"Pardon?"

"No need to get dressed,' Imperius clarified. "Destiny's call isn't for you, I'm afraid," he added. "Not this time, anyway."

Chauncy just stared at the man uncomprehendingly.

"Is Chaos home?" the old wizard inquired.

"Huh?"

"Chaos Little," Imperius stated. "Your son. Is he here?"

"Um…yes," Chauncy answered. He frowned, closing the front door behind him, then crossing his arms over his chest. "Why do you ask?"

"I'm here for him," Imperius explained.

"Why?" Chauncy pressed.

"I need to speak with him."

"Why?" Chauncy demanded.

"Destiny calls," Imperius replied. Chauncy's eyes narrowed.

"For Chaos?" he asked incredulously.

"Indeed," Imperius agreed. His expression darkened then, and he stood as tall as his stooped back would allow. "Our world is in grave danger," he warned rather dramatically. "The…"

"But he's only thirteen!" Chauncy interrupted. Imperius glared at him, clearly annoyed at having had his favorite monologue cut short.

"You were ten when I came to your door," he pointed out.

"He can't even take care of himself," Chauncy pressed, glancing back into the kitchen. Chaos was still at the table, blowing on his sausage and eggs, thus helping to prove Chauncy's point. "He still wets the bed!" Chauncy added, which was true. And that wasn't even the worst of it, unfortunately.

"He'll learn," Imperius replied. "As did you, when it was your turn."

"I was thirty-four," Chauncy argued.

"This time, destiny cannot be deferred," Imperius warned. "To do so would be to risk the very fate of the world!" Which, Chauncy knew from Valtora, was a standard destiny-delivering finisher-line.

"Come back in twenty-one years," Chauncy snipped.

"This cannot wait!"

"Uh huh," Chauncy replied. "Worked last time."

"The fate of the…"

"Yeah yeah," Chauncy interrupted. "Heard it all before."

"Chauncy Little!" Imperius scolded. After which Chauncy walked back into the house…and promptly slammed the door in the old wizard's face. And locked it.

There was a *thump*, followed by another *thump*, and then muffled cursing. And then, to his relief, silence. Chauncy sighed, shaking his head, then turning back to the kitchen.

"Who was that?" Valtora called out from the kitchen table.

"Um…just another salesman," he lied. "Wanting to hawk his wares at our shop."

"What was he selling?" Valtora pressed.

"Nothing I was buying," Chauncy answered.

And that, dear reader, was how the end of the world began.

Chapter 1

Now that we've established how things have gone horribly wrong, we'll attend, dear reader, to the story not of Chauncy, but his son. For this particular tale is of a different sort, in that it will only be peripherally concerned with Chauncy, the usual focus of our tales. In short, this is Chaos's destiny, and as such, *he* is our focus, at least for the moment.

That being said, let us commence with Chaos's singular point of view. Which was that, sitting at the kitchen table, blowing for what seemed like forever on his too-hot eggs and sausage, he'd rather be doing anything but.

This sucks, he thought, glaring at his breakfast. The same old breakfast every single frickin' day, part of the same old frickin' routine. He lifted his glare to his father, who came back from whoever he'd been talking to at the front door, dressed – as usual – in his silly chef's apron. And at Mommy, who sat at Fury's left, also as usual.

Everything the same as the day before. The same, same, same.

Chaos blew on his sausage and eggs, then heaved a heavy sigh.

"What's wrong pop-pop?" Mom asked.

"Nothing," Chaos lied. There was no point in trying to explain just how *boring* it all was to him, this dull morning routine. He turned to glance at Epic, dressed as usual in his gray suit and black undershirt. The same clothes Epic wore every day. He was perhaps the boring-est of them all, having never once offered Chaos a surprise.

He felt something hop in his lap, and saw a white cat there. It was Glare, his cat, and the only creature here he didn't mind seeing. He ran a hand down her back, and she turned toward him, pointing her butt at Chauncy. Who promptly made a face, avoiding eye contact. For Glare's butthole had a tendency to open up and reveal an extraordinarily irritated-looking eyeball...which was the very reason that Chaos had chosen her from Devorah Doverah's dozen feline companions.

"Get down," Dad scolded, making a threatening motion at the cat, who promptly leapt off Chaos's lap.

Chaos sighed again, twiddling his eggs and sausage with his fork glumly, knowing that the best part of his day had already passed, when he'd taken his bath. One that, not to be *too* graphic, had also involved the twiddling of eggs and sausage, previously covered by his cat.

"Don't play with your food," Dad chided.

"Every other animal does," Chaos argued. Mom's eyes immediately lit up.

"He's got a point," she stated, taking Chaos's side.

"Honey..." Dad began.

"But only predators," Mom continued, switching sides. "And they do it *before* they kill it and eat it."

"Right," Dad replied, "So..."

"But what better way to enjoy your food than to play with it?" she continued cheerily, building up the argument nicely. Mom was honestly the only not-boring person in Chaos's family, except for Fury sometimes. Even Chaos couldn't be sure what Mom would do next, which was awfully refreshing. Because everyone else was awfully predictable. And what's more, they seemed to actually *enjoy* living this awful way.

"How about by tasting it?" Dad shot back, clearly irritated at her now. Which was odd, because he rarely *was* irritated with her. Chaos perked up at this change in the morning routine, eyeing Dad curiously.

"Why can't he do both?" Mom pressed, undeterred by her husband's unexpected mood.

"He isn't," Dad snipped.

"I don't want it," Chaos grumbled, shoving the plate away.

"Then starve," Dad snapped. Which was quite unlike his dad. So while Dad's sour mood was irritating, the novelty of it was entertaining. Chaos naturally decided to take a stroll down this metaphorical road to see where it went.

"I'd rather starve than eat *this*," he declared, shoving the plate away further, almost to the center of the table.

"Gasp!" Mom gasped, putting a hand to her mouth. She glared at Chaos. "Say sorry pop-pop!"

"No," Chaos replied, stirring up the pot a bit more.

"You'd better," Dad warned, upping the ante right back.

"Why?" Chaos inquired, upping it in turn. "What're you gonna do about it?" he sneered, taking it to the extreme.

"Now listen here you little…" Dad began.

"Shit," Mom swore, bolting up from her chair. "We're gonna be late to open the shop!"

Chaos perked up even further, the thought of the day's normal flow being disrupted tantalizing indeed.

"We'll make it," Dad assured, causing Chaos to slump back into his usual position. "Come on everyone," Dad prompted, promptly removing his chef's apron and hanging it up. Which gave Chaos an unfortunate view of what was hanging down. Particularly given the presence of a certain demonic mod named Tip, the presence of which Dad had never deigned to explain.

"Dad!" Chaos complained, averting his gaze.

"Pee-pee!" Fury exclaimed with typical glee, pointing at Dad's decked-out weenie. Dad ignored all of them, going upstairs to get dressed, then coming down in his usual uniform. A purple, sparkly wizard's robe, Staff of Wind in his right hand.

The same uniform every day, everything done the same exact way. For Chaos's life consisted of waking up, eating breakfast, walking to the shop, studying while Mom and Dad worked, then going home for dinner, then to bed. Week after week, month after month, year after year. In fact, the last time he'd done anything else was when he'd been four, and gone on an adventure to save…well, himself, really. And the rest of his family, peripherally. It'd been the single most exciting time of his life, save for when he'd been three, and single-handedly destroy that awful white cube and helped defeat the president of Evermore.

Good times, but far too few, and far too long ago.

"To the shop, family!" Chauncy exclaimed.

"Yay!" Fury cried, hopping off Mom's lap and rushing to her father's side. For unlike Chaos, no matter how many times she did something, it was always as exciting as the first time. Epic said nothing, walking dutifully to the door. Zora followed behind her son, shambling in her usual fashion.

"Yay," Chaos muttered, standing from his chair and shambling after his family. In a remarkably similar way as Zora, in fact. Which made perfect sense; he felt precisely as if he was a zombie, going through the motions of living long after he'd stopped really living. Dad turned to shoot him another venomous glare.

10

"We'll talk later," he vowed ominously. Chaos didn't reply, but felt a thrill at the prospect of going toe-to-toe with his father, some nebulous time in the future.

So it was that Dad led them all out of the house, down the front steps of the porch, and then rightward along the sidewalk toward the center of the city of Southwick. Another boring day in Borrin. A day like any other, or so Chaos assumed. But as fate would have it, this particular day would soon prove anything *but* boring…and soon, he would leave Borrin behind.

For as Chauncy Little should have known all too well, deferring destiny was a dangerous act indeed. An act that, in this particular instance, would prove not just dangerous…but downright deadly.

* * *

The Little's family shop was located in downtown Southwick, on the far side of a circular courtyard of perfectly manicured grass. And a statue of one Archibald Merrick, the founder of the city, and of the Evermore Trading Company. Chaos watched from the very back of the family line as Mom reached the statue, dutifully punching it with her diamond fist. As she did every day, to the same effect. Which was to cackle, then snuggle against Dad's shoulder. They continued their usual route to the sidewalk, looking both ways for oncoming carriages, then crossing the street as a family. Up to the front door of A Little Magic, a store founded by Chaos's grandmother, who he'd never met. Dad produced a key, then unlocked the door, then put his shoulder into it to pop it open, as per the usual.

"After you, m'Lady," Dad told Mom.

"My *hero*," Mom replied, on cue.

Into the shop they went, Chaos again taking the rear. Mom got the broom from the closet, and it was Epic who swept the floor clean. A job that'd used to be Dad's, then Chaos's. But while Chaos had bored of the task, Epic seemed to enjoy it immensely, obsessively cleaning every last dust bunny from the shop. In a kind of grim, terribly earnest sort of way, as if it were his sworn duty to do so. Chaos didn't even bother to watch, knowing that he would never be able to understand his strange half-brother. For Epic seemed for all the world to be half-zombie, with Zora as his mother. The boy was like a little grownup, always serious and stiff and a total slave to his routines.

11

"Chaos," Dad prompted, in a tone that promised a grave discussion. "We need to talk."

This was, of course, something that would cause a normal son to suffer a twang of terror in his testicles, and to dread the coming conversation. But Chaos was no normal boy, and as such, the prospect of a dramatic interaction was, for him, an exciting thing. So much so, in fact, that he took his time in shambling behind the counter to his father, not so as to defer pain, but rather to prolong the anticipation. For, as he'd discovered quite early in his few years of being alive, anticipation of a thing was most often far more enjoyable than the thing being anticipated. As such, he drew it out for as long as he possibly could…much like he'd done while enjoying himself during that morning's bath.

At length, he reached his father's side, and Dad glared down at him.

"I spend a lot of time making you breakfast," he began.

"A few minutes," Chaos replied. Accurately.

"At least I make an effort to make you happy," Dad compromised. Which was true enough. But Chaos sensed an opportunity to increase the drama, and took it as he often did.

"It's your job," he retorted. Also accurately. But insultingly at the same time.

"I don't *have* to make you breakfast," Dad argued.

"If you didn't, you'd be a bad dad," Chaos pointed out.

"And you'd be a bad son if you weren't grateful," Dad argued. Which basically told Chaos he was, in fact, exactly that. Chaos glared at him.

"So now I'm a bad son," he stated. Which was perhaps accurate, but more entertaining than being good. For being good meant being predictable, by listening to rules and such. By acting the same every day, by doing what was expected of him all the time. Ho hum. Hum drum. Until he frickin' died.

"You could be better," Dad argued.

"I'd rather die," Chaos replied. Which wasn't technically true, but was quite satisfactorily dramatic. Dad rolled his eyes.

"Stop saying that," he protested. "People will start believing you."

"Good," Chaos stated, even though it wasn't. "Because I *mean* it," he added, just for the heck of it. Dad opened his mouth to reply, almost certainly in anger. And Chaos hoped that he did. But instead, Dad closed his eyes, took a deep breath in, and behaved himself, to Chaos's chagrin.

"Why are you acting like this?" Dad inquired, with a fake calm that rubbed Chaos the wrong way. Chaos said nothing in reply, which was rude. Dad waited. And waited. And waited some more. But still Chaos said nothing, which made the veins on Dad's temples bulge. "You know what?" he snapped, pointing at the door. "You can walk home and be all by yourself if that's how you wanna act."

"Fine," Chaos replied. "Works for me."

"And for me," Dad declared. "If you're going to act like this, I'd rather not have you around."

"*Bye*," Chaos snipped, turning and stomping toward the door.

"Hope to see you soon," Dad called out after him, with remarkable insincerity.

Chaos reached the door, pulling it open with a big ol' *dong*, then slammed it behind him so it rattled. And then stopped in his tracks, for to his great surprise, there was someone in front of the shop. A old man. A *very* old man. One tall and stooped, dressed in a blue pointy hat, a blue cloak, and wielding an impressive staff. The old man eyed Chaos, stroking his long white beard with his free hand.

"Imperius Fanning!" Chaos gasped, his jaw dropping in surprise. For the great Arch Wizard of the Order of Mundus was quite literally the last person he'd expected to see. Today or any other day, for that matter.

"If it isn't Chaos Little," Imperius replied. "It appears that I'm right on time, as usual."

Chaos just stood there, gawking at the wizard, feeling a burst of joy at this marvelous surprise.

"You're wondering why I'm here," Imperius stated.

"Well yeah," Chaos replied. Imperius knitted his bushy white brows, scowling down at him in an imperious fashion.

"Our world is in grave danger," the great wizard warned, his tone darkening dramatically. "A great villain is destined to rise, and will bring death and destruction to all the land. If you do not meet your destiny in the darkest depths of Grissam, they will destroy everything you know and love!"

Chaos blinked.

"Huh?" he asked. For he hadn't really been paying attention. Imperius grimaced, clearly irritated that his monologue had not been given the attention it'd deserved. Still, he repeated said monologue, and this time Chaos attended to it with more care. And then frowned, furrowing his own eyebrows.

"Who?" he asked.

"Who what?" Imperius counter-asked.

"Who's the villain?"

Imperius paused.

"I don't know," he admitted. Chaos crossed his arms over his chest.

"Then how do you know any of this is going to happen?" he pressed.

"My gut tells me," Imperius explained. "It's magic...and it's right every time."

"Oh," Chaos replied. "Makes sense." He paused. "What's Grissam?"

"A country far south of here," Imperius replied. "Where your mother was born, in fact."

"Oh," Chaos repeated. "So...how do I, uh, get there?"

"By going far south of here," Imperius answered. Which was the obvious, but not terribly specific, answer.

"My dad will never let me go," Chaos stated. "He doesn't trust me to use my magic yet."

"You'll never learn to use it by not using it," Imperius pointed out. "There is a time in every boy's life where he must defy his parents and forge his own path," he added. "And *now* is that time for you, irrespective of your father's wrath."

"Yeah, but am I really forging my own path if I'm just doing whatever you're telling me to do?" Chaos asked. Which was a really good question if he said so himself.

"I told you to meet your destiny," Imperius replied. "The path you take to it is up to you."

And with that, Imperius vanished into a burst of blue sparkles, which fell to the street and faded away. Which left Chaos alone on the steps of A Little Magic, feeling marvelous indeed. His day had started like every other day, and he'd fully expected it to end in the same predictable way. But as fate would have it, there was far more in store for him than he'd ever imagined possible.

A grand surprise...something Imperius had decided to call his destiny. A future that not even Imperius could see, but could only guess at. An honest-to-god *mystery*.

"Grissam," he murmured, a little thrill running through him.

He stepped onto the street, walking for a bit, then turning south down the main street leading to the massive silver doors set into the massive, two-hundred-foot-tall wall separating Borrin from the kingdom of Pravus. It was the Gate, the only entrance into the magical kingdom. Doors that only King Pravus could open...or a wizard.

I'm a wizard, he thought, breaking into a smile.

If Grissam was far south of here, then it had to be even farther south than Pravus, which was south of Southwick. Which meant that Chaos would have to travel all the way *across* Pravus...a distance not even his father had ever traversed. It would take a map, food stores, water, sensible clothes, and considerable planning to make such a journey.

He eyed the Gate, then turned to look north, across the courtyard in the direction of his house. To walk all the way there, get all that stuff, then walk all the way back would be a lot of work. *Too* much work. The mere thought of getting all that stuff and doing all that planning was exhausting to him. So instead, he turned back to the Gate, breaking out into another grin.

Nah, he decided. *I'll wing it.*

So, sticking with the plan of not having a plan, Chaos stuffed his hands in his pockets and starting walking toward the Gate. Yes, he would meet his destiny, just as Imperius had asked him to. After all, the old man's magical gut was to be trusted, and to defy it would be disastrous, for Chaos's family if not for him.

But by golly, he was gonna do it *his* way.

Chapter 2

Chaos strolled down the street toward the silver double-doors of the Gate, still gripped by that special thrill bestowed by the spirit of adventure. And while he'd trudged toward his soul-crushing day at A Little Magic with a slumping over of the shoulders and with his eyes downcast, now his shoulders were firmly pulled back, his eyes lifted to gaze at his destination. He even smiled at passers-by as he passed them by, which made them smile in return. Most of them, anyway; a few eyed his happiness with suspicion, which said more about them than about him.

In any case, he soon found himself nearing his destination, and slowed, then stopped, gazing up at the fabled double-doors. While a part of him yearned to rush through, the better part of him wanted to draw this out. Anticipation, after all, was the good stuff.

So he stood there, gazing at the doors. The sun shone on them, throwing the countless carvings on their surface in stark relief. He smiled at them, wondering what lay beyond them. Not the inevitable road and the grass and trees and such, for this was pretty much the same everywhere, at least in his experience. No, it was what might *happen* after he ventured through the Gate that excited him so.

"Can I help you?" a gruff voice asked. A voice that didn't seem to want to help him at all. Chaos turned his head, realizing that a city guard was staring at him. Or rather *glaring* at him, with arms crossed over an armored chest.

"Nope," Chaos replied. Because it was true. "No thank you," he added, remembering to be polite. Still, he was irritated that the guard had interrupted his enjoyment of this moment, the thrill before the opening of the Gate's magical double-doors. The beginning of the solving of a mystery, the very start of a grand...

"Step back," the guard ordered wearily.

"Huh?"

"Step back," the guard repeated. "No tourists beyond this point."

"Oh, I'm not a tourist," he replied. "I live here."

"Oh," the guard replied, his stony expression not changing. "Well in that case, no *citizens* beyond this point."

"But I have to go through," Chaos stated, gesturing at the doors.

"Good luck with that," the guard replied dryly. "Doors are magically locked."

"I know," Chaos stated. "I can unlock them."

"Yeah right," the guard grumbled.

"I can," Chaos insisted. "I'm a wizard," he revealed rather proudly. For it was a rare thing to be, at least in Borrin.

"Uh huh," the guard replied. "Get lost kid."

"I *can* unlock them," Chaos insisted, getting a bit more annoyed. "Watch," he added, stepping forward. But the guard stopped him with an outstretched arm.

"I said get lost," the man stated menacingly.

"I'm a wizard," Chaos insisted. "I have to get through. It's my destiny," he added.

"Right."

"It's true," Chaos stated. "Imperius Fanning himself said so."

"That's what they all say," the guard complained. "Every last kid who comes to the Gate. 'Imperius sent me. I'm a wizard. Let me through, I'm the *chosen* one,'" he added with a pair of rather rude air quotes.

"But…"

"I said beat it, kid!" the guard snapped, shoving Chaos back. Chaos stumbled, then fell onto his butt on the pavement, his buttocks smarting with the blow. He glared at the guard, his irritation turning to anger.

"Asshole," he spat.

"Asshat," the guard shot back. Chaos got to his feet, clenching his fists.

"Lemme *through*," he commanded, striding forward.

"Come at me and you'll spend a night in the city jail," the guard warned. He smirked. "Soft little boy like you is gonna be *real* popular in there, believe me," he added. Whatever the heck that meant.

"I'm not soft, I'm hard," Chaos replied. "And if you don't let me through, I'm gonna have to show you just how hard I can be!" For it occurred to Chaos that, being far from the shop – and therefore far from his father's Chaos Ring – he now had the ability

17

to use his magic. Something he hadn't been able to do in years, actually. Ever since returning from his last adventure, when his magic had inadvertently attempted to murder the Arch Wizard of the Order of Mundus.

"Go home kid," the guard ordered.

"Fine," Chaos replied, smoothing out the wrinkles in his pants, then lifting his hands to wiggle his fingers at the man. "Face my magic, moron!"

The guard rolled his eyes…just as Chaos concentrated, willing the universe to give him a surprise. Chaos felt a *shift*, as if the grand order of the universe had just been mixed up, a tiny, teeny, little itsy bit.

"Surprise!" he cried, which was his magical exclamation, in lieu of abracadabra or ka-zam or such.

The guard stood there, arching an eyebrow at him. Chaos smirked, lowering his hands to his sides. But to his surprise, nothing seemed to happen. Which wasn't exactly the surprise he'd been hoping for.

"Wow," the guard breathed sarcastically, even putting his hands to his cheeks in feigned surprise. "You really *are* a wizard."

Chaos grimaced, his cheeks flushing.

"I *am*," he insisted. "Let me touch the door and it'll open, I'm telling the truth!"

"Bye bye," the guard said, waving at him disrespectfully.

Chaos shot the man a dirty look. And if looks could kill, the man would have surely died on the spot, and not well. It would've been a particularly messy death to be sure. But alas, deadly glares were Bloodshot's specialty, not his. So, with no choice in the matter, Chaos turned away from the guard – and the Gate – trudging back the way he came.

"Frickin' stupid piece of *crap*," he swore. To which an adult gave him a nasty look. He ignored said look, stuffing his hands in his pants pockets and walking back toward the shop. Anger soon turned to depression, however. For in addition to having been rebuffed, he'd tried using his magic…and it'd failed him. Maybe after years of not using his powers, they'd grown weaker. Or maybe they were gone. Permanently.

The thought was terribly depressing, and Chaos felt glum indeed as he continued down the wide street. He immediately began to blame his parents. After all, they'd forbid him from using his powers ever since he was four, and had forced him to be around the Chaos Ring to ensure that any attempt at magicking would fail. Thus he'd been kept safe from the chaos his magic inevitably created, and his family had been kept safe too. Excruciatingly so.

And now his magic was gone, and his mission had failed before it'd even had a chance to begin. His destiny, it appeared, was to never meet his destiny. This was it. The end.

Thunk.

The sound echoed through the city, but its origin was from behind. Chaos stopped, then turned, seeing the silver double-doors as before. Except this time, one of them swung inward just a bit, to the surprise and consternation of the guard who'd denied him. And through that open door, a figure stepped.

It was a woman, Chaos realized. Tall and slender, she had long blond hair that extended all the way to her butt, and eyes as blue as the cloudless sky. She wore a dress so white that it seemed to glow in the sunlight, one both simple and at the same time elegant. She smiled at the guard gawking at her, then stepped around him, continuing forward toward Chaos. Who stood there gawking as well. She seemed familiar somehow, although why, he couldn't say. But when she spotted him standing there, her smile broadened.

"Chaos!" she exclaimed, walking a bit faster toward him, her eyes sparkling with joy. He blinked, taken aback. But before he could react, she'd reached him, and embraced him in a warm embrace. One that felt like a comfy blanket wrapped around him, safe and wonderful and warm and just…nice. He found himself hugging her back.

"Um…hi?" he replied. She pulled away, beaming at him.

"It's okay," she told him. "I understand why you wouldn't recognize me. You don't need to be ashamed."

"I'm not," he replied automatically. Which was a lie.

"I'm Olivia," she told him. "Addie's oldest daughter. I knew you when you were three."

Chaos's eyes widened.

"Olivia!" he exclaimed, remembering her now. "What're you doing here?" For after helping to defeat the Order summoned by Evermore seven years ago, she'd gone to live in Cumulus, the capitol of Pravus.

"I'm visiting my mother," she answered. "And I hear I have two new brothers," she added.

"Yeah," Chaos replied. One of them was his best friend Wesley. Who, despite his lame name, was otherwise pretty cool. The other was Quincy, who'd been born about eight years ago.

"It's so good to see you," Olivia told him, flashing him another warm smile. A smile that was practically magical to behold, for it made *him* want to smile, despite everything that'd happened moments before. "What are you up to?" she asked.

"I was trying to get through the Gate," he replied, and then realized a bit too late that he should've kept that piece of information to himself. Olivia was an adult, after all, and would almost certainly tell his parents.

"What for?" she asked. He hesitated, and she put a hand on his shoulder, giving him an earnest look. "You can tell me," she told him. "You have nothing to fear in doing so."

And so earnest was her expression that darn it, he believed her. So his tale gushed out of him, and he told her everything. About Imperius, and his attempt to go through the Gate, and the guard's meanness toward him.

"I wasn't *that* mean," the guard said in his defense. For Chaos realized that the man had followed Olivia and had been listening. Like, the whole time.

"I understand why you didn't want Chaos to leave," Olivia told the man. "And how frustrating your job can be. It's not your fault that you did what you did, or felt what you felt."

"Oh," the guard mumbled, his cheeks flushing. Olivia turned back to Chaos.

"And I understand your feelings too," she told him, putting a hand on his cheek. "You have every right to feel the way you do, Chaos. And to rediscover the magic that's been denied you."

"Uh," Chaos mumbled, feeling awfully...*vulnerable* for some reason. There was something about the way Olivia looked at him that made him feel both terribly nervous and yet wonderful at the same time. As if she had the terrible power to reveal the darkness within him...a darkness that, around her, he wanted desperately to hide and yet to be free of at the same time. She turned back to the guard then.

"He's telling the truth," she informed the man. "He is a wizard, and requires entry into the kingdom of Pravus."

"Oh," the guard replied. "Um...sure."

"Go on Chaos," Olivia prompted, giving him another one of her wonderful smiles. "Find your destiny."

"Really?" Chaos asked, eyeing the Gate, then her. "You...won't tell on me?"

"I won't," Olivia promised. She paused then. "Your father is a good man," she told him. "After everything he's been through, he'll do anything to protect you. But to find yourself, you'll need to face the dangers he would protect you from."

"Thanks," Chaos replied with a smile. She beamed at him.

"I'm so proud of you," she told him.

"But...I haven't done anything yet," he protested.

"You're on your way," she countered gently. "The first step is the one that so many people never take...and it's the steps that are the journey."

With that, she pulled his head in, giving his forehead a sweet, gentle kiss, and then embraced him. After which she pulled away, giving him one last smile before waving goodbye. Then down the street she went, toward the courtyard in the city center. Chaos realized he was gawking at her, and then turned back toward the Gate, realizing that the guard was gawking at her too. Not in the way that guys usually gawked at pretty girls, but as if the man had been blind before, and could now see.

"Wow," the guard breathed.

"Yeah," Chaos agreed. He blinked then, wiping sweaty palms on his pants, then eyeing the Gate. "Can I, uh...?"

"Sure," the guard replied. Without a trace of cynicism or sarcasm. "Good luck," he added.

"Thanks," he replied.

And with that, Chaos walked up to the double-doors of the Gate, eyeing the rightmost one. It'd closed after Olivia had gone through, and he paused before touching it, struck with sudden fear.

What if I can't open it?

If that was true – if his magic was gone, and he was no longer a wizard – then his journey would end right here, despite Olivia's help.

"Go on kid," he heard a voice behind him say. He turned, seeing the guard standing there. The man gave him an encouraging smile. "You can do it."

Chaos smiled back, then turned back to the door. He took a deep breath in, gathering his courage.

You can do it, he told himself, for the guard's smile – as well as his voice – had become Chaos's own, at least for the moment.

21

And so Chaos extended his hand, pressing his palm on the door.

Thunk.

His smile grew, relief coursing through him.

I am *a wizard!*

The door opened a bit, and Chaos turned back to the guard, giving a little salute. The guard smiled back, saluting in turn.

"Good luck," the man offered.

"Thank you," Chaos replied.

With that, he took his first step into the magical kingdom of Pravus, or at least his first step in quite a while. And with that single step, his adventure began.

Chapter 3

Chauncy glared at the door to his shop after Chaos slammed it shut, having half a mind to stomp up to it, throw it back open, and give his wayward son a piece of his goddamn mind. In fact, he would've done it, had Valtora not put a hand on his shoulder from behind.

"Don't do it," she told him. "Killing him now will feel good, believe me. But you'll regret it in the end. Eventually."

"Ha ha," he grumbled. But he sighed, returning to his stool behind the counter. Then sighed again. "I just don't get it," he admitted. "What the hell's wrong with him?"

"He's thirteen," she replied. "He's going through the change."

"The what?"

"The change," she repeated. "You know, zits and fur and fluids and stuff. I went through puberty when I was like eight."

"Eight?" he asked incredulously.

"Yeah. When did you go through it?"

"I dunno, when I was fifteen?" he guessed. Which he'd assumed was normal, but now wasn't so sure.

"Well everyone in my family went earlier," she replied. "He's just feeling his oats," she added. "I bet that's why he's being such a dick."

"I don't think so," Chauncy stated.

"Wanna make a bet?" she proposed, her eyes lighting up. He grimaced, knowing better than to do such a thing. For when Valtora won a bet, the price to pay was always spectacularly inappropriate. His childhood crush Addie had gotten two children out of such bets, and he'd suffered a remarkable number of other indignities as well. Indignities that he'd ended up enjoying thoroughly to be sure, but on account of the potential for soul-crushing shame, would never *ever* want anyone else to know about.

"No thanks," he replied.

"Pussy," she accused. He ignored her, and at length she pouted, realizing the jig was up. "Aww."

"I just wish he'd be like he used to be," Chauncy said, sighing again. And recalling the smiling, effervescent boy Chaos had been. A lot longer ago than Chauncy would care to think about. "I wish I could reach him."

"Eh, he'll come around," Valtora assured him, dismissing his worries with a dismissive gesture. "He just has to go through some shit first."

"I hope you're right," Chauncy muttered. "I just wish he wouldn't act like such annoying little…

Dong!

The shop door opened, and Chauncy half-expected Chaos to barge in. But it was a customer…a teenage boy named Dewey. He was tall, gangly, and possessed of a rather large nose and large lips, and had a face full of acne that to be frank, made him tough to look at. Puberty had struck the boy hard a year ago, and his face hadn't recovered from the blow quite yet. And might never do so, Chauncy knew.

"Welcome to A Little Magic!" Chauncy greeted with all the false cheer he could muster. Which, after decades of working with the public, wasn't too terribly much.

"Hey," Dewey replied, refusing to look anyone in the eye. Particularly Valtora, who he did glance at furtively, though most definitely not in the eye. Ever since puberty, he'd decided to focus on other things. Namely two things a bit below. Suffice it to say that, for Dewey, they were artifacts of enormous power that he found more magical than anything Chauncy sold in the store.

"Hey Dewey," Valtora greeted, leaning over the counter and giving the boy a naughty smile. One that Chauncy was quite sure Dewey would never see. For the boy's eyes had locked on the chasm Valtora had created, which she'd done quite intentionally. She liked nothing more than to torture the boy, having a fair amount of evil in her heart. And a fair amount of fair flesh insulating it. Chauncy elbowed her under the counter, and she stopped leaning, much to Dewey's obvious disappointment.

"What can I do for you?" Chauncy asked.

"Just browsing," Dewey mumbled, walking up to the shelves, then making a show of studying each of the products displayed. All while stealing glances he thought Valtora And Chauncy wouldn't notice, of course. For the only thing Dewey was interested in getting was the one thing he couldn't buy. Not from Valtora, anyway.

24

At length Dewey had made his way through the entire store, and Chauncy passed the time by counting how many glances Dewey stole. When he'd run out of stuff to pretend to look at, the boy left without a word.

"How many this time?" Valtora asked.

"Two hundred and seven," Chauncy answered.

"Ooo, he's getting bolder," she noted.

"It's been a few days since he came," Chauncy pointed out.

"Probably literally," Valtora replied with a grin. Chauncy rolled his eyes, but couldn't deny her logic. They both knew the male psyche very well, in that a particular kind of evil built up in a man's mind the longer he went without release. The very opposite of hunger, which was an urge to take in what one didn't have, it was the urge to get rid of what one had accumulated. Men and women were a bit different in this regard. For while the urge only grew stronger and stronger for Chauncy, for Valtora it grew until about three weeks, after which the urge went away completely. A phenomenon she hadn't experienced since a little after Chaos had turned three, thankfully.

"I meant to the shop," Chauncy grumbled.

"Uh huh," Valtora replied. She eyed Dewey through the shop windows as the boy walked down the street. "He better get laid soon," she stated. "Honestly, we should probably help him."

"He's what, fourteen?" Chauncy shot back. "Way too young if you ask me."

"Pfft," Valtora scoffed. "I say he's waited too long already."

"What?"

"Animals have sex when they hit puberty," she pointed out. "Humans are the only ones that make their kids wait. Like half a decade or more," she added, making a face.

"So?"

"Can't have a boy wait too long," she explained. "If he doesn't have sex with actual people soon, he'll start developing all sorts of crazy, nasty habits."

"Like what," Chauncy shot back, crossing his arms over his chest.

"Like weird fantasies and compulsions 'n shit," Valtora answered.

"*No*," Chauncy argued, still sucking at doing so.

"Oh yeah," Valtora insisted. "The Dark One told me all about what happens to hard-up boys. Give it a couple years, and the only

25

thing that'll get poor Dewey off is thinking about being ritualistically gangbanged by cross-dressing redheaded zombie centaurs wearing purple top hats. Even when he's having actual sex. Like, for the rest of his friggin' life."

"Zombies!" Fury exclaimed, thankfully choosing the least offensive of Valtora's words.

"Graarrghh," Zora graarrghed, spattering drool on the counter.

"You can always tell," Valtora mused. "They close their eyes during the act, so they can picture it in their minds."

"Whatever," Chauncy grumbled.

He glanced at Epic, who was sitting on the stool to his left. The boy was sitting with perfect posture, hands folded on his lap. Just staring out of the windows of the shop, probably gazing at the passers-by who were going about their various lives. But with Epic, it was hard to know.

"What are you thinking, Epic?" he asked the boy, eager to change the subject. Epic turned to face Chauncy, his gaze sending a chill down Chauncy's spine, as it usually did.

"I'm waiting," the boy replied, which wasn't really an answer as to what he was thinking, but did explain what he was doing. Chauncy thought about pressing the issue, but decided against it, switching to a considerably more candid conversationalist.

"What are *you* thinking, Fury?" he asked.

"Bubbles!" she cried exuberantly. blowing some bubbles from her bubble-making wand. While the wand wasn't magical in the literal sense, what it did was magical to Fury indeed. For after blowing said bubbles, she watched – enraptured – as they floated across the shop, making their way slowly to the floor. Chauncy had to smile, for his daughter was terribly cute. But not terribly deep, he was a bit reluctant to admit. Epic, on the other hand, had depths that neither he nor Valtora could seem to fathom. For the boy simply refused to talk most of the time, which was, for Chauncy, profoundly irksome. But on balance, Epic was unfailingly polite, which made it hard to get too mad at him.

Chauncy sighed, picking his fingernails as he eyed the door to the shop, waiting for the next customer to come in. Or maybe he was waiting for Chaos. He couldn't help but think that he might have been an itsy-bitsy bit too harsh on the boy.

"Think he'll come back?" he asked Valtora.

"Shrug," Valtora replied. While shrugging.

Chauncy continued to pick at his fingernails, cleaning under them. And then, once cleaned, he began to eat them.

"Think I was too harsh on him?" he asked.

"Pfft, no," Valtora replied.

"He said he'd rather die," Chauncy told her. "You don't think he'd *actually* try to kill himself, would he?"

"Nah," Valtora reassured. "He's angry, not sad."

"Huh?"

"Angry people want to hurt others," she explained. "Sad people want to hurt themselves."

Chauncy considered this, and found it to be rather wise.

"Huh," he murmured.

"Not just a pretty face," Valtora said with a pretty smile. "I'm like, deep as *shit*."

"Shit!" Fury exclaimed happily, blowing more bubbles.

"Language," Chauncy warned the girl.

"Oopsie," Fury apologized. "Sowwy Daddy."

Chauncy couldn't help but smile at his adorable little girl, and he watched as she continued to blow bubbles happily. She was almost *always* happy, in stark contrast to her name...and the fury she'd shown as a newborn baby. His gaze fell to the curved fang hanging from the necklace around her neck. The Fang of Rage, it was an artifact he'd created during their very first father-daughter walk, during their last adventure. As best as he could tell, it had the power to absorb anger. Which meant that, if it was anything like his other creations, it had the power to release that anger as well. Something it'd never done, thank goodness. Heck, he wouldn't even begin to know how it *could* be released.

"You're *sure* I wasn't too hard on him?" Chauncy pressed. Valtora rolled her eyes dramatically, not because she was particularly pissed, but because she thoroughly enjoyed hyperbole. Much like Fury, incidentally.

"Let it *go* Chauncy-poo," she ordered. He paused, then sighed.

"Fine," he grumbled.

They waited for a while longer, but to his surprise, no customers came to the shop. Which was weird, because his shop was usually hopping at this time of day. It took him a moment to remember why.

"It's Founder's Day!" he blurted out, standing up from his chair.

"Oh," Valtora replied. "Shit!"

"Shit!" Fury exclaimed, and promptly put her hand over her mouth in horror.

Founder's Day, you may recall, was one of the most important holidays in Southwick, and in Borrin in general. For it was the day that they celebrated Archibald Merrick, the founder of Southwick...and incidentally, of the Evermore Trading Company. And while Chauncy had no love for Archibald or his late son Gamsies – or the company they'd founded – *not* celebrating the holiday would alienate their blindly patriotic customers. And as every business owner knew, while holidays started off as celebrations of cultural importance, they all quickly devolved into marketing opportunities for the purposes of guilting people into buying stuff for each other in an empty show of caring and love. As such, A Little Magic had a great deal to gain from not going against the grain.

"I'll go get the costumes," Chauncy stated. "And the signs to put in front of the shop."

"Sit down," Valtora ordered, patting his seat. "I'll have my doppelganger do it."

"Oh," he replied, sitting back down. "Right."

Chauncy sat there while the doppelganger left, picking at his fingernails. He shifted in his chair, still feeling rather antsy. As to why, he wasn't sure.

"What's wrong baby?" Valtora asked, clearly sensing his continued unease.

"I don't know," Chauncy answered. "I've got a bad feeling is all."

"About what?"

"I don't know," he repeated.

At length, the doppelganger returned, bursting through the door with a *dong*, Founder's Day costumes and signs in hand. Chauncy busied himself with putting on the requisite green suit and golden tie, then in setting up the signs outside. Then he returned to his seat, still ill-at-ease.

Everything's going to be fine, he told himself.

But if he'd only known what destiny had in store for his son – and by extension, himself – he'd have realized that this was a damn lie. Everything *wasn't* going to be okay. Not by a long shot.

For in the end, someone he loved dearly was going to die.

Chapter 4

On the occasion of King Pravus the Eighth's fifteenth anniversary of being crowned king, all of the lords arranged for a grand celebration to be had in honor of him. Not by virtue of any sort of affection, Pravus suspected, but by virtue of the usual bitter recipe of custom and obligation. It was ever the way of human nature to do whatever one was used to doing, and as such, the lords did just that. Which was to throw a massive party in the name of their supposedly beloved monarch. To be fair, there was almost certainly a component of fear involved, for to *not* celebrate the occasion in a rather offensively opulent fashion could be construed as an insult. A metaphorical middle finger extended to the current king.

Luckily, while most politicians were male, the vast majority were particularly unmanly sorts, and as such, no one had the balls to consider making such a statement. Real men, after all, were in the habit of actually doing things, while politicians merely engaged in the act of appearing to do so. All through the strategy of give and take…mainly giving others blame for one's own failings while taking responsibility for others' successes. Those who were most believable in these acts ascended quite reliably to the top of the food chain, so to speak, and were showered with riches earned by the work of those they victimized.

In any case, today was the day of said anniversary celebration, and as such, Pravus was compelled to attend. Even though he would've preferred to extend his own middle finger to it all, and not just in a metaphorical sense.

"You look dashing cousin," his cousin Templeton declared, beaming at him from his right. While both of them beheld Pravus in all his majesty, reflected by his ridiculously ornate full-length mirror in his royal dressing room. Pravus eyed said reflection, admiring the way his black and gold uniform clung to his remarkably developed muscles, displaying the vast majority of them in all their glory. Including the one he enjoyed working out the most, which most of his subjects would wrongly assume was an overcompensating codpiece.

"Naturally," he purred, eyeing himself approvingly. Then he shifted his gaze to Templeton to eye his cousin. The man was dressed in black and gold like Pravus, well-built in a wirier kind of way. But what he lacked in sheer size he made up for in proportion and symmetry. And the way his ridiculously narrow waist flared out into those perky little buttocks, barely contained by those tight black pants!

Why, it was enough to prove that Pravus's "codpiece" was anything but.

"Ready?" Templeton inquired.

"Ready to suffer through it all," Pravus groused. For there was nothing more pompous and boring than pomp and ceremony, of that he could be sure. He sighed heavily, slouching his shoulders for once.

"We'll suffer together then," Templeton declared with a smile, hooking his arm in Pravus's.

"My trusty spotter!" Pravus stated with a smile of his own. For his cousin's eternal exuberance was infectious indeed, a ray of sunshine that warmed whatever it graced.

"If your load proves too great, I'll carry it instead!" Templeton exclaimed. And oh! If only he would consent to do such a thing, Pravus could die a happy man. As it was, such an act was forever doomed to remain a fantasy, albeit one that Pravus had used for the past couple of decades with remarkable efficacy.

Just then, there was a knock on the door.

"Come in," Pravus prompted.

There was a pause, and then the door cracked open, and none other than Desmond – Pravus's trusty man-servant and part-time advisor – peered in.

"My liege," the old man greeted, pushing the door open further, then bowing before his king. He gave similar treatment to Templeton, though for a lord, his bow wasn't quite as deep. "My lord."

"What is it Desmond?" Pravus inquired wearily, though he knew the answer already. Which explained his weariness. For even the thought of the grueling charade to come was enough to bring Pravus to the brink of contemplating suicide.

"It's time," the old man replied.

"Oh *wonderful*," Pravus replied snippily.

"That which begins will also end," Templeton declared with a smile. Pravus had to smile back, for to frown in the face of his cousin's indomitable cheer was nigh impossible.

"Indeed cousin, and well said," Pravus replied. He sighed, turning to the mirror and smoothing out a few non-existent wrinkles in his uniform. Then he turned to Desmond. "Lead the way," he commanded.

And so Desmond did, because he had to. In that way, Pravus realized, he was not so different than his servant. Pravus had finer things and more money and prestige and other such nonsense. But in the grand scheme of things, they were both servants to their respective roles. The punishment for Desmond defying his role – an unthinkable act, of course – was to take away his influence in the form of money, his freedom, or his life. The punishment for Pravus neglecting *his* role was perhaps even worse: having to endure the endless torture of his conscience.

Pravus sighed, doing as his role told him to do, while Desmond did the same. Off they went, down the various opulent hallways with riches that were really only there to convince others of Pravus's relative importance. Such was the strangeness of the human mind that, if he were the same person with the same ideas and action, yet operated out of a hovel, no one would take him seriously. Mankind – and womankind – were ever slaves to symbols of hierarchy, assuming that those who had more were relatively superior.

Suddenly Pravus found the finery exhausting, as well as the role he'd played for the last decade and a half.

"To think that I have to do this for another few centuries," he mused, the thought almost more than he could bear. For with the potions of youth he'd quaff every time he aged a bit too much for his liking would keep him alive for far longer than a normal person.

"A few centuries of going to the gym will help soothe the pain," Templeton replied with a sunny smile. Because of course he would find the upside to everything. Pravus had to smile back, but he didn't say anything in reply. For the incredible *sameness* of each of his days was starting to wear him thin. Templeton must have noticed Pravus's unlifted mood, for he gave a concerned look. "What's wrong my liege?" he inquired.

"It's just…" Pravus began, then stopped, both physically and verbally, to collect his thoughts. Then he gestured at the hallway around them. "Is this all there is?"

"I don't follow," Templeton replied.

"Being king," Pravus clarified. "Waking up to do the same old thing, over and over again?"

"Depressing, isn't it," Desmond droned. For this precisely described the old man's life.

"Well I suppose anything can get old after a while," Templeton conceded.

"Even the gym?" Desmond inquired, raising an eyebrow.

"Don't be stupid Desmond," Pravus snipped. For the idea was sheer nonsense.

"Perhaps it isn't so much that you're doing the same old thing, but that you haven't done anything new in a while," Desmond proposed, ignoring Pravus's rather rude retort. Pravus frowned, rubbing his broad, chiseled chin.

"Perhaps you're right," he replied.

"It's been a long time since our last adventure," Templeton agreed. And indeed it had been; about nine years, in fact, since they'd faced Devorah Doverah and Kyral on the field of battle. Which in that case, had been a field of grass. "Perhaps your soul craves an adventure, sire."

"I do believe you're right," Pravus replied, taken aback by this insight. For while he'd been feeling a bit down as of late, until now, he hadn't quite figured out why. But now that his plight had been made obvious by the observations of others, it was clear what he had to do. "I *do* need an adventure," he declared, striking a rather heroic pose. Something he also had not struck in some time.

"Yes, well," Desmond stated. "Adventures don't just appear on command. Not even for kings," he added. "Besides, we have a celebration to…"

And then there was a burst of blue sparkles, and a man appeared before them. A disturbingly old man with a stooped back and slouchy shoulders, and muscles so tiny they were barely up to the task of keeping him upright. A sad figure the man attempted to conceal with an admittedly fine blue cloak. One accessorized with a blue pointed hat and a wooden staff with a blue crystal on top. A very fine uniform indeed, though worn by a very worn man.

"Imperius Fanning?!" Pravus blurted out incredulously. Imperius smirked.

"In the flesh," he confirmed.

"What in blazes are *you* doing here?" Pravus inquired, so taken aback that he utterly forgot to make the old man bow or kneel.

"Following my gut," Imperius answered.

"This can't be good," Desmond noted. Which was probably true, but on the other hand, it was quite possible that even good things couldn't be good for Desmond, given his depressive disposition. For he was the exact opposite of Templeton, who could find something good about something bad. Good and bad were relational rather than intrinsic to a thing.

"It's neither good nor bad," Imperius replied, confirming Pravus's perspective. "It is what is."

"And what is it?" Pravus inquired irritably. Not because he was irritated by Imperius, but because he'd been interrupted while already irritated. It wasn't so much that he was projecting his irritation on the wizard, as projection wasn't really a thing. It was merely that irritation was his current way of being. Imperius gave Pravus a grave gaze.

"Our world is in grave danger," he warned, his tone darkening rather dramatically.

"Again?" Pravus interjected irritably. Imperius gave him an enormously irritated look. "Go on," he grumbled.

"A new villain is rising, and will soon gather his hordes," Imperius continued ominously. "One day they will spread across the land like a great plague, and destroy everything you know and love!"

"Oh *really*," Pravus replied. Imperius glared at him.

"Yes really," he stated. "It is my gut's prophecy."

Pravus stared at the man, then sighed, rolling his eyes.

"Alright. Fine." He paused. "So?"

"So what?"

"Who is it?" Pravus asked. "This new villain that's going to do all these terribly bad things?"

This time, it was Imperius who paused.

"I won't say," he replied. Pravus blinked.

"Pardon?" he asked.

"As to the identity of the villain, I won't say," Imperius sort-of-repeated. "You will learn their identity another day."

Pravus folded his massive forearms over his chest, glaring at the wizard. Who, on account of being the most powerful wizard in the most powerful group of wizards in the land, was not at all intimidated by this.

"So if you're not going to tell me who this villain is, what's the point of warning me?" Pravus snipped. "I can't do anything about it if I don't know who to kill."

"To stop this eventuality from occurring," Imperius replied rather testily, "…you must embark on an adventure of your own. One with your cousin here," he added, inclining his head at Templeton, "…in lieu of traveling alone."

"An adventure?" Pravus stated, perking up a bit. For an adventure suited his heroic persona quite nicely.

"Do tell!" Templeton requested with his usual verve.

"Your destiny is to venture forth into Old Langsroth," Imperius declared in a rather dramatic tone. "To the catacombs beneath the great city."

Pravus furrowed his brow.

"Old Langsroth?" he inquired.

"The Old Langsroth of legend?" Templeton pressed.

"Indeed," Imperius confirmed. "For only there will you uncover the means to defeat what may be the greatest villain of your generation…and save the world from utter devastation!"

Pravus considered this, rubbing a chiseled chin.

"Would it perchance get me out of this party?" he asked. Hopefully.

"It would," Imperius replied.

"Very well," Pravus declared, placing his hands upon his twenty-eight-inch waist and flaring his lats dramatically. Whilst engaging his glutes and pecs, naturally. "We shall venture forth to Old Langsroth at once!"

"To meet our destiny!" Templeton agreed zestily.

"Shall I inform the lords?" Desmond inquired. Pravus blinked, having completely forgotten that the old servant was still here.

"Do so at once," he replied. "But first, fetch our fire dragon!"

"You must go by horse or by foot," Imperius interjected. Pravus blinked again.

"Pardon?"

"By horse or by foot," the old wizard repeated. "Not by wingéd steed."

"Why not?" Pravus semi-protested.

"My gut tells me you shouldn't," Imperius answered. "And you must go without the protection of your uniform," he added. "And without your magic sword or crown."

Pravus eyed him skeptically.

"Really," he grumbled.

"Really," Imperius confirmed. Pravus sighed, knowing full well that to go against Imperius's gut was to invite tragedy.

"Very well," he decided. "I'll get changed at once. Desmond, fetch our steeds!"

Chapter 5

Having strode through the Gate, passing beyond the Great Wall into the kingdom of Pravus, Chaos found himself feeling better than he had in a long, long time. The wide-open landscape before him – stretching off into the distance as far as he could see – felt like the wide-open landscape of his mind. As if he'd been walking in tight alleyways for most of his life, passages that told him where to go. Narrow streets that limited possibilities, telling him where he could and couldn't go. But now the road he strode upon was wide, and what's more, was not at all necessary to follow. There was nothing stopping Chaos from stepping off the well-beaten path, for the purposes of beating a path of his own.

It was heady stuff, this sudden freedom, and it filled him near to bursting with giddiness. So he stopped for a moment to enjoy the marvelous sensation, and to take in all the scenery. Which while it looked for all the world like the grasses and shrubs and trees and dirt he'd become accustomed to, with his sudden freedom, it all seemed refreshingly new.

"*This* is more like it," he declared, sweeping his gaze across the land. No buildings. No lawns. No roads traveling in straight lines. Even the ground wasn't level in any particular place, unlike the streets and sidewalks of Southwick. This land went up and down and this way and that, doing whatever the heck it pleased.

And it pleased Chaos very much to see it…and to have joined the things in doing what they desired.

"Alright," he declared, cracking his knuckles. "Time to meet my destiny."

So he strode southward, his shoes crunching on the dirt of the road. One step in front of the other, each bringing him one step closer to his destination. Or rather, his destiny, in an adjacent nation. Or so he assumed, because he hadn't really looked at a map to see where Grissam was in relation to the kingdom he was currently in. But that hardly mattered, of course. In fact, not knowing was part of the fun.

Chaos smiled as he strode, taking in the scenery. Every once and a while he looked back, not because he was having second thoughts, but to see how far from home he'd gone. The thought of not being able to see the Gate or the Great Wall at all – of his home being completely gone, at least as far as his eyes were concerned – was terribly exciting. How he imagined being on a raft in the middle of the ocean might feel.

Unfortunately, given that the wall was two hundred feet high, getting far enough away to not be able to see it anymore took quite a while. So long, in fact, that after an undetermined amount of time, this particular leg of the journey started to lose its sheen. As such, what had started as an exciting expedition quickly devolved into a chore. Which by definition made it a bore.

"Well this kinda sucks," Chaos grumbled, his stride having turned into a trudge. He kicked a nearby stone, watching as it rolled randomly over the ground. Then he walked a ways more, kicking another rock, then another as he went, making a game of it. After each rock's random path grew tiresome, he made a game of seeing how far he could kick them. While vaguely following the path ever southward. With his body thus occupied, his mind was free to roam. Randomly at first, which was just the way he liked it. But then his thoughts turned to something he *didn't* like: the fact that, when he'd tried to use his magic back at the Gate, nothing had happened.

It occurred to Chaos then that, after so many years of not using his power, it might've gotten a fair bit weaker. Or even worse, that he might have lost it altogether. A thought that made him immediately think dark thoughts about his parents, particularly his dad. It'd been his father that'd insisted on Chaos not using his magic, after all, and who'd also insisted on wearing the Chaos Ring everywhere to suppress Chaos's magic just in case.

He knew that Dad loved him, but also that Dad hated his magic, because his magic had been powerful and unpredictable. If there was one thing that made his father uneasy, it was not knowing what was going to come next.

"Jerk," he grumbled, thinking back to his last conversation with his dad. "But you were a jerk too," he told himself, which was true. He found it easy to be a jerk when others were a jerk to him. And others tended to become jerks when he was one. A vicious cycle, a circle of jerks begetting jerks. And while that could be fun in the moment, it never seemed to end well.

Chaos sighed, kicking another stone, then another, making his way ever forward. The thought that his magic was gone returned to him, along with a pang of anxiety that this thought rightly caused. He was struck with the sudden urge to try to use his magic again, just to see if he could do it. But the thought that it might *not* work gave him pause. If he tried using his magic, but failed, then he would prove to himself that he was a failure as a wizard. And that kind of proof was the last thing that he wanted to be confronted with. So Chaos made the decision to *not* use his magic. For in not using it, he could at least pretend that he still had it. Which was ever-so-slightly comforting. Ish.

"Imperius said you were a wizard," he told himself. Which was a lie. "You need to meet your destiny," he added, telling the truth to balance things out. So he put one foot in front of the other, kicking stones as he went, determined to do what he'd been tasked to do.

Chapter 6

When the bell tolled across Southwick indicating the arrival of five o'clock, Epic did the honors of flipping the sign at the window from "open" to "closed." Everyone left the shop then, Chauncy locking the door behind him. Everyone except for Chaos, of course. A fact that made Chauncy's gut squirm, for he'd been anxious for Chaos's return. So it should come as no surprise, dear reader, that Chauncy was eager to return home to see his son. Which was why he set a brisk pace back home, resisting the urge to employ the powers of his staff to fly there ahead of the rest of his family.

"Slow *down*," Valtora said-complained, shooting him a glare she probably didn't mean. And promptly turned said glare on the statue of Archibald Merrick, which she slugged with her diamond fist. Right in the hip, which cracked. But held, to Valtora's clear dismay. "Next time," she vowed, glaring at said cracked hip as they past. And promptly seemed to forget about it altogether, smiling as they continued their walk. But Chauncy knew damn well that Valtora remembered every vow she'd ever vowed. And that she'd pretty much succeeded at making all of those vows come true, at least eventually.

Chauncy did slow down, though in doing so, he only prolonged his angst. As such, he enjoyed his usually enjoyable walk home from the shop not at all. When they'd neared their home, he found himself quite relieved, and picked up the pace to be the first up the porch steps to the front door. He unlocked and opened it, gesturing for everyone else to go through.

"After you," he told his wife.

"My *Chauncy*-poo," she gushed, batting her eyes at him. Fury was the next to step through, batting her eyes as well.

"My *Daddy*-poo," she gushed, mimicking her mother.

"Aww," Chauncy replied with a smile. Next came Epic, who said nothing at all, merely marching into the house with the usual grim determination he displayed for everything he did. Chauncy went through then, closing the door behind them.

"Chaos!" he barked, shouting up the stairs.

He waited, but there was no reply.

"Chaos?" he shouted again.

"Ooo," Valtora said, putting her hands on her hips. "You're gonna be in *trouble*." For she loved nothing more than to stoke the flames of an argument. Something that Chaos had apparently inherited, irritatingly enough. But while Valtora never meant her arguments, and performed them for the purposes of entertainment, Chaos seemed to mean every word. Which wasn't entertaining at all.

"Come down here right now," Chauncy warned in his gravest fatherly baritone, feeling his ire rising. "Or you're going to regret it, young man."

Still no reply.

Chauncy felt his ire rise past the point of keeping his calm, and thus he found himself stomping up the stairs, his mouth set in a grim line. He reached the top, turning rightward to stomp up to Chaos's door, which was closed. He banged thrice upon said door, again with no reply. And so he threw the door open, stepping into the room fully prepared to lose his *shit*.

But when he opened his mouth to let said shit out, he discovered that doing so would be a waste of time. For Chaos's room was utterly empty.

"What the *fuck*," he stated rather than asked, turning about and checking the bathroom, then his room. Then he went back downstairs, finding Valtora in the kitchen getting dinner prepared.

"Is he down here?" he asked.

"Nope," Valtora replied. "Not in his room?"

"Nope," Chauncy answered.

"Maybe he went outside," she stated. "Want me to get my doppelganger to hunt him down?"

"Sure," Chauncy replied.

"Fine," Valtora stated. "You make dinner."

So Chauncy did, taking over for his wife. He sizzled some steak and boiled some rice, and opened a can of rather unfresh fish for Zora to enjoy. The smell was something that would prompt any normal person to gag, but having smelled it daily for years now, it bothered Chauncy not one bit.

When he'd finished the task of preparing his family's meal, Chauncy doled out portions on plates, setting them on the kitchen table.

"Dinner is served!" he declared with fatherly gallantry, puffing his chest proudly at his accomplishment. Which of course paled in comparison to saving magic itself, or defeating such villains as the Evermore Trading Company or Devorah Doverah. But if one only celebrating one's biggest accomplishments, there would rarely be an occasion to celebrate at all. Celebrating successes of all sizes meant understanding that it was the process of succeeding that mattered. Of putting one's mind to something and seeing it through. And if it was in service to others, in the spirit of love, then celebration was surely due.

With his declaration, his family convened at the kitchen table, Valtora and Fury with glee, Epic rather grimly, and Zora in a manner severely delayed. They all sat at the table for their Little dinner…save for one conspicuously absent member.

"Have you found Chaos yet?" Chauncy asked Valtora. She frowned prettily, then shook her head.

"Doppelganger is still out in the city looking for him," she notified. "Getting tough in the dark."

Chauncy frowned, feeling his guts squirm. A feeling which made the rest of him squirm in his seat.

"This doesn't make sense," he protested. "He wouldn't stay out this late at night."

"He might," Valtora countered.

"I don't think so," Chauncy shot back.

"Well, he *is* a wizard," she told him. Chauncy blinked, then recalled his meeting earlier with another wizard. One Imperius Fanning, to be precise. He crafted a carefully neutral expression then, so as not to give anything away. He was, after all, guilty of a rather serious omission to Valtora. And Chaos, of course.

"What do you mean?" he inquired. Neutrally.

"You sent him away," she explained.

"So?"

"You're wearing the Chaos Ring," she pointed out, pointing at his left middle finger with her diamond left hand. He looked down, seeing that he was indeed wearing the Chaos Ring. A ring that suppressed Chaos's magical abilities. He felt his guts squirm again, and then spasm with fear.

41

"You think…that he used his magic?" he asked, fear turning into dread.

"I mean, that's what I would do," she told him. He grimaced, knowing it was true. And that, technically speaking, for so many reasons, he was the one responsible for Chaos's current situation. But it was ever the property of those in charge to deny responsibility for their own mistakes, placing blame squarely upon those they managed. The function of management was, in theory, to lead by example and organize the solutions to problems. But in reality, it was a position often focused on self-promotion and underling demotion. In short, a kind of professional coward.

"If he did use his magic, he's in deep trouble," Chauncy warned, executing this classic managerial style flawlessly. "He knows he isn't supposed to," he added. "We've made that *quite* clear."

"He's thirteen," Valtora countered.

"That's no excuse," Chauncy retorted. Though everything he'd just said *was* an excuse…for why he wasn't to blame.

"You're the one who sent him away," she pointed out.

"Because he was being insufferable," Chauncy argued, crossing his arms over his chest.

"And now he's dangerous," Valtora shot back. "And that's on you."

He glared at her.

"And how is that on me?" he demanded with righteous indignation. Which was, as you may recall, one of The Dark One's favorite evils. For there were none more prone to evil acts than those who were utterly sure they were right.

"You could've sat him in a corner," she pointed out. Which was, he realized with dismay, a very good point.

"He was being outrageous!" Chauncy complained, standing up from his chair and glaring down at her. An act that made little Fury Little start to cry. Chauncy threw his hands up in the air. "And now you've made her cry," he declared.

"Uh huh," Valtora replied. "*Totally* me."

"So I'm responsible for *this* too?" he blurted out incredulously.

"It's okay Fury," Valtora said, ignoring his reply rather rudely, while attending to their crying child. "Daddy's just having a bad day."

"Oh come *on*," Chauncy complained. But Valtora continued to ignore him. As did Epic, who continued to eat in silence, as usual.

42

Even Zora didn't make eye contact, staring blankly at the tabletop, drool dripping from the side of her mouth. "You know what?" he declared, shoving in his chair. "I'm done arguing with you."

"Why...is...he...yelling?" Fury gasp-cried, burying her face in Valtora's chest. And while such displays of weeping had usually been acting in Chaos's case, Chauncy knew that Fury felt them keenly and truly, sensitive soul that she was.

"Because he's wrong and he knows it," Valtora cooed, stroking the girl's hair. While giving Chauncy a look.

"For the love of..." Chauncy began, then bit his fist, which served to bite back whatever awful thing he'd been about to say. He turned away from the destruction that, to be fair, he knew in his heart that he'd caused. And then went to the front door, opening it and stomping onto the porch, shutting the door behind him. He went to the porch stairs then, sitting down and cursing the world at large. The heavens twinkled down at him with absolutely no comment on this turn of events, content to just be.

It wasn't long before Chauncy's fury fizzled, however. And in its place he felt a pang of regret. For he knew that Valtora was right...far more so than she could ever know, in fact. He *was* wrong. He'd been the one to kick Chaos out, when he should've kept him close. He'd been the one to lose his temper at breakfast in the first place, because of Imperius's impromptu visit. And he'd committed perhaps the most dangerous act any man or woman could possibly commit:

Going against Imperius Fanning's gut, and denying destiny.

Now Chaos was who-knows-where doing who-knows-what, instead of answering the call of destiny.

This time, destiny cannot be deferred, Imperius had warned. *To do so would be to risk the very fate of the world!*

Which was, Chauncy could no longer deny, precisely what he'd done.

Chapter 7

Preoccupying himself with games of kicking rocks and seeing how far they would go, Chaos continued his journey ever southward through the magical land of Pravus. In this rather distracted way, a surprisingly long period of time passed, such that, when Chaos lifted his gaze from the ground, he realized that it was quite late. And what's more, getting rather dark. That hardly mattered in the city of Southwick, where the streets and houses were always well-lit. But in the wilderness, it turned out that dark was a bit darker than Chaos had realized it could be. So dark, in fact, that he could hardly see.

"Well crap," he swore. Glancing back, he couldn't see the Gate or the Great Wall in the distance. And while that meant that he'd accomplished his goal of traveling a long way from Borrin, it also made him feel like home didn't exist anymore. That he was stranded here, in a strange wilderness, with no safe place to go. Or more importantly, to sleep.

But at least he had the path, his guide in this strange land. Or so he thought; when he looked down, he saw no path at all. Nor to his left, or his right, or behind him. Either he'd veered off quite a bit from it, or he simply couldn't see it anymore.

"Crap," he repeated, feeling suddenly ill-at-ease. And then shivered after a sudden, chilly breeze. The temperature was dropping, which was unfortunate, because he was wearing a short-sleeved shirt and shorts. He hadn't brought any warmer clothes...or a blanket, or a pillow, or a sleeping bag. Or food and water, he realized as his stomach growled, demanding its usual scheduled meal. "Shit," he cursed. And then glanced around him, to ensure that no adults were present. Which of course there were none. "Shitty shit crap *shit*," he added gratuitously, because he could. And while the freedom to swear to his heart's content was a novel treat, it couldn't distract him from his dire plight for very long.

Night was falling, and if he didn't do something soon, he'd suffer having to sleep outside, in the darkness. On dirt, which was hard, and thus hardly comfortable.

But what could he do?

Chaos considered his options, biting a hangnail as he did so. But nothing came to him. Which meant that he was doomed to suffer a night in the dark without shelter. And perhaps even an untimely death by being torn apart by some kind of grisly-looking monster. This thought grabbed his attention, and being that it was night – and therefore hard to see – his mind's eye was free to do the seeing for him. And it conjured up images of monsters lying in wait within every shadow, their fangs dripping with spit and their claws coated with blood. Claws that were eager for a second coat, so to speak.

"Fuck," he swore. For it was the most powerful of swears. "Shit," he added, because in contrast to the former, he knew what it meant. He found it strange that the most forbidden of words were all focused on natural bodily functions, ones that every person and animal was compelled to perform. Like shitting, which one did by way of their asshole, and pissing. "Fuck" was a word he still didn't quite get, but Mom told Dad to do it to her all the time when they were wrestling at night. He was starting to think it had something to do with his newfound favorite tub-time activity, but he had absolutely no desire to find out if he was right.

In any case, it seemed that any activity that was instinctual was bad, in that it reminded people that they were, in the end, animals. This was unthinkable to most in Borrin, who insisted they were something quite superior and special. And so instinctual activities were viewed with suspicion and contempt, and given special words that no one was supposed to say.

"Focus," he told himself, scrunching up his brow. It was what Dad always told him when his mind inevitably wandered. But focusing did nothing at all, for he still found himself in the same predicament. So he *un*focused, and lifted his gaze to the night sky instead. "What do I do, Grandma Light and Grandpa Space?" he asked. For while he'd never spoken with his Magus grandparents, he knew they were always there with him. Or rather, he knew that Dad had told him that this was so. But Space and Light didn't reply. "Fine," he grumbled, kicking a rock. It tumbled madly across the ground like tossed dice, coming to a stop.

Dice.

Tossing dice was, of course, the way to get a random number. A surprise. And surprises were his forte.

"All right," he told himself, cracking his knuckles. "Let's *do* this."

And then he focused on the heavens, sensing their very essence, their grand, infinite infinity-ness. A vast, orderly doing. *Too* orderly.

His eyes narrowed, and he focused further, *undoing* a bit of it, like pulling a loose string on a shirt that'd seen better days. He felt the fabric of the universe unravel, then knit itself back up…but not in the way it'd been. Then he relaxed, breaking out into a smile.

"There," he declared, putting his hands on his hips. And then he waited for a surprise. And that's precisely what he got; for to his surprise, he got no surprise at all. Which was surprising indeed. "What the *hell?*" he complained, stomping his foot. For his magic had once again failed him. "Fine," he decided, striding forward with his chin thrust forward and his hands balled into fists. "I'll just walk all *frickin'* night."

And so he set out to do just that, with the kind of determination only fury could bring.

Unfortunately for Chaos, fury was the kind of emotion that burned fast and bright, and as such it was gone in a flash. Which left him feeling utterly drained. And hopeless, for his situation was dire indeed. Utterly exhausted, his eyelids drifting closed over and over again, he lowered himself to the ground, no longer caring if he was attacked or eaten alive. He curled into a ball, closing his eyes. And immediately felt the world slipping away, until it was gone, gone, gone.

* * *

To Chaos's surprise, he woke up not dead.

He opened his eyes, then squinted, finding the light shining down on him far too bright. It took him a moment to realize he was lying on his back, on what felt like hard ground. He groaned, shielding his eyes with his forearm, waiting for them to adjust. Then he cracked an eye open, seeing endless blue sky above him. It took him a few more moments before he remembered why he was lying on his back outside, instead of on his comfy bed at home. When he did, he drew in a sharp breath, sitting upright and looking around.

There was short grass and wildflowers all around him, and forests flanking him in the distance. The path he'd taken was nowhere to be found, to his dismay. He must've veered off of it quite a ways in the dark last night.

Chaos got to his feet, brushing dirt off his pants and shirt, then stretched a bit. His muscles were terribly sore and stiff. But on balance, he wasn't dead or horribly maimed, which was a win in his book. He took a moment to find the sun and orient himself south-ish, after which he started off on the continuation of his journey.

Grrrarrrgh, his stomach growled, reminding him of Zora. At this point, the thought of eating her favorite meal – mildly decomposed fish brains – was more enticing than he'd ever thought possible. The last meal he'd eaten was a good twenty-four hours ago, which was easily the longest he'd ever gone without eating.

"This sucks," he grumbled at his grumbling stomach. He kicked a pebble, but missed, nearly losing his balance. "Suck suckity *shit*-piss," he swore, because he could. There were no consequences to the use of language when alone, after all. Words lost their power when there was no one else to hear them. But the consequences of not attending to *real* things – like food and shelter and whatnot – were powerful indeed. Chaos soon found that no amount of swearing could banish his discomfort for long.

So he suffered…and suffered. Until the thought of turning back and going home became a very tempting change of plan.

It was only then that he spotted something far in the distance: a few buildings flanking a road to his left. *The* road, he guessed. The one that he'd sort of followed all this way.

"*Yes!*" he exclaimed, breaking out into a run. He veered onto the road, running toward the buildings ahead. And ran. And *ran*. But the buildings were far further away than he'd estimated, and he soon ran out of steam, stopping to huff and puff, bent over with his hands on his knees. At length, he started running again, and then stopped. And then he decided to walk. Step by step he made his way toward the buildings, which numbered precisely three. At great length, he reached a sign before the buildings, which he read with great difficulty:

"Village…of…Erp," he read. "Pop…ulation…fifty-three."

He took a moment to recover from this mental exertion, processing what he'd read. This was the town of Erp, which had fifty-three people in it, apparently. Soon to be fifty-four, at least temporarily. Assuming the sign was current. Erp's village center

47

had three buildings, one of them a store, another with a sign that said "Inn," which had one too many "n's" as far as Chaos was concerned. Such that he was wary of going in it. The third had a sign that read "Bar," which was weird. Maybe it sold bars of metal or something. In any case, the mystery of "Bar" made Chaos want to know more, so he went right for the building's bright red front door. It opened right as he reached it, a large, potbellied man stepping through. One with a mostly bald head and big, meaty fingers, wearing brown…everything. The man gazed down at Chaos, chewing on a piece of straw.

"The hell are you doin' here?" he demanded, with a voice that hinted at more than a few missing teeth.

"Nothing," Chaos replied. Which was the truth.

"You can't come in here," the man told him, crossing his big arms over his chest, then spitting out the straw.

"Why not?"

"It's a bar," the man answered, as if it were obvious. Chaos stared at him as if he were stupid. Which was, on account of his appearance and demeanor, a strong possibility.

"No it's not," he retorted, gesturing at it. "It's a building."

The guy rolled his eyes.

"So you're a smart guy, eh?" he grumbled.

"Yep," Chaos replied.

"Get lost," the man said, taking another piece of straw from his pocket and picking his teeth with it. While standing in the doorway, preventing Chaos from getting past.

"I already am lost," Chaos argued.

"Then find yourself somewhere else."

"I'm hungry," he stated. "Where can I get food?"

"In the inn, duh."

"In the…?" Chaos began, turning to glance at the rather bland looking two-story building behind him. It was awfully familiar, though as to why, he couldn't say. Its sign did in fact spell "Inn," which food was in. Apparently.

"Git," the big man prompted, stepping forward rather menacingly. And while as a toddler Chaos would've been not a single bit disturbed by this – he'd practically murdered Imperius Fanning with his magic, after all – now he was appropriately afraid. For his magic was on the fritz, so to speak, if it even existed anymore. So it was that he left for the "Inn" more quickly than a brave person would. And unlike the bar, the "Inn" was easy to get into. Appropriately enough. Chaos strode through the doorway, seeing a big, tall man with a big beard standing behind a counter.

"Mornin'," the man greeted gruffly. "I'm Gerald and this is my inn. What can I do for you?"

"I'm hungry," Chaos declared. Gerald grunted.

"Breakfast is in the dining room to the left," he stated. "Six copper."

Chaos blinked.

"Huh?"

"Six copper pieces for breakfast," Gerald explained. "That's how much it costs."

"Um…" Chaos mumbled, shifting his weight from one foot to the other. "What if I don't *have* six copper?"

"Then you don't get breakfast."

"But I'm hungry," Chaos pointed out.

"Food costs money," Gerald shot back.

"I'm starving," Chaos corrected. Incorrectly, though it felt that way.

"I'm running a business," the man replied evenly. "Not a charity."

"What if I was dying of hunger?" Chaos argued testily. Probably because he was hangry. "Would you feed me then?"

"You're not," Gerald replied. "So I won't."

"So you'll let a child suffer?"

"Yep," Gerald answered. "Consider it a free lesson. Maybe you'll learn to bring money next time."

Chaos put his hands on his hips, glaring at the man. And then noticed a waitress to his left, picking up a plate of untouched bread from a table and walking it toward a trash can.

"Can I eat that?" he asked, intercepting the woman before she could toss it. She smiled at him, offering him the plate.

"No," Gerald answered, stopping her with a glare.

"But why not? She's just going to throw it away," Chaos reasoned.

"It's not yours," Gerald explained. "You didn't pay for it."

"But it's just going to go to waste," Chaos protested.

"This is a business, not a charity," he repeated. "You want to eat, you have to pay."

"But…"

"Get out of here," Gerald ordered, pointing at the door. "I'm done arguing with you."

49

Chaos opened his mouth to issue a retort, but Gerald gave him a supremely threatening look, one that made Chaos think better of it.

"Thanks for the help," he grumbled. And then turned and walked out. He made his way back to the road, striding southward away from the town of Erp. "Stupid *jerk*," he spat, kicking a rock. Then he paused. "*Jerks*," he added, because there'd been two. Still, as he left the two townspeople behind, his anger seeped away, until he wondered if it had been *him* who'd been less than kind. He could've been nicer, after all. Or offered to clean up or wash dishes or something to pay for a meal. Things he hated to do, because they were awfully boring, especially when he had to do them every day back at home. But for a meal, he'd have cleaned the whole dang "inn," at least in his current state.

But he couldn't go back now. He'd burned those bridges, so to speak. In being a jerk, he'd guaranteed that others would be a jerk right back. Which was precisely how he'd treated his dad, now that he thought about it. He'd poked the bear just to get a reaction, not caring if it was good or bad. Good reactions were more effort to get than bad ones, especially when he feeling bad himself. So, feeling bad, he made others feel bad, which made him feel even worse.

Which was quite the enlightening realization, but did absolutely nothing to feed his hunger.

"Assholes," he muttered, for being enlightened wasn't at all a cure for being human. "Bitch-ass bitches," he added, using one of his mother's favorite naughty lines.

Then, having nothing else to do but walk and hope, Chaos did just that. Ever southward, toward whatever destiny was in store for him.

Chapter 8

Having been prompted to set off on a rather vaguely defined adventure by none other than the destiny-delivering Imperius Fanning himself, Pravus found himself striding mightily down the halls of his castle, the ever-faithful Templeton at his side. Their destination was the royal stables, where their steeds were kept. For while Pravus had ordered Desmond to have said steeds fetched, with the siren call of adventure...well, calling...he found himself too eager to wait. Such that he broke out into a jog, so filled with vim that it made him vigorous.

"Fancy a race, sire?" Templeton inquired, picking up the pace to match his king. Pravus flashed him a smile.

"You read my mind, cousin!" he declared.

"When adventure calls, we run!" Templeton declared with vim of his own.

"Indeed, Templeton!" Pravus cried, bursting forward in an all-out sprint. But then he saw someone turn the corner at an intersection ahead; none other than Lord Ballister, the most powerful lord in the kingdom.

"Your Highness!" Ballister called out, holding up a hand. Pravus seriously considered trampling the man, but decided against it. For when dealing with Lord Ballister, it was better to proceed gingerly. Thus he skid to a stop. Reluctantly.

"What?" Pravus snapped, peeved at this interruption of his heroic gumption. Whilst eyeing Ballister's unfortunate beard. The man had grown fond of growing it out, such that it nearly reached his belly now. And unlike a few years ago, there was not a hint of gray in his hair, on account of a potion of youth Ballister had recently quaffed. So what remained was a veritable ocean of ginger waves, shining with a disturbing, rusty sheen.

Awful. Just *ghastly*. Pravus didn't even bother to suppress his reaction. Which he suspected was an aghast expression.

"The envoy from Grissam has arrived," Ballister stated, eyeing Pravus's plain gray shirt and pants with clear confusion. For the man had only ever seen Pravus in his king's uniform or gym attire, at least since he'd been crowned. Pravus glared at Ballister, crossing his arms over his chest.

"The *envoy?*" he snipped. For an envoy was a second-string ambassador. A backup to be used for inconsequential matters. In short, an insult.

"The ambassador was indisposed," Ballister explained.

"Then I shall dispose of his envoy," Pravus decided decisively, with a dismissive wave of his royal hand. "Now if you'll excuse me, I have actual important matters to attend to."

"But your Highness," Ballister began.

"Ta-ta," Pravus interrupted, stepping past the man and wiggling his fingers in a rather rude goodbye. And with that, he broke out into a sprint again, knowing full-well that the man would never be able to catch him.

"Wait…!" Lord Ballister cried out after him. But Pravus, being king, and thus not subject to orders from his subjects, decided not to subject himself to any more delays. For the subject at hand was destiny…and for a hero such as himself, the clarion call of adventure beckoned far more powerfully than any meager lord's demands.

"To the stables and our steeds!" Pravus cried, picking up his pace.

"At record speed!" Templeton agreed, matching pace beside him. And with that, the two men raced out of the castle, making their way toward the Royal Stables.

But while Pravus's impatience brought him to adventure sooner than he might otherwise have, in refusing to listen to Lord Ballister's protestations, he'd made an error most grave. An error that would haunt him for years to come…and that would bring tragedy upon his land.

Chapter 9

The evening of Chaos's disappearance, Valtora's doppelganger failed to find the boy. Chauncy stayed up the whole night flying with thrusts of his Staff of Wind, searching the city for his son. While calling out his name, unlike the doppelganger, who couldn't speak. But other than usher in news of a strange voice crying out "chaos, chaos!" in a rather haunting voice – news that terrified the city of Southwick the next morning, who couldn't see Chauncy in the darkness of night – the search had proven to be in vain.

So, with the sun starting to rise at the horizon, Chauncy had gone back home dejectedly.

He'd laid on the couch then, too ashamed to lay next to his wife – or rather, wives – in their hot-pink marital bed. And though he was utterly exhausted, he found that his guilt would not let him sleep. So he tossed and turned, and then tossed some more, until he heard the opening of his bedroom door on the second floor.

Chauncy closed his eyes then, pretending to sleep. For in his shame, he was loathe to be confronted by his failure to find Chaos, having driven the boy away in the first place. Not to mention the utterly asshole-ish things he'd said at the dinner table the night before.

Footsteps came down the stairs, rather gentle, indicating that it was Valtora. For Fury came down with a series of *bams*, Zora with a few *bangs*, and Epic without any sound at all. Chauncy rolled over to face the couch cushions, burying his face in them. Which was awfully cowardly, and thus, felt awful.

"Hey Chauncy-poo," he heard Valtora greet. To which he continued to fake being asleep. "Cut the shit," she added. "I know you're awake."

He groaned, shifting his weight as if just starting to wake up. Then he rolled over, squinting at her, then blinking rapidly, then yawning and stretching his arms. A tactic he'd used often when awoken by Fury's cries as an infant, after Valtora had gotten up to take care of the issue. Which was a terrible thing to do, but then

53

again, Valtora had done the same back to him. While most people hoped to marry a wonderful person, it was far better for one's peace of mind to marry someone a bit terrible. Wonderful people made others feel constantly bad about themselves; with Valtora, Chauncy could be his flawed self and avoid judgement, because she was just as bad, if not worse.

His display, to his dismay, convinced Valtora not in the least. At least if her triple eyeroll was any indication.

"You done?" she asked, putting a hand on her hip.

"Hmm?" he asked, yawning again for good measure.

"Get *up* already," she ordered. "Before I punch you in the dick."

Chauncy rolled out of bed right quick, knowing that she wasn't above hitting him down below. With Rooter always available to heal him, Valtora's threats of violence carried a bit more weight, if less permanence.

"Dick!" Fury cried gleefully from the top of the stairs, then came bounding down. Epic followed in stealthy silence, wearing his three piece suit yet again.

"What's wrong?" Valtora asked. Chauncy gave her a funny look.

"What's wrong?" he asked. "How about our son is missing because I drove him away?"

"Oh," she replied. "I thought you were too much of a pussy to face me because you acted like a total ass last night."

"Ah," he mumbled, his cheeks flushing.

"Like, throwing a temper tantrum and blaming everyone for everything you did and shit," she continued. But not in the customary accusatory way of standard wives. Instead, she accused – and accurately insulted – him with inappropriate cheer. "Like a little punk-ass *bitch*," she added, no doubt to stoke the flames a bit.

"Bitch!" Fury echoed, distressingly. But having spent his ire the night before, Chauncy had none left for this morning. Instead, he lowered his head in shame.

"Sorry poopy-dooz," he muttered miserably.

"Pfft," she replied. "So are you gonna make us breakfast or what?"

He blinked.

"What?"

"Make us breakfast," she repeated, as an order this time.

"But we have to find Chaos!" he protested.

"Not on an empty stomach we don't," she argued. "Eat first, search later."

Chauncy glanced at his children, who had already taken their seats at the kitchen table. And had witnessed their whole exchange, embarrassingly enough. Chauncy had always wanted to be the kind of father that his children would look up to, a powerful, authoritative man that was also funny and kind. To his dismay, he *still* wanted to be that kind of father. Because he wasn't.

He sighed then, trudging over to the kitchen to do his duty while his family watched. Well, most of his family, anyway. For Chaos was gone...to where, no one but Chaos knew. And it was up to Chauncy to make things right.

* * *

After feeding his family, everyone got ready for the day, which would normally mean preparing for another day at the shop. But today they got ready in an entirely different way, which was to say that they prepared for a more robust search effort than the night before. Valtora sent her doppelganger out to start another sweep of the city, while she and the rest of the family went to the backyard, where Valtora's hot-pink carriage – beautifully restored via funds from the Order of Mundus a few years back – was parked.

"Whooooa!" Fury breathed as she entered the carriage, all wide-eyed at the blinged-out interior.

"I know, right?" Valtora replied, smiling smugly at her accomplishment. For the carriage's construction had been a labor of love, whereas its destruction years back by Kyral – the self-described Lord of the Mirror Realm – had been a labor of hate, or at minimum, inconsideration. For most wrongs against others were a matter of a lack of consideration rather than outright malice, and outright malice was usually a matter of acting on ignorance. And it was safe to say that being inconsiderate was a simple matter of ignoring or being ignorant of the lived experience of others.

"SPARKLES!" Fury exclaimed, clutching her hands under her chin. Thus proving that she was in a remarkably different headspace than Chauncy was in. He loved her to pieces, but she was as deep as a puddle.

"Get in," Valtora told everyone. Rooter, Fury, and Epic filed in, while Valtora and Chauncy set out to summon Peter, Valtora's

55

faithful steed. With a burst of water from his Wetstone and the rays of the sun striking said mist just-so, a rainbow was generated.

"Come, Peter!" Valtora cried jubilantly.

But to Chauncy's surprise, Peter didn't come. No matter how many times Valtora told him to.

"Huh," he stated, rubbing his chin. For Peter had never failed to come before when thusly summoned. Valtora put her hands on her hips, looking rather pissed.

"What the hell?" she blurted out, stomping her foot. "Now what are we gonna do?"

"Go on foot?" Chauncy proposed. Valtora gave him a look.

"With *our* kids? Hell no," she replied.

"Well, um," Chauncy began, trying to come up with another plan. But Valtora beat him to the punch.

"Guess we'll just have to go to the Order of Mundus," she decided. Chauncy blinked.

"What?"

"Impy will know what to do," she explained. "He's got scrying orbs and shit that'll find Chaos in no time."

Chauncy felt the blood drain from his face, and immediately opened his mouth to protest. But again, Valtora interrupted him.

"I'll fly there," she decided unilaterally, sprouting her black metallic wings from the tattoos on her back. "Shouldn't take more than a couple days."

"No!" Chauncy blurted out as she began to flap said wings. She frowned.

"Why not?" she demanded. "It's a good plan."

"I mean, a few days is too long," Chauncy argued. "Chaos could be dead by then."

"What Daddy?" he heard Fury ask from inside the carriage. He realized that she was half hanging out of it, a mortified expression on her face.

"Dead tired," Chauncy clarified. "Like, super sleepy," he added when she clearly didn't know what that meant.

"Oh," she replied, turning away to mind her own business. Which mostly consisted of wide-eyed admiration of the carriage's sparkly interior.

"You got a better idea?" Valtora shot back. Chauncy paused, wracking his brain. For he knew that if Valtora reached Imperius, the jig would be up, and she'd realize the full extent of his misdeeds. But terror made his mind go blank, and he just stood there with his mouth half-open, staring at her. Blankly. "That's what I thought, she stated triumphantly.

"Well," he began, but she spread her wings, flapping them and rising from the ground.

"Bye," she said with a wave. "Make sure the kids don't die."

And with that, she flew up and away, heading south toward the Gate. Without even looking back. Or saying goodbye to her children, or giving them kisses or hugs, or any of the usual maternal things. She wasn't even close to the best mother in the world, as she would readily attest to. A fact that didn't bother Chauncy in the least, considering that – being not even close to the best father in the world – her imperfections made him feel far less guilty about his own. For again, the secret to feeling like a good person was to marry someone a bit worse than you were.

"Fuck," he swore. In front of his children, which was less than ideal.

"Fuck!" Fury shouted gleefully, for to be fair, it was a fun word to say. Chauncy stared at his retreating wife glumly, not even bothering to scold his daughter. He was struck with the sudden urge to fly after Valtora, but doing so would mean leaving his children unattended. To the people of Borrin, leaving a child unattended for even a minute was considered profound neglect, an act that might lead to kidnapping or even death. Despite the fact that kidnappings and deaths were quite rare, society had agreed that no child should ever be out of eyesight of a responsible adult, on pain of that adult promptly losing custody.

So Chauncy just stood there helplessly as his wife left him behind, knowing full-well that she would discover the truth soon enough. And then he'd have to face the full weight of her wrath for him having lied to her. Which, in comparison to having essentially screwed over the fate of the world, was, to him at least, by far the greater sin.

Chapter 10

After being driven from the village of Erp, Chaos continued his journey ever southward, following the winding dirt path. At length he didn't even have the strength to *not* follow it, falling into a kind of dull-minded trance. His stomach – which had ached terribly before – quieted down at last, which was a relief. But as it turned out, his relief was brief. For as morning transitioned to noon, and then noon to late afternoon, his hunger returned, until eating was all he could think about. He found himself fantasizing about the breakfast he'd refused to eat the morning before, the mere thought of which made him salivate profusely.

He imagined himself eating it one tiny bite at a time, savoring every last delicious little morsel.

At length even this passed, and he transitioned to beating himself up. Psychologically, that was. For in choosing to wing it during this trip, he'd done his past self a favor by decreasing his workload, but his present self a terrible disservice.

"Idiot," he grumbled at his past self. While knowing full well that his past self couldn't hear him. "Thanks a lot," he added, kicking a stone. It tumbled madly across the ground, but he ignored it, continuing forward one step at a time. A part of him knew that the wisest thing for him to do would be to turn around and go back home. But the far less wise part of him felt that to do so would be to admit defeat, and as usually occurred in these instances, wisdom was overruled by pride.

So Chaos continued, one step in front of the other, until the sun had nearly touched the horizon. With each step, he was acutely aware that he was one step further from safety…and a step closer to calamity.

Darkness fell over the land, the blue sky transitioning to a red-purple sunset, and then darkening until countless stars were visible in the heavens. Far more stars than he'd ever seen in Southwick. He stared up at them as he walked, his feet aching and his legs feeling like lead. He was pretty sure he'd developed blisters on his soles, which made him wince with each step. Eventually his eyelids began to close of their own accord, and he felt himself slipping off into unconsciousness. Which was inconvenient, given that he was still standing. So he went a few yards off the side of the road, finding some fallen leaves and collecting them into a makeshift bed. And with that, he curled up on it, closing his eyes and drifting off to...

Aaaaoooooooooo...

Chaos's eyelids snapped open, the hackles on his neck rising on-end. He laid there, pricking his ears. The sound had been from somewhere behind him, and far away. But not as far as he would've liked.

Aaaaoooooooooo...

He stiffened, the haunting sound echoing through the night air. It was the sound of a wolf howling, he realized. And it seemed closer than it'd been before. Sitting up, he peered into the darkness the way he'd come. But unlike the city of Southwick, nighttime in the wilderness was terribly dark; he couldn't make out much of anything in that sea of inky blackness.

Aaaaoooooooooo...

His heart leapt into his throat; the sound was *definitely* closer now.

Crap, he swore silently, scrambling to his feet. His heart *thumped* in his chest, and he strode away from the noise, following the path southward. The howling had to be the better part of a mile away, but it was impossible to really tell from the sound alone. Still, the thought of a pack of wolves on the hunt made him want to be nowhere near where they were, and so Chaos picked up his pace, jogging down the road. The blisters on his feet hurt with every step, but he hardly noticed now.

Aaaaoooooooooo...

The sound was much *much* closer now.

Terror seized Chaos, and he broke into an all-out run, barreling down the road as quickly as he could. He heard more howls from behind, and glanced back. At first he saw only darkness.

But then he saw glowing silver-blue eyes flashing in the moonlight, only a few hundred feet away...and heard the *whump-a-whump* of canine paws thumping rhythmically against the road.

"Crap!" he blurted out. And then cursed, realizing that if he hadn't given his position away before, he'd done it now. He pushed himself to the limit, gasping for air as he sprinted.

Aaaaooooooooo...

He glanced back again, and saw that the strangely glowing eyes were closer now, less than a hundred feet away...and he could make out the faint silhouettes of the wolves' bodies as they charged after him. They were closing the distance rapidly, their ears flat against their heads.

"Crap!" Chaos gasped, his lungs on fire as he ran. He spotted a few trees ahead and to the right, and veered off the road, running toward them. If he could just reach the trees in time, and climb up one of them to safety...

He heard one of the wolves growl behind him, so close that it couldn't be more than a few dozen feet away. He cried out, charging at the tree with the lowest branches ahead, his breath coming in ragged gasps. It was only twenty feet away now. Ten.

Come on...

He reached out for the lowest branch as he neared the tree...and then felt a sharp pain in his left upper arm as jaws closed around it, yanking him violently backward.

Chaos didn't even have time to scream.

He toppled backward, landing flat on his back on the ground. The wolf dragged him away from the tree by the arm, its teeth sinking deep into his flesh...even as another wolf pounced on him, its front paws landing on his belly. Air blasted out of his lungs, and he tried to shove the thing off him with his free hand. But it was incredibly heavy...and when he shoved its chest, his hand sank into something cold and wet...and *slimy*.

The wolf atop him turned around until its face was above him, its eyes glowing with a pale silver-blue light. Or rather, its eye. For its right eye was missing...and that wasn't all. The entire right side of its face was missing, including its ear...and its skull was visible, maggots hanging out of its right eye socket.

"Holy!" Chaos blurted out, trying desperately to twist away from the thing and escape. But its paws pinned his chest to the ground.

The horrid creature stared at him for a moment longer, its fangs bared, slick drool dripping from its lower jaw.

Then it lunged forward, opening its maw to clamp down on Chaos's neck.

Chapter 11

After blowing off Lord Ballister, King Pravus and Templeton made their way to the Royal Stables, mounting their respective steeds. Both geldings, or stallions that'd had their most precious parts removed. Pravus preferred riding geldings over stallions, at least when it came to the equine kind. Stallions were awfully territorial, while mares were on occasion temperamental, but geldings were as reliable as could be.

So it was that the two men found themselves riding out of the massive silver double-doors of Cumulus and continuing onward via the King's Passage, toward Old Langsroth. An ancient city far to the south, in a little country now called Grissam. A country that hadn't been so little in its heyday long ago. Before King Pravus the First had founded the kingdom that now bore his name, the Kingdom of Langsroth had been one of the most powerful countries of antiquity. A kingdom that Pravus had been forced to learn about as a child, which at the time had seemed pointless trivia. The Kingdom of Langsroth had been destroyed long ago, only its capitol city of Langsroth remaining. The city had fallen into disrepair, abandoned by the country of Grissam that'd claimed a small part of the old kingdom's land. No one had dared lived in Old Langsroth since…and for good reason.

Old Langsroth was cursed.

Or at least, that's what a bunch of long-dead academics had written in the histories. Honestly, Pravus didn't have much faith in history, it being composed mostly of stories composed by people who believed the stories told by other people. Politics had taught Pravus that everyone lied all the time, as much to themselves as others. Not to mention that only the powerful had a voice, and crafting a convenient narrative to maintain that power constituted the main job of the aristocracy. Thus a true account of the past was impossible, and history was a heaping pile of elitist horse manure.

"Smell that air!" Templeton stated cheerfully, his black hair swept back rather fetchingly in the breeze.

"Fresh and sweet!" Pravus replied with equal cheer, smiling at his cousin. For it was ever Templeton's way to appreciate the good in things, big and small.

"I daresay it's the perfect day to start an adventure," Templeton mused. "If I were a superstitious man, I'd proclaim it a good omen."

"But you're not," Pravus pointed out.

"No," Templeton agreed. "But I can appreciate the appeal of it."

"You mean taking comfort in fictions?"

"I mean that the external world cares for us," Templeton corrected. Pravus frowned at this as they rode.

"Go on," he prompted.

"Omens are signs that the world sends us to foretell future events," Templeton explained. "They imply that the universe is alive and cares for us."

"Hmm," Pravus murmured. Then he shook his head. "No, I'd wager they're mankind's desperate attempt to predict the future, to better prepare for it."

"A point of view not inconsistent with mine," Templeton pointed out.

"If the world truly cared for people, it wouldn't speak in riddles."

"Fair enough," Templeton conceded.

They road for a while longer, and Pravus eyed his cousin, eventually arching an eyebrow.

"But?" he pressed, sensing that the man had more to say.

"I believe that the world *does* care for us," Templeton stated. "In that we, being of and a part of it, care so much for each other."

Pravus considered this, and found it to be true, at least in part.

"But we also hate each other," he argued.

"Only out of ignorance," Templeton replied. "Love and joy are the basis of our beings."

"Certainly in your case, dearest cousin," Pravus said. "But not in others."

"I daresay I've never met a baby that didn't smile, or laugh joyously when tickled," Templeton argued. "Even the greatest of villains began as a baby. And as a baby, love, joy, and nurturing were their fundamental needs."

62

"I suppose you're right," Pravus conceded, inclining his head. "Once again you find the good in others, sweet cousin. Would that I only possessed your indomitable cheer!"

"You have me as your companion," Templeton declared with a sunny smile. "So you have it whenever you need!"

Pravus couldn't help but smile back, and found his spirit soaring as he rode beside his best friend. He gazed at the King's Passage extending far into the distance, feeling the *pull* of adventure drawing him gradually closer to his destination. It was a wonderful, weighty feeling, to embark on a journey to accomplish great deeds. But for the first time, it was less for his kingdom than it was for himself.

"You feel it too?" Templeton inquired.

"I do," Pravus confirmed.

And so, with the grand spirit of adventure filling their hearts, the two men rode ever southward toward Old Langsroth, to meet Pravus's destiny.

Chapter 12

Chaos watched as the horrible wolf's jaws opened wide, its long, curved fangs gleaming in the moonlight. It lunged at his throat, ready to tear out his windpipe…and he didn't even have time to scream.

He closed his eyes, waiting for the end…and instead, he heard a *yelp*, accompanied by a flash of brilliant golden light. The weight from the paws on his chest vanished.

Chaos opened his eyes, seeing the starry night sky above, the wolf who'd nearly torn his throat out gone. Stars twinkled in the night sky, even as there was another flash of gold light, another *yelp*, and then a blood-curdling howl.

"Urrnnghh!" a voice grunted, followed by a bone-crunching *fwumpcrack!*

Chaos heard the sound of retreating paws, and then a momentary silence, after which footsteps approached. He saw a face appear above him then, leaning over him and peering down at him. A girl's face, rather pretty, with eyes that seemed to glow with a golden light in the darkness, and long golden hair that cascaded down to tickle his cheeks.

"Damn," the girl declared. "You were about to get fucked *up*."

She just stared down at him, and he grunted, then rolled onto his stomach, wincing at the pain this caused in his right upper arm. He got to his feet unsteadily, glancing around him. The wolves were gone, having beaten a hasty retreat…leaving him alone with whoever the heck this girl was. She was about his age, or maybe a little older, and two inches taller. She had long legs and a short waist, and was slender as could be. But she had muscle, he noted. More than he did, to his immediate dismay. And she was awfully pretty, in a dangerous-looking sort of way. She wore a sleeveless golden top and golden pants, and carried a big ol' silver mace in one hand. One that had runes that glowed with a gold light that slowly faded to darkness, and that was coated with blood and bits of flesh and fur.

"You're welcome," she told him, looking him up and down. And ultimately chose down as the proper direction to look at him.

"Uh...thanks," he mumbled, rubbing his injured left arm. It was slick with blood, and hurt something terrible.

"Come on," she prompted, turning away from him and striding the opposite way he'd been going. "Before they come back."

"Uh..." Chaos replied rather lamely, still surprised that he was still alive. But he followed her, catching up and walking beside her. While clutching his injured arm, which hurt something fierce...and hurt more with each step he took.

"You going to finish that thought or not?" she asked.

"Uh," he repeated. "Thanks for saving me."

"You already thanked me."

Aaaaooooooooo...

Chaos glanced back, the haunting sound giving him goosebumps.

"There's more," he warned.

"No shit."

"We should get out of here," he told her.

"We are," she replied. If she was at all concerned about the howling, she certainly didn't show it. In fact, she walked with a kind of swagger, her golden eyes steely as she strode. Which was strange, because she couldn't be much older than he was.

"Shouldn't we like, run or something?" he asked.

"You already tried that," she shot back, giving him a sidelong glance. He grimaced. "They come after us, we fight," she stated. Then she eyed him up and down. "*I* fight," she corrected. He looked at the flanged mace resting against her shoulder.

"You sure you can beat those things?"

"Only thing I'm sure of is myself," she replied. Which wasn't really a direct answer to his question, but good enough. Maybe.

"What were they?" he asked.

"Looked like zombie wolves to me."

"They sure did," he agreed.

"Never seen zombies with those color eyes," she noted.

Chaos glanced back, peering into the darkness, trying to make out silver-blue wolf-eyes. But he couldn't see anything.

"Why aren't they coming after us?" he asked.

She shrugged.

"Aren't you worried?" he pressed.

"No."

"We could die," he pointed out.

"We will," she replied. He blinked.

"We...will?"

"Eventually," she clarified. He rolled his eyes, following alongside her, still clutching at his injured arm. The wolf's fangs had left small holes in his shirt, with slick mushy clots and blood seeping from them. The pain was steadily worsening, throbbing horribly with every movement.

"I should've brought Rooter," he grumbled. She raised an eyebrow. "He's a...he heals people," he clarified. "With magic."

"Why didn't you?" she asked.

"I um...didn't think about it," he admitted, his cheeks flushing. There was no way for her to notice in the dark, however. Or so he assumed. Still, she gave him an odd look. As if he were odd.

"Why were you here?" she asked.

"I'm traveling to Grissam," he answered.

"On foot," she stated, continuing to give him an odd look. "At night."

"Uh...yeah," he replied with another blush, lowering his gaze and scratching the back of his head.

"With no provisions," she noted. "Or weapons."

He didn't bother to answer, because the answer was embarrassingly obvious.

"So you're retarded," she concluded.

"*No*," he answered rather defensively. And indignantly, because that was a terribly off-putting word that his father had insisted he never use. Even though Mom used it like, all the time.

"Then you're an idiot," she decided.

"I'm not," he retorted. To his dismay, she didn't reply. "I'm not," he insisted. Still no response. He decided to change the subject. "What were you doing out here anyway?" he asked.

"Hunting zombies," she answered.

"Why?"

"Paladin," she stated, tapping her chest with her free hand.

"Huh?"

"Holy warrior," she translated. "I kill zombies for Vita."

"Vita?" he asked.

"The goddess Vita," she clarified. He just stared at her blankly. "Goddess of Life," she added. "Zombies are abominations. The dead should not live, so Vita calls upon one paladin each generation to take them back to their natural state."

66

"By killing them," Chaos deduced.

"Right," she replied. Then she frowned. "You've never heard of Vita?"

"Nope," he admitted.

"You grow up under a rock?"

"I grew up in Borrin," he replied. Her eyebrows shot up.

"You're from beyond the Gate?"

"Yeah," he replied. "I'm a wizard," he added rather proudly. She gave him a supremely doubting look. "I am," he insisted.

"Okay," she replied, clearly not believing him.

"I'm on a quest," he continued, gritting his teeth against another jolt of pain in his left shoulder.

"To do what?"

"To…ah…" he stammered. "To find my destiny, I guess."

"And that is?"

He paused.

"I don't really know," he confessed. "Imperius Fanning just told me to go to Grissam to find my destiny. He never told me what it was."

She gave him a funny look, her golden eyes seeming to glow slightly in the moonlight.

"What?" he pressed.

"Nothing," she replied, turning her gaze forward again. He did as well, and spotted a faint golden light in the distance. Or rather, a dome made of golden light to one side of the road. It was large enough to fit a horse in…which was exactly what *was* within it. A beautiful golden horse with a golden saddle and bulging saddlebags.

"Is that yours?" he asked.

"That's Gwendolyn," she replied. "And she isn't *mine*," she added. "She's my companion."

They walked up to the dome, and the girl stepped into it, the dome's golden light making her silver mace shimmer. She tied her mace to a saddlebag, then closed her eyes and lowered her gaze, seeming to pray. The golden light promptly faded. Then she mounted the horse – Gwendolyn – in a single athletic movement, grabbing the reins.

"Come on," she told Chaos, patting the saddle behind her.

He walked up to the horse, then quickly realized that with his injured shoulder, he wouldn't be able to get on the horse. Not without suffering tremendous pain, anyway.

"Ow," he blurted out on the first attempt, clutching at his shoulder. She hesitated, then sighed.

"Hold on," she grumbled, closing her eyes again. When she opened them, they were glowing bright gold...and a beautiful gold light shone from her fingertips. She leaned down then, putting a hand on his injured shoulder. The gold light seeped from her fingers, spreading across his shoulder. Then it seemed to flow into his flesh through his puncture wounds.

Chaos gasped, a wave of the most incredible feeling washing over him. It was like a mother's sweet love...or the feeling of utter comfort when cuddling under a warm blanket at night. It was the feeling not just of safety or security, but of being totally *cared* for. The knowledge that, in this moment, at least, everything was going to be okay.

"Oohhhh," he moaned, his eyes rolling back in his head quite involuntarily. Much as they'd done in his bath the other morning.

Then the feeling began to fade, and he tried to hold on to it, desperate for it to stay. But try as he might, it left him...and left him feeling its absence keenly.

"Now try," she told him, patting the saddle again.

Chaos blinked, then realized his shoulder didn't hurt anymore...and that his wounds were gone. He rotated his shoulder gingerly, then more aggressively, breaking out in a smile as he did so. Then he realized that his feet no longer hurt, or his legs. Or anything, for that matter. He didn't even feel hungry anymore, or tired.

In short, he felt fantastic.

He scrambled up into the saddle behind the girl, doing so embarrassingly badly. But at length he made it.

"Hold on to my waist," she ordered. "Don't get sassy."

He did so, feeling awkward. She snapped the reins, and they started off down the road in a trot.

"What was that?" he asked. "What you did to me, I mean."

"Vita's blessing," the girl replied. "She gives me the power to Lay on Hands once a day."

"Lay on Hands?"

"Total healing," she explained. "Cures all infections, diseases, injuries, hunger, sleepiness...everything."

"Wow," he murmured. "Thanks."

"Once I use it, I can't channel her power until I get some sleep," she warned. "So if we're attacked again, you're screwed."

68

"Ah," he mumbled, glancing back. "Can Gwendolyn outrun a wolf?"

"For a bit."

"Great," he grumbled, glancing back. He couldn't spot any wolves in the darkness, and hadn't heard their haunting howls for a while now. But still, his guts squirmed uneasily.

"You got a name?" she asked.

"Chaos," he replied.

"Your name's Chaos?" she pressed.

"Chaos Little," he confirmed. He paused. "What's yours?" he asked.

"Destiny," she replied.

Chapter 13

Chaos spent the rest of the night riding with Destiny along the road leading southward, Gwendolyn trotting tirelessly hour after hour. As the sun rose peeked out from under the horizon, Chaos was surprised to find that he still wasn't tired at all. This despite the fact that he'd been awake for over twenty-four hours now, and hadn't eaten in days. Sure, he was a little sore from riding Gwendolyn all night, but other than that, he felt perfectly fine.

"That's some pretty powerful magic," he mused. "Laying on Hands, I mean."

Destiny stirred, but didn't say anything. She'd been quiet for most of the trip, only answering questions she deemed worthy of being addressed. But when it came to statements meant to start a conversation, she usually didn't take the bait.

"Aren't you tired?" he asked.

"No," she replied.

"You've been up all night," he pointed out.

"Vita's blessings rejuvenate me."

"Oh," he mumbled. "How does that...work? Her blessings, I mean."

"When I was six, I sensed Her presence for the first time," Destiny explained. "She chose me as her paladin, to support life in its intended form."

"Like not zombie-form," he guessed.

"Right."

"So how do you, uh, use your magic?" he asked.

"It isn't my magic," Destiny countered. "It's Vita's."

"So how do you use *her* magic?" he pressed.

"I am Her vassal and Her vessel," she explained. "I pledge myself to Her and She acts through me."

He waited for her to elaborate, but she did not.

"Um...so you're what, like her flesh puppet?" he translated. She twisted around to give him a dirty look.

"No," she replied. "She doesn't control me. When I need Her, I open up to Her and connect with Her. Then Her power flows through me."

"Like opening a dam to let some water out," he stated.

"In a way."

"Why'd she choose you?" he asked. She shrugged. "How long have you been killing zombies for?"

"Since I was eight," she answered. "About six years."

"Wow."

Chaos considered this, finding himself feeling glum. To think that he'd wasted the last six years of his life going through the same old routine day after day at the shop, living the same day again and again...all while Destiny had been honing her skills as the chosen champion of a goddess. The simple act of doing different things had lead to two entirely different lives...and his was by far the worse. A few hours around Destiny had already made him feel absolutely useless. A feeling he absolutely hated.

I need to start doing *things*, he told himself, jutting his chin out firmly. What those things were, he wasn't exactly sure. But he knew he needed to get on it, and soon. Otherwise he'd end up being a useless adult, doing nothing while heroes like Destiny changed the world. For it was clear that Destiny was the kind of person that made things happen, while he was someone that things happened to.

He fell silent then, the *clip-clop* of Gwendolyn's hooves putting him into a kind of trance. The sun continued its rise to their right, sending warm rays across the land. At length, Destiny brought them to a halt, dismounting and rummaging through one of the saddlebags.

"Get down," she ordered. "Breakfast."

Chaos did so, albeit far less gracefully than she had. She pulled out a big bag of nuts and two leather flasks, handing one to him.

"Water," she told him, taking a swig of her own flask. He did as well, finding the water warm and...not great. But it was wet, and being the first thing he'd drank in days, it was good enough. She poured out some nuts into his hands then, and they both stood there munching on them for a bit. After which she placed everything back in the saddlebag, and then went to the saddlebag on the other side, pulling out what looked like a sleeping bag. She threw it on the ground, then got inside, lying on her side and closing her eyes.

71

"What should uh, I do?" he asked.

"You should let me sleep," she replied. "Don't wake me up unless something's coming to kill us."

"Right," he mumbled.

And with that, she began to snore. Chaos watched her for a bit, not knowing what else to do. He didn't feel tired at all on account of the whole Laying on Hands thing. In fact, he felt positively wonderful, as if every possible appetite and need had been taken care of.

So, with nothing to take care of, Chaos had nothing to do but wait.

* * *

When Destiny finally awoke hours later, she got up wordlessly, putting the sleeping bag back in the saddlebag, then eating some more nuts and drinking more water. That done, she promptly lowered herself to her knees on the grass.

"What are you..." Chaos began.

"Morning buffs," she replied, closing her eyes. "Shut up."

Chaos's jaw snapped shut, for he'd been about to ask what morning buffs were. So instead of talking, he watched as she lifted her hands in a position of prayer.

Suddenly, her posture changed, and she took a deep breath in. When she opened her eyes, her irises were glowing with an intense golden light. This spread throughout her body, a glow coming from just under her skin.

Then it pulsed, and the light vanished.

"What was that?" he asked.

"Vita's Dribbling Rejuvenation," she answered. "A blessing that gives me a continuous supply of vigor, so I don't get fatigued."

"Wow," he murmured. "That's pretty awesome."

She closed her eyes again, opening them to reveal glowing golden irises. This time, however, that glow spread a fraction of an inch *above* her skin, then seemed to crystallize to form translucent glowing plates over her body. These vanished, and she stood.

"What was that?" he asked.

"Vita's Crystal Skin," she replied. "Magic armor that can take a few hits before cracking. Its why I don't have to wear heavy armor," she added, gesturing at her golden shirt and pants. "I can still move quickly and without being encumbered, but I'm protected."

"Whoa," he breathed. "I wish I could do that."

"What *can* you do?" she asked. He blinked, then blushed.

"Um…"

"Didn't mean it as an insult," she reassured him. "You said you're a wizard. What can you do?"

"Oh. Um, well, I can do…surprises," he answered.

She just stared at him.

"Like, chaos is my magic," he continued. "I can make unexpected things happen. Unexpectedly," he added. Lamely.

"So your magic is to surprise people?"

"Sort of," he replied. "Like, one time I dropped a meteorite on someone's head because they were bothering me."

She arched an eyebrow.

"You murdered someone because they annoyed you?"

"He didn't die," he clarified. "It was Imperius Fanning. I was four, and he, uh…it's a long story."

She continued to look at him with an arched eyebrow.

"I also…" he began, then stopped. He'd been about to tell her about how he'd gotten Zora pregnant with Epic, but considering that she was a paladin, and duty-bound to destroy all zombies, informing her of Zora seemed like a bad idea. "…did other stuff," he concluded, scratching the back of his head and lowering his gaze.

"I still don't get it," she admitted.

"You have to see it to get it," he told her.

She ended the conversation then, praying one more time, then touching Gwendolyn. The same golden light pulsed under the horse's skin, then faded.

"Vita's Dribbling Rejuvenation?" he guessed.

"Yep," she confirmed. "Let's go," she prompted, mounting Gwendolyn. He mounted the mare as well, only slightly less awkwardly than before. Off they went then, continuing their journey south.

* * *

Late morning gave way to afternoon as Gwendolyn brought them southward, the horse never tiring in its rather quick pace. Vita's Dribbling Rejuvenation proved potent magic indeed, allowing Gwendolyn to exert herself for hours on end without any rest needed. At length, grassland with its few scattered trees gave way to a grand forest to the southeast. One with trees as large as he'd ever seen.

"What's that?" he asked, pointing to the forest.

"The Great Wood," Destiny answered. Chaos's eyes widened. For it was ever the path of destiny to venture off to the Great Wood, plunge deep into the Cave of Wonder, and find the power within oneself to complete one's quest. At least according to his parents.

"We're going there?" he asked.

"We're going to Grissam."

"But every time my dad went on an adventure, destiny brought him to the Great Wood," Chaos protested.

"Well *this* Destiny isn't going to," Destiny grumbled. "We're going to Grissam. Where I live. And that's that."

"But…"

"You want me to drop you off?" she asked, twisting around to give him an arch of the eyebrow. He grimaced, knowing full-well that he'd probably get lost without her. Or get dead. "That's what I thought," she grumbled, facing forward again.

Chaos sighed, watching as they followed the road, passing the Great Wood by. Then he frowned, realizing that if he *did* go to the Great Wood, he'd just be doing what he'd done before. He'd already been there three times, at least according to his parents. *Not* going there meant doing something new…which is exactly what he'd wanted all along.

He sat up a bit straighter, breaking out into a smile. For now he had no idea what to expect. A fact that suddenly made the coming adventure seem magical indeed, in contrast to the last nine or so years of his life. Most of his life had been absolutely wasted, as far as he was concerned. But now he was correcting that situation, for in finding his destiny, he was sure to come into his own, and become the powerful wizard he was fated to be.

With that, Chaos faced the future not with reticence, but acceptance. And so he continued onward with Destiny toward his destination, eager to see what would happen next.

Chapter 14

After his wife's abrupt departure to the Isle of Mundus, Chauncy found himself suffering the perfect torture of being both anxious and depressed. For anxiety was suffering the future before it came, and depression was suffering the past well after it was gone. He had ample cause, of course, to suffer from both, as he'd acted badly and would very soon suffer the consequences of said bad actions.

But in the *here* and *now*, there was nothing he could do about either the past or the future. Other than obsess about them, which he did. So his suffering of the past was multiplied, and that of his future as well.

Fuck, he thought as he lay in bed the morning after Valtora's departure, staring at the ceiling. He'd hoped beyond hope that Chaos would've returned yesterday, but his hopes had been in vain. The boy was gone, and Chauncy's imagination had seen fit to conjure up all sorts of gruesome reasons as to why he hadn't come back, asshole that it was. In fact, even thinking this caused it to ramp up its efforts to torture him, generating fresh new scenarios to explain Chaos's absence.

Chauncy found himself beginning the usual cycle of anxious thoughts, like psychic itches that demanded to be scratched…only to become *more* itchy, and so on. Then there came a knock on the front door.

His heart skipped a beat, and he leapt out of bed, rushing to get dressed. Not in his usual special underwear and wizard's robe, but in mundane clothes. This done, he dashed downstairs, dodging a few socks left there by ZoMonsterz. He swung open the door, expecting to see Chaos on the other side…and instead, he saw someone else entirely. Or rather, two someone's. A trim, bald, elderly man standing next to a gaunt elderly woman with hair as short as a man's, both of them raising their eyebrows in surprise at Chauncy's abrupt door-opening.

"Chauncy!" the old man blurted out. "How in the gosh diggity-darn *heck* are ya?"

"Uncle Willard?" Chauncy asked, hardly believing his eyes. Uncle Willard beamed at him, spreading his slender arms out wide.

"Chauncy boy!" Willard exclaimed. "Come give your big ol' Willy a *hug*."

* * *

Having gotten a single limp hug from Uncle Willard's wife Gretchen and more than a few from the man himself, Gretchen went upstairs to wake up the kids. Meanwhile, Uncle Willard rushed into the house, flapping his hands a bit as he ran into the kitchen. The two men sat down at the kitchen table, and Uncle Willard gave Chauncy a big smile.

"Well isn't this *fun*?" he asked. "What's it been, fourteen years since we met up?"

"Sixteen I think," Chauncy replied.

"Too long," Willard mused. Then he winked. "At least, that's what Gretchen always tells me."

Chauncy glanced over his shoulder, seeing Gretchen leading the kids into the kitchen. While shaking her head at him. And gesturing with her index finger and thumb, spread apart a disturbingly small distance.

"Um," Chauncy began.

"So where's *wifey*?" Willard asked. "I heard you got yourself a straight-up *vixen*."

"She's out," Chauncy answered. "Um, business trip," he lied.

"Oh well isn't that a shame," Willard said with a pout. "Isn't that a shame, Gretch?" he asked, twisting around to glance at his wife, who was busy cooking breakfast. She ignored him. "That's a shame," Willard repeated, turning back to Chauncy.

"She'll be back," Chauncy stated.

"Oh *good*," Willard replied. "We'd just love to meet her!"

"Yes," Chauncy replied, still a bit taken aback, and what's more, distracted. "Good," he added, having already forgotten what Willard had just said.

"A shame about your grandmother," Willard said, his expression turning grim. He sighed. "We were on a little cruise when it happened, weren't we Gretchen?" he asked. Gretchen continued to cook, having apparently checked out of the

76

conversation. "We didn't hear about it until weeks after the funeral," he continued. "We came here to visit, but you were off on some sort of journey. Not that we knew that at the time," he added. "We made it to Southwick just after the goblins raided the city. Thought you were…" He ran a finger across his skinny neck, then stuck out his tongue and pretended to be dead.

"Still alive," Chauncy stated, fidgeting a bit.

"Where's your eldest?" Willard asked, looking around. "Heard you had a ten-year-old."

"Thirteen," Epic corrected. Flatly. "He ran away."

Willard blinked.

"He what now?"

"He ran away," Epic repeated.

"Um," Chauncy began.

"He ran away from home?" Willard blurted out incredulously.

"Yes," Epic replied. "Father yelled at him and said 'If you're going to act like this, I'd rather not have you around.' And then Chaos left and hasn't come back."

"My goodness," Willard exclaimed, putting a hand to his mouth in horror.

"That wasn't exactly how it…" Chauncy began.

"How long has he been gone for?" Willard interrupted.

"Two days," Epic answered, before Chauncy could. Chauncy grimaced, wanting nothing more than to tell Epic to go to his room. But while unfair flexing of his authority was something he could get away with when there was no one else around, with company present, he was forced to be well-behaved.

"My *goodness*," Willard repeated, putting his hand to his mouth again.

"Father lied," Epic continued. "Mother did not go on a business trip. She went to find Chaos."

Chauncy glared at his son, opening his mouth to protest. And then closed it, realizing that there was absolutely no way for him to make this situation any better by doing so. So he just sat there like a lying little bitch. Because in truth, that's precisely what he was.

"Well I'm sure she'll find him," Uncle Willard stated, dismissing all of this with a rather dramatic wave of his hand.

"I don't know," Chauncy confessed, his eyes growing moist. He lowered his gaze in much-deserved shame. "He was really, really angry with me."

"Whatever for?" Willard inquired. Chauncy shrugged.

"I don't know," he admitted. "He's just…he's just angry all the time. He seems to hate his life, and I don't know why."

"Oh, that's just a phase, isn't it Gretch?" Willard asked his wife. Who'd finished making breakfast, and had doled it out to Epic and Fury, who sat at the table. Gretch just stood there, not eating, staring off at nothing.

"I'm not so sure," Chauncy countered.

"Well of course not," Uncle Willard replied. "You haven't lived through it yet."

"Oh," Chauncy replied. Which was not agreeing, but also not disagreeing. And as such, a perfectly wimpy retort. His forte, as Valtora would certainly attest to.

"Hi!" Fury exclaimed, smiling and waving exuberantly at Willard. "What's *your* name?"

"Uncle Willard," he replied. "But you can call me Big Willie."

"Don't," Gretchen blurted out. Which was the first thing Chauncy had heard her say.

"Big Willie!" Fury cried gleefully. After which Gretchen lowered her face to her hands. And kept it there.

"Accurate," Willard told Chauncy, throwing him a wink.

"So anyway," Chauncy stated.

"Well the way I see it, if Chaos left, it'd make sense if *both* of you went to look for him," Willard stated. "After all, you can't really be present as a father if you're worried to death about Chaos."

"True," Chauncy had to admit.

"I tell ya what," Willard declared, slapping the tabletop. "Gretch and I will stay and take care of the kids. You go find Chaos, Chauncy-boy!"

"Uh…really?" Chauncy asked.

"Sure!" Willard stated. "Gretch and I raised three boys together," he added. "We're old pros, aren't we dear?"

Gretchen kept her face in her hands, just standing there.

"You go off and find your boy," Willard insisted. "We'll take care of everything."

"But the shop," Chauncy protested.

"Easy-peasy," Willard stated. "I'll just write a cutesy wootsy little ol' sign saying we'll closed for a few days."

"Oh," Chauncy mumbled. "Um…okay."

"Go on," Willard urged, making shooing movements with his hands.

"Now?"

"No time like the present," he pointed out. Chauncy paused, then did get up.

"I guess I'll get changed," he decided. And with that, he grabbed his wizard's robe from the closet, then went upstairs to change into it. Back downstairs he went, grabbing his Staff of Wind. "You sure you'll be okay?" he asked Willard.

"Okay?" Willard replied, giving him a look. "We'll be *fabulous*, don't you worry."

"Okay," Chauncy decided. "Um…I guess I'll see you later kids," he added.

"Bye Big Daddy Nyum-Nyums!" Fury exclaimed, using her pet name for him. She jumped out of her chair and rushed up to him, and leaping into his arms and giving him the kind of hug that truly meant something. His heart melted, and even Gretchen clutched at her heart, so moved was she by Fury's love. Then Fury pulled away, tousling Chauncy's hair, and gave him a big ol' adorable smile. "Love you," she told him. And clearly, *clearly* meant it.

"Aww, love you too," he replied with a smile of his own. Then he glanced at Epic. "Buy buddy," he offered.

"Farewell Father," Epic replied. "Until we meet again."

Chauncy disengaged from Fury, who went back to the table to finish eating, then turned to the door.

"Oh Chauncy-boy?" Willard asked.

"Yes?" Chauncy replied.

"How long do you suppose you'll be gone?"

"Um…I dunno, maybe a day?" Chauncy guessed.

"Take your time," Willard urged. "We'll be here when you get back, won't we Gretch?" Who didn't reply.

"Bye," Chauncy said. And then he opened the door, venturing outside…and saw Valtora's doppelganger standing there at the doorstep before him. "Oh, hey," he greeted.

The doppelganger greeted him back…by slapping him right across the frickin' face.

Chapter 15

After another full day's journey, Chaos and Destiny dismounted to make camp. Which meant Destiny curling up in her sleeping bag while Chaos was forced to curl up on the grass. Another consequence of his decision not to prepare for the trip. As it turned out, winging it had certainly made his journey more interesting…but mostly by making it far more painful than it had to be.

As such, it took far longer for him to fall asleep than if he'd been nestled in a sleeping bag of his own. But fall asleep he did, waking at the crack of dawn.

After another breakfast of nuts and water – and Destiny casting her morning buffs – they got back in the saddle, continuing southward. This time, Chaos found himself not at all in the mood to talk, and Destiny was more than happy to settle into a comfortable silence. In this way, they continued onward, until Chaos saw an unexpectedly familiar sight: a two-hundred-foot-tall stone wall, and golden double-doors nearly the same height. They looked exactly like the Gate between Southwick and Pravus, save for the fact that the doors were golden rather than silver. The road they were traveling on led right up to it, and Destiny dismounted, praying silently. Then she stopped, eyeing Chaos.

"If you're a wizard, you should be able to open the Gate," she stated. She gestured at the doors then, prompting him to do so.

"Can *you* open them?" he asked, feeling a bit irritable. For he was *not* a morning person.

"Vita's magic allows me to," she replied. "Go on," she added, gesturing at the doors again.

"Fine," he grumbled. He walked up to the double-doors, putting a hand on one of them.

Thunk.

The door swung open, and Chaos beamed Destiny a self-satisfied look, crossing his arms over his chest.

"*Told* you I was a wizard," he declared.

"I don't believe what I'm told," she replied. "I believe what I'm *showed*."

Chaos paused.

"That was actually a pretty good line," he had to admit. Destiny ignored him, getting back on Gwendolyn's back and gesturing for him to do the same. With that, their faithful steed took them through the Gate, which closed on its own behind them. Then they continued their journey ever southward.

* * *

It was late morning by the time Chaos noted the ground sloping upward. At first slightly, then more steeply. He supposed that it was only by virtue of Vita's Dribbling Rejuvenation that Gwendolyn was able to continue forward without quickly tiring. At length the terrain leveled off, revealing a rocky landscape with sheer, dull red rock walls rising up on either side. It was as if a great big hill had been carved out in the middle, the six-foot-wide road passing through the chasm left within.

"Wow," Chaos murmured, taking in the scenery. It was far more interesting than the flat grid of streets and nearly identical-looking buildings in Southwick. All in the same style, most painted with one of a few muted colors. In contrast, this land was wild, the road the only human element. A land mostly untamed by the obsessive orderliness of mankind's collective hand.

"Impressive, isn't it," Destiny replied.

"Did people carve out this chasm, or was it natural?" he asked.

"Neither," she answered. "The giant Harsgrof cut it in half with his famed sword Hillsplitter."

Chaos chuckled.

"Good one," he told her. She twisted around to glower at him.

"Not a joke," she told him. "He cut the hill in half to help the humans pave a wide enough road for their armies, so they could wage war on Old Langsroth."

"A giant cut the hill in half?" Chaos asked. "Come on."

"It's true."

"I've seen a giant," he informed her. "My friend Rocky. No way he could've cut a hill in half."

"How tall is he?"

"I dunno, maybe twenty feet?" Chaos guessed.

"That's a dwarf giant," she told him. "Real giant is much bigger."

"Like how big?" he asked.

"Big enough to hold a sword that'd cut this hill in two," she answered dryly.

"Oh."

Chaos eyed the twin walls flanking the road with newfound respect, then looked up between them at the blue sky, imagining a great big sword crashing down on them. Then lifting up, rubble falling from its massive blade, until the sky was visible once again. It would take a sword a quarter mile long to do it, he wagered. Which meant that Harsgrof must've been at least a thousand feet tall.

"Where is he now?" he asked. "Harsgrof I mean."

"In Old Langsroth," she replied. "Long dead."

"How'd he die?"

"The same way the army that marched into Old Langsroth did," she answered. He paused, waiting for her to elaborate. Which she didn't.

"And how was that?" he asked.

"You really don't know anything about our history, do you," she stated rather than asked.

"No," he admitted. "I grew up in Borrin," he added. "All they care about is themselves."

A moment passed.

"That's a terrible life," she said at last. "Vita teaches me to treat others as myself. Generosity is the greatest good."

"Then why are you so mean to me?" Chaos joked.

"I'm being honest with you," she corrected. "Protecting you from the truth with comfortable lies is mean."

"Is it though?"

"It is," she replied immediately. "Most people think they lie to spare other people's feelings. But they're really just sparing their own feelings. They don't want to feel uncomfortable seeing other people get sad or angry about the truth, even though being confronted with the truth is the only way for them to better their lives."

Chaos paused, trying to parse this.

"You sure you're fourteen?" he asked.

"Vita chooses old souls."

Gwendolyn brought them ever-forward, until the walls on either side of the road ended abruptly. Beyond, the road began to slope downward, revealing a magnificent sight below. For, a few miles ahead, the road led to a grand city. One built on what looked like a large, squat mesa a hundred feet tall, made of the same red rock as the hill they'd passed through. Buildings made of the same red stone rose from this flat surface, most only a few stories tall, but some much taller.

"Whoa," Chaos breathed, taking in the majestic sight. It was a city utterly unlike Southwick, and thus, utterly fascinating. "What's that?"

"Tabula," Destiny answered. "The capitol of Grissam."

"Wait, we're in Grissam?" he asked.

"Not yet," she replied. "But when we get to Tabula, we will be."

* * *

A tireless Gwendolyn brought Chaos and Destiny down the hill, traveling another five miles before reaching the base of the mesa upon which Tabula was built. A winding, upsloping path led from the ground up the front of the mesa, and Gwendolyn took them up to its start, which was guarded by burly-looking men wearing red and gold chainmail armor. On their red helmets were golden symbols of swords pointing downward.

"Afternoon Destiny," one of them greeted. "Who's the boy?"

"A rescue," she answered. Which was true.

"He'll have to register at the Visitor's Center," the guard stated rather apologetically. To which Destiny said not a thing. The guard eyed her, then his fellow guard, then Chaos. Then he inclined his head. "Keep doin' what you're doin'," he told Destiny. "Vita be with you."

Destiny nodded, then continued past the guards, going up the path. It was a good sixty feet wide and made of flattened red rock, the same rock as the mesa itself. The slope was gentle enough to allow a carriage to be pulled up it, which necessitated a much longer path than would have been necessary for strictly human use. At length they made it all the way up, the path leading them to a red stone wall blocking the way into the city. A single arched gateway served as the entrance, more guards…uh, guarding it.

"Afternoon Destiny," a few greeted in unison, one even waving. "Who's your friend?"

"A rescue," she answered. Again.

"You ah, gonna take him to the Visitor's Center?" one asked. To which Destiny simply continued forward, passing under the arched entranceway. "Oh," the guard mumbled. But to Chaos's surprise, no one tried to stop them, or interfere in any way.

"Why didn't you answer?" Chaos asked as they left the guards behind.

"If I said 'no,' they'd be obligated to do something," she replied. "By leaving it ambiguous, they can say they reminded me and assumed I would do it."

"Oh," he replied. "Are you going to register me?"

"No, takes too long."

"What if they find out?" he pressed. "Will we get in trouble?"

"They know I won't do it, so they won't check," she answered. "No one wants to get on the bad side of a paladin of Vita."

She led them forward, and the grand city streets of Tabula lay before them. Red stone buildings lined narrow cobblestone streets, most between one and four stories tall. Colorful signs over the doors of many of the buildings advertised shops and pubs and such, with throngs of people going in and out of them. Colorful banners had been strung from the roofs of buildings on either side of the street, adding a bit of flair. Something that Chaos could appreciate after being raised by a mother whose magic was to bedazzle things.

"Wow," he breathed, gazing at all the people. Far more than he'd seen on the streets of Southwick, except for maybe on Founder's Day. Mesa was a smaller city, but was far more jam-packed with buildings and people, and was far more chaotic as a result. "I like it."

"You wouldn't if I wasn't with you," Destiny countered.

"Why?"

"Tabula isn't the safest city," she explained. "Especially at night. Three gangs are fighting to control the streets, and when they fight, nobody wins."

They rode Gwendolyn further into the city, turning down a narrower side street, which wound this way and that between buildings. Again, it was totally unlike Southwick, whose streets had been built in a boring grid. All straight lines and flat land, supremely organized and efficient...and thus, barely worth visiting.

Tabula's winding streets, on the other hand, made it impossible to see what was just around the corner…and what *was* around the corner was surprise after surprise. Colorful shops of all shapes and sizes, and people of all shapes and sizes too, clad in clothes that were wildly different than what he was used to. Some of the more unfriendly looking types wore darker leather shirts and pants, and regarded Chaos and Destiny with unfriendly looks.

"Don't stare," she whispered, prompting Chaos to keep his eyes to himself. Mostly.

The smell of horses and their excretions filled the warm air, which was nasty but at the same time pleasant. For at least it *did* smell lived-in, unlike Southwick's sanitation-obsessed odorlessness. The stink was mixed up with the tantalizing scent of fresh bread being baked or meat being grilled, along with a bunch of other smells that Chaos couldn't place.

All in all, it was a feast for the senses, and Chaos soon found himself a bit overwhelmed. There was so much going on that he couldn't take it all in, though he desperately wanted to explore it all.

"So what are we doing here exactly?" Chaos asked, fidgeting in his seat.

"What you should've done before you set out on your quest," she answered. "Prepare."

"Right," he mumbled, his cheeks flushing. She steered Gwendolyn toward a shop ahead and to the right, stopping the horse near the entrance.

"Come on," she told him, dismounting. He did as well, landing on the street. She immediately left Gwendolyn behind, striding toward the shop entrance.

"She won't leave?" he asked.

"No."

He followed Destiny into the shop, which had rows of shelving that were quite cramped compared to A Little Magic back home. It was packed with customers…also unlike A Little Magic. Most of the customers were mangy-looking men who eyed Chaos with obvious distrust. But they all greeted Destiny, clearly deferring to her.

"What is this place?" Chaos asked.

"The Great Flat Blade," Destiny answered.

The shop sold all sorts of equipment an adventurer might need, like knives big and small, swords, whips, maces, hammers, flails, bows, crossbows…and armor. Lots and lots of armor. Leather armor, chainmail, scale mail, and even a set of plate mail.

"Ooo," Chaos oooed, his eyes widening. For to him the sight of such goods was even more magical than the wares in a magic shop. "Plate mail!" he exclaimed, for it was his favorite kind of armor, theoretically.

"Plate *armor*," she corrected. "You need an arming doublet first," she told him, leading him down an aisle. Chaos frowned.

"A what?"

"Padded garment under your armor," she explained. "What size are you?"

"Uh…I don't know," he confessed. "My Mom usually buys clothes for me." Which, on immediate reflection, sounded really *really* lame.

"How old are you again?" she asked, confirming his self-reflection. She grabbed a folded-up tan garment, eyeing him, then handing it to him. "Try this on."

"Um…here?" he asked, looking around. She gave him a funny look.

"In the changing room," she corrected, pointing to the back end of the shop. There were several doors there, all marked as changing rooms, one for men and three for women.

"Oh."

He went to the dressing room, opening the door and stepping through, then locking it behind him. Stripping off his clothes – which stank, he realized with fresh dismay – he tried on the arming doublet. It fit perfectly, and was quite light. He took it off, putting on his stinky clothes, then made his way back to Destiny.

"It fits," he announced.

"Tell me your size then," she ordered. He blinked, then looked down at the doublet, blushing again. For the first time in his life, he realized the full extent of how very useless he was. Mostly because for most of his life, he'd let everyone else figure things out for him. He'd always considered buying clothing and such to be boring, and therefore something he should pawn off onto his parents. In forgoing the everyday boring stuff, however, he'd made himself useless at everyday things.

And since everyday things were done every day, he was, as a result, useless every day.

Crap, he told himself, beating himself up. She must've noticed his grimace.

"Don't beat yourself up," she told him. "It's not your fault you're useless."

"Uh...it isn't?" he asked. "I'm not useless," he added defensively, a bit too late. She shrugged.

"It's either who you are or how you were raised," she reasoned. "Probably both."

"I'm not useless," he repeated, blushing furiously. Even though he'd just *just* called himself so in his thoughts. She didn't reply, which made things that much worse. Instead, she led him down another aisle, this one with different kinds of armor displayed.

"You're slow," she told him.

"No I'm..."

"...so you'll need armor that protects you more than keeps you agile," she finished. "But you're too weak to use plate armor. Scale armor and mail are too heavy too. But leather armor won't offer enough protection for someone with no fighting skill."

"Can you think this through in your head maybe?" he grumbled.

"We'll have to go with mail," she decided, eyeing sets of chainmail. Or rather, what he called chainmail and *she* called mail. "Go on," she prompted, gesturing at the sets. He paused, then grabbed one. "Is that your size?" she asked. Chaos grimaced, checking the tag, and saw that it was not. He blushed yet again, going through the sets until he found the right size, then bringing it to the changing room. Trying it on, he found it profoundly uncomfortable...but he supposed that was because he wasn't wearing the arming doublet underneath. It was also prohibitively heavy. Like, half as heavy as he was. He took it off, returning to her.

"You're right," he admitted. "It is too heavy."

"Find a mail helm," she ordered, ignoring his statement. Rather rudely, he thought. But he did as he was told, trying a few on before finding one that fit. "Now gloves," she ordered, which he found after trying a few on. "Leather pants and boots," she prompted.

At length, he found everything she'd asked him to find, which was quite a lot of stuff. And quite expensive, he noted after glancing at the price tags.

"Um...I don't have any money," he confessed.

"I figured," she replied.

He watched with well-deserved mortification as she went to the front of the shop and paid for his stuff. For unlike him, she did have money. Because unlike him, she'd come prepared. There was, he realized suddenly, a considerable amount of power that being prepared provided. One as powerful as magic, really.

That done, they left the shop, returning to Gwendolyn. Who hadn't budged an inch, or been stolen. In fact, everyone seemed to back away as Destiny drew near them, deferring to her much as the guards had. She placed his stuff in one of Gwendolyn's saddle-bags, then mounted the mare. Chaos followed suit, finding himself a bit more capable of doing so. A process that was still embarrassing, but not as time-consuming. Destiny snapped the reins, and off they went down the street.

"Why does everyone act like that around you?" he asked.

"I'm a paladin," she answered. "I protect them from zombies."

"Oh."

"I'm also the only one that'll go into Old Langsroth," she added. "Everyone else is too scared to."

"You mean the place that that giant was trying to help people destroy?"

"Right," she replied.

"Why won't anyone else go there?" he asked.

"Old Langsroth is cursed," she explained. Which wasn't a great explanation at all, really.

"How?"

"That takes some knowledge of history," she answered. "I assume you don't know anything about the Kingdom of Langsroth."

"Nope."

"It existed about two thousand years ago," she explained. "Langsroth occupied a huge territory that included what we call Grissam today. It was the most powerful country in the world at that time."

"Okay," he replied.

"A necromancer was born in Langsroth," she continued. "He was driven out of the city when the authorities discovered him practicing dark magic, and everyone assumed he'd left for good. But instead, he'd gone underground, making a home in the sewer network beneath the capitol city."

"Why didn't he just leave?" Chaos asked.

"I haven't asked him," she deadpanned. "In any case, he mastered the dark arts underground, then used them to get revenge on the city that'd rejected him. He cursed a single citizen, and that curse spread throughout the city, dooming it."

"Cursed?" Chaos asked. "How?"

"With the Fallen Sky," Destiny replied. "It turned everyone in the city into zombies. A city of undead."

"Wow."

"The city fell, and the rest of the kingdom rose up to try to reclaim its capitol," she stated. "But anyone who went into the city was cursed, doomed to walk the earth for eternity as a mindless animated corpse."

"Is that what happened to the giant?" he asked.

"We don't know," she confessed. "Harsgrof went with the armies of Langsroth to reclaim the city, but never came out. We assume he died...or worse."

"Oh."

"The Kingdom of Langsroth lost the war against its own capitol, and was so weakened by the attempt that neighboring countries invaded and took it over. A few hundred years ago, Grissam was founded, and here we are," she concluded.

"So...what happened to the capitol city?" he asked.

"It was renamed Old Langsroth," Destiny answered. "And it remains to this very day."

He frowned.

"Wait, you mean the curse is still there?" he pressed.

"That's right," she confirmed. "The curse of Old Langsroth still remains. A city of the undead."

"Huh," he replied. "So you go there to fight zombies?" he guessed.

"I do," she confirmed. "And so will you."

He blinked.

"Wait, what?" he blurted out. "Why me?"

"You said Imperius Fanning told you to go to Grissam to meet your destiny," she answered.

"Yeah," he replied. "So?"

"I'm Destiny," she stated. "And you've met me."

"I don't think that's what Imperius meant," Chaos argued.

"Vita told me to take you in," Destiny argued. "She wants me to take you to Old Langsroth."

"To do what?" he pressed.

"To do what I do best," she replied. "Kill zombies."

Chapter 16

King Pravus found the journey to Old Langsroth a rousing adventure indeed, but in a surprisingly different way than the usual soaring flight on the back of his old friend, the fire dragon. This journey was, to the purely practical eye, a mere horseback ride across terrain, interrupted by meals and nights spent making camp. But to those wise enough to understand the magnificence of mundane things, it was far, far more.

For one, the journey was something he'd never done, riding and camping with only Templeton at his side. What's more, it represented a disruption of his day-to-day existence, something entirely new. This was, he believed, because to have lived the same day every day was to have barely lived at all. Without something new serving as the space between words in the story of one's life, the whole tale ran together as meaningless nonsense.

"Why, I don't believe I've ever felt so alive as this," Pravus mused as they sat on a boulder near the road. After finishing a set of bicep curls with a large stone.

"Strange, isn't it?" Templeton mused, implicitly agreeing with his king. Whilst performing squats with a large stone of his own.

"It is odd, to spend our days attending to purely living," Pravus professed, setting his stone down, then grabbing a bit of beef jerky from his fanny-pack. An excellent source of protein for demanding muscles, and essentially an imperishable food, if stored correctly. Templeton finished his set, and Pravus offered him some jerky. Templeton accepted this post-workout gift with grace, chewing happily.

"I suspect this is the core human experience," Templeton philosophized. "And thus our spirits are drawn to it so."

"To travel and eat and sleep?"

"To make a living living," Templeton replied. Pravus frowned, biting off a piece of jerky, then chewing on this. Literally and figuratively.

"I don't follow," he admitted.

"The natural occupation of a living being is attending to one's wants and needs, and those of their family," Templeton explained. "Our society has taken us away from this, making us specialize in a very specific aspect of living."

"To mutual benefit," Pravus noted.

"Perhaps," Templeton replied. "We spread the responsibility for each aspect of our own life across a huge number of people, such that we depend on each other to fulfill our wants and needs."

"Instead of doing so ourselves?" Pravus guessed.

"Indeed," Templeton confirmed.

"A man cannot be as good at everything as he can be at one thing," Pravus argued. "In doing one thing extraordinarily well, he lets everyone benefit from his focus."

"And at the same time, his soul suffers, unless he truly loves what he does…and loves doing it almost every day for most of his life," Templeton countered gently. Pravus frowned, taking another bite of jerky.

"You're referring to my current predicament," he realized. Templeton smiled.

"Just so, cousin."

"I *have* often pondered the life of a man," Pravus mused. "Particularly those outside of my kingdom. I hear they work for eight to twelve hours a day at doing the same task, over and over again."

"I've heard the same," Templeton replied.

"A most unnatural condition for a man to be in," Pravus stated with a shake of his kingly head. "Even when a man is doing what he loves, few would ever do it for so long without breaks to do other things."

"Indeed," Templeton agreed. "A natural thing, to go from one task to the next, never spending too long on one thing."

"Why, if I were tasked to go to the gym for eight hours a day, every day, even I might soon find it contemptible!"

"What we love is medicine in moderation, yet poison in too great a dose," Templeton declared.

"Well said, cousin!" Pravus replied. "I do believe you're right."

"But I daresay there's no recourse in a society such as Borrin," Templeton lamented. "As long as they worship at the altar of efficient productivity, the individual is doomed to suffer at the hands of the collective's demands."

92

"Until he or she can afford their freedom," Pravus agreed. "Or be born with it, like the aristocracy."

"A lottery of birth that few win," Templeton mused. "So most must spend most of their lives saving to buy said freedom."

"A life so onerous that they feel compelled to spend their money instead, on bits of fleeting happiness to numb the pain."

"Thus they are never truly free," Templeton concluded. "A incomplete life indeed."

"A life never fully lived," Pravus said with a sigh. "Let us recoil in horror at a fate like this for ourselves!"

"I daresay this adventure will do us both a bit of good, and fill the void we've been suffering," Templeton declared with a smile. Pravus arched an eyebrow.

"You've suffered it too, cousin?"

"I have," Templeton confessed. "I adore my children, and love spending time with them. But my life is them and the aristocracy, with little time to satisfy my...solitary interests." He gazed off at the scenery, striking a handsomely pensive pose indeed. One that made Pravus fall in love with the man all over again. "I'm a father, a husband, and a lord...with precious little time to be not a role, but myself."

"Hmm," Pravus hmmed.

"Without time to be myself, my self longs for that time," Templeton continued. "And my roles risk becoming a source of resentment."

"I've never found you to harbor resentments," Pravus noted. "Or any other ill thought."

"Only in my mind," Templeton replied, turning to face him. "Even the best of men experience the full spectrum of human emotion."

"Just so," Pravus concurred. "But I daresay the lion's share of your emotions are happy ones."

"My nature is to focus on the good," Templeton agreed. "While acknowledging the bad it sometimes hides behind." He stood then. "Shall we be off, my liege?"

"We shall," Pravus decided. "Onward, dearest cousin!"

"To high adventure!" Templeton declared with gusto. "And when we return to Cumulus, may we find ourselves better men for having experienced it!"

Which would have been a timely ending to the conversation, and a rousing return to riding. But just then, Pravus heard the telltale *clippity-clop* of horses' hooves on the road. Getting louder, which meant they were coming his way. He spotted a good dozen horses ahead, carrying rather rough-looking riders clad in leather armor. These men slowed as they approached Pravus and Templeton. One of them led the way, a man whose leather armor was red instead of brown, and was quite obviously their leader, for his shoulders were squared and he was possessed of the typical steely-eyed, slightly squinty look leaders gave.

"Well well," the man stated, stopping his horse a few yards away. "Lookee what we got here."

"Gentleman," Templeton greeted, though by the looks of them, they were anything but. The other eleven or so men slowed their horses, and Pravus couldn't help but notice that they formed a loose circle around him. He stood from the boulder he was sitting on, putting his hands on his hips. And then proceeded to pose rather heroically, flaring his lats and puffing his chest. A display not unlike a peacock, which sent a message to those who saw it. In this case, not one of mating, but of potential prey not worth the effort.

"Ooo," one of the men stated. "Watch out Gilgon," he warned, clearly addressing the leader. "That one's *scary*."

"Be a lot scarier if he had a weapon," Gilgon mused, eyeing Pravus, then Templeton. Neither of whom did have a weapon, on account of Imperius having advised them not to carry one. An ill-advised advisement, Pravus realized.

"We mean no harm," Pravus declared mightily. "As long as you mean the same. Carry on," he added, dismissing them with a gesture. Gilgon's eyebrows rose at that.

"Funny, that seemed like an order," he stated. "Didn't it seem like an order?" he asked one of his men.

"Sure did," the guy replied.

"Not an order but an advisement," Pravus corrected. "We have nothing to offer, and you have nothing to offer us."

"I beg to differ," Gilgon retorted, eyeing Pravus's waist. Or rather, the bulging coin purses hanging from his belt. Purses that, in retrospect, would have been wiser to conceal. Pravus gave Gilgon an imperious glare.

"Leave at once," he commanded. "I will not ask again."

"You didn't ask," Gilgon retorted. "That was a command."

"We don't want any trouble," Templeton stated, ever one to de-escalate a situation.

"Neither do we," Gilgon replied. "Hand over your money and there won't be any."

Pravus's eyebrows rose.

"You rhymed," he noted. "Are you wizards?"

Gilgon blinked.

"What? No," he scoffed. He held out one hand. "Hand them over," he ordered.

Pravus gave the man a withering glare.

"No," he replied.

"You really willing to die for your money?" Gilgon asked.

"I'm willing to die for my principles," Pravus replied. "I would rather die than live as a victim to so-called men like you."

"Ooo," one of Gilgon's men replied disrespectfully.

"You talk real brave," Gilgon mused.

"Bravely," Pravus corrected, being a stickler for grammar. "My actions follow my words."

"I bet you squeal like a little girl when you're stuck though," Gilgon continued, pulling a dagger from a sheath at his waist. He fingered its edge. "Most of the biggest, baddest looking men do."

"My cousin doesn't squeal when penetrated, he grunts," Templeton corrected. Which was true. For Devorah Doverah had penetrated Pravus with the Sovereign Spear years ago, to which Pravus had uttered a manly "urrghh."

"And how would you know? Have you penetrated him?" Gilgon inquired with a smirk. His men chuckled at that.

"No," Templeton answered. Though Pravus rather wished that were not so. For he'd spent most of his post-pubescent life wishing for that very act, one that would surely have resulted in manly "urrghhs" far more pleasant that the Sovereign Spear had prompted.

"Guess we'll just have to find out for ourselves, eh?" Gilgon stated, sheathing his dagger. He nodded at the others, who dismounted, unsheathing shortswords from their hips. One-handed swords of mediocre length, they were toothpicks compared to Pravus's magical greatsword. He reached behind his back, pantomiming the act of drawing it, which summoned it from the ether into his hands.

Or rather, it should have. But the act did nothing, for he'd left his magical uniform and crown and such at home. Or rather, the act did nothing for *him*, but gave great amusement to Gilgon and his band of dastardly men. Who pointed, then laughed. Then pointed again, and laughed, tears dripping down a few of their cheeks. Pravus tried not to blush, with no success. A foreign feeling for him indeed.

"It appears we are outnumbered," Templeton warned. "And out-armed."

"Then our bodies shall serve as our weapons," Pravus replied resolutely. "And our arms will be arms enough!"

The men stared at them both, then burst out laughing again. Pravus fixed them with an imperious glare, waiting for their mirth to be spent. After which they brandished their swords, a few of them stepping toward them.

"Hand over the money and no one gets hurt," one of them snapped.

"No," Pravus replied.

"It is not the cost so much as the price we'd pay in giving it," Templeton explained. "A price of accepting victimhood...and allowing you to create victims of others afterward." He shook his head. "For the good of others, we must stop you."

"That's what heroes do," Pravus concurred. "Well said, cousin!"

"Can we like, kill them already?" Gilgon grumbled, clearly having had enough.

"Do your worst, villains!" Pravus cried, adopting a fighting stance. Which is to say, a wrestling stance. The man nearest him rolled his eyes, then lunged forward with a feint. One that was awfully slow compared to Templeton's rapid thrusts, and as such, fooled Pravus not in the least. The enemy lunged a second time, this time committing to his thrust...and Pravus pretended it was a wrestling match, and that the man's sword was a hand reaching for him.

Pravus dodged to the side and forward, facing the man's back, and grabbed his waist, picking him up and twisting his torso, slamming the man onto his head. And not gently.

The man's neck *snapped*, the sound echoing through the air, and he laid there, unmoving on the grass. Pravus picked up the man's sword, tossing it to Templeton, who caught it.

"My thanks cousin," Templeton stated. "But I'd rather you have it."

"I'd rather wrestle," Pravus replied.

"Back-to-back then?" Templeton proposed with a mischievous smile. Pravus smiled, then obliged, pressing his back against his cousin's. They eyed the remaining men sidelong, and Pravus adopted his fighting stance again.

"Who's next?" he inquired.

The nearest men glanced at their fallen comrade, who wasn't moving. Or breathing. Then they stared at Pravus, clearly having second thoughts.

"How about we try *more* than one at a time?" Gilgon suggested. "Like two, or three, or even frickin' five, 'cause there's like six times as many of us?"

"Right," one of his men replied. "Surround 'em!"

The men formed a circle around Pravus and Templeton, loose at first, then tighter as they drew closer.

Then they attacked!

They rushed forward, and Templeton reacted immediately, thrusting expertly with his borrowed shortsword. A weapon quite different than his usual fencing-like blade, but still deadly in the man's hands. He impaled one of the vagabonds through the solar plexus, just below the breastbone, then slashed another's throat. All in the length of time it took for three of the men to attack Pravus with a triple-sword-thrust!

"Behind you!" Pravus cried, ducking beneath the blades and diving at the men's legs, tackling them all at the same time. Templeton spun around to deflect the blades from impaling his back, thank goodness, then spun back to block more attacks affronting his front.

One of the men Pravus tackled dropped their sword, and Pravus snatched it before getting to his feet. He felt a sharp, burning sensation in the middle of his upper back…and a feeling of warm, spreading wetness there.

He clenched his teeth against the sudden pain, then swung his sword at one of the three men he'd tackled, even as they scrambled to their feet. The blade severed the man's head from his shoulders in a spray of blood, and Pravus followed up with a second slash, severing the sword arm of a second combatant.

The third man facing Pravus noted these developments, and decided to turn and flee, wisely. But a fourth who'd managed to sneak up on Pravus's left side did not.

Instead, he thrust his sword at Pravus's right left shoulder, and Pravus barely saw the attack in time, batting it away. But the blade still managed to slash his shoulder in a glancing blow.

Pravus thrust his sword through the man's belly, then kicked him away, facing the remaining men grimly. With the one he'd killed and the two he'd maimed – and the five that Templeton had slain – there were only four vagabonds remaining. And Gilgon, of course.

"Our odds keep getting better and better," Templeton noted.

"Indeed cousin," Pravus agreed, eyeing Gilgon. "Surrender at once, villains, or share the fate of your fallen comrades!"

Gilgon eyed Pravus's blood-soaked blade, then his own fallen men.

"Come on boys," he told his men. "These two aren't worth it."

And with that, the vagabonds beat a hasty retreat, vanishing off into the distance on their steeds. Pravus watched as they fled, then turned to Templeton.

"Are you injured, cousin?" he inquired.

"No sire," Templeton replied. "But you are." He studied Pravus's injuries. "Only flesh wounds, thank goodness," he stated. "Do they hurt?"

"Yes," Pravus admitted. "But I daresay being vulnerable makes me feel more alive than I've ever been." Which was true. Since he could remember, he'd been protected from harm by various magical uniforms, and had thus rarely endured any physical pain other than that of lifting weights. To be vulnerable meant being mortal...which, upon confronting, had one of two effects. The first was the most common, to stimulate fear of death. But the other was what Pravus felt, a realization that mortality was something not to fear, but a reminder of how precious his life was.

"Shall we be off?" Templeton inquired.

"We shall," Pravus answered. "To Grissam...and to destiny!"

Chapter 17

After buying his armor, Destiny took Chaos through the maze-like streets of Tabula, going first to a shop selling backpacks and such, and then to a shop selling dehydrated foods and other non-perishable nutrition. Then they went to a camping shop, purchasing all sorts of useful things, like matches and flint and hunting knives and water flasks and water purifying tablets and such. Not to mention a sleeping bag, a foldable tent, and much, much more. Most of the items were small or collapsible, fitting in his pack or hanging from it. The biggest exception – literally – being a shovel, of all things. At the end of their shopping spree, he was more prepared than he'd ever been. For anything.

"Wow," he breathed as Destiny finished helping him organize his pack. "You really thought of everything."

"I've been doing this a long time," she told him, tying the shovel to the saddlebag.

"How did you learn about all this stuff?" he asked.

"I asked people," she answered. "And I made a whole lot of mistakes."

"Mistakes?"

"Nothing as bad as what you did," she stated. "But going out into the wilderness and not having what you need teaches you to get it for next time."

"Makes sense."

"The world is my teacher," she lectured. "When I fail, it doesn't sugar-coat anything. It lets me know I failed."

"Kinda like you," Chaos noted ruefully.

"I learned to teach from the way the world teaches," she explained. "The world doesn't sugar-coat its lessons, but it doesn't get mad at you for failing either. It never *calls* you a failure. It doesn't label you or categorize you. It just lets you know that what you did didn't work."

"Huh," he murmured. "That's…kinda nice."

"The opposite of mean," she replied, giving him a significant look. He smiled.

"Guess you aren't mean after all," he told her.

"Come on," she prompted, mounting Gwendolyn once again. He hopped on, far more ably than he'd done initially, and they trotted down the street, turning this way and that. Eventually he realized that they were heading out of the city...via the same arched entranceway they'd entered through.

"Wait, we're leaving?" he asked.

"Yep."

"Already?" he pressed.

"We got what we needed," she reasoned. "Why waste time?"

He paused, then found he didn't have a very good answer to that. Other than being able to sleep in an actual house with a roof over his head. And a comfy mattress under him. And eating a meal or two that didn't consist of nuts and stale, warm water. They weren't *bad* reasons, but bringing them up would only make him seem soft and weak. Which to be fair, he was, at least compared to Destiny. But he didn't want to *seem* that way, especially to her.

"Yeah," he replied. "Let's *go*."

Gwendolyn followed the wide path leading down the front of the mesa, eventually reaching ground level.

"So, uh...where are we going?" Chaos asked.

"Old Langsroth," Destiny answered. As if it were obvious.

"Naturally," he replied, in an attempt to save face. Whether it worked or not, he couldn't tell.

"You ask a lot of questions," she told him.

"I..."

"...that make you sound stupid," she finished. His mouth *clicked* shut. She did not follow up with the "even though you're not" statement he would've liked to hear. Which put him in the unenvious position of having to say it.

"I'm not," he protested. Stupidly.

To this she didn't deign to reply, which irked him even more. Mostly because it left it quite open as to whether she thought that he was stupid or not. This was of course better than her telling him that she *did* think he was stupid, but worse than her telling him he wasn't. Still, it was human nature to feel profoundly uncomfortable with not knowing, and so Chaos pressed the issue.

"You don't think I'm stupid, do you?" he asked.

"I think you've done stupid things," she answered. "You'd have to do something smart to prove that you're not."

Which meant, to Chaos's dismay, that he had not. At least not yet, anyway. He clenched his teeth, sitting up a bit straighter in the saddle, determined to prove his not-stupidity. He would do something really *really* smart.

You'll see, he thought, glaring at the back of her head.

What commenced then, dear reader, is a process I'm sure you're quite familiar with. A process everyone goes through whenever insulted with the truth. Immediate anger, followed by fantasies of some sort of revenge. A silent arguing of one's case, followed of course by counter-insults to prove the other person's greater faults. Then the nagging feeling that the insult held a kernel of truth, but that it could've been presented in a more constructive way. And at last, the hope to rise above one's failings, and mend the relationship in doing so, resulting in forgiveness and smiles all around.

All of this took quite a bit of time, such that by the time Chaos got his proverbial head out of his ass, he realized it was nearly nightfall. And that he had absolutely no idea where they were, or for how long they'd been riding.

"Where are we?" he blurted out, looking around. The scenery had completely changed. Whereas before they'd been traveling across dry land with lots of red rock, now they'd ventured into a rather strange land. Or rather, *nearly* ventured. For they were riding on the lushest grass he'd ever seen, down a gentle slope toward an utterly flat area ahead. An utterly *huge* flat area, extending as far as he could see. It was flat, he realized, because it was water. A huge lake from which a thin mist rose.

"The Great Flat," she answered. "Old Langsroth is a few miles ahead."

"But…we don't have a boat," he protested.

"We'll manage," she replied dryly.

He opened his mouth to protest again, but realized that it was perhaps his habit of blurting stuff out the minute it came to his mind that made him appear stupid. And that stopping to think for a bit was sort of the definition of being smart. So he closed his mouth instead of blurting, studying the Great Flat. Its surface rippled gently, reflecting the colors of the sunset overhead. At the shore, there was no sand, but merely waterlogged grass.

Okay, he thought.

Then, to his surprise, Destiny brought Gwendolyn all the way up to the water's edge...and then had the horse trot into it. Or rather, over it. For, to Chaos's further surprise, the horse's hooves only went in a few inches deep, allowing her to continue forward. Not just a few yards, but a few *hundred* yards across the water's surface.

"How...?" he blurted out.

"Vita's blessings give Gwendolyn the power to walk on water," Destiny explained.

"Wow," he breathed. "That's amazing!"

She twisted around to glance at him, giving him a look he didn't like one bit.

"I was kidding," she grumbled. "The water's shallow."

Chaos blinked, then looked down, peering at the surface of the water. Beneath it, he could make out Gwendolyn's hooves touching dark dirt. And not only that, but he realized that there were bushes and tufts of long grass poking out of the water all around him.

"Oh," he mumbled, his cheeks flushing. And once again, he felt stupid. He'd spent most of his life being pretty sure he was pretty smart, but if the world was the best teacher, then it's lesson so far had been to question this assumption.

Crap.

They road further into the Great Flat, Gwendolyn's hooves splashing in the water rhythmically. Chaos kept his mouth shut, eyeing the terrain in lieu of putting his foot in his mouth again. There were tall cliffsides on either side of the water, and ahead, the land was shrouded by the mist. Above, the sky was partially cloudy, but a few miles ahead, dark thunderclouds loomed.

The urge to ask questions was almost overwhelming, and Chaos struggled to keep his big mouth shut.

Shut up and pay attention, he scolded himself. *Stop being dumb.*

He studied the area further, trying to imagine how it came to be. As far out as they went, the water never got deeper, which meant it was a huge lake but only inches deep. On reflection, this made no sense, for the water should've just evaporated away. Unless it was being fed by a water supply like a river, of course. But if that were the case, he'd imagine that the water would be deeper.

"What water source feeds the Great Flat?" he asked. After saying it in his head a few times to make sure it wasn't a dumb ask.

"The Fallen Sky," she replied.

"Is that...what is that?" he asked.

"An eternal rain that falls on Old Langsroth," she explained. "It floods the Great Flat, which never dries up."

"Makes sense," Chaos replied. "Why does it always rain there?"

"Old Langsroth was cursed two thousand years ago," she reminded him. "It was the greatest city in the world at that time, the capitol of the Kingdom of Langsroth. A powerful wizard was born there, but his magic was forbidden. The Wizard Council of Langsroth cast him out of the city when he was barely more than a boy, and he vowed to get revenge. According to legend, he didn't return for sixty years, and everyone assumed he'd forgotten or died."

"Huh."

"But then he *did* return...as the most powerful wizard Old Langsroth had ever seen. He created the Fallen Sky, a storm that cursed the city, dooming it for eternity."

Chaos considered this.

"So the wizard got revenge on the city by flooding it?" he asked.

"Worse," she replied. "Legend has it that he cursed the highest-ranking Elder of the Wizard Council, making it so that any time he bled, that blood would rise as a mist into the sky above Old Langsroth...and take a part of his soul with it."

"Wow."

"The wizard slit the Elder's throat, and the man bled out," she continued. "His soul left his body, and his body died...and his blood formed a small cloud above the city."

"With his soul still in the blood?" Chaos asked.

"Right," she confirmed. "Then that blood fell as rain, drenching some of Old Langsroth's citizens...and cursing them in the same way. So that every time they bled, the same thing would happen to them. And the more blood-rain they were exposed to, the easier it became for them to bleed."

"And then their soul-blood rained down, cursing more and more people, who had *their* blood drained, and so on," he guessed.

"That's right," she replied.

"So...I thought you said there were zombies in Old Langsroth," he said. "How did they get there if everyone just died?"

"The blood-rain possesses the collective souls of everyone else who's been cursed," she answered. "And as people bleed out, they get thirsty. *Very* thirsty," she added.

"So wait...they *drink* the blood?"

"And if they do, it only makes them bleed even more," she stated. "And lose more blood, which makes them thirstier, and drink more blood, and so on."

"So they die," he translated.

"And when they do, their souls are bound in their blood, cursed to rain down, then rise up, then rain down again and again, forever," she concluded. "While their soulless bodies wander the city as the Fallen, drinking and wading in the blood, whose collective soul-power keeps them animated."

Chaos processed this for a bit.

"That's...really dark," he stated at last.

"The wizard got his revenge on Old Langsroth," Destiny stated, "...and ever since, it's been a cursed city of the undead."

"And you're a paladin, which means you want to destroy them," Chaos reasoned.

"Right. But every time I kill a zombie in Old Langsroth, the blood heals it and reanimates it," she stated. "It's the Fallen Sky that's the problem...and as long as it exists, Old Langsroth will continue to be cursed."

"So...you have to stop the curse of the Fallen Sky?" he guessed.

"That is the sacred destiny Vita charged me with," Destiny confirmed. "And I would give my life to fulfill it."

* * *

After Destiny's telling of the sordid tale of Old Langsroth, they fell into a long silence, Gwendolyn's splashing hoof-falls the only sound. As they traveled across the Great Flat, Chaos found his gaze lingering on the clear water.

"Wait," he stated. "So why's the water here clear? If it's flooded from the Fallen Sky, shouldn't it be made of blood?"

"It rains down as blood," Destiny replied. "But after it leaves the city, the soul-energy leaves it, and it transforms into regular water."

"So the rain is only blood if soul-energy is in it?"

"Right," she confirmed.

"Huh."

The mist became denser as they continued, and it wasn't long before Chaos noticed dark shapes jutting up from the water, partially obscured by the mist. They were buildings, he realized; the crumbling ruins of what remained of them, anyway. With the rapid approach of nightfall, it was getting harder to see. And the air was growing much cooler, to the point where Chaos found himself shivering despite the warmth radiating from Destiny's back. They traveled between the ruined buildings, Gwendolyn's hoofbeats echoing off the dark stone walls. Chaos felt a chill run through him, and realized he was holding onto Destiny's waist a bit tighter than he had been.

"We're reaching the city outskirts," she warned. "You'll start seeing them soon."

"Seeing what?"

She didn't reply, much to his consternation. The buildings were closer together now, some with recognizable doorways, but most so old and ruined that he couldn't make out their original design. Ahead, he spotted something huge rising up from the mist: a tall wall made of black stone, extending to the left and right all the way to the cliff walls on either side of the Great Flat. Innumerable crumbling ramparts rose up from the top of the wall like the broken teeth of a monster's lower jaw.

"The wall of Old Langsroth," Destiny announced. "The city lies beyond."

"Wait...so we're going into Old Langsroth?" he asked, feeling more than a little unnerved by the thought. Zombies were bad enough – except for Zora, of course – but exposing himself to cursed blood-rain was far worse.

"We'll stay here in the outskirts first, close to the wall," she told him. "A few zombies got out of the city and can't find their way back in to drink the pure Fallen blood."

"Pure Fallen blood?"

"The blood that's rained down and undiluted," she explained. "Just outside of the city, the floodwater has traces of the Fallen blood in it. The zombies spend all their time drinking it, desperate for the real stuff. They're the weakest of the zombies, and regenerate the slowest."

"Oh."

"We'll deal with them first," she told him.

"But won't they still regenerate eventually?" he asked.

"Eventually," she agreed. "But you suck at fighting," she added. "So they'll make good practice for you."

Chaos grimaced, not at all liking the substance of her statement or how it was delivered. But it was true, and arguing about it would only worsen her already dim opinion of him. Which was that he was a bit dim.

She pulled back on the reigns, signaling Gwendolyn to stop, then dismounted, gesturing for Chaos to do the same. He did so, landing in the shallow water with a splash, and she gestured at the saddle-bags.

"Get your gear on," she ordered.

He retrieved his chainmail armor – or rather, what she called "mail," and started to put it on when he remembered that he had to put on the arming doublet first. He almost put the mail on the ground, then realized that would make it very wet, and so he stuff it back in the saddle-bag. After which he had to take it out again, because the arming doublet was underneath it. He took out the arming doublet, shoved the mail back in the bag, and then slipped on the arming doublet. He made the mistake of glancing at Destiny whilst doing this, and saw her watch him. And then shake her head. And continue to watch.

He grimaced, reaching for the saddlebag again to get the mail…then paused, making sure this was the right next move. Determining that it was, he put it on, followed by his mail helmet and gloves. He was already wearing his waterproof boots, thank goodness.

"Okay," he stated. "I think that's everything."

"Weapon," she prompted.

"Uh…" he replied, looking around. Of all the things they'd bought, a weapon wasn't one of them.

"Shovel," she clarified, gesturing at the shovel she'd bought, still tied to the saddlebags. Chaos blinked.

"A shovel?" he asked incredulously. "As a weapon?"

"Weapons are tools that solve a problem," Destiny told him. "The best tools have more than one use. A shovel can do a lot of damage in the right hands."

"Not sure my hands are the right hands," he confessed.

"Not yet," she told him, untying the shovel and tossing it to him. He caught it in both hands. "But with time, they may be." She turned about then, striding through the shallow water toward the tall black stone wall far ahead. "Come on," she prompted. "Time to hunt."

Chapter 18

Chauncy *squeaked* as his wife's doppelganger slapped him full-force in the face. So hard, in fact, that the meaty sound of said slapping echoed through the morning air. And threw him bodily to the side, such that he fell onto the porch, bruising his shoulder and hip.

He laid there, stunned, seeing stars.

"Ow," he whined. And then spotted the doppelganger staring down at him, hands clenched into fists. His sphincter snapped shut, perhaps in preparation for an attempt to violate his nether region. Scrambling to his feet, he thrust his staff before him defensively...and then realized he'd dropped it on the porch.

But instead of winding up for another slap, the Inkling crossed her arms over her chest instead. And then shook her head.

"Um," he began. And then lunged for his staff, rising again and holding it in front of him. "I can explain!"

The doppelganger just stood there, tapping its foot. Chauncy paused, suddenly realizing that he didn't really know exactly what Valtora had discovered. If he told her everything, he might give something away that could've remained a secret. But if he hid something, he'd almost certainly worsen his situation.

"So, did you talk to Imperius?" he asked, trying to feel out the situation.

The doppelganger raised her right hand to slap Chauncy again, and he blocked frantically with his staff...only to be slapped with her left hand instead. Which made him stumble against the wall of the house, then bounce off.

"Hey!" he blurted out, backpedaling quickly. "Okay, okay! Fine!" He rubbed his smarting cheek. "Imperius came to give Chaos his destiny and I thought he was too young so I told him off and now I've ruined everything and cursed the world!"

He paused.

"And I'm sorry," he finished. Lamely.

The Doppelganger glared at him for a bit longer, then lowered its arms, stepping toward him. He flinched, but in lieu of hitting him, it hugged him instead. And *then* hit him, one last time. But afterward, it helped him up. Then hugged him again, confusingly.

"So um, what now?" he asked.

"What indeed," a voice behind him stated.

Chauncy *screeched*, whirling around and holding his Staff of Wind at the ready. But to his surprise, it wasn't an enemy. Probably. For it was none other than Imperius Fanning. The old wizard stood before him with his magnificent staff in hand, regarding Chauncy as if he'd just bitten into a turd-covered lemon.

"We meet again, Chauncy Little," Imperius declared in his deep voice.

"Imperius!" Chauncy exclaimed. "Um," he added, fidgeting a bit. "So, uh...sorry?"

"Difficult words are easier to say than difficult actions are to do," Imperius replied stonily. "Whether your apology is sufficient is entirely up to you."

Chauncy gave him a blank look.

"Up to me how?" he asked.

"In due time," Imperius replied mysteriously. Chauncy glanced at Valtora's doppelganger, then back at Imperius.

"So um, Chaos has gone missing," he announced. "We can't find him anywhere."

"That's because he's on his adventure," Imperius replied. "Following destiny to the cursed land within Grissam."

"Oh," Chauncy replied. "So he's okay?"

"Alive and well," Imperius confirmed. "For now. Whether that remains true, time will tell."

"So he's in danger?"

"Mortal danger," the old wizard confirmed.

"We have to help him!" Chauncy exclaimed.

"The best way to help him is to *not* help him," Imperius proclaimed. "To interfere with his quest will spell his doom...and doom the world to utter annihilation."

Chauncy paused.

"Really?"

"Really," Imperius confirmed.

"Oh," he mumbled. "So...you want us to do nothing?"

"Correct," Imperius replied. "You are not to interfere with Chaos's quest."

"But he's only thirteen!"

"Even so," Imperius stated. "His journey is his alone."

"You don't understand," Chauncy insisted. "He's...not..."

Imperius arched an eyebrow.

"...useful," Chauncy finished with a grimace. For Chaos's uselessness was entirely his fault. "Ever since the...meteorite incident, we've..."

"Constrained him?" Imperius guessed.

"Right."

"Stunted him?" Imperius added.

"A bit," Chauncy had to admit.

"Made him safe and secure by making it so he couldn't use his magic, living a mundane life he grew to despise day after day?" Imperius continued, to Chauncy's further dismay. For it was precisely what Grandma Little had done to him all those years, with the best of intentions, of course. It'd driven him near to suicide, in fact...a hint of which Chaos himself had...well, hinted at.

I'd rather die, he'd said. And while he most certainly hadn't meant it, it made far more sense to Chauncy now.

"You're right," he realized, a chill running down his spine. He swallowed past a sudden lump in his throat. "I'm just like Grandma Little."

"The evil we do trying to do good," Imperius mused, placing both hands on the crystalline head of his staff. "Protecting our children from risk...and thus reward."

Chauncy's shoulders slumped, and he lowered his gaze to his feet.

"So...what do I do?" he asked. Imperius sighed, putting a hand on his shoulder.

"Nothing," he replied. "Which will be the very hardest thing for you."

With that, Imperius vanished in a burst of blue sparkles, which fell to the ground and vanished. Chauncy stood there, staring first at his feet, then at the street ahead...and then far south, to the two-hundred-foot-tall Wall and its silver-doored Gate. He imagined Chaos out there somewhere, lost and alone. Or worse, *not* alone, with someone less than ideal. Someone who might take advantage of him or his powers. Likely a man, of course. Old and creepy. Like Mr. Schmidt, their lotion-loving customer, but worse.

A *buggerer*.

The thought of it made Chauncy's guts squirm, and he gripped his Staff of Wind, turning to the doppelganger.

"Sorry hon," he told it, knowing Valtora would hear through its inky ears. "When it comes to the people I love being in danger, nothing is the one thing I can't do."

And with that, he thrust the butt of his staff downward, flying upward in a burst of wind, soaring high above the rooftop of his little home. Upward he went, thrusting until he was soaring south toward the Wall...and the Kingdom of Pravus beyond.

Chapter 19

Chaos followed Destiny through the night-shrouded Great Flat as she led them through the ankle-deep water toward the wall of Old Langsroth, struggling to do so. His armor was terribly heavy, weighing at least thirty to forty pounds, in addition to the weight of the shovel he was carrying. With the extra difficulty of wading through the water, he found the going…well, difficult. Such that he soon fell far behind Destiny.

"Um," he called out. She stopped, turning around. "Having trouble here."

"Right," she replied, walking up to him. She closed her eyes in silent prayer, her hands glowing gold. Then she touched him…and he felt a surge of sheer power run through him.

"Whoa," he breathed.

"Come on," she prompted, turning about and leading him forward once again. Chaos paused, then trudged after her. Or rather, he walked, with startling ease. For the armor that'd felt so heavy a mere moment ago now felt as light as a cloud. As did his shovel. The gold light faded.

"What was that?" he asked.

"Vita's Boundless Strength," Destiny answered. "The weakest version of it, for now." Chaos caught up with her, striding beside her, and threw her a smile.

"I gotta admit, your magic is pretty awesome," he told her.

"Vita's blessing is," she corrected.

"Thanks," he told her.

"You're welcome," she replied. And then stopped, holding out an arm to bar his way. "Hold up," she said, then gestured ahead. Chaos frowned, peering through the darkness. But he couldn't see anything. "Zombie ahead and to the right," she informed him, pointing…ahead and to the right. He peered harder, but still couldn't see anything.

"Sorry, I can't see it," he whispered. "Do you have a light?"

"Zombies are like moths," she replied. "They're attracted to anything shining in the darkness."

"Oh," he replied. "How do you know there's a zombie there?"

"I sense it," she answered. "That's how I found you. I sensed the undead wolves and tracked them."

"I was wondering about that."

"You're lucky I was all the way over in Pravus at the time," she told him. "I don't usually venture that far out from Tabula." She strode forward, slower than before, putting a finger to her lips. Chaos nodded, and they made their way toward the ruins of a small building. It was about half the size of Chaos's house, and all four walls were still standing. The wooden door had long since rotted away, leaving a small open entrance, beyond which was utter darkness. "Inside," she mouthed, then pointed to his shovel.

He stared at the doorway, then at her.

"Now?" he mouthed.

"Now," she confirmed silently.

Chaos turned back to the doorway, adjusting his grip on the shovel. Its handle felt slick in his sweaty hands, and he hesitated, glancing at her again. She gestured for him to get a move on, and he took a deep breath in, then steeled himself for what was to come.

You can do this, he told himself.

He stepped forward, his boots sloshing in the water, until he was only a few feet from the doorway. Beyond was utter darkness, which presented a problem. If he couldn't *see* the zombie, how was he supposed to fight it? He glanced back at Destiny, who rolled her eyes...and then banged her mace on her shield.

Clang clang clang!

"What are you...!" Chaos blurted out.

"Graaargh," a horrid voice inside the building graarrghed.

Chaos blinked.

"Zora?" he called out in disbelief. But when a pale figure shambled out of the darkness inside the building, making their way toward the doorway, he found that it was not his undead stepmother at all. It was a man, old and skinny, his flesh half-decomposed, crawling on his hands and...well, his belly. For he had no legs, and was terribly, awfully pale, and his eyes were glazed over and half his scalp was missing.

"Ew," Chaos blurted out, making a face. And taking a few steps back. For in addition to looking awful, the man smelled awful too.

113

"Graarrgh," the zombie rasped.

"You gonna hit it or what?" Destiny prompted.

"Uh," Chaos replied, taking another step back and holding his shovel with sweaty hands. The zombie crawled with comforting slowness, its belly half immersed in the water. "You want me to hit it?"

"I want you to kill it," Destiny replied.

Chaos watched the thing for a bit longer, feeling a bit bad for it.

"Can it even hurt us?" he pressed.

"Not the point," she shot back. "You need to learn how to fight. On things that can't hurt you before fighting the ones that can."

"Oh," Chaos replied. "Makes sense." He paused, grimacing at the zombie. "Sorry guy," he added.

And then he swung his shovel as hard as he could at the thing's face.

Clang!

The head of the shovel hit the zombie right across the goddamn face. The impact tore the shovel from his hands…and tore the zombie's face from its bones. Chaos cursed, retrieving the shovel and scrambling back from the creature. Half of its face hung in a loose flap that dangled into the water, the exposed bone crumpled inward.

"Ugh," he blurted out. "Urrghh," he added, dry heaving a bit.

"Again," Destiny ordered.

"Urgghkay," Chaos replied, swallowing back some bile. "Sorry," he added, swinging the shovel again, this time in an overhead chop. The shovel shoved the zombie's head into the water, splashing Chaos, and tore most of its remaining scalp off.

"Again," she prompted.

Chaos complied, swinging the shovel again and again, until the zombie's skull had caved in completely. Its arms spasmed, then twitched a bit, and then went still.

"Whew," Chaos said, wiping a sweaty forehead with the back of his hand.

"Killing is a lot of work," Destiny noted.

"Sure is," he agreed. "My mom makes it look so easy."

Destiny blinked.

"Excuse me?" she asked.

"Uh…nothing," he replied. "So what now?"

114

She turned away from the zombie he'd killed, facing the other buildings around the one it'd come from. To Chaos's horror, more zombies were emerging from the buildings.

Dozens of them.

"My banging woke the dead," she told him. "Put them back to sleep."

* * *

"Crap!" Chaos blurted out.

Zombies shambled out of the black stone buildings toward him and Destiny, some walking, others limping or crawling. All of them distressingly nude, and severely decomposed looking. Their pale skin hung from their bones, some with an eye missing, or faces half torn off. Others had missing limbs like the first zombie Chaos had dealt with. They came from all sides, converging on Chaos and Destiny like a slow-motion wave of impending death.

"Stay calm," Destiny advised. "Don't let them surround you. If they come up from behind and grab you, you're in trouble."

"So...what do I do?" Chaos pressed.

"Move," Destiny answered, as if she were explaining something terribly simple to a terribly simple child. "So that they're all in front of you."

"Right," Chaos replied.

He did just that, jogging through the ankle-deep water the way they'd come, until all of the zombies were in front of him...or at least not behind him. Destiny didn't follow, to his surprise. But the zombies didn't seem to notice her, coming toward him instead. Also to his surprise.

"Why aren't they coming for you?" he called out.

"Vita's Invisibility to Undead," she replied. "Only works on weak undead though. Also, shut up. Unless you *want* to attract more of them."

Chaos grimaced, shifting his weight from one foot to the other, holding his shovel at the ready. His heart pounded in his chest, sweat dripping down his flanks. The two dozen-odd zombies came toward him, all shuffling and limping and crawling and such, their dead eyes locked on him. The closest were thirty feet away, and closing in. Not quickly, but steadily. The ones that could walk were coming the quickest, and given the distance involved, this caused them to pull away from the slower zombies. Which, he realized, made it so that he'd be facing fewer zombies at a time. So he backpedaled further, making that gap bigger...and now only the fastest three were even close to him.

All right, he told himself, faking a confident smirk. *Time to tear off some frickin' zombie faces.*

He planted his feet wide, winding up as the first zombie came within a few feet of him: a scrawny, elderly woman with very bad teeth. Who was naked, and flappy and floppy in all the places Mom was not. With a grunt, Chaos swung his shovel at her sunken face. Hard.

Clang!

The zombie's head snapped to the side, her neck breaking with a sickening *crack*. She fell onto her side on the flooded street with a second *crack* as her hip broke, probably. Chaos followed this first swing up with an overhead chop at her head, but missed, hitting her neck instead. With the sharp edge of the shovel head, by accident. With Vita's Boundless Strength powering the attack, the metal cut right through the zombie's broken neck...and decapitated it.

Chaos felt a surge of nausea, but didn't have time to puke. For the other two zombies had reached him...a middle-aged man with one arm and a boy about his age, respectively. The man reached out with his one arm, grabbing Chaos's shovel.

Crap!

Chaos tried to tear his shovel away, but the zombie's grip was incredibly strong. But in pulling, he pulled the man off-balance, and the zombie fell to the street with a splash. Which was a problem, because he took the shovel with him, tearing it out of Chaos's hands.

"Your body is a weapon," Destiny called out. "Use it."

Chaos let go of the shovel, backing away from the two zombies. The boy-zombie lunged at him, by far the faster of the two. Chaos reacted without thinking, kicking the kid in the chest. The kid fell onto his back...but Chaos did as well, losing his balance and falling to the street. Cold water surged through his armor, soaking him...and chilling him to the bone.

"Gah!" he blurted out, scrambling to his feet. Which would have been impossible if it hadn't been for Vita's Boundless Strength, given the weight of his armor. He reached for the shovel, but it was still clutched in the older zombie's iron grip. So he did the only thing he could think of, and stomped on the guy's wrist.

Over and over again. The bones there cracked, the zombie's forearm curving in an S-shape. But still the bastard wouldn't let go. So Chaos stomped again and again and again, then stepped on the guy's shoulder, grabbing the shaft of the shovel and yanking it as hard as he could.

The zombie's rotten flesh tore, its hand coming off at the wrist. Still clutching the shovel, to Chaos's dismay. He tried prying its fingers free from his weapon, but it was no use.

Then the two zombies started rising to their feet...even as three more approached. The first zombie-woman he'd decapitated rose as well, grabbing her head by the hair with one hand, so that her face was facing him.

"Hurrgghh," Chaos dry-heaved, backing away quickly. "Hurrghhblarrghh!" he added, a jet of vomit spewing from his mouth. Which was terribly embarrassing, in that it wasn't heroic at all.

"Focus," Destiny chided.

Chaos swallowed, then vomit-swung his shovel, knocking the woman's head from her hand. It flew off to the side, tumbling in the water, and the zombie's body stumbled, then fell. The other two zombies made it to their feet, and Chaos bashed their faces in with a symphony of *clangs*.

Then the rest of the zombie horde drew near, crawling or limping toward him, while glaring at him with dead-eyed hate.

Chaos stumbled backward, wiping his sweat-drenched forehead with his free hand. His heart was racing, his breaths coming in short gasps.

"Getting...tired!" he called out.

"Take a rest if you want," Destiny replied. While staying right where she was.

"Ha...ha," he gasped, grunting as he swung at the nearest zombie, crawling at him on all fours. Its head snapped to the side, and it rolled onto its back, but the other zombies simply crawled over it. He swung his shovel madly, trying desperately to fend them off. But his arms felt like lead now, his blows doing less and less damage.

Which was a problem, because even the ones he struck just got back up.

"Need...a...little...help!" he yelled, smacking a zombie-toddler in the temple. The blow was so weak that the toddler shrugged it off, barely even stumbling. A good six zombies reached out for him with pale zombie hands, less than a yard away now.

"Seriously, just step back," Destiny said.

Chaos blinked, then realized he could do just that.

He backpedaled, then turned and jogged away, putting a good thirty feet between him and the front of the zombie horde. Which gave him plenty of time to drop his shovel, lean over and rest his hands on his knees, and gasp pathetically. Which he did for a good minute before the zombies drew near again. So he just picked up his shovel and backpedaled more, doing the same thing.

Idiot, he scolded himself. For once again, he'd nearly died by being remarkably stupid. Which made him wonder if he really *was* stupid, and no one had ever. had the heart to tell him so. Which was a kindness, but also a disservice, for he'd always assumed he was smart. And perhaps that was the stupidest thing that stupid people did, not knowing what they didn't know, or who they were.

At length he recovered somewhat, then grabbed his shovel, facing the zombies again. He realized then that there wasn't a single one that'd stayed down, not even the headless woman. His shovel had injured them, but to the undead, injuries were merely inconveniences.

"I can't stop them," he confessed. "And they're wearing me out."

"Then you've learned your first lesson about fighting the undead," Destiny replied. "Now watch and learn."

With that, she held her shield and mace, striding toward the back of the zombie line. And what happened next was precisely what you'd imagine would happen when a badass frickin' paladin of Vita took on a group of undead.

Chapter 20

Chaos leaned against the cool stone wall of one of the ruined buildings outside of Old Langsroth, staring glumly at the scattered pieces of undead bodies lying in motionless hunks in the flooded streets, half-buried by water. Destiny finished off the last of the zombies by exploding its head with her mace, after which she walked up to him, not at all short-of-breath. Or sweating, he noted with dismay. He couldn't help but feel absolutely useless once again, as well as emasculated. After all, he'd been beaten by a *girl*, as his best friend Wesley would have jeered.

"Hey," she greeted, stopping before him, while posing badass-edly.

"Hey," he mumbled back. Posing slouch-ily.

"Couple things," she stated. "You use your arm muscles too much when you swing. Use your hips instead."

"Uh...how?" he asked.

"Rotate them," she answered. She demonstrated a few swings with her mace, pivoting to put her hips into each one. "You won't tire out so fast then," she told him. "Try it."

He did so, swinging his shovel, and she immediately corrected him. By setting her mace and shield down, then grabbing his hips and rotating them forcefully.

"Hey!" he blurted out.

"Learn to use your hips," she told him. Then she smirked. "Trust me, you'll thank me later."

"When I can swing real hard?" he asked.

"Sure. Yeah."

He tried a few more swings, and she corrected him a distressing number of times before she was somewhat satisfied.

"That's better," she told him. "Now use it on a zombie."

"They're all dead," he noted.

"They were dead before we got here," she pointed out. "They're still animated."

"They're not moving," he argued. Which was kinda literally the definition of animated.

"For the moment," she agreed. "The water here has diluted Fallen blood in it though. It'll heal them."

"How...uh...long does it take?" he asked, eyeing the scattered corpse-pieces warily.

"Out here, a few weeks," she answered. "These are the weakest undead. They were only ever exposed to dilute Fallen blood."

"So the ones in Old Langsroth are stronger?"

"Oh, you have *no* idea," she replied, giving him a look that did a much better job at answering his question.

"Well crap," he muttered. "If I can't beat these..."

"...pathetic zombies," she interjected rudely.

"...then how am I going to beat anything *inside* the city?" he finished.

"Practice," she answered.

"Right," he grumbled. "It can't be *that* easy."

"It isn't about easy or hard," she countered evenly. "It's about consistency."

"With my attacks?"

"With training," she corrected. "Whatever you do each day is what you'll get better at. Choose who you want to be and do that."

He frowned.

"How can I do what I want to be if I'm not what I want to be yet?" he asked.

"Act how the person you want to be would act, and try to do what they'd do. Eventually you'll get good enough to do it well."

Chaos considered this, rubbing his chin.

"Huh," he murmured. "Was...that what you did?"

"Yes," she confirmed. "That was why Vita chose me."

"Because you acted like the person you wanted to be?"

"Because I was already doing it instead of keeping it a dream," Destiny corrected. "Most people spend their lives dreaming about the future rather than living their dreams. They never start, so they never arrive."

He nodded, realizing that she was right. He'd been doing just that, living the same boring day over and over again back home, dreaming of a day that things would be different. It'd taken Imperius to give him permission to start his journey...and it'd taken Destiny to force him to try things even though he sucked at them.

It'd been his lifelong dream to become a great wizard. The great wizard, in fact, that Imperius had foretold he would become. Which meant that if he wanted to *be* a great wizard, he had to start wizard-ing. Even if he sucked at it. Right now.

Chaos took a deep breath in, standing a bit taller and squaring his shoulders.

"Right," he declared. "So I need to use my magic."

"To make a surprise?" she asked.

"Right."

"What good is that?" she pressed. He frowned.

"What do you mean?" he asked. "The power of chaos is like, super powerful."

"Making surprises," she stated.

"Right," he replied. She stared at him, clearly doubting his proclamation. "It *is* powerful," he insisted. "Imperius Fanning even said so."

"Maybe it is," she conceded. "But that doesn't make it useful."

He blinked.

"No," he protested.

"Yes," she retorted. "When you use your magic, do you know what'll happen?"

"No," he scoffed. "Then it wouldn't be a surprise. Duh," he added, pettily.

"And so you have no idea if what you're doing will be bad or good," she pressed.

"Right."

"So how is that useful?" she asked.

"Because," he answered. And then paused. "Um," he added, for the sake of procrastination. "When something bad is going to happen – inevitably bad – it shakes things up so that something good might happen. Or at least *less* bad."

"So your magic is useful when you're in deep trouble with no way out, and you're willing to roll the dice on a surprise that may or may not help," she translated.

"Yes," he concluded proudly, crossing his arms over his chest. "It's come in handy before," he pointed out. After all, Zora never would've gotten pregnant, and Imperius Fanning never would've been hit by a magical meteorite if it hadn't been for him.

"So what do you do to prevent yourself from getting into a no-win situation where you'd *need* to use your magic?" she inquired, crossing her arms over her chest in turn.

He thought this over, then shrugged.

"I dunno," he admitted.

"Right," she replied. "Like I said, your magic is mostly useless. Or useless in most situations."

Chaos opened his mouth to protest, then thought better of it.

"So I *shouldn't* practice my magic?" he asked.

"You should," she countered. "But if your magic is a power of last resort, you need to practice skills that prevent you from having to use it in the first place."

"Like...fighting?" he guessed.

"Like fighting," she agreed. "You want to be a great wizard? Fine. But your magic isn't the kind of magic that you'll be able to use very often, at least as things are right now. Maybe we're missing something and your magic is more useful than we know. But for now, you need to be useful without it."

He sighed, then nodded.

"Okay," he agreed. "Teach me, oh master," he requested, bowing only slightly sarcastically.

"Tomorrow," she replied. "If you want to be an effective human, get the basics right. Eat well, get enough sleep, and exercise...and right now, it's time for sleep."

* * *

After leaving the Great Flat the way they'd come, Chaos and Destiny rode Gwendolyn to solid, unflooded ground. Destiny chose to make camp a few hundred feet away from the shore, building a fire, then retrieving her sleeping bag and setting on the ground. Chaos did the same, and after a meal of dehydrated stuff, he took off his mail and snuggled into his brand new sleeping bag. Within moments, he heard Destiny's soft snoring, barely audible over the crackling of the fire.

Chaos sighed, rolling onto his back and staring up at the stars. They twinkled down at him, the crescent moon casting the ground in a pale white light. A soft breeze flowed over him, which was a little cool, but his sleeping bag was like a warm cocoon, and he relished it. He'd never paid much attention to his comfy bed and warm blanket at home, and had certainly not appreciated it. But after suffering the elements these last few nights, he found himself silently thanking the sleeping bag. And not only the sleeping bag, but the shopkeeper who'd sold it to him, and Destiny, who'd paid for it. And the people who'd made the sleeping bag, hunting animals for skins, then curing them or whatever. Then sewing the skins together, growing and picking cotton for the warm insulation inside – or caring for birds to get their soft down – and so on.

It occurred to him then that it had taken a great number of people working together to make this sleeping bag that served him so well. And that these people – doing vastly different jobs – had collected the basic materials needed to craft useful things. It'd taken a multitude, all planning to accomplish their tasks, then carrying it through to completion. And a craftsman to design the sleeping bag and use all of these materials to bring their design to life.

It was, Chaos realized, the exact opposite of chaos. An order that he'd hated back home, but served him so well now.

What good is your magic?

Destiny's question made him squirm, and he rolled onto his side, bringing his knees to his chest. What use was chaos when order had so much power? What purpose was his power if his power destroyed order, like it'd destroyed the Order – that big white cube of abstraction – years ago?

All my magic can do is destroy, he thought, and the thought was profoundly depressing. He'd destroyed the Order, sure, but he'd also almost got Imperius Fanning killed, and had nearly gotten his family killed as a result.

His father could make all sorts of useful magical items, and his mother's magic was to make existing things awesome. Imperius's magic had saved the world countless times, and even Gavin's magic knitting needles had proven surprisingly useful.

If Chaos's magic was so useless, how could he ever hope to measure up to them?

Chaos rolled over onto his other side, wishing that he'd gone to the Cave of Wonder. His father and mother had told him of how the magical cave had shown them the way every time they'd gone inside. He really *should* have gone, he realized. Even if he hadn't lost his magic completely – which was a very real possibility – he had no idea what to do with it.

He set his jaw firmly, realizing what had to be done. After he finished doing whatever it was he was doing with Destiny, he would go to the Cave of Wonder, destiny – and Destiny – be damned.

123

Chapter 21

After several days of travel – without being molested by any more bandits – King Pravus and Templeton had left Cumulus far behind, and found themselves riding up the gentle slope of a large hill early in the morning. They came to the top of it, and were rewarded for their efforts – or rather, the efforts of their horses – with a magnificent view. One of a great big red mesa a hundred feet tall, with a grand city built atop it. They stopped their steeds to take in this view, and Templeton issued forth a low whistle.

"Marvelous!" he exclaimed.

"Magnificent!" Pravus agreed. "Congratulations, dearest cousin," he added. "We've made it to Tabula, capitol of Grissam!"

"I've heard stories and seen illustrations," Templeton said, "...but to see it with my own eyes, why, it gives me goosebumps to behold!"

Pravus smiled, beholding his cousin beholding Tabula. While wishing he could be holding Templeton in an entirely different way. It was so often the case that the more time one spent with a friend, the less one liked them. But despite the last few days of Templeton being ever-present, the man appeared no less magical to Pravus than he always did. A joy and a curse, for he could only enjoy Templeton at arms' length, when he would so desperately prefer to enjoy him in an overlapping sort of way.

They regarded this scene silently for a moment, not wanting to spoil it with distracting conversation. For Pravus knew that feeling a scene in one's soul required a sort of psychic space, a taking in rather than a putting out. It was, he knew, impossible to do both at once, except perhaps in the bedroom.

At length Pravus turned to the right, spotting the ruins of a large stone building a few hundred yards away on the top of the hill.

"What do you suppose that was?" he asked.

"If I recall from my schooling, it was a temple," Templeton stated. "The Temple of Vita," he added. "A Magus revered as a god, as they often are."

"Ah."

They both stared at the ruins for a bit.

"Strange, to worship a Magus," Pravus mused.

"How so?"

"A Magus is merely a man or woman who became what was magical to them," Pravus explained. "Worshipping a person means putting oneself far beneath them. It devalues the self, declaring that another person is far more important than you. In who they are, not what they do."

"You may be right," Templeton replied. "Better to admire and be inspired by others than to put oneself down in relation to them."

"I've always thought so," Pravus agreed. This had been the purpose of his muscly statues erected around his gymnasium. Not as idols to be worshipped, or as a way to make others feel that they were less because they didn't look that way. But rather as exemplars of the potential of the human body...a reminder that, with hard work, remarkable things were possible. Why, if a single boy or girl gazed upon those statues and was inspired to love what Pravus and Templeton loved – and reap the reward of a muscly physique, and in due course inspire others to do the same – then Pravus would consider it money well spent.

"Old Langsroth should be a day's ride or so from Tabula," Templeton estimated. "Shall we go directly to, or stop in the city for a respite?"

"A respite would be divine," Pravus replied. He paused then, his lips curling in a naughty smile. "What say we put our commoner's garb to good use and play the part?"

"A fine idea indeed!" Templeton declared merrily. "A rare treat, to cast off the weighty mantle of the aristocracy!"

"Why, it may prove an adventure in and of itself," Pravus stated. "Come, sweet, dearest Templeton! To Tabula at once!"

Chapter 22

The morning after their first foray into the Great Flat – and the ruins of the town outside the wall of Old Langsroth – Chaos woke to find Destiny already up. He rubbed his eyes, then watched, still in his sleeping bag, as she did her thing. Which was to feed Gwendolyn, wipe down her saddle, and then check inside the saddlebags.

"What are you doing?" he asked.

"Taking inventory," Destiny answered.

"Why?"

"Provisions are our lifeline," she explained. "We starve, we die."

She finished this, then got to work polishing her mace and checking the leather wrapping around its handle. All while Chaos yawned, stretched, and then sat there watching.

"We both have the same amount of time," Destiny grumbled. "How you're using it is why you won't succeed."

Chaos grimaced, getting out of his sleeping bag, folding it up and putting it back in one of the saddlebags. Then he stood there, watching her.

"Um…what else should I do?" he asked.

"Maintenance," she answered. "Check your armor and your weapon."

"They're fine," he replied. "They're like, brand new."

"Get in the habit of checking them," she shot back. "Or one day you'll get a surprise you won't like."

"Fine," he grumbled. He did as he was told, going through his armor and checking the little metal links. They were fine, of course. "It's fine," he declared.

"How's the oil on the boots?" she asked. He frowned.

"Oil?"

"Mail is metal," she told him. "Metal rusts. Oil stops it from rusting. Your mail was oiled, but you walked in water for a while. Water makes rust form faster."

"Oh," he mumbled. He checked the boots, sliding a finger across. "Um, not too slippery?"

She went to the saddlebags, retrieving two cloths, one white and the other black, and threw them at him. He caught it, and then she tossed a flask at him. A very heavy one.

"Dry the mail with the white cloth. Re-apply oil with the black one," she instructed.

Chaos did so, drying, then putting a fresh coat of oil on his boots. Despite his irritation, after a while he found himself actually enjoying the process, taking his time taking care of his stuff. It made him pay attention to his armor, and appreciate the little details of its construction. When he was done, he handed the cloths and flask of oil back to Destiny.

"Thanks," he told her. "Sorry," he added.

"You weren't taught right," she replied matter-of-factly. "Not your fault."

"My parents never let me do stuff by myself," he admitted. "Not after I was four, anyway. After I dropped that meteorite on Imperius, they stopped me from using my magic and kept me close to them all the time."

"They made you useless to yourself and others," she translated.

"Yeah," he replied, blushing a bit. "I guess you're right." He sighed then. "I hate it. That I'm useless, I mean."

"You're not stupid," she offered. "Just ignorant. You can be taught. Learn how to be powerful and you'll have the power to become who you want to be."

"By doing what?"

"Developing rituals," she answered. "The things you want to be able to do the most? Make them the first thing you do each day. Every day, whether you feel like it or not."

"The same thing every day?" he pressed, making a face. "Sounds boring."

"It is sometimes," she conceded. "But sometimes 'boring' is what it takes."

"Huh."

"If all you go for is excitement, you'll never get good," she continued. "Because any one thing isn't exciting after the first few times." She paused. "With a few exceptions."

127

"Like what?"

"Pretty sure you've already figured that out," she replied with a smirk. He blushed furiously. "Now check your shaft."

He blinked.

"Of your *weapon*," she clarified.

She helped him check his shovel, inspecting the shaft, then its connection to the head. Then he checked the head for dents or rust. If the head of the shovel broke off, it'd be an unwelcome surprise, Destiny reasoned, and Chaos had to agree she was right. She taught him how to inspect and care for each part of his armor, then took out a sewing kit to teach him how to repair any tears in his arming doublet or clothes. Simple stuff. Mundane. Boring, or so he'd imagined they'd be. But each thing he learned was itself something new, and becoming gradually more self-sufficient was awfully exciting.

When at long last their inspection was complete, she let Chaos eat. Then he put on his armor, after which they mounted Gwendolyn. With the weight of his armor, this was a difficult feat, and Chaos needed Destiny's help to do it. This done, Destiny guided the horse back into the shallow water of the Great Flat. The horse's hooves splish-splashed as they went, the sun shining brightly in the near-cloudless sky.

"Going to kill more zombies?" Chaos guessed.

"Yep."

"All right then," he stated. "I'll do my best."

"Don't need to," she replied. "Just put in the work."

"Huh?"

"You can't do your best all the time," she explained. "And if you try to, you'll just wear yourself out. Do a little less than your best and you'll be able to keep that up without burning out."

"Huh," he murmured. It was an odd way of thinking, especially after growing up in Borrin. For in Borrin, everyone was always pushing people to do their very best, all day every day…especially employers and schools. Anything less, in fact, was considered lazy and grounds for reprimand. To be urged to do *less* than his best was rather refreshing, and gave him the space to fail with far less worry. For if he did his very best and failed, it was awfully depressing. "I can definitely do that."

"We'll see," she replied, but not in a doubting way. It was merely a statement of fact. He realized then that, while he'd imagined that she'd been judging him – and quite harshly – this whole time, in the end it'd been *him* who'd done the judging. With every misstep, he'd judged himself negatively, and assumed that she was doing the same.

"What do you think of me?" he asked bluntly. And quickly, before he could change his mind.

"You're naïve and sheltered and unconfident," she answered. He grimaced.

"Kinda wish I hadn't asked."

"But you're not annoying," Destiny added.

"Great," he grumbled.

"It's a big deal, actually," she admitted. "Most people would've irritated me by now."

"Oh," he replied. "Um…thanks." He managed a smile, though seeing as she was riding in front of him, she couldn't see it.

They made their way across the Great Flat, and in the sunlight Chaos was able to appreciate much more of the terrain than the previous night. Whereas before it'd appeared rather menacing, now it was quite beautiful. White mist floated over the water a few feet, but above that, his view was clear. Such that he could easily see the ruins outside of the great black stone wall of Old Langsroth far ahead, broken buildings poking out of the mist.

But beyond the wall, the sky was filled with low-hanging clouds so dark they were almost black. Clouds that formed a slowly rotating spiral, like an upside-down whirlpool in the sky. Closer to the center of the whirlpool, the clouds were blood-red in hue; and from those clouds, a red haze extended all the way down to the city.

It had to be the Fallen Sky…and the blood raining down from it.

A chill ran down Chaos's spine at the thought of the wizard who'd cursed the ancient city, for the man must have been extraordinarily powerful. A wizard whose power was far more useful than Chaos's, in fact. For Chaos could only make a surprise in the moment, while this long-dead wizard's magic had endured across countless generations.

Once again, he felt *less than*, and it made him terribly depressed.

At length, they made it to the ruins they'd been to last night. But instead of stopping Gwendolyn and dismounting, Destiny guided the horse toward the great wall far ahead.

"Where are we going?" Chaos asked.

"Zombies de-animate during the day," she replied. "Except under the Fallen Sky."

"Wait, we're going inside?" he blurted out, fear gripping his guts.

"We'll stay near the exit," she assured him. Ineffectively, for he found himself utterly unassured. "Don't worry, I'll use Vita's Trickling Regeneration on you."

"What's that?"

"It heals you slowly over time," she answered.

"Nice."

"But it won't heal you if you die," she added. Which was honest, but not nice at all. Chaos's unease continued, an icky feeling in the pit of his stomach just below his breastbone. Still, he had little choice but to stay where he was, perched on Gwendolyn's back. For to try to go against Destiny would mean violating Imperius's command. An act that could only result in something far worse than whatever Destiny had planned.

So it was that they rode toward the massive wall ahead, one so long that it spanned the entire width of the Great Flat, merging with the cliff walls on either side. True to Destiny's word, no zombies shambled out to bar their way, and it wasn't long before they'd come within thirty feet of the wall. Its black stone was slick and had a reddish hue, Chaos discovered, and water poured down its surface in a steady stream. One that went all the way to the pool of water at the base of the wall. But to his surprise, the water there was tinged deep red, a color that faded the farther away from the wall it got.

He realized then that the "water" streaming down the wall wasn't water at all. It was blood.

"That's the Fallen blood," Destiny stated, as if reading his mind. "The further from the wall we get, the more dilute it is in the water of the Great Flat. That's why the zombies out here are weak," she explained.

"Because they only drink dilute blood," Chaos deduced.

"And touch it," she added. "Fallen blood absorbs through the skin. It's attracted to skin, actually."

With that, she dismounted, her feet splashing in the pink water.

"Come on," she prompted. Chaos eyed the pink water warily.

"What if *we* absorb it?" he asked.

"Nothing," she answered. "Unless we bleed. Then a part of our souls will bleed out too, and rise to join the Fallen Sky. Come on," she prompted.

Chaos stayed where he was on Gwendolyn's back.

"Um, no thanks," he stated. "Not into losing my soul."

"Don't worry," Destiny replied. "If you bleed, I can draw on Vita's power to bring any part of your soul you lose back into your body."

"Oh," Chaos replied. With that, he dismounted, landing in the reddish water.

"Unless you bleed out more than half of your blood," she stated. "Then most of your soul will be outside of your body, and it won't work."

"Why not?" Chaos asked, wishing he'd stayed on the horse.

"Because Vita's power draws your soul to wherever most of it is," Destiny explained. "If most of it is outside of your body, her power will pull the rest out too."

"So don't bleed more than half my blood," he stated.

"Right."

"Right," he muttered. "*Super* excited to be here."

"Stay here Gwen," she told the horse, patting her nose and giving it a kiss. Which was, Chaos realized, the first time he'd seen Destiny show the slightest hint of affection toward another living thing. Then Destiny strode leftward, and Chaos followed behind, grimacing at the cool wetness that spilled into his waterproof boots, as the water was up to his knees now. *Bloody* water, which was gross. And cursed, which was terrifying, to boot.

They'd gone about a hundred yards when Chaos spotted a large, arched stone…well, archway ahead, with a metal grated door-thingy that was closed. Destiny walked right up to it, then stopped.

"This is the entrance," she told him.

"How do we open the door?" he asked.

"It's a portcullis," she corrected. "We lift it."

She closed her eyes, lowering her head and bringing her hands together in prayer. Her hands glowed with a golden light, and she opened her eyes – which were also glowing, rather prettily he thought – and she put a hand on his shoulder. A feeling of warmth and a marvelous tingling sensation spread through him, and suddenly his armor, which had been oppressively heavy, felt as light as silk.

131

"Whoa," he breathed. "What was that?"

"Vita's Boundless Strength," Destiny replied. "A stronger version. Now lift the portcullis."

"Alright," Chaos agreed. He bent down, grabbing the portcullis, then lifting.

"No no," Destiny admonished. "Squat, then lift with your legs. Don't bend over and lift with your back."

"Oh," Chaos replied. He did so, and heard the screech of metal on rusty metal as the portcullis lifted. Vita's Boundless Strength proved not to be, as Chaos soon discovered, for lifting the portcullis was difficult indeed. But lift it he did, until it was as high as he could lift it.

"Hold it up while I go through," Destiny instructed, doing just that. "Now go through," she added. Which he did. He dropped the portcullis, and it fell with a *clang*. One that echoed loudly, much to his chagrin. "Lower it slowly next time," she grumbled.

"Sorry," he mumbled, lowering his gaze in shame. For the loud noise was sure to attract zombies, as she'd told him yesterday.

"Failure is a teacher, not a judge," she replied evenly. "Every failure will make you better, if you learn from it."

Chaos nodded, meeting her gaze.

"What now?" he asked.

"Now we kill zombies," she declared.

Chapter 23

Having utterly ignored the warnings of Imperius Fanning, Chauncy thrust his Staff of Wind repeatedly, soaring high over the kingdom of Pravus. The wind howled in his ears as he flew, the landscape a good hundred feet below flying by with reasonable rapidity. It was, on reflection, a far more efficient way to travel than Nettie and Harry's carriage or Peter's back, or Rocky's for that matter. A thought that reminded him that he hadn't seen Rocky for years now, since their battle with Gamsies and the Order. Where the big guy had gone, he didn't know, and it made him feel awfully guilty that he hadn't sought Rocky out. But then again, Rocky hadn't sought *him* out, which was Chauncy's petty way of justifying his own lack of initiative.

In any case, Chauncy found himself flying quite rapidly over the terrain of Pravus, making his way ever southward toward Grissam, the country to Pravus's south. A fact that he'd memorized long ago in school, when he'd eagerly memorized the countries near Borrin and their capitols, along with their official plants and such. Useless information, he'd realized as an adult. Utterly pointless for him to learn. But the fact that he knew anything about countries beyond Borrin's borders was unusual, for the country was notorious for being self-obsessed. His prepubescent efforts proved fruitful in the end, guiding him toward Grissam. A country he'd certainly never been to, and knew next to nothing about. Other than that the capitol was Tabula, and the official plant was the Weeping Lilly.

But his repeated thrusting grew tiring after a while, and Chauncy soon had to take a break. Which meant descending, then making a gentle landing on some grassy terrain. He lowered his staff to the ground then, stretching out his sore shoulders. For while his hips were quite capable of endless thrusting on account of performing multiple such workouts a day, his arms were decidedly not.

So Chauncy rested, shaking his arms out for a bit, whilst looking around. To his surprise, he found himself in a rather familiar place. Pleasantly familiar, in fact. For to his right, he spotted the magnificent tree line of the Great Wood.

"Oh," he blurted out, surprised to find himself here. For every other time he'd arrived at the Great Wood, it'd been after a fair bit of traveling. He paused, eyeing the tree line, feeling suddenly torn. If he went into the forest and delved once more into the Cave of Wonder, it might give him some guidance on what to do. On the other hand, it would delay his journey, and if something horrible happened to Chaos and Chauncy was just a bit too late to prevent said horror, then he would never be able to live with himself.

Chauncy hesitated, engaging in a bit of the ol' wringing of the hands, unsure of what to do. Which meant that he did nothing, as usual. For to make a decision was to commit to the consequences of said decision. But in the same way, to *not* make a decision was also a decision, with consequences of its own.

Which meant that each branch of action – going to the Great Wood, skipping the Great Wood, or just standing here a-wringin' – was equally consequential. A fact that made choosing even *more* difficult for him. For if he chose incorrectly, Chaos might die.

Chauncy frowned then, an idea coming to him.

Chaos...of course!

The best way to choose would be to choose randomly. And even better, to have something else make the random choice for him. That way, he could blame said something else for the decision, and escape culpability. And like so many who found themselves in questionably-earned positions of authority, escaping culpability was his main priority.

"Right then," he decided.

He reached down for his staff, then set the rules for his decision: he would throw the staff up, and if it landed facing toward him, he would go into the Cave of Wonder. If away, he would go directly to Grissam. Thusly prepared, he threw the Staff of Wind upward, making it twirl as much as he could. It flew high into the sky, then fell back down, landing on the ground. Pointing away from him, he found.

"Right then," he repeated, willing the staff to fly back into his hand. "To Grissam it is."

And with that, Chauncy thrust downward, flying into the air, making his way ever southward. Still, as he thrust rhythmically, he couldn't help but think that he'd made a mistake. For in making randomness choose for him, he'd made the choice to do so. There was no escaping the fact that in the end, it was *his* choices that would be to blame if anything went wrong.

Chapter 24

Chaos stood next to Destiny just inside the portcullis that served as the entrance to the ancient, cursed city of Old Langsroth, knee-deep in blood-tinged water. He felt it flowing in a rather powerful current out of the portcullis, pulling at his legs. The water here was not pure water at all, but red and thicker and stinking of nasty metal. In other words, it was diluted blood...glowing a faint crimson.

"Hurrghh," Chaos dry-heaved, covering his mouth with one hand.

"Get it over with," Destiny grumbled, taking a few steps forward away from him.

"Hurrghblaaargh!" Chaos obliged her, quite unwillingly, spewing his half-digested breakfast into the water. It flowed away in a raft of chunky chunks, exiting via the portcullis. "Glarghbuuurp," he vomit-belched. After which his eyes watered, and he stood there hunched over, dry heaving a bit more.

"You done?" Destiny asked.

"Mhmm," he replied. And as it turned out, this was a lie. For he vomited one more time. "Mhmm," he repeated afterward, hoping his body would comply this time. Which it did, to his relief.

"This blood is still dilute," she told him. "Pure blood falls from the center of the Fallen Sky. Out here, it mixes with regular rainclouds. The closer we get to the center of Old Langsroth, the less dilute it'll be."

"Great," he grumbled. "Can't wait."

"You'll get used to it," she assured him. "Come on."

She strode forward, against the current, and Chaos followed reluctantly behind her. Beyond the portcullis was a stone hallway a good fifty feet long, and flooded all the way up to above Chaos's knees. It was also awfully dark after a few yards in, despite the morning sun. For the sun could not penetrate the dense clouds of blood that were the Fallen Sky; thus Old Langsroth had been plunged into eternal darkness.

Even as Chaos thought this, the golden inscriptions on Destiny's mace began to glow, casting the tunnel ahead in warm light.

They trudged forward, fighting the powerful current flowing against them. Chaos supposed that it would've been nearly impossible for him to stride against the current in his heavy armor had it not been for Vita's Boundless Strength, once again proving that Destiny's magic was more useful than his. It was dependable. Practical. Predictable.

And predictable, it turned out, could be powerful.

Chaos sighed, the weight on his soul too heavy for even Vita's Boundless Strength to help him bear. And so his spirits fell, and he soon found himself plunged into the darkest of thoughts. Thoughts that he was useless. That this whole journey was hopeless. That he'd never become who he wanted to be...or even worse, that who he was simply wasn't enough.

I'll never be as good as her, he thought as he followed behind Destiny.

In fact, he had no real idea of what the heck he was really doing here, following Destiny into some zombie-infested place. Or any clue as to whether this was what he was actually supposed to be doing. For Imperius had only said to find his destiny in Grissam, and while he'd found Destiny, she certainly wasn't *his*. It occurred to Chaos that he might be on the wrong track, so to speak. Dad had been told exactly what his destiny was each time Imperius had arrived. He'd been given a specific goal to complete. But Chaos's destiny, it seemed, was merely to meet, not complete. So what the heck was he supposed to do now?

Chaos bumped into Destiny's back, and realized that she'd stopped in her tracks, just before the end of the long hallway, where an open arched doorway greeted them. Beyond was a large open space, the sound of rainfall pattering on the surface of the water greeting his ears. It was oppressively dark, and as such, he couldn't make out much of anything beyond. Other than a subtle red glow from the blood in the water, a glow that grew brighter the further into the space he looked.

"Focus," she admonished. Which was a nice way of telling him to get his head out of his ass, as Mommy often told Daddy to do. He did so, metaphorically thank goodness, focusing his attention on the present moment. Which was that he was entering a mysterious open space of oppressive darkness bathed in a lake of blood, in a city swarming with bloodthirsty undead.

Shit, he thought. Which was something he wasn't supposed to say, but thinking it was entirely fine. His thoughts were his own, even if his speech was policed. Not that Destiny gave a darn. Probably. She only cared about what really mattered. Which didn't include what he thought or said, but what he *did*.

Destiny put a finger to her lips for silence, then let her mace's light die out. This left the meager bit of indirect sunlight from beyond the wall as the only source of illumination. Which was unfortunate, given that it was about fifty feet away now. He could barely make out Destiny's figure, though she was right next to him. Chaos kept his mouth shut, even though it was unlikely anyone would be able to hear them over the sound of water rushing out of the portcullis. Not to mention the low howling of the cool wind the water brought with it.

Chaos waited…and then Destiny grabbed his free hand, tugging on it gently, then moving forward.

He followed behind her as she made her way out of the tunnel, and immediately felt cold raindrops pelting him. The scent of dilute blood came with it, and he did he best not to gag. Ahead, he saw a large open area. Lightning flashed overhead, allowing him a split-second to make out a lake that spread out as far as the eye could see, with a hint of buildings rising up from the water beyond. Some of them merely peaked roofs, which didn't make sense, because the water was barely more than a foot and a half deep. Beyond that, he couldn't see much at all, on account of it being so dark.

Destiny leaned in, bringing her lips to his ear.

"Follow behind me," she whispered. "You veer off, you die."

Chaos swallowed, then nodded, feeling a chill run down his spine. She turned left, hugging the tall stone wall there, which was clearly the inner surface of the wall surrounding Old Langsroth, and he followed right behind her. He had the sudden, powerful realization that he really, *really* didn't want to be here. And as such, that he wanted to get this over with as quickly as possible.

Another few flashes of lightning lit up the city, revealing glimpses of what lay beyond the wall and the partially-submerged buildings ahead: a vast city ringed by the water, rising up from it in a great circle a good hundred feet away. The buildings closest to them were one story tall, but beyond those they were two stories tall for a few blocks, then three, then higher and higher the closer to the center of Old Langsroth they got. And each level of the buildings was like another city in and of itself, the buildings connected by sky-bridges that served as streets for each level. It was a city unlike any he'd seen, with each level's streets interweaving intricately with the levels above and below it. The sky-bridges were supported by elegant stone columns, with streets often running between them in the levels below. Streets that were, in turn, supported by columns with streets running between them below that, and so on, in a vast, interconnected network.

"Wow," he breathed. Earning him an elbow in the side, and a vicious glare from Destiny.

His mouth snapped shut, and he followed behind her as she continued to follow the wall. Not in a straight line, but weaving this way and that, in a slow, careful manner. He did exactly what she did, remembering her warning. At length she turned right, wading through the thigh-deep water toward the center of the huge city. There were more flashes of lightning, and Chaos used them to get a brief look around. There were, to his surprise and relief, no zombies in sight. Which was odd, because he'd expected the place to be crawling with them.

Chaos hesitated, then tapped Destiny on the back of her shoulder. She paused, turning around to glance at him. He leaned in a bit awkwardly to speak in her ear.

"Where's all the zombies?" he whispered.

"Resting underwater," she whispered back. "We're stepping around them."

Chaos blinked.

"We are?" he whisper-hissed. She just gave him a look. "How many are there?" he pressed.

"A city's worth," she answered. "Don't trip over one, and don't make noise."

Chaos swallowed with some difficulty, his butthole puckering a bit. He nodded silently, suddenly wishing he'd never asked. Knowledge was not always power, unlike what he'd learned back in Borrin. It was only power when one ignored human nature, which was to be fearful of just about everything, especially other humans. And especially *especially* undead humans living in a city flooded in a lake of frickin' blood.

Crap, he thought to himself, terror rising within him. And it was all he could do not to crap in his pants. It was only the thought of Destiny's disgust that gave him the sphincter-strength to stop said cowardly dribbling of poo...along with the thought that the zombies all around them might be able to smell it too.

There was another flash of lightning, followed a good ten seconds later by a low rumble of thunder. One that was certainly loud enough to wake the dead, but didn't.

Destiny continued their trek, weaving left and right, and Chaos followed her movements exactly, just as before, but with far more fear this time. He regretted having asked her about the zombies' location, and realized now why she hadn't told him until he'd asked. Knowledge was power, but ignorance was bliss, and thus ignorance promised a happier, if less effective, life.

At length Destiny stopped, turning around to whisper in his ear again.

"We're stepping onto a skybridge over the lower levels of the city," she told him.

"Lower levels?" he mouthed.

"The city goes up," she stated, gesturing forward as a flash of lightning lit the progressively taller buildings ahead. "And it goes down."

"How far?" he whispered.

"As far as it goes up," she answered.

Chaos blanched, peering down into the water. He couldn't make out anything beneath it, even when the lightning flashed. The light merely reflected off the bloody water's surface, leaving what lay below it a mystery. That the water went down hundreds of feet was terrifying, considering his armor made him a human anchor. The thought of him losing his footing and sinking to the bottom gave him a sinking feeling, appropriately enough. Still, as she turned away from him and strode forward, he followed behind dutifully, choosing to trust in Destiny rather than continue to resist.

It wasn't long before they neared the nearest of the buildings, a narrow one-story white stone building with a peaked black roof, about a third as big as Chaos's home. There were a few windows whose panes had long since shattered, and a closed stone door partially submerged in pinkish water. Destiny walked right up to the door, then turned to Chaos.

140

"I defeated a zombie in here the last time I came," she told him. "It'll have regenerated a bit by now, but it should still be weak enough for you to beat."

"Great," Chaos grumbled.

"Get ready," she warned. "When I open the door, rush in. Don't make too much noise, or you'll wake the dead."

"Um," he replied, eyeing the head of his shovel. "It's gonna make noise."

"I mean don't scream," she clarified. "Most of the zombies are underwater, so they won't hear much. Especially over the rain and thunder."

"Ah."

"Ready?" she asked.

"Not really."

"Too bad," she replied. And then grabbed the doorknob, pushing the door open.

Chaos cursed under his breath, charging into the doorway, his heart pounding in his chest. He plunged into the utter darkness beyond…and promptly tripped over something, falling headlong into the water.

His breath locked in his throat, ice-cold water soaking through his armor and arming doublet. He scrambled to his feet, Vita's Boundless strength the only thing allowing him to do so despite his armor's formidable weight. Destiny closed the door…and he was plunged into darker darkness than before. Only the intermittent flash of lightning came through the windows, barely illuminating the flooded room. He heard the sudden sound of water dripping from the rightmost corner of the room, and a flash of lightning revealed why.

A pale zombie was rising from the water, its bloated face turning to face him with bloodshot eyes.

Chaos cursed, stumbling backward from the horrid thing, and nearly fell backward into the water in the process. He went to raise his shovel…and then realized he wasn't carrying it. He must've dropped it when he'd fallen.

"Shit," he swore, squatting and plunging his hands into the water, searching the floor for his weapon. While keeping one eye on the zombie, or at least trying to. For without lightning, the room was pitch black. He could hear the thing wading through the water toward him, and cursed again, scrambling to find his shovel. But he couldn't find it.

He felt something grab his left shoulder, and he whirled around, just as lightning flashed through the windows…

…and saw the zombie's face inches from his, its mouth opening to reveal awful, broken teeth!

"F…" Chaos began. But his curse was cut short. The zombie lunged at him, sending him stumbling backward…and he slammed back-first into the wall.

Then it grabbed his face with one hand, yanking his head back and exposing his throat…and sank its rotten teeth into it. The zombie's broken teeth pierced Chaos's flesh, sinking into his windpipe.

Chaos *screamed*.

He shoved the thing backward as hard as he could, and to his surprise, it flew backward as if shot from a cannon, slamming into the opposite wall. A fact he only knew because the front door swung open, revealing Destiny standing there in the doorway, her eyes glowing with a golden light.

"Uh…!" Chaos blurted out, freezing in place.

"I told you not to scream!" Destiny hissed…even as zombies rose from the inky-black surface of the water, dozens of them all around her.

"Uh…!" he repeated, pointing at them in a panicky sort of way. She just rolled her eyes, then closed them, lowering her head in prayer. A dome of golden light appeared all around her, then shattered into billions of tiny sparkles…

…and the zombies fell back below the surface of the water like so many limp noodles, vanishing from sight.

Destiny opened her eyes, glaring at Chaos, who grimaced, feeling like a complete idiot. And as his father had often told him, he should trust his feelings, because feelings were never wrong.

"Sorry," he whispered.

"Get your shovel," she grumbled. He did so, rummaging under the water until he felt his fingers strike something hard. He retrieved his weapon, blushing furiously…while rubbing at his injured neck. She strode up to him. "Let me see."

He tipped his head back, and she paused, waiting for a flash of lightning to get a good look at it.

"Barely punctured the skin," she told him, turning around and walking out of the building. He followed behind her, and she turned to face him again, her hands on her hips. "Never taken a hit before, have you," she guessed.

142

"Um…not really," he confessed.

"It would've been better if I'd trained you to *before* coming here," she stated. Not in a self-incriminating sort of way, beating herself up for her mistake. Rather, she said it as if it were something to do next time, a lesson learned…and nothing more.

"Yeah," he agreed. Partially because it was true, and mostly because it shifted the blame from him.

"Let's go," she told him.

"Where?"

"Back to where we made camp," she answered. "You're not ready for this yet."

Chaos didn't reply, but was all too happy to comply. He followed her as she went the way they'd come, making her way toward the tall black stone wall far ahead. They began the journey across the long skybridge over the hidden depths of the city, crimson rain pelting them as they went.

Then Destiny stopped, freezing in place.

"What?" Chaos asked.

"Back!" she ordered. And then shoved him in said direction before he could comply. He stumbled backward…just as a huge *thing* burst out of the water to their right. It was a massive, pale creature that looked like a dozen or so zombies glommed together into a single body…and had veins and eyes that glowed with an unholy red light.

The thing arced over their heads, extending an arm down toward Destiny…one with far too many joints, as if three arms had been glued together, wrist to shoulder. It grabbed Destiny's long golden hair, even as she lifted her mace to attack…

…and then it finished its arc over the submerged skybridge, plunging below the surface of the water, taking Destiny with it.

Chapter 25

By the time Pravus and Templeton made it to the entrance to Tabula at the top of its grand mesa, Pravus was feeling mighty fine. For there was little in life that was as grand as exploring a faraway land, and entering into Tabula was, at least to him, an adventure in and of itself.

"A charming city, don't you think?" Pravus stated, eyeing his cousin riding at his side.

"Indeed, my...cousin," he replied, nearly adding Pravus's honorific instead. They'd both agreed to travel incognito, to avoid unnecessary attention and delays. And also to enjoy feeling like common men for the first time in their lives. To experience what everyday commoners experienced, to walk a mile in their proverbial shoes! Why, it was every bit as exciting as facing an army of evildoers or a dastardly wizard.

They rode their respective horses to the arched entranceway to the city, what appeared to be the sole entrance and exit through a red stone wall surrounding Tabula. A few guards were doing their duty, in that they were verbing their role's noun.

"Afternoon," one greeted in a mildly aggressive way. Whilst lazily putting his hand on the hilt of his sheathed sword. "Haven't seen you two around before," the guard noted. "What brings you to Tabula?"

"A fine meal," Templeton declared with a warm smile.

"And some fine steel," Pravus added, doing his best not to gaze down at the guards with haughty, kingly disdain. Instead, he adopted the most neutral gaze he could, which was surprisingly difficult for him.

"Steel?" the guard asked, fingering his hilt. Whilst eyeing Pravus's physique, Pravus noted. Not in the sort of way that promised further fingering, but with a mix of admiration and jealousy. And a touch of fear, naturally. For as a guard, the guard would have to guard against him, if Pravus chose to act up.

"We are adventurers," Pravus explained. "Headed to Old Langsroth to meet danger head-on!"

The guard gave him a doubting look.

"Old Langsroth?" he replied. "Why?"

"To meet danger head-on," Pravus repeated, peeved that he'd been forced to do so. Still, in the spirit of being incognito, he stopped himself from giving the man a monarchal glare, instead choosing a neutral stare.

"We would appreciate it very much if you could direct us to the nearest eatery and weapons shop," Templeton stated with customary civility.

"You'll have to register at the Visitor's Center first," the guard replied gruffly. "And no funny business while you're in town," he warned.

"Adventuring is our business, not comedy," Pravus replied evenly.

"Bring them there," the guard told one of his fellow guards, who nodded, then stepped through the entranceway into the city, gesturing for Pravus and Templeton to follow. Which they did, passing under the archway and into Tabula itself. What lay beyond was a bustling city, with gobs of citizens swarming down narrow streets that wove between quaint red buildings several stories tall. It was all quite utterly unlike Cumulus – or any other city in Pravus's kingdom – and thus a delight for the senses.

"What novelty, eh cousin?" Pravus declared zestily.

"I daresay we've waited too long to seek it," Templeton admitted. Not in the regretful sort of way most would, but rather with the cheer of someone who'd reunited with an old friend after a long time apart. For it was ever Templeton's nature to focus on what was gained rather than what was lost, and as such, he never lost sight of what he had.

"Why, I could spend hours merely exploring this place," Pravus mused. Templeton gave him an impish smile.

"I say let's do just that," he replied.

"But the mission," Pravus protested.

"This is not a mission but an adventure," Templeton reminded him gently. "And the purpose of an adventure is the adventure itself."

"Wiser words have rarely been spoken!" Pravus declared.

145

"You taught me them yourself, at the gym," Templeton replied. "Not with words, but with each rep and set."

Pravus beamed at his cousin, and then realized that there was a rather large crowd of people on either side of them, who'd stopped to stare at them. And then exchange glances with each other. And then resume staring. It occurred to him then that the good people - and not-so-good people – of Tabula had likely never seen men of such massive muscular development, and were understandably rendered utterly awestruck by the sight. He puffed out his chest, not in the spirit of bragging, but to give them a show. One that would stick in their minds, and inspire a few to develop themselves too.

"I suppose you're right," Pravus stated. "Come Templeton!" he prompted valiantly, prompting his steed to move forward at greater speed. "Let us seek out a good meal…and then make haste to the armory!"

* * *

It didn't take long for Pravus and Templeton to find a restaurant in Tabula, one that served the city's signature cuisine. For Pravus knew very well that, when in a foreign country, it was always best to seek out a restaurant serving local food that locals tended to frequent. Such that, instead of getting a fake experience catering to outsiders, one experienced the truest form of a country's cuisine. His late mother had given him this advice when he'd been but eight years old, and he'd never forgotten it, though until now, he hadn't had the occasion to follow it.

After this, Pravus and Templeton gave their server an extremely large tip, as Pravus was well known for. Then they were off to the armory, which they found after a considerable – albeit leisurely and thoroughly enjoyable – amount of exploring. The Great Flat Blade, the shop was called. And it *was* great. A massive emporium of swords, halberds, non-magical staves, whips, daggers, axes, clubs, and more. And bows and arrows and crossbows and such. And on the other side of the store, a simply spectacular array of armor sets.

It was this that stole Pravus's attention, for while a greatsword was his weapon of choice, he'd never had to consider wearing armor before, what with his nigh-invincible monarchal uniform always protecting him. The sheer variety of types and styles of armor available were absolutely astounding…and he found himself hypnotized by the sight of them.

"So many choices!" he breathed. Templeton smiled.

"Ah, the sweet paralysis of choice," he mused. Pravus smiled back.

"Just so," he agreed. "Why, I could spend hours pouring over these."

"Then pour to your heart's content," Templeton replied. "And do not stop until you are satisfied."

"I'd hate to bore you while I peruse, dearest cousin."

"I shall enjoy perusing myself," Templeton replied. "And if perusing loses my interest, witnessing your enjoyment will more than suffice!"

Pravus beamed at his cousin, feeling a swell of emotion…accompanied by the sudden urge to kiss the man, if at least on the cheek. He stifled this urge only with the greatest of effort, turning to the displays of armor instead. He spotted one of the Great Flat Blade's staff members eyeballing them in a standoffish sort of way; upon making eye contact, the man cleared his throat noisily, reluctantly stepping up to them.

"May I be of assistance good sirs?" he inquired, in a tone rather reminiscent of Desmond's. In that it sounded as if his will to live had long since died. A common ailment of those cursed to deal with the general public on a regular basis, Pravus had come to notice. For the general public was generally awful.

"Indeed my good man," Pravus replied. "I require armor of the highest quality, at once."

The man looked Pravus up and down.

"I'll need to take measurements."

"Nonsense," Pravus replied. "I know them by heart." With that, he rattled off measurements of every body part, save for the one he enjoyed the most, each to the nearest half-inch. The man looked quite taken aback.

"Such a narrow waist and large chest and shoulders will require numerous modifications," he warned. "I'm afraid it'll take some time."

"Time I don't have, but money I do," Pravus replied. "I offer triple the price of everything I buy, if you can have them modified by tomorrow."

The man blinked rapidly.

"Triple?"

"Quadruple then," Pravus decided.

"Have...you the coin?" the staff member asked, looking terribly sorry to have done so. "Terribly sorry sir," he added, "...but I'll need payment up front."

"Naturally," Pravus stated. And then showed the man the voluminous contents of his overflowing coin purse. The man's eyes widened.

"What armor catches your eye?" he inquired.

"Something devilishly heroic," Pravus replied. "And *weighty*." The man broke out into a smile.

"Follow me," he replied.

Chapter 26

Chaos stood on the submerged skybridge in his cold, wet armor, staring at the huge glowing red circle in the water to his left. One that faded rapidly as the…whatever the hell that huge zombie had been…plummeted far below the surface.

Then the light winked out altogether, leaving him alone in the darkness.

He stood there, staring off into the darkness, his heart *thumping* in his chest. He waited for something to happen. For Destiny to rise up from the water in a ray of golden light, and then lead him back out of Old Langsroth. But something *didn't* happen. Which left him in the unfortunate position of being in the middle of a skybridge he couldn't see over vast depths, wearing a suit of armor that would punish any misstep by pulling him to the bottom of the blood-tinged water, ending in certain death.

And even if he *did* manage to cross the skybridge, he'd soon wade into an army of undead lying in wait below the surface…and one wrong move and he'd wake them up, and be devoured extremely painfully. Also ending in certain death.

So Chaos did the only thing he could think to do in this situation. Which was to pee involuntarily.

Shit, he thought, in lieu of releasing a little poo too. *Fuck*, he added, for it was the very worst word he knew.

He stood there, warmth spreading across his groin, the sharp tangy smell of piss in the air. Rain pattered down on him, lightning flashing from the Fallen Sky far above. He turned his stare to the water where the horrible zombie-creature had vanished beneath, its surface still a-churning. It occurred to him then that the thing might come back for *him*. And thus that standing here doing nothing was a decision to wait for it to do just that.

His stomach twisted itself into knots, and he hesitated, glancing back the way he'd come, then forward again.

Okay, he told himself, trying to focus. *What would Destiny do?*

She would tell him to stop being so damn helpless and do something. But doing the *right* something was the key. And there was no way he'd know which decision was right until it confronted reality…and to fail this time would surely be deadly.

Think!

The way forward would be almost impossible to navigate, what with the floor being littered with countless submerged undead lying in wait. So the only options were to stay here or go back…and the only benefit to staying here was that Destiny would know where he was. Assuming she was still alive, which was unlikely, considering she hadn't emerged from the dark depths of the water. The thought that she might actually be dead should have been terribly depressing, but his fear would allow no other emotion in.

The drawback of staying here was that the horrible creature might return. So that left going back to where he'd been, in that little building with the zombie who'd bitten him. If he dealt with it, he could throw it out of the building and close the door. Which would theoretically keep the rest of the zombies out.

"Right," he decided under his breath. It was the only good-ish option left. So he took it, carefully turning around and wading back toward the building. He took each step carefully, knowing that it was possible that he was veering off to one side or another, and that a misstep would send him plummeting off the edge of the skybridge. His slow-going prevented this fate, and he made it all the way to the closed door of the small building he'd been in before. He reached for the knob…then paused, remembering the zombie inside. The memory made him touch his still-smarting throat, and to his surprise, he found it wet with blood. He wiped it away…and felt more blood trickling down his neck, slowly but surely. He pressed his fingers against it to stem the flow, but when he let go, it kept bleeding.

Focus, he told himself. A little cut wasn't his biggest problem, getting to safety was. Out here, who knew what other zombies might be lying in wait under the water? In the building, he would be relatively safe.

Chaos steeled his nerves, gripping his shovel tightly in one hand, then reaching for the doorknob with another. He took a deep breath in, then shoved it open, stepping inside…

...and saw the zombie lunging for him with its awful teeth bared!

Chaos swung his shovel instinctively, smacking the thing's temple with a loud *clang*. It flew to the side, slamming into the wall and ricocheting off, then falling to a heap on the floor, vanishing below the water.

Chaos lifted his shovel above his head, sending it down in a vicious chop where the zombie had fallen. It struck something soft-ish, and he lifted it up, doing it again and again.

Then he stumbled backward, his lungs burning with the effort.

"Asshole," he swore, spitting on it. Or rather, the water covering it.

Then he realized that the door was still open. He needed to get the zombie out and then close it. Of course, the thought that the zombie would slowly regenerate was disturbing; if he threw it off the edge of the skybridge, on the other hand, it wouldn't be able to come back for him. Probably.

He hesitated, then reached down into the water, feeling his fingers touch something soft. He pulled on it, and it stretched quite a bit...and then he felt it tear off. He stumbled backward, catching himself...and saw what he'd torn off of the zombie. He'd thought it was a finger, but alas, this proved a fallacy.

"Gah!" he blurted out, chucking it out of one of the windows. He blushed then, wiping his hand on armor. Though it hadn't been the first dick he'd pulled on – he'd discovered the joys of doing so rather recently, to his delight and secret, horrible shame – having pulled on two was one more than he'd ever wanted to pull on in his lifetime.

Chaos collected himself, then reached down again, in a decidedly different place than he had before. His hand wrapped around something he could confidently say was a wrist, and he pulled on it, dragging the zombie behind him. Which was easy to do, on account of Vita's Boundless Strength.

So instead of dragging the zombie to the skybridge, he decided to chuck it instead.

He flung it as hard as he could, sending the thing flying to the left of the skybridge. It struck the water with a splash, then sank beneath the surface, never to be seen again. Hopefully.

That done, he turned back to the building, ready to go inside...and realized that he was very much not alone.

For there, rising up from the surface of the water all around him, were zombies. Male zombies, female zombies, even child-zombies. Dozens of them.

All staring at *him*.

"Fuck," Chaos swore.

Chapter 27

Having defied Imperius Fanning, Chauncy found himself flying through the air, far above the two-hundred-foot wall below. One that looked remarkably identical to the one separating the Republic of Borrin from the kingdom of Pravus, complete with a double-doored Gate. In lieu of opening said doors, he simply flew over them, continuing onward. Beyond, he saw a great big hill, one cleaved in two by a narrow path. Beyond this, he spotted a city. One situated upon a great, flat hill. A mesa, if he remembered correctly from his schooling.

He continued toward said city, thrusting his Staff of Wind repeatedly, though his arms were getting quite tired from the act. Until at last he'd situated himself above said city, whereupon he relaxed for a bit. This sent him accelerating downward at an alarming rate, the wind screaming in his ears. He waited until he was a mere hundred yards above the city before resuming his a-thrustin', slowing his descent rapidly. He landed with nary a *thump*, touching down gently in the middle of a bustling city street. Much to the surprise of everyone around him.

Including the city guard, unfortunately.

"Hey!" one of said guards barked, unsheathing a very sharp-looking sword and brandishing it threateningly. A few more followed suit, rapidly forming a ring around Chauncy. "Don't move!"

"Oh," Chauncy replied, taken aback. He hadn't considered that anyone would have an issue with a random wizard landing in a foreign land. But as it turned out, their issue with him was considerable.

"On your knees, wizard!" one of the guards ordered. "Drop the staff!"

"Um," Chauncy replied. And promptly stood there, because as you're well aware of by now, dear reader, Chauncy's first instinct in

153

the face of sudden danger was to do nothing. And what he lacked in bravery, he made up for in consistency.

"I said drop it, or else!" the guard warned, taking a step closer. The ring around Chauncy shrank as the guards drew near, and more guards joined their ranks, having clearly been alerted by the commotion.

"I don't want to hurt anyone," Chauncy began.

And then something slammed into his left calf from behind, and his leg buckled, sending him falling onto his back on the ground.

Pain shot through his calf, and he screamed, clutching at his leg. To his horror, the wooden shaft of a crossbow bolt was sticking out of it. The sight of which made him scream again.

Guards swarmed around him, one of them grabbing his Staff of Wind, which he'd dropped. Another rolled him onto his belly on the street, yanking his arms behind him and tying his wrists. A third guard decided to plant a boot on Chauncy's lower back, pinning him to the street.

"Ow!" Chauncy cried out. "Stop!"

"Should've dropped the staff, asshole," one of the guards shot back.

* * *

Within an hour of arriving in Tabula, Chauncy found himself in a small, un-comfy cell within the city prison, his wrists and ankles bound with uncomfortable rope. Rope that bit into his flesh, and what's more, itched quite a bit. There was no window in the cell, only a bucket for his waste. Which of course, he didn't need, considering that he had Tip. The demonic mod for his rod lived off his waste, consuming it before it ever had the chance to exit his body. Which was convenient, because Chauncy's cell had other cells on either side, with prison bars separating them instead of walls. Pooping in front of an audience was something Chauncy simply couldn't do, for performance anxiety practically guaranteed he'd choose death by fecal impaction over the relief of relieving himself.

"Lawyer," a voice called out. And sure enough, Chauncy spotted a guard escorting a short, balding, frumpy-looking man down the hall toward his cell. The man stopped in front of said cell, eyeing Chauncy.

154

"I'm Herby," he announced. "Your appointed lawyer."

"Great," Chauncy replied, feeling relieved. "This was all a big misunderstanding!"

"Trial is in two days," Herby stated. Chauncy blinked.

"What?"

"Two days," Herby repeated. "Your trial."

"Two days?" Chauncy blurted out. "But I didn't do anything!"

"Section 12-A of the Tabula penal code states that any person attempting entry into the city via circumvention of standard entry procedure will be fined no less than two hundred gold, and a minimum of sixty days in prison."

"What!?" Chauncy shot back. "You can't..."

"Section 35 of the penal code states that any wizard utilizing magic without prior authorization will be subject to a fine of no less than one thousand gold, and a minimum of six months in prison," Herby continued, rudely interrupting him. Chauncy's eyes widened.

"No!" he protested.

"Yes," Herby replied.

"No!" Chauncy repeated, stomping his foot.

"Yes," Herby repeated.

"I didn't do anything wrong!" Chauncy insisted.

"Did you fly over Tabula and land in the middle of the city?" Herby asked. Chauncy paused.

"Yes," he admitted.

"Does flying require magic?" Herby continued. Chauncy paused.

"Yes, but..."

"Then you used magic illegally to land illegally in Tabula," Herby concluded. "Illegally."

"I didn't know," Chauncy protested. "I was just trying to..."

"Lack of knowledge of a law does not make breaking that law any less illegal," Herby interjected. "By section 3Z of the..."

"It was an honest mistake!"

"Okay," Herby replied. Unhelpfully. "I'll see you the morning before your trial." And with that, he turned to leave.

"Wait!" Chauncy protested. Herby paused, then sighed, turning to face him again. "You're my lawyer, right? Can't you do something?"

"I'm a court-appointed lawyer," Herby answered.

"Right," Chauncy replied. "So can you help me?"

Herby looked at him as if he was stupid. Which he was reasonably sure that he wasn't. Or at least that his question wasn't.

"I recommend you cut a plea deal," the man...well, recommended. "Admit to all charges, and the judge might go lenient on you."

"I mean, can't we win the case?" Chauncy clarified. Herby rolled his eyes.

"I don't have time for this," he grumbled, turning away.

"But...you're my lawyer!"

"I'm a public defender," Herby countered. "I'm a lot of people's lawyer."

"But..."

And then Herby promptly – and rudely – left.

Chauncy watched the man go, powerless to stop him. For with his staff taken and his hands tied behind his back literally, his hands were tied figuratively as well. There was nothing he could do. He was at the mercy of the court.

And while he was stuck here – for months, or even years – Chaos's life was in danger, and there wasn't a damn thing Chauncy could do about it.

Chapter 28

Impossible!

It was the only word Destiny had time to think as the Zhimera burst out of the water to her right, a pale mass of zombie body-parts fused to each other as one huge organism. A bald head with eyes glowing bright red with the Fallen Blood coursing through the thing's veins. It had another head fused to its chest, and four arms with shoulders, upper arms, forearms, then shoulders, arms, and forearms again, before terminating in hands that had fingers with six knuckles each.

An undead from Central Langsroth, closer to the center of the Fallen Sky's storm. Where the blood was purer. Less dilute. And the undead were far more powerful.

The Zhimera arced over the skybridge and over Destiny and Chaos's heads, blood-tinged water raining down on Destiny's face. She shoved Chaos backward, out of the Zhimera's grasp...and it grabbed her left arm instead.

Then she felt it yank her to the left, pulling her off the skybridge. She plunged into the water, enveloped by ice-cold blackness.

Destiny's throat locked up, her body reflexively protecting itself against inhaling water...and she felt herself sinking rapidly, the Zhimera dragging her all the way toward the bottom of the city hundreds of feet below. The pressure in her ears spiked, sharp pain lancing through them as her eardrums ruptured. She could see nothing. Hear nothing. All was cold wetness...and falling.

Terror seized her. For in that moment, she knew that *this* was what it felt like to die.

Pray.

The thought tore through her fear, and she closed her eyes, focusing inward...and outward. Beyond the mere circumstances of her particular life, beyond this mortal experience. Within and without, she felt Vita's presence…and it spread over her, comforting her like a warm, heavy blanket.

When she was one with Vita, fear could have no hold on her heart. With Vita, there was only life…and love. Even death was merely a means to more life, the end of an experience, but the beginning of another. A mourning and a celebration both, something precious lost but also gained.

She gave a silent prayer, asking for Vita's blessing. A gift of Vita's Undead Repulsion, a field that would send nearby undead fleeing, struck with terror of humans that humans normally had for them.

Destiny opened her eyes, seeing herself bathed in golden light…and felt the Zhimera's grip on her arm slip away.

She blew bubbles, watching for the direction they rose. Then she swam in that direction, the golden light fading gradually away. With her heavy mace threatening to pull her back down into the depths, swimming upward proved terribly challenging. Her lungs began to burn, her body hungry for air, but she ignored the discomfort, knowing that only one thing mattered now:

Up.

Destiny focused on that singular direction, letting everything else fade away. There *was* nothing else other than up…and she went there, even as her head began to swim, the urge to open her mouth and take a breath in growing rapidly. Until it threatened to become bigger than her *up*. Until taking a breath in became more important than living, the *now* more important than the future.

Up!

She clawed through the water desperately, her lungs on fire now, the urge to breathe overwhelming. Then she lost herself to it, opening her mouth to take a breath in.

* * *

Chaos stood outside of the small stone building he'd just thrown his zombie throat-biter out of, watching in horror as dozens of zombies rose from the water all around him. And all of them facing him, their dull, baleful gazes locked on his. Facing this horde, Chaos couldn't help but think that things couldn't possibly get any worse.

Then he felt a *shift*, and his armor suddenly felt much, much heavier.

It was, he realized with a pang of terror, the end of Vita's Boundless Strength. A strength he'd just reached the boundary of, unfortunately enough.

"Crap," he blurted out, taking a step back. The zombie horde started wading toward him, reaching for him with their pale arms in zombie fashion. While making sounds that weren't quite graarrghs, but close enough. Chaos cursed again, backing through the doorway into the small building. And then pushed on the door to close it.

It didn't budge.

Chaos pushed harder, and the door barely budged, water sloshing with the effort. He realized then that the door was partially submerged, and was terribly difficult to move as a result. Something he hadn't noticed when imbued with Vita's Boundless Strength, but was now all too apparent. Which was unfortunate, because the zombies were slowly approaching, the nearest one only a few yards away…and they were clustered so close together that there was no way he would be able to push through them, especially with his heavy-ass armor on.

But if he couldn't close the door, then he'd be trapped inside…and the zombies would have him for dinner.

"Come *on!*" he complained, shoving harder. The door moved, but barely, only half-shut now. "Rrrghh!" he grunted, backing up, then ramming into the door, to little effect. He kept pushing, closing it inch-by-inch, even as the zombie horde inched closer.

He'd nearly closed it when a zombie-hand snaked through the narrow gap…and then another, and another.

Crap!

There was a *thump* as zombie-bodies struck the door, and it began to swing inward, their sheer weight opening it back up. Chaos cursed, pushing back on the door as hard as he could, but to his horror, the door inched open. Ever-so-slowly, but surely…and if it kept opening, he knew he would surely die.

But try as he might, his might was no match for the combined weight of the zombies on the other side of the door. The door inched open a bit further…and then the zombies started pouring in.

Chaos scrambled away from the door, watching in horror as the zombie horde entered the building. In a slow-motion charge, which only made it worse. In the face of his quite certain impending death, he did the only thing he could think of doing.

He *screamed*.

And then shrieked. And then stumbled backward until his back struck the rear wall of the room. After which he shrieked again and screamed and said "no no no" and such. All while sobbing hysterically. And while this was certainly a common reaction to one's upcoming grisly death via zombie horde, 'common' was not at all heroic.

Thus sealing his exceedingly common fate as a non-hero, Chaos watched in terror as the agents of his death drew near.

Then he realized that the zombies were all clustering near the rightmost wall of the room, where he happened to be. Which left a sizable gap to his left for him to dodge around them and make it to the doorway…which the last zombie just-so-happened to be stepping through. It was remarkably stupid on the zombies' part, and thus totally on-brand.

So, being smarter than a zombie, Chaos saw his chance and took it, removing and chucking his helmet and chest armor at the zombies nearest him, then juking around the zombies and rushing at the one who happened to be blocking the doorway. He shoved it backward as hard as he could, then rushed through the doorway past it, continuing onward toward the great wall of Old Langsroth. Zombies shuffled toward him on either side, but they were far too slow to catch him…and those who got too close, he simply shoved away.

"Ha!" he exclaimed, feeling rather satisfied with himself. And then he ran right off the edge of the stone floor, plunging into the water. Which was unfortunate, because he was still wearing his heavy leather leggings and boots.

Terror gripped him as he plummeted through the water, going deeper and deeper into icy darkness. He clawed upward, but it was no use; he continued to sink at an alarming rate, the pressure in his ears growing until it was unbearable.

Help!

He cried out in a spew of bubbles, reaching down to try to pull his boots off. All while the burning in his chest intensified, the urge to take a breath growing stronger with every passing second. He managed to peel one boot off, but the second wouldn't come free.

In that moment, he knew he was going to perish.

Chaos cried out again, reaching up futilely for the surface. And in that moment, he said a kind prayer of his own. Not to a god, but to the universe. To not let this go to its inevitable conclusion, which was for him die...but instead, to give him a surprise.

But just as he did so, he spotted a golden light below. One that grew in size and brightness as it zoomed upward toward him. His vision blackened, his lungs screaming for air...

...and then the golden light enveloped him, and he felt himself shooting upward suddenly, right before oblivion claimed him.

Chapter 29

Chaos opened his eyes to bear witness to golden light.

He squinted, shielding his eyes with one hand, then blinked, his eyes adjusting. He realized that he was sitting with his back propped against a cool stone wall, his legs and waist immersed in icy water. The golden light faded, but its source remained.

A golden-haired girl clad in a golden shirt and pants, a mace and shield in her hands.

"Destiny?" he breathed, staring at her in disbelief. After all, she was supposed to be dead.

"I leave you alone for three minutes," Destiny replied, shaking her head. But she didn't seem all that upset. "You're missing half of your armor," she noted. He got to his feet rather shakily, finding that she was right. His helmet and chestpiece were gone, as was one boot. And his shovel, to...boot.

"Oh," he mumbled. "Sorry, I uh..."

She waited.

"I um, they were heavy, and the strength you gave me ran out, and I was surrounded by zombies, and..."

"My fault," she interjected. He blinked.

"It is?"

"You're weak," she replied. "I shouldn't give you equipment you'll constantly need Vita's blessings just to use."

Chaos considered denying this insult, then decided against it, mostly because it was accurate.

"We need to leave," she told him, striding rightward to follow the wall. He hesitated, then followed her, limping a bit with his one boot.

"Where are we going?" he asked. "How did you survive that...thing?"

"To the Temple of Vita," she answered. "That thing was a Zhimera," she added. "I survived it with Vita's blessing."

Chaos paused, considering which answer to his questions to question first.

"Zhimera?" he asked.

"A zombie chimera," she explained. Chaos stared at her blankly.

"Huh?"

"A chimera is a combination of creatures," she lectured. "A Zhimera is a combination of zombies. A single main zombie that tore off body parts from other zombies, and attached it to itself."

"So that's why it had all those extra joints and stuff," Chaos realized. Then he frowned. "How does it...attach stuff?" he asked. He could hardly imagine that zombies would have the brains to sew. And he would know, considering that he'd spent most of his life living with Zora. A fact which made him realize that he was, in fact, sort of an expert on zombies, for he'd lived with one for the last ten years.

"I don't know," Destiny replied. "But I imagine it has something to do with the undiluted power of the Fallen Blood."

"You mean the stuff that rains in the middle of the city," Chaos translated.

"Right," she confirmed. "The Fallen Blood has more power the purer it is. I can only assume that it has the power to combine zombies in Central Langsroth. But..."

"But what?" Chaos asked.

"Zhimeras never venture into the outskirts of the city," Destiny said. "They stay in Central Langsroth, where the blood is purer. They crave the Fallen Blood, and would never go this far out, where the blood is so diluted."

"Oh," he replied. "So...what was it doing all the way out here?"

"I don't know," she admitted. "But I should have been able to feel it coming sooner." She shook her head. "Something must have blocked me from feeling its presence until the last second."

"Like what?"

"Magic of some kind," she guessed. "Dark magic."

He frowned.

"You're saying that there's a wizard living here?" he asked.

"Maybe," she answered. "Either way, I'm going to find out."

They reached a familiar arched opening to a tunnel to their right, one that plunged through the wall a good fifty feet. The current here pulled them forward, and Chaos had to brace himself, taking mincing steps to avoid being pulled off his feet. They made it the fifty feet to the closed portcullis; the golden rays of the sun

163

peeking between the black bars of the portcullis made Chaos's heart soar; he was all-too-eager to leave this awful, dark, *stank* place behind.

They reached the portcullis, and Destiny paused for a bit of prayer. Then, glowing with golden light – which was surely Vita's Boundless Strength – she lifted the gate, gesturing for him to pass through. She went next, letting the portcullis drop with a *bam*.

And with that, their abbreviated, awful adventure to Old Langsroth was done.

Chapter 30

King Pravus rode his stallion alongside Templeton, their horses' hooves *splish-splashing* in the water of a great, shallow lake of sorts roughly a day's journey from the city of Tabula. It was really more of an oversized puddle than a lake, the water barely ankle-deep. But in its reflection, he could see the items he'd purchased from The Great Flat Blade: a truly epic a suit of purple-pink platemail armor, and a purple-pink greatsword of epic proportions, nearly as large as the magical golden greatsword he'd become accustomed to. He carried said sword in a scabbard on his back, which was a rather inconvenient place, it turned out. For a blade of its length was nearly impossible to unsheathe from one's back without a fair bit of torso contortion, and would have been much easier to carry on one's hip. But being a creature of habit, Pravus accepted this inconvenience for the sake of familiarity. And awesomeness, and epic-ness, and heroic-ness and such. The armor was also formidably heavy, far more so than any normal man might find comfortable. But in its impractical heft, Pravus gained a constant workout, in that every moment required exertion merely to carry it. The only armor he'd eschewed was a helmet, for he found them profoundly uncomfortable.

Thusly clad, Pravus and Templeton made their way across the Great Flat toward the great wall dividing Old Langsroth from the rest of the world…and toward Pravus's destiny.

"Nearly there, eh cousin?" Templeton declared, flashing Pravus a knowing smile. Pravus couldn't help but smile back in kind.

"Indeed, Templeton!" he replied. "Our destination is nigh!"

And then, to his surprise, he spotted something ahead: a gold-colored horse upon which two riders rode. Pravus frowned, slowing his steed's speed and watching as the other party drew nearer. It was, he discovered, a young teenage girl dressed in gold, with long hair of similar color…and a strikingly handsome dark-haired boy about the same age, wearing a an arming doublet, leather pants, and one leather boot.

"Hello!" Pravus boomed, his voice carrying easily after years of making monarchal speeches. The girl slowed her horse, and the two parties stopped a few yards from each other.

"Who're you?" the girl asked bluntly.

"I am…Markarian," he lied, using the epic pseudonym he'd concocted.

"And I am Viggo," Templeton greeted, doing the same.

"We are adventurers doing a bit of adventuring," Pravus explained.

"In Old Langsroth?" the girl asked.

"How did you know?" Templeton inquired. She gave him a look.

"The Great Flat leads nowhere else."

"Indeed we are," Pravus proclaimed, puffing out his chest. "I take it you're coming from there?"

"Yep," she replied. "If I were you, I'd turn around. A Zhimera ambushed us near the wall."

"A what?" Templeton inquired.

"Something you definitely don't want to meet," she answered.

"Perhaps this 'Zhimera' will say the same about us when we cross paths with it," Pravus stated. "In any case, we will forge ahead, for it is our mission to do so!"

"Indeed!" Templeton agreed, exuberantly.

"Your funeral," the girl replied with a shrug. And promptly led her horse forward, passing Pravus and Templeton by. Pravus watched them go, then turned to Templeton.

"Did you see that boy?" he asked. "Half his armor's missing."

"And he had no weapon," Templeton noted.

"No wonder they feared this 'Zhimera,'" Pravus mused. "Shall we, sweet cousin?"

"We shall!" Templeton replied.

And with that, they surged forward on their trusty steeds, making their *splish-spashing* way toward their final destination.

* * *

Chaos turned around in his saddle, eyeing the two men they'd just passed. A big man in purple-pink platemail with a purple-pink sword, and a smaller man wearing black leather armor.

"Wow," he stated, not knowing quite what else to say.

"Gay," Destiny replied.

166

Chaos paused, not sure if her statement was in the spirit of explanation or an expletive.

"He's gay," Destiny added. "The big guy."

"Really?" Chaos asked. He'd never met a gay person, at least that he was aware of.

"Definitely."

"How can you tell?" he pressed. She twisted around in her saddle, giving him a look.

"Really?" she asked.

"Because he wore that armor?" Chaos guessed.

"That's...part of it," she replied. "You really can't tell, can you?"

"I mean not really," he confessed.

"Huh."

They rode for a bit longer, and Chaos stirred.

"Was the other guy?" he asked. "You know..."

"Gay?" she guessed. "Nope."

"How can you tell?"

"I just can," she answered with a shrug. "Some people can, some can't."

"So...the big guy...likes...uh, wrestling other guys?"

"Mmhmm."

"Weird," Chaos murmured. For the prospect of "wrestling" another man was...well, weird to him. He'd never really considered it.

"Wrestling women would be weird to him," she countered. "We like what we like."

Chaos paused.

"What do you like?" he asked.

"Guys," she replied.

"Huh," Chaos stated.

"Why huh?"

"I just didn't expect you'd like...well, anything," he admitted.

"You're really that oblivious."

"Huh?" he asked, utterly confused.

"Nothing," she replied.

They continued riding, and Chaos frowned, stuck with the idea that he'd missed something. And what's more, something important. The idea nagged at him, until he couldn't take it anymore.

"Why am I oblivious?" he asked.

"Beats me," she replied. He paused.

"I mean *how* am I oblivious?" he clarified. She didn't answer for a long while, to the point that he thought she wouldn't. But eventually, she did.

"You don't get out much, do you?" she guessed.

"Not really," he admitted. "Most of the time I just stay at my parents' shop."

"You go to school?"

"Homeschooled," he replied.

"Any friends?"

"Um…I have a best friend," he stated. "His name is…"

"So you're sheltered," she interrupted. He paused.

"I mean I guess so."

"Meet many girls?" she asked. He frowned.

"No, not really," he answered. "Not my age, anyway."

"You like girls?" she pressed. He blinked, taken aback by the sudden change in questioning.

"Uh," was all he could say. While blushing furiously.

"That's a yes," she replied. A paused. "You're shy, aren't you."

"*No*," he retorted.

"Uh huh."

"I am *not*," he insisted, although it was a damn lie. For, having not engaged with the opposite sex very often, he was frankly terrified of it, especially if they happened to be terribly attractive. His mind's eye, however, had engaged with the opposite sex on a remarkable number of occasions, usually during his morning bath.

To Chaos's consternation, Destiny didn't reply. Which put him in the unenviable position of having to defend his non-shyness. Which he did not verbally, but in his own head, coming up with all sorts of arguments as to why she was wrong. While voicing precisely none of them, proving her right.

Gwendolyn continued the journey across the Great Flat to dry land beyond, making her way toward Tabula far, far in the distance. But as they drew nearer the city, Gwendolyn veered off toward a hill a few miles from the city. Eventually they reached the base of said hill, and with the benefit of Vita's Dribbling Rejuvenation, Gwendolyn made the trip up its slope without any need for rest, coming to the top of it by the time the sun was starting to set. And at the very top of the hill, Chaos spotted the ruins of what appeared to have been a great temple. Destiny guided Gwendolyn to said ruins, stopping in the middle of them.

The ruins were arranged in a rectangle, with crumbling stone columns supporting half of the stone roof that remained. At the far end of the rectangle stood a lone statue, one of a rather spectacularly shapely woman with her hands by her bare bosom, cradling a clump of dirt, upon which grew a small plant. Chaos tried not to stare at the statue, but found himself doing so anyway. Because boobies. And more importantly, *nipples*.

"This is the Temple of Vita," Destiny declared, dismounting Gwendolyn. She walked up to the statue, putting a hand on its thigh. "She grew up in a small cabin here, on this hill."

Chaos didn't reply, still transfixed by matters previously mentioned. At some point – a bit after he would've preferred – he realized Destiny was staring at him.

"Huh?" he asked, assuming a blank expression.

Destiny rolled her eyes.

"I was just…" he began, blushing furiously.

"I didn't roll my eyes because you were staring at Vita," Destiny stated. "I rolled them because you tried to hide it."

Chaos just stared at her, not knowing how to navigate this particular predicament. Destiny ignored his plight, turning back to the statue of Vita.

"Even in desolation, life flourishes," she stated. And Chaos couldn't disagree. For even here amongst the ruins of the temple, vines crawled up the stone columns, and moss grew over the cracks in the stone. Weeds did as well, and a few trees had planted themselves within the ruins, breaking through the stone floor to reach upward toward the sun. "There are no ruins in nature," Destiny declared.

Chaos nodded, realizing that she was right. Life flourished everywhere, even in deserts. Except…

"Except for Old Langsroth," he countered, recalling the cursed place. Destiny lowered her gaze.

"Most life can't grow there," she stated. "Not until the curse is lifted."

"Is that why Vita wants you to lift it?" Chaos asked.

"That's right," Destiny answered. "The dead should support the living, not the other way around."

"Huh?"

"We eat the flesh of plants and animals," she explained. "And when we die, we'll decompose. Life will grow from us. The dead support the living."

"Ah. Makes sense." He paused, trying his best not to sneak another glance at the statue. But as it turned out, his best was not good enough. "Um…so why are we here?" he asked.

"I need to connect with Vita," Destiny replied. She gazed at the statue. "This is where I feel closest to her."

"But…why connect with her?"

"I need her wisdom," Destiny explained. "Something's going on in Old Langsroth…something more than just the Fallen Sky. I need to figure it out…and I need to figure out your place in all of this."

"Oh."

"And I need to train you up," she continued. "I was wrong to bring you to Old Langsroth so soon. I should've prepared you better." She turned away from the statue to face him. "I was so eager to take on the Fallen Sky that I let it cloud my judgement. I could've gotten you killed."

Chaos grimaced.

"It's my fault," he countered. "I…"

"Cut the crap," she interjected. His mouth snapped shut with a *click*. "You're being considerate and I appreciate it. But I own my mistakes…and that's why I learn from them."

He paused, then inclined his head, not knowing what to say. He'd never had the experience of a girl taking responsibility for something they could've easily blamed on someone else. Then again, he hadn't had the experience of being with a girl, other than Fury and Mom. And Zora, who didn't really count.

"You're bleeding," she noted, eyeing his throat.

"Oh yeah," he replied. "It's not that bad."

"It is too," she countered. "Your soul is leaving with your blood, remember?"

"Oh," Chaos mumbled, putting a hand to his throat.

"Hold on, I'll heal it," she reassured him, closing her eyes to pray. A beam of golden light shone from the heavens, touching his throat…and the bleeding stopped. "I'm going to pray now," she told him. "Don't interrupt unless it's an emergency."

"What should I do?" he asked.

"Get some rest," she advised. And with that, she lowered herself into a cross-legged position at the feet of the statue of Vita, closing her eyes. Chaos watched her for a bit, then stole a furtive look at the statue. He committed its construction to memory, for the purposes of enhancing his bath-time relaxation, naturally.

170

Which was quite natural for a boy to do, though he didn't quite know that, and would never *ever* admit to it.

Then he reached into Gwendolyn's saddlebags, retrieving his sleeping bag, then taking off his chain armor. And with that, he laid down and went to sleep.

Chapter 31

King Pravus and Templeton rode their steeds across the oversized puddle that was the Great Flat, making their way toward an imposingly tall black wall far ahead. The black stone ruins of a town just outside said wall jutted out of the shallow water, obviously a town where the peasants had once lived. As they drew nearer, Pravus spotted an archway built into the wall, with a closed portcullis there.

"Ancient construction," Pravus noted. "No gatehouse to guard the main gate."

"But a generous talus," Templeton noted, referring to the sharply-upsloping stone reinforcement at the base of the wall. A fortification that ensured long term stability, and prevented enemy forces from undermining the wall.

"Generous indeed," Pravus agreed. "An excellent curtain wall, overall."

"Look at the machicolations," Templeton said, gesturing at the top of the wall. It jutted out a few feet, and there were gaps in the floor of this overhang where stones and such could be dropped onto enemy forces. "They're diamond-shaped."

"How odd," Pravus replied. "Not very practical."

"But aesthetically pleasing," Templeton noted.

"Indeed," Pravus had to agree. He could hardly blame the ancient kingdom's architects for choosing form over function. The most efficient method of doing something was not always the best way, after all. A man could forge nails every hour of his working life, and make more nails per hour than a blacksmith who crafted a variety of things. But such a job would suck the soul out of any man, transforming him into a means to an end. Akin to a zombie, such a man would be a lord's dream...but no man had a right to demand such a thing of their fellow man.

The function of a human being, after all, was to serve as a kind of symphony, not a single instrument sounding out the same note for eternity. Such would be a life barely worth living.

At length they passed through the ruins of the town, arriving at the portcullis Pravus had previously perceived. Pravus dismounted, his armored boots making a little splash. Templeton followed his lead, and they both strode up to the portcullis.

"Care for bit of the ol' deadlifting?" Templeton inquired, shooting Pravus a smile.

"By all means, give it a go," Pravus replied, gesturing for Templeton to do so. Templeton assumed the position, squatting to grab the bottom of the portcullis, his back in the neutral position so as to prevent injury. Then he pushed – with his legs first, for the first half of a deadlift was a leg press.

Templeton grimaced, lifting with all his might, and the portcullis rose upward slowly. But its weight proved too heavy for his cousin to heft, and Templeton lowered the portcullis, then stood up straight with some difficulty, flashing Pravus an apologetic smile.

"I fear I can't be a gentleman and open the door for my king," he lamented.

"A gentleman is defined not only by deeds, but by intent!" Pravus replied. "I'll give it a try."

With that, Pravus removed his gauntlets, handing them to Templeton. Then he stepped up to the portcullis, bending down and gripping its metal bars tight. In an over-under grip, to accommodate the considerable weight. Then he focused, preparing himself for the trial to come…and pressed upward with his legs.

The portcullis proved a proper challenge, but such was Pravus's power that he lifted it until he was standing up straight. Then he transitioned to a military press, pushing the portcullis all the way up over his head.

"Bravo cousin!" Templeton cried.

"Perhaps…we…should prop…it open?" Pravus gasped, enjoying the burning of his muscles.

"At once!" Templeton replied, rushing to grab some black stone blocks from the ruins around them. He stacked these under the portcullis on either side of the gate, then helped Pravus hold the portcullis up so that Pravus could step inside. Then they both lowered the portcullis behind them, until it rested on the stones they'd placed.

"Whew," Pravus said, wiping the sweat from his brow.

"A fine challenge, eh cousin?" Templeton quipped with a twinkle in his eyes.

"The finest I've had in days," Pravus proclaimed, putting his gauntlets back on.

"Shall we?" Templeton inquired, gesturing forward, down a tunnel through the wall some fifty feet long. Water flowed in a considerable current against them, pouring out of the city beyond.

"We shall," Pravus replied.

They headed down the tunnel, the current providing a welcome resistance to each step. Along with his heavy armor, it made for a mild full-body workout.

"Getting dark," Templeton noted. "Shall I illuminate the way?"

"It may behoove us to brave the darkness while we can yet see," Pravus replied. "A light will let the enemy spot us before we spot it."

"Just so," Templeton concurred.

They made their way through the tunnel, eventually reaching its end. It opened up into a flooded area of unseen proportions, such was the darkness that bathed the land. High above, Pravus saw a swirling vortex of clouds, which gained a deep crimson hue toward the center of said vortex. Rain fell from the sky in a gentle drizzle, occasional lightning illuminating the area. What said lightning revealed was a city immersed in water, rising up from it in a great circle thirty yards from where they stood. The buildings at the periphery were a mere one story tall, but the buildings went higher and higher the closer to the center of Old Langsroth they were. Elegant sky-bridges connected the buildings in the most curious way, seeming to function as streets for each level. Such that the city was really several cities stacked on top of each other, in a way. All supported by a truly impressive number of rather lovely, pale stone columns.

"Oh my," Templeton breathed.

"Magnificent!" Pravus exclaimed, albeit quietly.

"To think that our forebearers thousands of years ago could build something like this," Templeton mused, shaking his head in wonder. "What I wouldn't give to have a glimpse into their lives!"

"I concur," Pravus...well, concurred. "A shame that they continue in un-life, or so the story goes." For in addition to having learned about Old Langsroth from his studies back home, Pravus had been told a few tales from the people of Tabula during his short stay there. Tales of a city of undead, of cursed blood, and horrors beyond imagination. Tales which would have terrified most anyone, but had only served to fan the flames of heroism within Pravus and Templeton.

"Shall we go on?" Templeton inquired.

"Let us scout the periphery," Pravus prompted. "And get a lay of the land, so to speak."

"A wise approach indeed," Templeton agreed.

Pravus turned right, following the wall, and Templeton waded after him. The water was a bit higher than in the Great Flat, up to their mid-shins now. To Pravus's eye, it seemed to glow with the faintest reddish hue, so barely there that he suspected his eyes were playing tricks on him. But when he glanced toward the buildings in the distance, he saw that the reddish glow seemed brighter there. And furthermore, that the hue was precisely the same as the center of the stormy vortex high above.

Interesting, he thought…just as he tripped over, well, something. He stumbled, catching himself just before he fell.

"What's wrong?" Templeton asked.

And then a pale head rose from the surface of the water where Pravus had tripped, followed by a mildly decomposed body.

"Zombie!" Pravus cried, making the motion of pulling a sword from a scabbard on his back. A motion that would have summoned his magical golden greatsword, but in this case, did nothing. He was forced to grab the actual greatsword from the actual scabbard on his back, which was quite difficult, seeing as it wouldn't slide all the way out easily, on account of the bad angles caused by impractical back-scabbards.

So, as the zombie finished its menacing rise from the depths, Pravus found himself fighting his sword instead of it.

"Confound it!" he complained, backing up a step as the creature lurched toward him. His foot struck something underwater, and he fell backward into the water, chilly fluid getting in all of his armor's crevasses. He gasped at the sudden chill, rising with some difficulty on account of his armor's ridiculously inappropriate weight…and saw another zombie rising where he'd tripped. And then another nearby. And what's more, one more.

"My liege!" Templeton cried, thrusting his slender sword expertly into the first zombie multiple times. But the creature tolerated said penetration without a blink of an eye, shambling toward Pravus anyway. Pravus cursed, kicking the thing in the chest and sending it flying backward into the water.

He felt something tug on his scabbard from behind, and turned around, sending another zombie hurtling to the flooded ground. Only then did he manage to unsheathe his sword at last.

"Ha!" he bellowed with triumphant might, swinging it at the nearest zombie-neck. The attack took the zombie's head right off, and its parts fell, vanishing below the water. But more zombies rose from the depths, hissing and growling and graarrrghing and such.

"I fear our noises have awakened them," Templeton warned. Pravus swung his sword again, decapitating another zombie, then another.

"Let them rise," he declared zestily. "So that we might...ngghh...fell them again!" And with that manly grunt, he executed another attack, one that executed another zombie.

"My thrusts do not fell them," Templeton noted.

"Cut off their heads," Pravus advised. And so Templeton did, his slender blade darting around in a rapid dance of death, sending a half-dozen zombie heads and bodies tumbling back into the depths. The zombies stood no chance against them, slow and dumb as they were. But what they lacked in almost everything, they made up for in sheer numbers. For as the rather noisy battle continued, more zombies were awakened, dozens of them rising from the water all around them.

And then *hundreds*.

"Sire!" Templeton stated in warning. Pravus eyed the small army of undead, enjoying a slight burn in his shoulders. Holding his sword out before him activated the anterior deltoid muscles in the front of his shoulders quite nicely, each swing utilizing his pecs, upper back, lats, and even the oblique muscles of his abdomen, to power each torso twist. A marvelous workout, a veritable symphony of muscular contractions, all cooperating to cleave his enemies in twain. He eyed Templeton then, a merry twinkle in his eye.

"Fancy a bit of high-intensity training?" he inquired. Templeton paused, then smiled back.

"I'd like nothing more," he replied. Called "circuit training" and many other things, it was inevitably deemed a completely novel and miraculous development by each new gym-going generation. At least by those lifters who didn't deign to study the past...which was most of them.

176

Pravus watched as the approaching hordes formed a ring around them, closing in on them slowly.

He relaxed, preparing himself for the gauntlet of physical activity to come. For his high-intensity intervals with Templeton were the stuff of legend at the gym back in Cumulus, trials that tested even the strongest and bravest of men.

"Ready?" he asked his sweet cousin.

"Ready!" Templeton replied with gusto. Which was the only way to approach high-intensity workouts, if one hoped to get the most out of them. Pravus waited for the horde of zombies to draw near, then gripped his sword tightly.

"Begin!" he cried.

And with that, the two began a dance of death, swinging their swords to decapitate zombie head after zombie head. Never stopping, never slowing. They marched into the army of undead, performing rep after rep of sword swings and thrusts.

Under the onslaught of such ceaseless exertions, Pravus's arms and back began to burn, each swing taking considerably more focus to perform. Until the weight of his greatsword became too great, such that he was barely able to heft it.

"Legs!" he gasped, kicking a zombie in the chest. Templeton transitioned as well, beginning the lower body portion of the workout. They kicked and punted zombies, knocking them back into their brethren and sending them tumbling into the water. This continued until Pravus's legs felt nearly dead, such that he was unable to lift them high enough to kick.

"Arms!" he cried, going back to a-swinging. More zombies lost their heads, but Pravus tolerated far fewer reps this time.

"Legs!" he gasped, kicking and punting again. His whole body felt like it was on fire now, his heavy armor threatening to pull him to the ground. He cried out, kicking one more zombie away. "Arms!" he groaned, his breath coming in ragged gasps now.

"Rrrnngh!" Templeton moaned in a masculine tone, one that normally would have gotten a rise out of Pravus. But so exhausted was he that he could only focus on the task at hand. Which was the greatsword in his hand.

"Arrggh!" Pravus grunt-cried, decapitating one last zombie. And then he stumbled, slamming his shoulder into the stone wall.

"My liege!" Templeton cried, still swinging, on account of his light armor and featherweight sword.

"Unnghh!" Pravus cried back, his thighs spasming, such that he sank to his buttocks in the shallow water. A zombie woman lunged at him, and while it did so with terrible slowness, it was still faster than Pravus could currently move. Thus she leapt upon him, and it was all he could do to hold her back by the shoulders. She raked her claw-like fingers at his face, scratching it...and then was hurled to the side by sweet Templeton, who followed up with a decapitating strike.

"Are you...alright?" Templeton gasped, helping Pravus to his feet. Pravus's legs wobbled, and he nearly fell again.

And, all around them, even more zombies rose from the water, albeit from further away. Still, there were hundreds and hundreds of them now, their pale faces reflecting flashes of lightning from the stormy sky...and they were all shambling toward Pravus and Templeton.

"Regroup!" Pravus commanded. Which was a politically expedient way to say "retreat." Which was itself an expedient way to not say "run away like the coward you are." But on balance, running away was sometimes the only prudent choice, allowing one to recover, then fight another day. Heroically retreating was far different than cowardice, for cowardice implied giving in to fear. An emotion that, even surrounded as they were by dreaded undead, Pravus did not feel.

So it was that they beat a heroic retreat, Templeton staving off undead whilst helping Pravus back into the tunnel. They made it to the portcullis, a legion of undead trailing behind, and ducked under it. Then they both lifted said portcullis from safely outside of it, kicking the stones they'd stacked to hold it open. The portcullis fell closed with a bang, locking the zombies within.

And with that, Pravus and Templeton's first foray into Old Langsroth was complete.

Chapter 32

When Chaos awoke from his slumber, he found that it was morning. Destiny was nowhere to be found, and neither was Gwendolyn. He felt a twinge of fear, and scrambled out of his sleeping bag, exiting the temple ruins…and found Destiny and her mare a few dozen yards outside of it. Destiny was in the in the process of making breakfast, and Gwendolyn was munching on some grass.

"Morning," he greeted, rubbing the sleep out of his eyes.

"Morning," Destiny replied. "Sit," she prompted. "Eat."

"Not hungry yet," he countered a bit irritably, continuing to rub his eyes. He hadn't woken all the way up yet, and was hardly in the mood to eat.

"Think ahead," she retorted. "If you don't eat now, you'll be hungry soon…and by then, we'll be riding again."

Chaos stopped a-rubbin', giving her an irritated look. For as his parents had often said, he was a lil' bitch in the morning. Still, he couldn't very well argue with Destiny's logic, not without losing status with her. Family he could treat as badly as he wanted, because they *had* to put up with him. Destiny, on the other hand, did not.

So it was that Chaos found himself sitting down by the little fire she'd made, chewing on some chewy strips of meat.

"Surprised you eat meat," he grumbled between bites.

"Why?"

"Shouldn't you be a vegetarian or something?" he asked. "You worship the Goddess of Life."

"Life feeds on life," Destiny replied. "Besides, plants are alive too."

"Yeah, but not *really*," he countered. She just stared at him as if he was an idiot. "I mean, a potato isn't alive."

"Put it in the ground and it sprouts," she pointed out. "Alive."

"Well…an *onion* isn't," he stated.

"Put it in the ground and it sprouts," she repeated. "Alive."

"Ok…an apple then," he argued, crossing his arms over his chest.

"A plant uterus filled with baby apple trees," Destiny shot back. "Alive."

"The apple flesh isn't," he pointed out.

"Yes it is," she replied. "Otherwise it'd decompose rapidly…and it wouldn't be able to ripen once it was plucked."

Chaos paused, wracking his brain for a counter to her retort. But he found himself coming up short. And what's more, with a little food in his belly, he was already feeling better.

"Well plants don't have feelings, so…" he stated.

"Wrong again," she replied. He frowned.

"No way," he protested. She just raised an eyebrow at him. "Whatever," he mumbled. "So what did Vita tell you when you, uh, prayed last night?"

"That there's a powerful magic working within Old Langsroth," Destiny revealed. "Magic beyond that of the Fallen Sky."

"Like what…a wizard?"

"Vita isn't sure," Destiny admitted. "She senses a strange presence there, in the center of the city. A…force of death. Beyond that, she cannot say."

"But she's a god," Chaos pointed out.

"The Goddess of Life," Destiny corrected. "Not the Undead. She can sense the presence of undead, but not any specifics."

"So…the Zhimera was able to shield its presence from us because of this 'force of death' presence?"

"Right," she confirmed. "And whatever this presence is, it had to have convinced the Zhimera to travel away from its favorite power source…the Fallen Blood in the center of the city."

"So we need to figure out what this presence is," Chaos deduced, putting his hands on his hips. "Which means we need to make it all the way to the city center."

"No, *I* need to figure out what this presence is," Destiny corrected. "Which means *I* need to make it to the city center. You're not going."

Chaos blinked. It was of course exactly what he'd hoped to hear, because the idea of going back into that hellhole was more than he could bear. But he couldn't exactly *admit* that, because it would give her the impression that he was a bit of a coward. Which, while certainly accurate, would be embarrassing. Thus, against his better judgement, he decided to protest. Weakly, so as

180

not to change her mind, but enough to seem upset with her decision.

"But…" he protested. He waited for her to interject, which she did not. "But…it'll be dangerous to go alone," he reasoned.

"It'll be more dangerous if I have to protect two people instead of just myself," she argued.

"I…"

"Face it, you're not ready," Destiny interjected, to his relief. "Come on," she added, starting to pack up. "I'm dropping you off at Tabula. You can stay at my place until I come back."

* * *

So it was that Chaos found himself back in Tabula, riding Gwendolyn to a small apartment building at the northwestern edge of the city. It was a rather rough part of the city, Chaos noted, with rough-looking people eyeing them as they rode. He personally would never have gone near said neighborhood alone, for fear of being beaten, robbed, and potentially murdered. But with Destiny nearby, nobody dared to give them any shit.

It seemed like *everyone* in Tabula was a teensy-bit scared of the girl, though she was barely older than him. Everyone respected her, in stark contrast to how people – including the guard at the Gate in Borrin, and the innkeeper in the town of Erp – had treated Chaos. It was, Chaos knew, because she was a self-made girl, disciplined, tough, and powerful. While he was precisely the opposite, depressingly enough.

So, after Destiny dropped Chaos off – with a generous allowance of money to pay for food and such, considering that she had no idea how long she'd be gone – she left him in her 1st-story apartment, a remarkably clean and well-cared-for one-bedroom place. He sat on the edge of her bed, which had been tidily made. Something he'd never done, but was oddly pleasing to see.

He stared at the wooden floor, which was also remarkably clean. Everything Destiny had was well cared for and organized, though she owned only what she needed. Once again, she'd proven that her way of life was better than Chaos's.

I suck, he realized. And the thought rang perfectly true. In contrast to Borrin – where adults taught that confidence and self-esteem didn't need to be earned, but merely *believed* – Chaos's adventure had taught him the opposite. Confidence was earned through competence, and gaining competence required hard work and discipline.

Which meant that a *lack* of self-esteem was a sign of a lack of competence...an important signal of work that needed to be done. Not something to get terminally depressed over, but simple information. He wasn't ready because he hadn't put in the effort.

If I want to be who I want to be, I have to do things differently.

No more putting things off or complaining about doing boring work. No more chasing after surprises all day, which were really just little bursts of pleasure to make the boring-ness go away. No, true, lasting pleasure was not found in novelty, for anything new quickly became old. Lasting pleasure came from a sense of accomplishment, not in accomplishing one thing, but in knowing that you were the type of person who *could* accomplish things.

To feel powerful required *being* powerful. And Destiny had showed him beyond a doubt that nothing was more powerful than good habits. Which were boring, because they were the same every day, but would allow him to eventually do surprising and wonderful things.

He stood up from Destiny's bed, his jaw set firm and his fists clenched at his sides.

"I might not be a great wizard," he declared. "I may never have powerful magic. But I can still become a powerful person," he added.

And that meant starting right here, right now.

* * *

To become the person he wanted to be, Chaos realized that he needed to follow his Destiny. In that he needed to think and act like she did...which meant that, first and foremost, he needed to get prepared. She'd left him with the pack full of the provisions she'd gotten him, but his chain armor had been useless to him, heavy as it'd been.

With this in mind, he left the apartment, taking the rather large amount of money she'd left with him. Hidden, of course, in his clothes, seeing as how rough the neighborhood was. In lieu of glancing around nervously, or keeping his eyes on his feet as he normally would, he decided to mimic Destiny. So he kept a steely gaze forward, his shoulders pulled back and his chest puffed out.

Not too much, but just enough to show that he wasn't afraid. Which was a lie.

To his relief, this seemed to work, and he made it out of the northwest section of Tabula unmolested. Such that he soon found himself in a familiar part of town. Ahead, he spotted a large building with a sign that said: "The Great Flat Blade." He went inside, finding himself in the shop he'd purchased his chain armor set at. He went right to the front counter, eyeing the burly-looking clerk there.

"Hello," he greeted. Confidently.

"How can I help you, kid?" the guy asked.

"I need lightweight armor," he replied. "A full set."

The clerk eyed him doubtingly.

"You got money?" he asked.

"Sure do," Chaos replied, displaying the robust allowance Destiny had provided.

"Kid your size'll want hardened leather," the clerk stated. "Lightweight, comfortable, and easy to run away in."

Chaos grimaced, but didn't reply. For despite the man's insinuations, it was precisely the kind of armor he needed.

"That way," the clerk stated, pointing to a far corner of the shop. Chaos inclined his head, venturing to said corner, and found the aforementioned leather armor sets there. Most of which were for adults, but a few that were for those of his size. Unfortunately, adults of his size were women, and as such, it took him a fair amount of time to find a set that didn't have...adornments that made their intended gender obvious. But he did, in a suit of leather armor that was black with some dark red stripes on upper arms. He tried it on, finding that it fit perfectly. So he took it off and brought it to the front counter.

"I'll take this," he declared, and paid for it. And while it was with money he hadn't earned, it was still his, and thus he felt quite grown-up to spend it.

"You need anything else?" the clerk asked.

"A weapon," Chaos answered.

"What'you know how to use?"

"Um...a shovel?" Chaos replied, blushing a bit. The clerk blinked.

"...oh," he stated. "Well...check out the camping aisle."

Chaos paused, and was about to ask the man where the swords were, then realized he had no idea how to use a sword. The only weapon Destiny had taught him to use was a shovel, and he didn't exactly have the time to take lessons learning another weapon. So a shovel it would have to be, at least until he met up with her again. He went to the camping aisle, finding a wide selection of shovels. One of which caught his eye: a black-handled shovel wrought of pure metal, with a silver head. It was the Omen-63 Tactical Shovel, the #1 rated survival shovel in Tabula, apparently. With a compass on the butt of the handle, which twisted off to reveal a small compartment that held a flint rod. What's more, the head of the shovel had edges that were quite sharp.

It was, to be frank, the most badass shovel Chaos had ever seen. And also the *only* badass shovel he'd ever seen.

He brought it back to the front counter, plunking down some more coins.

"The Omen-63, eh?" the clerk stated, eyeing the shovel approvingly. "When there's a problem, the answer is the Omen-63," he recited.

"Huh?"

"That's the tagline," the clerk explained. "Damn expensive, but it's a damn good choice. Last one in Grissam, I'd bet. They don't make 'em like that anymore."

"Thanks," Chaos replied.

He took his wares back to his apartment, putting the suit of armor on again. Again, it fit perfectly, and when he regarded himself in Destiny's full-length mirror, he had to admit he looked fine indeed. *Damn* fine.

"All right Chaos," he told himself, puffing out his chest. "Not bad."

He posed for a bit longer, feeling rather good about himself. Then he turned to his pack, which was lying atop Destiny's bed.

"Okay," he stated, putting his hands on his hips. "What now?"

He frowned, rubbing his chin, as he'd seen Dad do when he was pondering things. Destiny had gone to Old Langsroth without him, to destroy whatever evil had manifested there. His destiny had been to find his Destiny, which he'd done. But Destiny had told him – at least initially – that Vita had wanted Destiny to take him to Old Langsroth. And his destiny was, according to Imperius Fanning, to save the world. It was obvious that whatever was threatening the world was the evil that Destiny was facing. Which meant that, to fulfill his destiny, it wasn't enough for Chaos to *find* Destiny. He had to help her, too.

"I have to go back," he realized, a chill running down his spine. "I have to help Destiny to fulfill my destiny."

As soon as he spoke said words, Chaos knew they were true, though why, he didn't quite know. He only knew that, deep within his soul, he *knew*.

He had to face the evil within Old Langsroth with Destiny at his side…or the world as he knew it would surely end.

Chaos returned his gaze to the full-length mirror, squaring his shoulders and giving his reflection a steely-eyed, slightly squinty look. The kind of gaze a badass hero gave. And also Chaos.

"Right," he declared heroically. "Time to kick some zombie *ass*."

With that, he grabbed his pack, slinging it over his shoulder, then grabbed his Omen-63 Tactical Shovel. With his presumably trusty weapon in hand, Chaos left Destiny's apartment, marching southeast toward the city entrance. Such was his posture and squint of his eye that no hooligan dared intercept him, despite the exceedingly expensive – and top of the line – shovel that he carried. For the difference between predator and prey was attitude, and at the moment, Chaos's attitude screamed "don't fuck with me, m'kay?"

In this badass way, he made his way down the city streets, which were bustling with people as usual. As he passed an outdoor dining area of a restaurant, he couldn't help but overhear a conversation.

"He flew on a big ol' stick!" a rather robust bald man declared, taking a swig of an amber-colored drink. The woman he was sitting opposite frowned.

"A stick?"

"A big ol' twisty stick," the man confirmed. Chaos slowed his strut a bit to listen.

"You sure it wasn't a broom?" the woman asked. "Maybe it was a witch."

"Nah, it wasn't no broom," the man countered.

"Pfft," the woman scoffed. "You wouldn't know what one looked like."

"It was a guy anyways," the man argued. "What's a guy witch?"

"A warlock," the woman answered.

"He was wearing a purple dress though," the man admitted. "Real glittery. Maybe he was…one of *those*," he added, giving the woman a look.

185

"You sure it wasn't a woman?"

"He did scream like one when the city guard arrested him," the man stated. "Maybe it was a girl. Ugly as hell though, poor thing."

Chaos's eyes widened.

"They keeping her in a holding cell or at the prison?" the woman asked.

"Prison I think," the man answered. "Just in case she tries any magic."

With that, their conversation turned to other things, and Chaos sped back up, his heart pounding in his chest. He could hardly believe what he'd heard, but he'd heard it. There was only one person who fit the description that man had given.

Dad!

But how had his father found him? And why had he come all the way here?

There was only one way to find out, Chaos knew.

"Hey," he asked a passing woman. "Where's the prison?"

Chapter 33

After their high-intensity workout in Old Langsroth – and heroic retreat – Pravus and Templeton limped their way back across the Great Flat to the shore of the dry land beyond. That done, they licked their wounds, so to speak. Which were mostly muscular, on account of the excellent workout they'd done. In fact, the only actual wound sustained was a scratch that zombie woman had made on Pravus's right cheek. A shallow wound, one that wouldn't leave a scar, Templeton assured him. Not that a bit of magical healing salve back home wouldn't fix such an unsightly blemish.

So it was that Pravus found himself sitting on said shore with his cousin a few feet away, dabbing at the scratch on his cheek.

"Still bleeding," he noted with a frown. For it'd been quite some time since he'd sustained the wound. He applied pressure yet again.

"Perhaps the zombies' fingernails have an anticoagulant on them," Templeton posited. "One that makes the blood thin."

"Or the water," Pravus counter-posited, recalling the dull red glow the water had emitted. A crimson color close to blood, now that he thought on it.

"I suspect you're right," Templeton replied.

"I'll hold pressure for a bit longer."

They both sat there, recovering from their ordeal. Pravus's legs felt like dead weight, and his arms weren't much better. It was a marvelous feeling, really. To have fought to the very limits of his capabilities, and then heroically retreated across the great resistance of the Great Flat, his heavy armor threatening to fell him with each step! Why, it'd been glorious, if exceedingly painful. Merely remembering it brought a smile to Pravus's lips. A smile that clearly caught Templeton's eye, for he smiled back.

"Marvelous, wasn't it?" he mused.

"Indeed Templeton," Pravus agreed. "One of the very best!"

"A high-intensity workout for the ages!" Templeton declared.

"It really was something, eh cousin?" Pravus stated.

"Something special," Templeton replied resolutely, "...not only for the exertion, but in that I got to share it with you."

And oh! How Pravus's heart threatened to melt with this proclamation of cousinly love! Why, he was filled with the sudden and nearly irresistible urge to kiss the man, if only on the cheek, and not out of any sort of lust or romantic love – at least at the moment, surprisingly – but out of an expression of brotherhood and joy. While he could never have his cousin the way that he would prefer, as it was, their friendship was a closer relationship than most men could imagine having with their wives. Or husbands, or whatever.

"I can only concur, dearest cousin," Pravus replied, finding himself otherwise at a loss for words.

"Fancy a bit of stretching?" Templeton inquired. Pravus sighed, then nodded. For though it was the last thing he wanted to do – he would much have preferred to lie down and go to sleep – his internal resistance to the task was yet another trial to conquer. So conquer he did, settling in to a gentle stretching routine, one they'd done countless times before. Always after working out, for Pravus had found – after extensive personal research – that stretching before lifting tended to decrease one's strength.

When they were done with said stretches, Pravus found himself glad to have done them. For there was little in life that was quite as satisfying as stretching after a good workout...and then eating, of course.

"I'm famished," Pravus declared. "Shall we eat, cousin?"

"Our muscles cry out for sustenance," Templeton replied with typical cheer.

"Let us feed them!" Pravus stated.

He struggled to his feet, and they retrieved some jerky from their horses' packs. And some water, and soaked oats and such. A plain meal, one that many would turn their noses at, or consume only reluctantly. But to Pravus and Templeton, it was akin to a feast. After all, there was no man richer than he who had what he wanted...and nothing more. In this case, the meal was exactly what Pravus desired, and thus it was a wealthy man's repast.

He finished with a contented sigh, then pulled off his pink-purple platemail, one piece at a time. This done, he rested on his back on the ground, staring up at the clear blue sky. He felt a tickling sensation run down his cheek, and wiped at it, finding his fingertips wet with blood.

"How odd," he murmured, putting pressure on it again. He supposed it was an unnatural amount of bleeding for so superficial a wound, but then again, he hadn't actually been wounded very often in his life. His monarchal uniform had prevented any injury, save for the penetration he'd suffered by way of Devorah Doverah's Sovereign Spear. As such, he couldn't really say whether the duration of his bleeding was within the normal range. It was only a little dribble, but to be fair, a little in abundance could end up being a lot.

"Perhaps we should spend the morrow resting, then try again the day after?" Templeton proposed.

"A wise plan," Pravus replied. "For when it came to workouts, recovery was too-often ignored.

With this in mind, he turned to lay on his oozing cheek, to apply consistent pressure to it. Then he closed his eyes, and let the gentle breeze and the sounds of birds chirping lull him slowly and gently to sleep. For with Templeton at his side, he had no fear that anything would dare attack them. And if something did, he was quite sure that together, they would surely prevail.

Chapter 34

After finding the prison in Tabula, Chaos convinced the authorities within that he was, in fact, Chauncy's son...and to allow him to speak with his father for precisely five minutes. So it was that Chaos found himself standing outside his father's cell, a guard posted down the hallway to keep time.

"Son!" Dad cried, rushing up to the bars. His hands were tied behind his back, Chaos noted, and his Staff of Wind was nowhere to be seen.

"Hey Dad," Chaos replied, smiling despite himself.

"Thank goodness you're okay," Dad said, clearly relieved. "I was worried to death about you."

"How'd you find me?" Chaos asked.

"Imperius," Dad answered. Which made sense. "Are you okay? Are you hurt?"

"No," Chaos replied. Dad smiled again, then eyed his leather armor and his Omen-63 Tactical Shovel. He blinked.

"Is that...the O-63?" he asked.

"Uh...yes," Chaos replied. "How did you know?"

"How could you possibly afford that?" Dad demanded, rudely ignoring Chaos's question.

"Destiny gave me some money," he replied. Dad just stared at him blankly. "I'm going to Old Langsroth to find Destiny," Chaos added. Dad hesitated, then sighed.

"Imperius said your destiny was to go there," he conceded, clearly unhappy with that fact. He lifted his gaze to meet Chaos's. "But it's too dangerous, son."

"I have to go," Chaos insisted.

"Take me with you," Dad pressed. Chaos blinked.

"Um...how?"

"Let me touch you with my left hand," Dad explained. Which was, Chaos knew, Dad's *magic* hand. The hand that could let them switch bodies. Which would conveniently put Chaos in jail, which

190

was probably exactly what Dad wanted. Chaos felt a familiar bitter anger rise like bile within him, and he glared at his dad.

"You just want to trap me again, like you've done to me my entire life," he accused.

"I want to keep you safe," Dad corrected.

"You don't trust me," Chaos shot back. Dad grimaced.

"You can't take care of yourself," he argued.

"Whose fault is that?" Chaos retorted. Dad didn't answer...because he couldn't. Not without admitting whose fault it was. "I'm leaving now," Chaos announced, turning away.

"Wait," Dad blurted out. Chaos hesitated, then turned back around.

"What?"

Dad lowered his gaze, then shook his head.

"You're right," he confessed. "It *is* my fault." He swallowed visibly. "But after what happened with Devorah Doverah, when you dropped that meteorite on Imperius's head..." He sighed. "Your magic is too strong, Chaos. I'm afraid it'll get you in more trouble."

"How am I gonna learn how to use it if I don't use it?" Chaos demanded.

"The risks..."

"You're the one who put the entire universe in him, so that if you die, the universe dies with you," Chaos argued. "But you're gonna tell *me* my power is too dangerous?"

Dad paused.

"Fair point," he conceded. He licked his lips, clearly trying to think of an argument in his defense, but suddenly Chaos was done with him.

"I'm done with you," he declared, turning around again.

"Wait!" Dad blurted out. Chaos stepped away from the cell, and felt something tug on his Omen-63 from behind. He pulled away, turning to see Dad with his back to the bars, his tied-up hands shoved through the gap. "Don't go!" Dad cried.

"I need to do this if I ever want to be a hero like you," Chaos countered. He paused. "But like, confident about it too," he added. Dad grimaced, for they both knew very well that his dad was perhaps the most heroic coward alive.

"You don't have to be a hero," Dad countered.

"But I want to," Chaos shot back. "Goodbye Dad," he added. "I'll help you when I get back."

After leaving the prison, Chaos went back into town to finish shopping. While he already had provisions that Destiny had put in his pack, he figured that packing extra couldn't hurt. While he'd begun his adventure with no preparation at all, now he wanted to be over-prepared. So, in this way, he wasn't so much *inviting* chaos into his adventure, but preparing for it instead. Outside of the carefully secure quasi-prison of his life in Borrin, the world was full of surprises.

When they came, he would be ready.

Then, his pack...packed, Chaos slung it over his back, along with his Omen-63, and made his way out of Tabula, starting the long journey back to the Great Flat. The weight of his pack and his shovel seemed trivial at first, but after a few hours, they were anything but. Still, while Chaos would have previously bemoaned their weight, now he knew the value of it. For with each step he took carrying a burden, his ability to carry it would grow...until one day, he would be as strong and capable as Destiny.

Thus, with a simple shift of the mind, what was once burdensome was transformed, and Chaos found himself seeking out more burdens to bear, to see just how much he could take on. He strode away from Tabula, not stopping when he grew weary, or when his legs began to burn, or his feet became sore. Each discomfort presented a challenge, a kind of mental resistance to push past. Such that each step became a victory, minor as they were.

At length, Chaos stopped to eat, preparing rations from his pack as he'd seen Destiny do. Then he packed things up and continued his journey, traipsing across the land between Tabula and the Great Flat, with the plan to make it back to the wall of Old Langsroth before nightfall. A plan that he found himself incapable of executing; for on foot, the journey was considerably longer when not riding Gwendolyn.

So, as the sun set and the stars opened their eyes to gaze down upon the land, Chaos was forced to make camp. He set down his pack in a clearing, gathering stones to set in a ring around where the campfire would be. Then he gathered tiny twigs and brush and leaves, building a generous pile of kindling. He was about to grab two sticks to start a fire the way he'd seen Destiny do it, but then he remembered his Omen-63. Retrieving the flint rod from it, he struck it on a rough part of the metal shaft, sending a shower of sparks down onto the brush. After a few attempts, it lit...and then promptly blew out.

"Crud," he grumbled, trying again. This time, he added more brush as soon as he got a flame, protecting it from the breeze with his hand. A longer flame rose from the kindling, and he set small twigs and sticks atop it, then bigger and bigger pieces of wood as the fire grew. It wasn't long before he had a bona fide, actual campfire a-blazing, to his great satisfaction, and he sat before it, enjoying its warmth immensely.

Minutes passed, then over an hour, and Chaos was surprised to find himself perfectly content to sit there and gaze into the flickering flames. To do precisely nothing, which would, at any other time, have filled him with the anxious urge to *do* something. It was a marvelously peaceful feeling, and he couldn't remember the last time he'd felt this way.

"This is alright," he murmured, lifting his gaze and smiling at the stars.

No, it was more than alright...it was exactly what he'd been missing all this time. It *had* to be. Because now that he had it, he wanted for nothing. He was, in this moment, complete.

At length, Chaos's eyelids grew heavy, and he grabbed his sleeping bag, obeying his body's silent suggestion. Snuggling up, he let his eyes close, and surrendered to sleep's sweet oblivion.

* * *

Upon waking the next morning, Chaos found that the sun had just began to peak over the horizon. He slipped out of his sleeping bag, glancing at the fire, which was long dead. He yawned, then stretched, taking a moment to wake up fully. Without anyone to bother him with their presence or demands, he found himself in an unusually good mood for having just woken up. It occurred to him that perhaps this was what he needed in the morning; a moment to himself, a bit of the ol' quiet time, so that he could face the day with the proper disposition.

With no one to rush him, Chaos took his time taking down camp, folding his sleeping bag and stuffing it back in his pack. Then, on a whim, he took it back out, so he could better check the contents of his pack. He took out each item, checking it

193

methodically, and had no desire to rush the process as he normally did. The bulk of a child's life was to do whatever adults said, and to be punished if they didn't quickly comply. A servant's life, really...so it was no wonder why Chaos had chaffed under such a tyrannical system.

Now he was the author of his day. What he was doing was precisely what he wanted. Thus there was no reason to rush.

After a while, he'd checked each item in his pack, spotting a piece of food that'd gone a bit bad. He tossed this, then put everything back, grabbing his Omen-63 Tactical Shovel and setting off on his journey once again.

Grassland gave way to rocky terrain, with sparse grass sprouting between cracks in the earth. At length he spotted a few trees ahead, and made his way toward them. For he had the sudden urge to train with his shovel, and a small tree would provide a good target. If he was going to become a killer of zombies, he needed to get good. And getting good meant practicing over and over again.

He stopped by a tree with a trunk as thick as his arm, which really wasn't as thick as he would've preferred. Then he put down his pack, then holding his shovel before him. Winding up, he took a moderately-powered swing, striking the trunk with the edge of his shovel's head. To Chaos's utter surprise, it cut halfway through the trunk, embedding itself within.

"Wow," Chaos blurted out, bracing himself, then yanking the shovel free. He might as well have struck the tree with an axe. "Huh," he murmured, eyeing the Omen-63 with newfound respect. "No wonder why you cost so much."

He tried another chop, this time pivoting his back foot and really getting his hips into it. This time, the shovel struck a bit lower than before, cutting most of the way through. Chaos yanked it out with some difficulty, feeling rather proud of this accomplishment. But then he imagined what Destiny would say.

Better, but not good enough. Try again.

He set up to swing again, this time aiming for where he'd struck the first time. Then, using his hips more than his arms, he swung again. The shovel struck slightly above the mark, going halfway through.

Try again.

Chaos pulled the shovel free, then aimed and swung again, and this time he struck true. The Omen-63 cut straight through the tree trunk, felling it in a crash of branches and brush.

"All right," he declared triumphantly. Then he eyed another tree trunk, this one twice as thick as the first. "Try again," he prompted himself.

He performed the previous exercise, practicing horizontal swings for a bit, focusing not on chopping the tree down, but on making each strike hit where he wanted it to hit. For it seemed to him that accuracy was the most important thing to master first. After a few dozen strikes, he found his accuracy greatly improved…and his arms feeling like lead.

"Okay," he stated, stepping back from the tree and wiping his sweaty brow. "Stamina sucks. Got it."

Of course, he didn't have the benefit of months to improve his endurance, nor could he rely on Vita's Boundless Vigor. If he wanted to improve his stamina, he needed to fight smarter, not harder. But how?

He frowned, rubbing his chin and thinking it through.

"My arms are tired," he noted. "Mostly my shoulders. But my hips and legs aren't at all." Which meant that he needed to focus on powering his blows with as little shoulder use as possible, particularly if he wanted to last more than a few minutes against a horde of zombies. It also meant that he needed a way to fight if he got so tired that swinging the shovel wouldn't work anymore.

So he put the shovel down, then practiced kicking the tree trunk instead.

At first his kicks barely rattled the tree, but as he practiced, he learned to lean his weight into each blow, and kick with a bit more of a snapping action. Zombies were terribly slow and uncoordinated, after all, so a good kick to the knee or hip would send them tumbling to the ground. Or into their fellow zombies, sending a whole bunch to the ground. This would allow him time to recover, or to pick them off one and a time. Or perhaps most importantly, to run away.

Chaos found that, the more he thought about the problem of fighting zombies, the more solutions he came up with. And the more solutions he found, the more problems he thought up, and so on. Until he realized that he'd spent a good few hours on the task, in fact. But he knew that, in preparing, he was telling chaos to come get some. That Daddy was ready, bitches, come show me whatcha got. After all, in life, a fair bit of chaos was practically guaranteed. He had to plan for it…or die pathetically.

Then, quite tired physically – and tired of strategizing, at least for the moment – Chaos took a break to eat some of his rations. Then it was back to journeying.

The sun swung ever-so-slowly across the sky, and it had nearly set by the time Chaos came to the shore of the Great Flat, sending its rays across the water in reds and oranges like little flames dancing in the wind. Chaos had half a mind to forge onward, for Destiny awaited somewhere in Old Langsroth. But as tired as he was, he knew that to enter the deadly city now would be suicide.

So he made camp instead, making a fire a bit faster than before. Then he prepared dinner – tasteless rations, as usual – eating it, then retrieving his sleeping bag. Tomorrow was going to be a big day, he knew, and it was imperative that he get his rest. He would need every last bit of his strength and his wits if he hoped to survive the coming adventure; it was his responsibility to be at his best.

Chapter 35

The next morning, Chaos woke with the sun, climbing a bit stiffly and sorely from his sleeping bag. He took his time adjusting to the idea that he was, in fact, awake, then got to work with his new morning routine. A routine he found rather comforting, which was odd, for routine was, at least to him, another word for boring.

His pack checked, then slung over his shoulder, and his Omen-63 on his back, and his boots freshly re-oiled to maintain waterproof-ness, Chaos found himself ready for the next leg of his adventure: a return to Old Langsroth.

"Okay," he told himself, recalling his mental preparation the night before. He ran through his plans in his mind, a series of attacks and counterattacks, defenses, and reasons to flee and such. This done, he started striding into the Great Flat.

The shallow water *splish-splashed* as he walked, and to his satisfaction, his boots repelled the water without difficulty, leaving his socks and feet comfortably dry. Onward he went, enjoying the sun on his face and the breeze in his hair, and the faint scent of the fresh water. A scent he knew would soon change to one of blood and decay, unfortunately.

Still, this scent promised to be the least of Chaos's trials, and besides, he would endure it when it came. For now, instead of being filled with dreadful, morbid anticipation, he allowed himself to enjoy the present. Which was, presently, quite pleasant.

At length, Chaos spotted the great black wall of Old Langsroth in the distance, and he trudged toward it, setting a pace he could maintain indefinitely. There was no point in blowing through his body's energy reserves before they were truly needed, after all. As a result, it took another good hour for him to reach the wall at last...and its portcullis, which was open, to his surprise. Or rather, opening. For there were two men in the process of lifting it...or more precisely, one man lifting it while the other stacked rocks to prop it open. The one lifting the portcullis was clad in an eyeball-grabbing purple-pink set of platemail armor, a great big sword in a scabbard at his left hip. The other man was tall and slender, but obviously quite muscular, wearing a simple suit of leather armor, not unlike Chaos's own.

Chaos slowed his pace, eyeing the two men warily. They were, he realized, the two men he'd seen before, when leaving Old Langsroth with Destiny.

"Hey," he called out. The slimmer man turned to Chaos, and then the platemail-clad one did as well.

"Ah, hello," the slimmer man greeted. He finished propping the portcullis open, and then the two men strode toward him. He hesitated, then walked toward them as well, stopping when they were a few yards away. "You're the boy we met the day before yesterday," the slim man recalled. "On our way here."

"That's right," Chaos confirmed. "What are you guys doing here?"

"We've come seeking adventure," the bigger, platemail-wearing man declared. A formidably handsome man with a wide, chiseled jaw and short black hair, and eyebrows so perfect they had to be plucked. His face was only marred by a small scratch on his right cheek...one that was bleeding. "What's your name, boy?" he asked, putting his hands on his hips. Not in a "you're in trouble" kind of way, but rather as if he were striking a manly pose. And succeeding in doing so.

"Chaos," Chaos answered. The man blinked.

"Chaos Little?" he asked. It was Chaos's turn to blink.

"Uh...yeah," he replied. "How did you know that?"

"It is not the first time we've met," the slim man answered with a smile.

"Nor the second," the bigger man added. "You don't recognize us?"

"You didn't recognize me," Chaos pointed out a bit defensively.

"A fair point," the slender man conceded. "But to be fair, it was nearly a decade since we saw you last, and you were but a toddler then."

Chaos just stared at them blankly.

"I," the bigger man proclaimed, still posing, "...am King Pravus the Eighth, ruler of the kingdom that bears my name."

"And I am Lord Templeton, my liege's cousin," the smaller man stated. Chaos's eyes widened.

198

"Ohhh!" he exclaimed. "I remember you!"

And it was true. He had met the two men, both during the battle with Gavin Archibald Merrick Senior – or "Gamsies" as Mom had called him – and during the battle with Devorah Doverah. Heck, he'd even been invited to King Pravus's castle in Cumulus to have a banquet in his – and his family's – honor.

"How could you not?" King Pravus stated, continuing his pose. Which really was quite heroic, Chaos had to admit.

"Why are you heading into Old Langsroth?" Chaos asked. Pravus paused, eyeing Templeton.

"Do you suppose we should tell him?" he asked his cousin.

"Chaos is a Chosen One," Templeton reasoned. "I'd say we have more than enough reason to trust him."

"Indeed," Pravus replied. "Very well. None other than the great Imperius Fanning himself bade us travel to Old Langsroth to meet our destinies," Pravus revealed.

"Me too," Chaos replied.

"Really," Pravus murmured, rubbing his chin with one purple-pink gauntleted hand. "I suppose it makes sense that a Chosen One would join us in saving the world."

"Perfect sense," Templeton concurred.

"I'm looking for Destiny," Chaos told them. Pravus paused.

"Yes, we know," he replied. "We just said that we shared the same destiny."

"Or different destinies in a similar place," Templeton stated.

"No, I mean Destiny came in here, and I have to find her," Chaos countered. They both stared at him blankly. "Destiny is a person," he explained. "I met a girl named Destiny, and she's a person," he added when it was obvious this explanation was insufficient. "She's a paladin of the goddess Vita, and she went into Old Langsroth to destroy the Fallen Sky."

"Pardon?" Templeton inquired.

Chaos took them through a quick explanation of everything that'd happened to him, and the history of Old Langsroth as he knew it, and Destiny's theory that something or someone had gained control of the zombies in the cursed city. When he was done, the two men rubbed their broad chins, their gazes downcast.

"I say," Pravus...well, said. "This is more convoluted than we thought."

"Not a simple 'search and destroy' mission after all," Templeton agreed.

"I find it rather odd," Pravus continued with a frown.

"How so?" Templeton inquired.

"Since Chosen Ones have existed, their destinies have followed a familiar formula," Pravus explained. "Imperius Fanning declares a prophecy, the Chosen Ones go to the Great Wood, then the Cave of Wonder, then fulfill their task, self-actualizing in the process."

"Just so," Templeton agreed.

"Yet now Chaos here has a destiny to meet Destiny," Pravus continued. "Forgoing the usual formula altogether."

"And we have been granted destinies of our own," Templeton noted. "Which technically would make us Chosen Ones."

"Which is very unusual to say the least," Pravus stated, putting his hands on his hips. "Though I suppose it makes sense, given how many times we've saved the world."

"Helped to save," Chaos corrected. For according to his parents, King Pravus had always played a bit part in doing so.

"In any case," Pravus continued, ignoring Chaos's interjection, "...it is clear to me that we're dealing with a different kind of destiny."

"And a girl named Destiny to boot," Templeton mused, shaking his head. "How very strange indeed."

They both stood there, looking perplexed, and Chaos waited for them to be finished. Impatiently, as it turned out, for he quickly grew tired of waiting.

"We going in?" he asked, gesturing at the open portcullis.

"Ah yes," Templeton replied. "Ready, my liege?"

"Quite," King Pravus replied. "Come Chaos," he prompted. "We shall conquer the curse of Old Langsroth together...and together, we will find – and fulfill – our destinies!"

With that, the two man strode forward into the tunnel, and Chaos followed beside Pravus. They walked against the current, and Chaos glanced at the king as they made their way toward the partially submerged city.

"You're ah, bleeding," he noted. For the king most certainly was. A steady stream of blood drooled from a shallow cut on his cheek...bleeding that had been going on the entire time, in fact, and still hadn't stopped. Pravus touched his cheek, grimacing a bit.

"Yes," he replied. "The confounded cut won't stop."

"A zombie scratched his cheek with a fingernail," Templeton explained from ahead of them. "We suspect a substance on her fingernail that prevents proper healing."

"No, that's not it," Chaos countered.

"Hmm?" Pravus asked, applying pressure to his cheek.

"If your wounds get exposed to the Fallen blood, they won't stop bleeding," Chaos explained. "And that blood will go up into the Fallen Sky, taking a bit of your soul with it."

"Poppycock," Pravus replied peevishly. He let go of the pressure on his cheek, and still it bled.

"I'm afraid not," Templeton countered gently, eyeing Pravus's wound. Before their eyes, the blood transformed into a kind of barely visible mist, floating up into the air. A process so subtle that Chaos hadn't noticed it before. "Your blood is going up, my liege."

"It is?" Pravus asked, touching his wound again. He stared at his bloodied fingers then, and sure enough, the blood coating them slowly dissolved, floating up and away. "Egads!" Pravus exclaimed, staring in horror.

"Thank goodness it was a small wound," Templeton noted. He turned to Chaos. "How do we get it to stop?"

"We need Destiny to do it," Chaos answered. He hesitated then.

"What is it?" Templeton inquired.

"It's just that...well, if you bleed out more than half your blood, your...ah..." Chaos began, glancing nervously at Pravus.

"Spit it out boy," Pravus commanded.

"Well, your soul leaves with it," Chaos concluded. "And when that happens, you turn into a zombie."

* * *

Upon hearing of his soul's fate to join the Fallen Sky, and wander the flooded streets of Old Langsroth for all eternity, King Pravus and Templeton set off down the tunnel leading into the cursed city with a quickened pace. For it was clear that the only way to save his soul was to find Destiny before it was too late.

"There's zombies lying under the water everywhere," Chaos whisper-warned as they approached the end of the tunnel. "They react to touch and noise."

"That explains our first foray," Templeton stated with a reluctant smile. "I should have made a better effort at reconnaissance before coming here."

"The responsibility is mine," Pravus countered, with a grim lifting of the chin and steeling of his gaze. "I relied on exuberance and bravery to complete this adventure, when a more level head would have sufficed."

"Then I say that saving your soul is our new mission," Templeton declared valiantly. "And with the lessons we've learned, we shall complete it!"

Pravus had to smile at that, his eyes growing moist.

"Sweetest, dearest Templeton," he murmured, shaking his head in wonder. "You never fail to raise my spirits, even in my darkest hour!"

"Shhh!" Chaos scolded, glaring at the two. Their mouths snapped shut, and they continued down the tunnel in silence, eventually reaching the end. It opened up into the city itself, ever-shrouded in darkness. Chaos paused then, holding a hand out for the others to do the same. He eyed the surface of the water, rippling in the pelting rain. How on earth were they going to be able to navigate around hundreds – if not thousands – of submerged zombies? It was a question he'd pondered all last night.

And it was a damn good thing he'd come prepared, because he'd figured out an answer.

He gestured for the other two to take a step back into the tunnel, then opened his pack, retrieving a fist-sized rock. Which he wound up and threw as hard as he could to the left, roughly in the direction Destiny had led him the last time he'd been here.

"What...!" Pravus whisper-blurted, then put a hand to his mouth.

The stone struck the water a good two hundred feet away from them, with a plop that echoed through the night air.

Ripples spread outward from the impact, and soon Chaos could see zombies rising from the surface, their pale flesh reflecting the light of the lightning flashing high above. Dozens of zombies, all around the impact site.

They formed a ring around the site, like so many iron filings attracted to a magnet.

Okay, Chaos thought with a triumphant smile. *That worked.*

He retrieved another stone from his pack, throwing it half as far. This excited another group of zombies, who circled around the stone as before. But the noise from the further group of zombies attracted the nearer ones, or rather, they attracted each other. And thus started shambling toward one another, to meet in the middle. And then sort of stand around for a while, until they decided to lower themselves back under the water.

"Brilliant," Chaos heard Templeton breathe. He felt the man put a hand on his shoulder from behind. "Well done, Chaos," he added with a genuine smile. One that Chaos knew was from the heart. Chaos smiled back, feeling a rare kind of pride surging within him. It was heady stuff, to have come up with a plan that, purely with the power of his mind, had defeated a seemingly impossible foe. A mere evening's preparation had been all it'd taken…and in succeeding, it'd proven that preparation was a powerful kind of magic in and of itself. No, it was beyond the magical and physical, in that it allowed anyone to use these methods to achieve their goals.

With the power of preparation, even a wizard with middling magic could become powerful. And he hadn't even used his magic, assuming he still could.

Maybe I don't need magic, Chaos thought, the chill of Revelation's touch running down his spine. *I can be a hero without it.*

He grabbed another rock from his pack, throwing it near the wall to his left, a mere fifty feet away. Then he ducked back down the tunnel out of sight, peering out. Sure enough, it'd worked again…and this time, the zombies near the tunnel got up, shuffling toward the rock before settling down under the water again.

"Okay," he whispered. "I think the path should be clear."

"At least for a hundred yards," Templeton agreed. He turned to King Pravus. "Shall we?"

Pravus nodded, pressing a finger to his cut in a vain attempt to stop his soul from leaving him.

Chaos led the way, visualizing where he'd seen the zombies rise, then lie back down. To his relief, the path was indeed clear, and they made it a good few hundred feet before he stopped. Then he turned toward the center of the city, where he recalled the sky bridge being. Of course, he didn't know exactly where it was, but he'd thought of a way to find it.

He grabbed another stone from his pack, then threw it, watching as it landed fifty feet away. He waited for zombies to appear…but none did, which meant either that the rock had hit an area without zombies, or it'd missed the sky bridge and plummeted into the depths far below the surface.

Chaos grabbed another rock, tossing it a bit to the right of the first...and it plopped below the surface. This time, a few zombies arose in front of the site of impact, and shambled their way toward the rock. Two made it, but the rest dropped suddenly below the water.

Yes!

That meant the sky bridge was where the two zombies were standing, while the others had fallen off the edge into the depths.

"Okay," he whispered, turning to the others. "The sky bridge is there."

"We'll go first," Pravus stated, "...and take out the two zombies."

Chaos nodded, and they went forward to do just that. Then he paused.

"There might be more zombies between us and the sky bridge," he warned.

"Not many," Templeton countered. "We can handle it, eh cousin?"

"Naturally," Pravus replied, still pressing on his wound.

They continued forward, and to Chaos's relief, they stumbled upon no zombies on their way toward the two on the sky bridge. Who were facing away from them, conveniently. As he watched, the zombies started to lie down, just as Templeton and Pravus drew near.

Templeton went ahead, unsheathing his slender sword and decapitating both of them in a fraction of a second, while Pravus caught their bodies and lowered them gently to the ground. Their heads, unfortunately, made a bit of a splash, but to Chaos's further relief, no zombies were attracted by the sound. Probably because the rock had already drawn the closest zombies to the sky bridge, and as such, no other zombies were near enough to be alerted.

That done, they moved ahead on the sky bridge, taking each step cautiously, for fear of reaching the edge and falling off. Chaos gestured at the buildings ahead, specifically the one he'd been attacked in earlier. It provided a convenient visual landmark to ensure that he was traveling in a straight line across the bridge.

They made it across without incident, reaching the other side.

So far, so good, Chaos thought, feeling another burst of pride. Pravus turned to him.

"What now?" he whispered. Chaos paused, eyeing the buildings ahead.

"This is as far as I got," he confessed.

"Fantastic," Pravus grumbled.

"But Destiny said she needed to go to the center of the city," Chaos explained. "She said the ultimate evil was there."

"Well, we have our destination," Templeton stated with indomitable cheer. "We've merely to get there."

"Which part of the center?" Pravus snipped, eyeing the city in the distance. It was a good point; the closer to the center they got, the more levels there were, with the very center having eight stories of sky bridge roads interconnecting the buildings there. Chaos had assumed they'd need to make it to the top, for that was naturally where one's goal would be, at least classically speaking.

"There aren't many buildings in the center," Templeton reasoned. "Even if we have to search each level, it shouldn't take overly long to do so."

"Well, time is of the essence," Pravus replied, taking his hand off of his wound and grimacing at the blood there. He immediately pressed again. "Losing my soul here."

"We need to be careful," Chaos warned. "We don't know if there are any more hidden sky bridges underwater…and the city is as deep as it is high."

"Which means the source of evil could be underwater," Templeton reasoned.

"Then Destiny couldn't go there," Pravus countered. "All we have to do is find her, not the source of evil."

"Well, we still have to help her defeat it," Chaos pointed out.

"After my soul is saved," Pravus agreed.

"We'll have to make each step cautiously," Templeton warned. "I'll go first," he added bravely, clearly willing to sacrifice himself for his king.

"I'll keep using the stone-throwing trick," Chaos offered.

"At least until we can get to the second story of the city," Templeton added. "Then we'll be able to see our footing, and we won't have to worry about submerged zombies."

"An excellent plan," Pravus stated. "To the second story it is!"

"Shhh," Chaos shushed.

And with that, they made their way forward, their eyes on the two-story-tall buildings a city block away.

Chapter 36

The main sky bridge of the fourth story of Old Langsroth was wide enough to accommodate three carriages side-to-side, its white stone nearly perfectly preserved, though partially hidden beneath a layer of mold due to the constant moisture provided by the Fallen Sky.

Destiny strode across the sky bridge, her eyes on the center of the city far ahead...and more specifically, the huge building at its very top, the only building on the ninth story of the fabled city. It was the Temple of Langsroth, a building once dedicated to the magical arts...and where, Vita had told her, the ancient necromancer had cast the spell to murder the city's Elders, and create the Fallen Sky.

She could feel the power of the undead creature within the building, even from this far away. Which meant that it was more powerful than any undead she'd ever faced.

This is your destiny, she thought. *Your mandate from Vita.*

Her entire life had been in preparation for this. To end the curse of Old Langsroth once and for all. To allow the dead to rest, and for life to spring anew in this cursed place.

She felt the presence of other undead as she strode across the skybridge. Weaker undead, though still powerful in their own right. The upper levels of the city had few undead, the dumber and weaker zombies having long ago fallen off the sky bridges. This left the higher-powered undead, those who'd retained enough intelligence to navigate the upper levels of the city. Though again, they tended to stay near the water, where the Fallen Blood fell. This blood was still diluted by the water around it, but was the most concentrated form of the blood, other than the rain itself.

Destiny stopped suddenly, spotting something ahead, standing on the roof of a building one story above. A Zhimera...one standing with its eyes toward the Fallen Sky, its mouth open wide.

It's drinking, she realized.

Without a steady diet of the Fallen Blood, the Zhimera would eventually fall apart, the unholy magic keeping it together as one being leaving it. Being so far away from the blood below, this Zhimera was clearly drinking the rain to keep itself together.

She studied the thing, struck by how the simplest of laws could direct the behavior of living – and un-living – things. She herself was subject to the simple rules of eating and drinking, of sleep and other natural needs. But the rules of Old Langsroth were far simpler:

Crave the blood. Drink the blood. It falls from the sky.

She watched the Zhimera for a while longer, studying its composition. It was not the one she'd fought earlier, for this Zhimera had only two sets of arms and legs, with a long, segmented body that went head-chest-torso-chest-torso-pelvis-torso-pelvis. Its eyes glowed with an unholy crimson light, so powerful was the Fallen Blood within it. Indeed, even its veins glowed with that light.

Why is it out here?

The only answer from Vita was that there was another presence here. Something immensely powerful. And that it was up to her to destroy it...and to destroy the magic that perpetuated the Fallen Sky.

At length, the Zhimera stopping drinking, lowering its gaze...and locked its red eyes right on Destiny.

Damn.

It made a high-pitched screech, a horrid sound that echoed through the vast city, mingling with the low rumble of thunder and the pattering of rain.

Then it leapt off the roof of the building, landing on the sky bridge ahead...and broke out into an all-out sprint toward Destiny, moving with inhuman speed!

Destiny gripped her mace, lowering her head in prayer.

I need your strength, she thought, not in words, but in feelings. She felt a spreading warmth go through her, Vita's Boundless Strength surging through her muscles. Then she made a second request, and felt Vita's Crystal Skin harden her flesh.

She opened her eyes, seeing the Zhimera bounding toward her, its eyes glowing with a baleful crimson glare. She strode toward it, her jaw set firm. But she felt no hatred for the thing. It'd been a human being once, with hopes and fears and people who loved it.

Now it was a suffering thing, cursed by foul magic to hunger for eternity. For the soul it'd once had.

And no amount of drinking would ever return it.

I will set you free, she promised. *All of you.*

Chapter 37

King Pravus found himself following Chaos and Templeton across the flooded first level of Old Langsroth, not leading as he would've preferred to do. But after learning that his oozing wound was in fact a portal from which his soul was slowly dribbling out of his body, he'd found himself rather preoccupied with that fact. And with keeping his soul where it belonged. Sadly, with his focus thusly…focused, he found himself utterly incapable of leading with his customary heroic zeal. Which was irritating.

Chaos used his ingeniously simple trick again and again, finding and corralling zombies with the toss of a stone. Such that they were able to continue toward a staircase ahead, one spiraling up one of the many white pillars supporting the bridge-like roads above.

"Almost there," Chaos whispered. Unnecessarily, which only peeved Pravus further. But he kept his kingly mouth shut, focusing on doing the same for his cheek's cut.

To everyone's relief, they made it to the foot of the stairs unmolested, and began climbing it toward the second level. At the prospect of not facing another zombie, Pravus was relieved. For while he normally would've leapt at the chance to…well, leap into battle, the thought that he might be cut again – and bleed out even faster – gave him considerable pause.

Up the spiral staircase they went, reaching the top. Which put them on a wide sky bridge, a road wide enough to fit three carriages side-to-side. It was, Pravus had to admit as he gazed up at the bewildering network of buildings and suspended roads, an absolutely stunning architectural achievement, both in design and implementation.

Not to mention the fact that, despite millennia of disrepair, without a single copper piece paid to maintain it, the city still stood in remarkable condition. Almost pristine, even. In fact, the only damage to the city's aesthetic was, for the most part, purely cosmetic, a result of mold and blood staining the otherwise white stone.

"Incredible," Templeton murmured, clearly of a similar mind, and thinking along a similar vein.

"Indeed," Pravus had to agree. Softly. For while there were no zombies hidden from view now, the city was still teeming with undead. And while said undead were unlikely to be able to reach Pravus from here – zombies were notoriously bad at stairs, or so Chaos claimed – there was still the matter of their eventual escape. Meeting a vicious army on their way back down was hardly something that Pravus looked forward to, now that he knew what a single scratch could do. Which was tragic, because otherwise he would've relished the challenge.

They continued across the sky bridge, passing by buildings on either side. Some of which were only two stories tall, and had doorways that opened up onto the sky bridge. Other buildings were three or four stories tall, and got taller the further they went. But even these had their second stories accessible by the sky bridge, with doorways leading inside.

It was a remarkable way to fit the equivalent of several cities inside one. In fact, a part of Pravus not occupied with soul-saving was tempted to build a city like it in his own kingdom. Assuming he survived, of course.

"Hold up," Chaos whispered, prompting everyone to stop. The boy peered into the darkness.

"What do you see?" Templeton inquired.

"Nothing," Pravus grumbled. But he knew that children tended to have better night-vision than adults, so if anyone was going to spot danger first in this wretched place, it was Chaos.

"I thought I saw something moving," Chaos stated. "On the sky bridge ahead." But a fortuitous flash of lightning lit said area quite nicely, proving that Chaos was wrong. "Nevermind," he stated.

"Quite alright," Templeton reassured, putting a hand on the boy's shoulder. "Better to say something and be wrong than to suffer from silence."

Chaos nodded, and they resumed their trek.

It wasn't long before the boy stopped again, peering off into the darkness. There was another flash of lightning, again revealing nothing concerning.

"Huh," Chaos mumbled. He continued forward, but grabbed his shovel, holding it before him. A paltry weapon, utterly inappropriate to the task of fighting zombies, much less anything else. Why the boy had chosen such a weapon was beyond Pravus. But, seeing as it was Chaos they were dealing with, he supposed he had to expect the unexpected.

Pravus decided to unsheathe his own sword, which proved far easier when done from the hip than the back. Templeton took the hint, unsheathing his own fencing-like blade.

Forward they went, unmolested, which was nice.

"See anything?" Templeton whispered, keeping the lines of communication with Chaos open.

"Nope," Chaos replied.

And then the enemy attacked!

Chapter 38

Destiny charged down the fourth-story sky bridge toward the eight-limbed Zhimera, even as it *shrieked*, barreling toward her. She gripped her mace, winding up...and then swung it right as the unholy creature reached her.

The mace struck the side of the thing's face with a bone-crunching *crack*, sending it hurtling to the side. But its momentum carried it forward, one of its left shoulders smashing into Destiny's unarmored chest. Such was the force of the blow that she felt Vita's Crystal Skin crack.

She grunted with the impact, flying backward and to her right, and struck the street with a whump, the air blasting out of her lungs.

Destiny gasped for air, struggling to her feet...even as the Zhimera – who'd barreled past her, and had nearly fallen off the side of the sky bridge – recovered, turning to face her. It's left cheek had crumpled inward, but as she watched, it glowed bright red as the Fallen Blood within it surged to the wound. And before her eyes, that wound closed, healing rapidly.

Damn.

She gripped her mace, having managed to hold on to it only by virtue of Vita's Boundless Strength. Every breath sent stabbing pain through her left ribs, and she knew they were broken.

The Zhimera hissed, moving toward her more cautiously now. Which implied a kind of intelligence she'd never seen in a zombie before.

She sidestepped her way toward the center of the sky bridge, acutely aware of the consequences if she fell off. Then she changed her mind, edging toward the leftmost edge instead. This thing was clearly capable of healing rapidly – even more rapidly than she could, at least with Vita's Dribbling Rejuvenation. Only Laying on Hands would heal her more quickly...and if she did that, she wouldn't be able to use Vita's magic until she got some sleep.

The creature *hissed* again...and then it charged!

Destiny planted her feet wide, staying right where she was...and then threw herself to the right – away from the ledge – whilst swinging her mace at its face again. But the creature blocked the blow with one left arm...and then grabbed her with its second left hand...

...taking her right off the edge of the sky bridge with it.

Destiny cursed, grabbing the thing's arm with her free hand, then swinging her legs up to wrap them around its forearm, even as they both plummeted off the street toward the glowing red water far below.

Damn it!

Her gut flip-flopped as she fell...and then did it again as she swung *under* the street. For the Zhimera had grabbed onto the edge of the street with its four feet, which she realized were actually hands attached to its ankles.

It held her then, dangling over the edge of the sky bridge, its horrid glowing eyes boring into hers. It tried to shake her off, but she held on tight, hanging upside-down and glaring right back at the thing.

Then it grabbed Destiny by the hair with its other left arm, yanking backward. *Hard.*

Destiny grit her teeth against the sudden pain, tears blurring her vision. But she held on tight.

Go on, she told it. *Tear my goddamn hair off.*

Then it let go, and grabbed the arm Destiny was hanging on instead...and yanked on that instead. The shoulder popped out of joint with a sickening *thunk*, the skin there going taut as the Zhimera continued to pull.

It's trying to rip its own arm off!

Destiny cursed, doing a sit-up and grabbing onto the thing's arm, climbing up it as quickly as she could. The creature let out another awful *shriek*, an anguished sound that made her skin crawl. She ignored it, Vita's Boundless Strength allowing her to climb up the thing's unnaturally long arm with ease. Then she continued upward, reaching for the edge of the sky bridge...

...and the Zhimera let go of its grip on the bridge, plummeting toward the water far below.

Destiny kicked off the creature just as it let go, extending her hand for the edge...and just made it, hanging on as tightly as she could.

213

Below her, the Zhimera plummeted four stories to the water, giving one last ear-piercing *shriek*…and then vanished with a splash.

Destiny turned her gaze upward, adjusting her grip, then throwing her mace onto the sky bridge. Then she grabbed the edge with both hands, pulling herself up as well. She retrieved her mace, then wiped the sweat from her forehead, waiting for her heart to slow down.

Damn, she thought. *That was close.*

She glanced back over the edge, peering into the darkness, and could *feel* the Zhimera's presence far below. It was smarter than any zombie she'd met, which meant that the other Zhimeras probably were too. It would find its way back up to her if she stuck around long enough. And if it was *really* smart, it would bring some friends to the party.

She had no plans of being anywhere near here when it did.

Destiny turned back toward the center of the city, breaking out into a jog down the sky bridge…and then hear a voice shouting from somewhere behind and below her.

"Forward!" it cried.

A man's voice.

She slowed, then stopped, turning around. She heard rhythmic thumping then, following another voice.

"*Fuck fuck fuck!*" it cried.

"Fuck," she swore, sprinting back the way she'd come.

For it was Chaos's voice.

Chapter 39

When the enemy attacked, Chaos was the first to see it.

A great big *thing* rose up from the edge of the sky bridge to their left, what appeared to be a massive white pillar. But Chaos soon realized that it wasn't a pillar at all.

It was a *finger*.

More fingers appeared as the thing continue to rise, until a giant hand was revealed. A hand at least sixty feet wide, and twice as long. Or in this case, twice as tall.

It towered over them, and Chaos swore, backpedaling rapidly away from it…and nearly stumbled right off the opposite edge of the sky bridge in the process.

"Forward!" Templeton cried, charging down the sky bridge. Pravus joined him, and Chaos did the same. The massive hand's fingers curled downward, and it crawled onto the sky bridge like a horrible spider, even as they ran forward, leaving it behind.

Chaos glanced back, spotting something atop the hand. A zombie who appeared to be riding it.

"Oh *hell* no," he complained, breaking into an all-out sprint after the other two men, terror gripping him with its own awful hand.

The giant zombie hand skittered toward them, each finger-step it took making the whole sky bridge vibrate. And to Chaos's horror, it was much, *much* faster than they were.

Whump whump whump!

"Fuck fuck fuck!" Chaos swore, trying in vain to run even faster. But the hand gained on them quickly, closing the distance in mere seconds…and when Chaos glanced back again, he saw its massive index finger rising up directly above him, even as its other fingers kept it crawling.

Crap!

Chaos leapt to the left just as the index finger slammed down, smashing into the sky bridge so hard the stone cracked. A blow that would have instantly killed him, had he dodged a split-second

215

later. But even the shockwave from its impact sent him tumbling further to the left, toward the opposite edge of the sky bridge.

He corrected course, glancing back again...and realized that the giant hand hadn't slowed one bit. Instead, it loomed over them now, balancing on its thumb and pinky finger, its palm directly overhead.

"Oh sh..." he swore, just before the hand spread its fingers and thumbs wide, falling right toward them!

"To the perlicue!" Templeton cried, grabbing Chaos and veering to the right.

Then the hand *slammed* into the skybridge with an eardrum-splitting *BOOM*.

Chaos screamed, squeezing his eyes shut, and waited for the awful end. For the horrid sensation of ruptured organs and such to begin. And to look down at his body one last time, seeing a mangled mash of flesh with bones sticking horribly out of it.

But to his surprise, all he felt was a blast of air, and the sky bridge trembling beneath him.

He cracked an eye open, and found himself standing beside Templeton and King Pravus, utterly unharmed...in the space between the thumb and forefinger of the giant hand.

"Oh," he murmured, feeling enormously relieved. So much so that he relieved himself. And not at all subtly.

"Run!" Pravus urged, even as the hand began to rise around them. He promptly followed his own advice, and Templeton and Chaos followed behind him, each running as fast as they could. Which was far, far faster than Chaos could run. Seeing this, Templeton slowed, grabbing Chaos and giving him a piggy-back ride. Which was emasculating, but also appreciated.

"A bit wet," Templeton noted as he ran, nearly as fast as he'd been running before, which was impressive.

"Sorry," Chaos blurted out. And in that moment, he wanted to die of shame. A fate far preferrable than being squashed by a giant zombie hand, albeit with identical end results.

"Quite alright," Templeton reassured. "A natural part of the fight-or-flight response!" And such was the man's cheer and obvious goodwill that Chaos actually believed him.

They rushed forward at what Chaos would've assumed was superhuman speed, but when he glanced over his shoulder, he saw that the giant hand was even faster. For while they'd gained some distance from the thing on account of it standing back up, so to

216

speak, its rider quickly realized that they were still very much alive. A situation the rider was clearly determined to change.

"Incoming!" Chaos warned, even as the giant hand surged forward.

"We can't outrun it!" Pravus warned, skidding to a stop, then turning to face the monstrosity. "We must fight!"

"But my liege...!" Templeton protested. Still, he too skid to a stop, dropping Chaos to the ground, and Templeton re-unsheathed his weapon. Which Chaos couldn't do, because his shovel didn't have a sheath.

The giant hand rushed up to them, going sideways this time, like a giant crab. Which, given that it was a left hand, with its pinky closest to them, made it so that the next time it smashed them, they wouldn't be able to hide between the huge gap in its thumb and index finger.

"How shall we proceed, my king?" Templeton cried, the hand only thirty feet away now.

"Attack the rider!" Pravus answered. And then the hand was upon them!

It crawled right over them, so it was on top of them once again...but Pravus veered off to the leftmost edge of the sky bridge, where the tip of its pinky finger was. He leapt up onto it, which was damn impressive given the weight of his armor, then started climbing up it.

Which was great and all, but Templeton and Chaos were left directly under the massive thing's palm...and the hand spread its fingers wide, falling right toward them!

Chaos cried out, ducking down and holding his Omen-63 before him, and waited for the dark curtain of death to fall over him. The end. Ker-splat.

And waited. And...waited.

He opened his eyes, seeing the huge palm hovering inches above his head...and the silver head of his Omen-63 Tactical Shovel, embedded in said palm.

What the...

The hand jerked upward and backward, skittering away a bit, blood pouring out of a gash in its palm where the Omen-63 had penetrated it. Chaos stared at the shovel, then at Templeton, who was eyeing the shovel in wonder.

"Your shovel took the full force of that blow without bending," the man breathed. "What marvelous construction!"

217

"It's the Omen-63," Chaos explained. As if that explained everything.

"Look!" Templeton blurted out, gesturing at the hand. Or more specifically, at the pinky, which Pravus was charging up. The great big king unsheathed his great big greatsword, reaching the back of the great big hand and sprinting toward the glowing-eyed zombie rider perched there.

"Yes!" Chaos exclaimed, twirling his shovel so its silver head was facing down, then slamming it onto the sky bridge triumphantly.

But to his surprise, the silver head didn't *clang* off the stone, but rather sank into it. Like, all the way to the shaft.

What the...

Then, as he watched, the stone sank inward, as if sucking into the scoop of the shovel, forming a pit there.

Chaos jerked the shovel up, staring at the pit in the stone. And then gazed at his shovel in wonder.

"Ha!" King Pravus cried, reaching the rider at last.

But then the giant hand crouched down, so to speak...and then leapt straight up.

* * *

King Pravus cried out in triumph as he neared the giant hand's rider, winding up to perform an epic swing of his sword. To cut evil in twain, to save the day. But as it turned out, he was a bit premature, which was not usually a problem for him.

For the giant hand dropped beneath his feet, making him fall a few feet. And then it lurched upward violently, leaping high into the air!

Pravus cried out, slamming face-first into the back of the giant hand as it flew upward. Only by virtue of his deadlift-trained grip was he able to hold on to his sword. He got to his knees, plunging his blade into the back of the hand, then held on to his hilt for dear life. Just in time, for the hand reached the apex of its leap, then plummeted down.

It landed on the sky bridge, a ways away from Templeton and Chaos, thank goodness, the impact nearly throwing Pravus off.

"Ha!" he cried in triumph.

And then its fingers curled into a fist, and it executed a forward roll. One that was guaranteed to execute him.

Chaos watched in horror as the giant hand curled its fingers into a fist, then rolled forward toward them, Pravus still atop it.

"Hang off the side!" Templeton cried, grabbing Chaos's arm and yanking him toward the edge of the sky bridge. He dropped to a slide, right off the edge...and grabbed the edge with one hand.

Chaos, on the other hand, went right off the edge, falling toward the inky black water below!

But before he even had the chance to scream, his fall was halted abruptly. For Templeton clung to his arm, whilst hanging off the ledge...and the giant hand rolled by them.

"Up you go," Templeton stated, somehow managing to lift Chaos – with one arm! – all the way up to the ledge. Chaos grabbed it, setting his shovel atop it, then pulled himself all the way up. Templeton did the same, and they both glanced at the hand, which had rolled a good hundred feet away. But Chaos couldn't help notice that, while Pravus's sword was still embedded in the back of the hand, that Pravus wasn't there.

"Sire!" he heard Templeton gasp. Chaos turned, then spotted a purple-pink platemail-armored body lying motionless on the skybridge nearby.

Templeton rushed up to Pravus's side, kneeling before him, and Chaos did the same.

"My liege! Say something!"

Pravus opened his eyes, then gave a pained smile.

"I   yet...live,   sweet   Templeton,"   he   gasped. "My...armor...saved me."

Templeton broke out in an enormously relieved smile.

"I daresay a less hefty set would have been the death of you," he replied, tears brimming in his eyes at the thought.

"Just...so," Pravus replied. He grimaced, trying to get up, then screamed.

"What is it?" Templeton asked.

"Nnghhh, my back!" Pravus cried. He grit his teeth. "I...can't feel my legs!"

"We have to get you out of here," Templeton declared.

Which would have been a prudent plan, had it been possible. Which it wasn't, because the giant hand, having recovered from its roll, was in the process of rolling back toward them.

"Run!" Chaos cried, but it was too late. For the hand was already upon them.

Chapter 40

Chaos screamed as the hand rolled over them, dropping his shovel and covering his face with his hands.

But then, instead of the darkness of oblivion, he saw a flash of pure golden light.

He heard a WHUMP, then lowered his hands...and saw himself, Templeton, and Pravus surrounded by a glowing golden dome...and the giant hand flying backward with incredible speed, landing upside-down on the sky bridge over a hundred feet away.

Chaos stared at this sight in wonder, then turned, seeing something wonderful indeed: none other than Destiny, clad in her golden shirt and pants, mace in hand, her eyes glowing with a bright gold light.

The light faded, and with it, the dome that'd shielded them, and Destiny turned to gaze at Chaos. Disapprovingly, which at the moment, he was perfectly fine with.

"Hey," he greeted.

"Idiot," she replied. Which was rude, but accurate. "Why did you come back?"

"I...wanted to help you," he told her.

"Mission failed," she replied. He grimaced.

"I was worried about you," he argued. This caused her expression to soften, and she sighed, eyeing his armor.

"Not bad," she conceded. "You chose well." Then she frowned, eyeing the shovel on the ground nearby. "Is that...an Omen-63?" she asked.

"Um...yes," he replied, retrieving it.

"You bought that?" she pressed.

"Yes?"

"Do you have any money left?" she demanded. "That was supposed to last you six months! Including rent!"

"I...uh..." he stammered. "Oh."

"Huurrghhh!" a most manly groan interjected. They both turned, seeing Pravus still lying on the ground, Templeton kneeling over him.

"Who are these guys?" Destiny asked, striding up to them.

"King Pravus and Lord Templeton," Chaos answered. "They're with me."

"My liege is hurt," Templeton stated. "Is it within your power to heal him?"

There was a whump from behind, and Destiny turned. In the distance, the giant hand had rolled back onto its fingers...and its rider, though considerably squished, its body all mushy and bloodied, began to heal before their eyes. Its wounds glowed with the power of the Fallen Blood, mending rapidly...until the rider was once again sitting up, glaring down at them.

"Hold on," Destiny grumbled, striding toward the hand. "Stay here," she added when Templeton started to stand to aid her. Chaos, on the other hand, hadn't made a move to do so, and was only too happy to comply.

They watched as Destiny strode toward the hand, even as the hand skittered toward her. It picked up pace, charging at her at full speed. But instead of running away like a reasonable person would, Destiny sprinted toward it instead. And then wound up, chucking her mace at it with all her might, undoubtedly aided by Vita's Boundless Strength.

The mace hurtled at the hand, spinning 'round and 'round...and then smashed right into the undead rider's head.

Which exploded.

The giant hand went instantly flaccid, falling and tripping over its own giant fingers, and skid to a stop. Inches from where Destiny stood.

Chaos gawked at her, then turned to Templeton, who was also gawking. Destiny turned to them, ignoring their gawks, and strode up to Pravus, kneeling before him.

"Well done!" Templeton declared with gusto.

"Shut up," Destiny replied. Templeton blinked. "You'll wake the dead."

"Ah," Templeton replied. "You must be Destiny," he guessed, whispering this time.

"Yep," Destiny replied. She closed her eyes then, touching Pravus's cheek. "He's lost blood to the Fallen Sky," she noted.

"Can you help him?" Templeton asked. Quietly.

"Yes," she answered. And then a warm golden glow perfused her, spreading down her hand to Pravus's cheek. It flowed over Pravus, and then Chaos saw something descending toward them. A ray of golden light coming from the center of the Fallen Sky, to alight on Pravus's cheek. The king gasped, his eyes going wide...and then it was done. Before Chaos's eyes, the wound on Pravus's cheek mended shut.

"Urrghhh!" Pravus groaned. "Grrrmmfff! It stings!"

"His back is broken," Destiny revealed. "His nerves will heal, but slowly."

"Did you use Lay on Hands?" Chaos asked. Destiny gave him a look.

"Vita's Dribbling Rejuvenation," she corrected. "If I use Lay on Hands, I can't use magic again, remember?"

"Oh," Chaos mumbled. "Right." He paused. "Thanks for saving us."

"Yes, thank you again," Templeton whispered.

"You're welcome," Destiny replied.

"We should get moving," Destiny advised. "With all the noise you made, we're going to have lots of company soon."

"I'll carry you, my liege," Templeton offered.

"Thank you Templeton," Pravus gasped. "If I cry out in pain, ignore me!"

"Only with great difficulty, cousin!" Templeton replied.

"Shh!" Destiny scolded.

Templeton grabbed Pravus, and despite the man's considerable weight – and the incredible weight of his ridiculously heavy armor – Templeton did pick him up, carrying him across his back.

"Excellent...form," Pravus gasped.

"I learned from the best," Templeton whispered, with a smile.

Destiny stared at them, then rubbed her face wearily, then sighed.

"Alright," she grumbled. "Let's go." And with that, she turned, continuing down the sky bridge toward the giant hand. Which, without its rider, was dead instead of un-dead.

"Wait, the way out is this way," Chaos protested, gesturing in the opposite direction.

"We're not going out," Destiny replied. "We're finishing this."

"Wait, what?"

"We're going to the top of the city," she explained. "To end the curse of Old Langsroth once and for all."

"But Pravus," he protested, gesturing at the fallen king.

"He'll be fully healed by the time we reach the Temple of Old Langsroth," she reassured.

"The what?" Chaos pressed.

"The temple where the Elders of Langsroth lived," Destiny explained. "The ones who rejected the wizard who came back to curse them."

"A fitting place to start the curse," Templeton noted.

"I think it's where the curse *is*," Destiny explained. "Vita thinks the curse began with a single man, someone whose body was sacrificed to hold it."

"So the Fallen Sky isn't where the curse is?" Chaos asked.

"Nope," Destiny replied. "The Fallen Sky is *caused* by the curse, not the source of it."

"Oh."

"So if we destroy the source, it'll end the curse," Pravus reasoned. "Let's *do* it."

"Fine," Destiny replied, climbing up the giant hand to retrieve Pravus's sword, then leaping off and handing it to Templeton. That done, she strode down the sky bridge toward the center of the city. "Just do yourselves a favor," she added.

"Like what?" Chaos asked.

"Quit making so much frickin' noise," she replied...just as a zombie lunged at her from a doorway of a building to her right. She swung her mace backhand-style, smashing it in the skull...and sent it hurtling back into the building it'd come from.

"Fucking *badass*," Chaos breathed. Then grimaced, realizing he'd sworn in front of adults.

"I have to agree," Templeton replied.

"Let's go," Destiny grumbled, striding down the sky bridge, without waiting to see if they were following. Which was also badass, like the way she walked, the way she fought, and just...well, everything about her.

Chaos found himself staring at her in a rather different way than he had in the past, as if a lever within his brain had been toggled to "on." It was the kind of stare that naturally locked on matters above and below. In this case, firmly in the "below" territory, as she was facing away from him.

God damn, he thought, feeling some kind of way.

"Try to keep up," Destiny prompted.

Which, at the moment, was the direction Chaos's…erm, lever…was firmly set to.

Chapter 41

King Pravus found the journey up each of the remaining levels of Old Langsroth a terribly painful affair, his shattered spine healing far more slowly than he would've preferred. A process that involved the very worst pins-and-needles sensation he'd ever felt...one that lasted nearly an hour. In addition, every step that sweet Templeton took whilst carrying him sent jolts of electric nerve-pain down his legs, and even his groin. Which he could feel again, thank the gods.

But on balance, he was healing, so the alternative would have been far worse. And it wasn't long before Pravus managed to change his relationship with his pain, seeing it not as something to avoid, but as a kind of resistance much like the weight he loved to lift. It was a trial, this pain, and in accepting it, he saw fit to endure it...and even to grow from it. For in the process of completing this most difficult of trials, he would become a better man for it.

So endure he did, until the pain was gone...which was, as it turned out, at about the same time as they reached a long set of stairs leading straight up from the eighth story skybridge of Old Langsroth to the Temple of Langsroth. A journey that had involved Destiny and Templeton and even Chaos helping to dispatch several zombies – and two abominations called Zhimeras – along the way.

"I am healed, Templeton," Pravus declared. "You may set me down."

"At once, my liege," Templeton replied, and did just that. Pravus found that he could stand on his own two legs again, and in that moment, he appreciated them more than he ever had. For to lose something was to understand its true value, not merely intellectually, but viscerally.

In this renewed spirit of gratitude for his body, Pravus followed the others up the long staircase leading up to the Temple of Langsroth, studying the building's design.

It was, Pravus found, a simply massive building, a giant stadium-like cylinder of sorts with what appeared to be an open, domed ceiling. It was supported by massive columns that he assumed went all the way down to the water far, far below. It was a bit difficult to be sure, even with lightning flashes illuminating the city at irregular intervals, for the water was a deep red color this close to the center of the Fallen Sky, and thus difficult to see through.

"Slow down," Destiny prompted, taking the stairs one at a time, her mace held at her side. "I sense something ahead," she added. "Something…powerful."

"You may need this, sire," Templeton stated, handing Pravus his greatsword. Pravus smiled, thankful that Templeton had carried it all this way.

"My thanks, cousin," he replied, carrying it before him.

They continued up the stairs, slowly per Destiny's command, and then she stopped.

"We need to prepare," she stated, turning to face the others. "I'll bless each of you with Vita's Dribbling Rejuvenation, and Boundless Strength."

"Boundless Strength?" Pravus inquired, raising an eyebrow.

"It makes you much stronger," Chaos explained. "I was able to lift the portcullis with it."

Both of Pravus's eyebrows went up then.

"By the gods," he exclaimed, but not too loudly. "Imagine what it would do for us, cousin!"

"Particularly for you, my liege," Templeton breathed, clearly in the midst of imagining it.

Destiny lowered her head in prayer, and soon each of them in turn was infused with her golden light. A light that, upon being touched by it, spread throughout Pravus's body. He felt a most curious sensation then, as if every muscle in his body were instantly rejuvenated, any sense of soreness gone. And what's more, his armor immediately felt far lighter, to the point that it almost felt as if it weren't even there.

"Why, my platemail feels as if it were made of cotton!" Pravus exclaimed.

"Shh!" Destiny scolded.

"Nay, not cotton, but clouds!" Pravus added, though a bit more hushed. He executed a practice swing with his sword. "And my sword might as well be yours," he told Templeton. "No offense of course."

"None taken," Templeton replied with a gorgeous smile. "I prefer a thrust to a swing."

As did Pravus, in the proper context. Or rather, in an improper context, considering the circumstances.

"Okay," Destiny declared when she was done. "Get ready," she warned. "Whatever's up there...it's the most powerful undead I've ever felt."

"Then it is our sacred duty to defeat it," Pravus declared resolutely.

"Our destiny, per the great Imperius Fanning!" Templeton agreed grandly, albeit whilst whispering.

Destiny stared at both of them, then shook her head slowly. Almost certainly out of amazement at their heroic gusto, at least from Pravus's point of view.

Then they all ascended, one heroic step at a time, each step bringing them closer to their shared destiny. To defeat a great evil, and restore peace to the land...why, it made Pravus's heart soar just to imagine it! He glanced at Templeton, seeing the man smiling radiantly, his face practically aglow. For his cousin was surely experiencing the same elation, and anticipation for the heroic deeds to come.

Then, at long last, they made their final step in their ascension, and came to the wide stone landing before the entrance of the Temple of Langsroth!

* * *

Chaos mounted the last of the steps leading to the entrance to the Temple of Langsroth, the shaft of his Omen-63 slippery in his sweaty grip. For while King Pravus and Templeton were inexplicably eager to meet and battle a great evil, Chaos was anything but. But on balance, he kept moving forward toward said evil, cowardly as he felt. Which was perhaps an even greater show of bravery than that which Pravus and Templeton displayed, though Chaos didn't see it that way.

In any case, he found himself standing next to Destiny at the top of the stairs, gazing at a stone landing stretching out before them some fifty feet long and twice as wide. Ahead was the wide, arched entrance to the Temple of Langsroth, a circular, domed building over a hundred feet tall and easily two hundred feet in diameter. It was easily the largest and most ornate building in the city, which was certainly saying something.

But between Chaos and his destination stood a man blocking their way. An exceedingly pale man dressed in a crimson cloak, with long white hair and a long white beard. He gazed at them with eyes that glowed with an intense crimson light, casting the area around him in an unholy glow. And his cloak, Chaos soon realized, was not fashioned of fabric, but of constantly flowing blood. Blood that glowed with a fainter red hue than his eyes, but gave off light nonetheless.

Destiny continued forward, inexplicably, then stopped some twenty feet from this man. Who was, of course, obviously a zombie. Chaos hesitated, then stopped a few feet behind her and to her right, while Pravus and Templeton stood in solidarity to her left. Which made Chaos grimace, then take a few steps forward to do the same. Reluctantly.

"Welcome," the zombie-man greeted, his deep voice booming across the city. Which made Destiny grimace, particularly after spending the last hour or so telling Pravus and Templeton to shush.

"It speaks" Destiny observed.

"It does," the man replied coolly.

"It dies," she decided.

"It died," he corrected calmly. Destiny eyed him, holding her mace in a threatening manner.

"And you are?" she inquired.

"I am the Vessel for the Fallen Sky," he revealed. "The body of the man who sacrificed his own flesh and cursed this land." He paused. "You can call me Fallen."

"Just who I was looking for," Destiny replied. "Time to die."

"I died long ago," Fallen retorted. "When I sacrificed this body as the Vessel for the Fallen Sky."

"Time to die again," Destiny corrected. "Permanently."

Fallen regarded her with disdain.

"As long as the Fallen Blood fills my veins, I shall continue in my current form," he declared. "You cannot destroy me, girl."

"I am Destiny, paladin of Vita," Destiny shot back. "By her grace, I can...and will."

Fallen scoffed, crossing his arms over his blood-cloaked chest.

"Even Vita's power is no match for the curse of the Fallen Sky," he argued. "Generation after generation of her paladins have tried and failed."

"I brought friends," Destiny shot back. Which was a badass line, Chaos had to admit. Fallen turned his gaze upon him, and Pravus and Templeton. A gaze that made Chaos's skin crawl.

"Did you bring them to make defeating me more challenging for you?" Fallen shot back.

"Disparage us all you want, vile creature," King Pravus piped in valiantly. "We fight best not with our tongues, but our swords!"

"And…shovels?" Fallen added, gesturing at Chaos's weapon. Chaos blushed, pulling it close to his chest.

"Enough chatter!" Pravus declared. "Have at you!"

"Now now," Fallen retorted, holding up a hand. "Why on earth do you wish to defeat me?"

"You're evil," Pravus argued. As if that should've been obvious. Which to be fair, it really was.

"I am a Vessel for the Fallen Sky," Fallen countered. "I am not evil or good, merely a continuous, self-perpetuating process."

"A process that you yourself called a curse," Destiny argued.

"A curse is perpetual desire for what one wants but can never have," Fallen replied. "Or a hopeless desire to get rid of something one already has."

"Millions of Langsroth's citizens suffer under the Fallen Sky," Destiny pointed out. "They're soulless creatures, mindless roaming the city, desperate for your tainted blood."

"No more so than the living crave food and drink and sex," Fallen reasoned. "Appetites that, once sated, only satisfy briefly, before needed to be fulfilled again…and again, and again."

"That's life," Destiny shot back.

"That's un-life as well," Fallen argued. "Merely a different manifestation of the same pattern…one your goddess finds disturbing because it isn't her preferred manifestation."

"These people never asked for this," Destiny stated, gesturing at the city at large.

"And they never asked to be born," Fallen replied evenly. "We are as much victims of life as we are of un-life, are we not?"

"I am not a victim."

"Yet you suffer," Fallen pointed out. "All life is suffering, with moments of joy interspersed. Much as a 'zombie' – as you call them – experiences bliss when imbibing of the Fallen Blood."

"It's different and you know it," Destiny countered.

Fallen eyed Destiny with those unnerving, glowing red eyes, then sighed.

"Do you want to know why your goddess really hates us?" he inquired.

"I already know," she replied.

"I don't think you do," he corrected. "You see, Vita believes that souls should be selfish," he stated. "Every body is given one soul, and when that soul dies, it goes away."

"As it should be."

"But here, under the Fallen Sky, we share our souls," Fallen continued, gesturing up at the spiraling vortex high above. "They rise with the blood, mingling in the sky, then rain down to nourish the bodies those souls once inhabited. Not for a meager lifetime, but forever." He smiled, lowering his arms to his sides. "As rain falls from the heavens to nourish the earth, the blood falls to nourish the undead. And we all share in the souls of millions, as one great community."

"A community of mindless walking corpses!" Destiny spat. Fallen raised his eyebrows.

"My my, but that is mighty presumptuous," he scolded. "And rude."

"Rude?"

"That you judge a being's existence based on the degree of its intelligence," he explained. "Are not most of the lives that Vita cherishes unintelligent? Do you converse with grass, and fungus, and beetles?"

Destiny didn't answer, which was answer enough.

"Do you cast aside or destroy people who are simple?" he continued. "Is a person's worth commiserate with the complexity of their thoughts?"

"You're twisting my words," Destiny accused.

"Vita's way is wasteful," Fallen insisted. "A single soul for a single being, and when it dies, the soul goes away, never to live a life again!" He glared at her. "My creator offered a different way. A way for souls to experience life after life for eternity!"

"In a flooded, moldy city with blood raining from the sky, never to love or laugh or truly live again," Destiny shot back. "I'm done arguing with you," she added. "And I won't let you corrupt me with your twisted lies."

231

"I have not uttered a single lie," Fallen countered. "You merely can't tolerate the truth…because it goes against what you've been brainwashed to believe."

Destiny glared at him.

"You know what I believe?" she asked, pointing at him with her free hand. "You're undead. I kill undead. I kill you."

"How sophisticated," Fallen replied calmly. "When you die, you'll fit right in with the lesser undead."

"Attack!" Destiny cried, breaking out into a charge at Fallen, her mace held high. King Pravus and Templeton joined the charge without hesitation, and Chaos waited a bit, then charged behind them, quite halfheartedly.

But before they could reach Fallen, the rear of his blood cloak shot backward as a thin tendril…and then a massive disembodied right hand lunged through the wide arched entrance to the Temple of Langsroth, grabbing the man.

Then it pulled him backward, right through the entrance and into the temple, the temple double-doors slamming shut behind him…leaving everyone else standing there, weapons at the ready, with no one to attack.

"Well crap," Destiny blurted out.

Chapter 42

Chaos stood next to Destiny, Pravus and Templeton on her other side, all of them staring at the closed double doors that Fallen had been pulled through. Chaos glanced at Destiny, who looked none-too-pleased.

"So...what now?" he asked.

"We open those goddamn doors," she answered, striding toward them. Chaos hesitated.

"Shouldn't we, uh, have a plan first?" he pressed.

"Like what?" she shot back, not turning around. And continuing to walk toward the doors, a bit rudely.

"Well, we don't know what that guy is capable of," he reasoned.

"An excellent point," Templeton concurred. "We know little of his capabilities."

Destiny spun around, glaring at them.

"First of all, that thing is not a 'he,'" she argued. "It's a zombie. A collection of spirits that are trapped in the living world millennia after they should be, animating an evil wizard's corpse."

"Granted," Templeton stated. "But it is sentient."

"Because it's the Fallen Sky," Destiny replied. "That thing is just the sack of dead flesh the Fallen Sky is perpetuated by. Its heart, so to speak."

"I have no issue with destroying it," Templeton stated. "I merely believe it is reasonable to prepare properly in order to maximize our chances of doing so."

Which was awfully reasonable, of course. Destiny paused, then sighed.

"Of course," she agreed. "Sorry...he just...pissed me off, that's all."

"He attempted to diminish the goddess you cherish," Templeton stated. "I would feel the same if someone were to insult my king."

"Consider me touched, sweet Templeton!" King Pravus proclaimed, putting a hand to his heart.

Destiny gave Pravus a look that made it clear that she thought *he* was touched.

"So what's the plan?" Chaos asked.

"We can't know the full extent of his powers," Destiny reasoned. "But we can guess based on what we've seen."

"Which is that he can use the Fallen Blood to control zombie body parts, including that giant hand," Pravus replied.

"And heal like the zombie rider of that other giant hand," Destiny added.

"Unless you explode their head," Chaos piped in.

"Right," Destiny agreed.

"So we need to destroy his head to kill him," Templeton reasoned. "And presumably, by destroying the source of the Fallen Sky, it will end the curse."

"But first we have to open those big-ass doors," Destiny stated. "Even with Vita's Boundless Strength, I don't think I can do it."

"I'm willing to give it a go," King Pravus offered. Destiny gave him a doubting look.

"You may be strong, but those doors are huge," she pointed out. Templeton gave her a wry smile, walking up and patting her on the shoulder.

"It may not be obvious with his armor on, for it hides his physique," he told her, "...but if there is any man alive who can open those doors by virtue of his might, it is my liege."

"Well said Templeton," Pravus replied. "And I appreciate your confidence in me!"

With that, Pravus strode up to the double doors, then tore off his gauntlets, handing them to Templeton. Then he slid his finger through the small gap between the doors, curling his fingers around the rightmost one.

"Remember to breathe, sire!" Templeton called out helpfully.

Pravus paused, taking a deep breath in, and planting his feet wide. Then he scowled ferociously, his eyes locked on his hands...and *pulled*.

The door swung open rapidly, so much so that it flung all the way open, banging into the wall, then bounced back a bit.

"Oh," Pravus mumbled. "That was far easier than I expected." While looking rather put out that it'd been so easy.

234

"Bit of a let-down," Templeton admitted, scratching his head. "Those must be excellent hinges."

"Especially after millennia of disrepair," Pravus declared.

"Well done, long-dead builders, I suppose," Templeton congratulated.

"Well then," Pravus mumbled. He gestured past the half-open doorway. "Shall we?"

Destiny glanced at Chaos.

"You ready?" she asked. Which was considerate.

"No," he admitted. But then he smiled. "But I'm gonna follow my Destiny, even if it kills me."

She smiled back.

"It just might," she warned.

"Well, if I'm going to die," he replied, "...I'd rather do it at your side." Which was a fucking *awesome* line. She smirked.

"Tell you what," she stated. "We make it out of here alive, and I'll make it worth your while."

"Oh yeah? How?" he asked.

"Be a shame if you died and never found out," she replied with a wink.

Then she turned to Pravus, inclining her head.

"Let's *do* this," she prompted...and strode through the doorway into the Temple of Langsroth.

* * *

The interior of the Temple of Langsroth was massive, seemingly even more so than its exterior had implied. Composed of a single, circular room, it had white walls rising to meet a partially-domed white ceiling, one that was mostly open to the sky. A fact that allowed a continuous stream of Fallen Blood to rain down into the center of the Temple...which explained the knee-deep pool of blood covering the floor. Blood that glowed far brighter than the blood nine stories below.

But this was not where Chaos found his gaze drawn. Rather, it was to the center of the massive chamber. For there, resting on a massive, severed stump of a neck, was a truly enormous human head.

Or rather, it was the bottom half of a head, with its skull missing above its eyes, its brain removed. Atop its flat, empty cranium stood none other than Fallen, his legs having fused with the base of the giants skull, which was filled with a pool of blood.

But that wasn't all.

For upon the giant head's flesh were innumerable human limbs, arms and legs grafted on it all the way around. And attached to the giant's right temple was a limb composed of fused-together arms and legs, which was twenty feet in diameter and a hundred feet long. And at the end of this was a giant right hand, of all things. The same hand that'd plucked Fallen from where he'd stood earlier, bringing him back into the temple.

"Oh," Templeton blurted out as soon as this sight was seen.

"Fuuuuuuck," Chaos added, appropriately.

"Focus," Destiny snapped, readying her mace.

"Welcome to the place where it all began," Fallen declared, his voice booming throughout the chamber. "Bear witness to the very source of the Fallen Sky!"

"Fuck," Chaos repeated.

"Stand firm, my friends!" Pravus urged, wielding his greatsword mightily. "We must remain brave in the face of danger!"

"Well said, my liege!" Templeton replied, assuming an equally mighty stance. "Prepare to be cleaved in twain by the blades of justice!"

"Heroic ejaculations will not save the day," Fallen replied, using an unfortunate term for an abrupt, exclamatory utterance. One that Chaos only knew by virtue of his mother's predilection for dictionary reading. "Prepare to donate your sorry souls to the Fallen Sky."

"Our ejaculations are merely a prelude to victory!" Pravus countered valiantly.

"Indeed!" Templeton concurred. "And might I add my own ejaculation to this heroic chorus!"

"You most certainly may!" Pravus exclaimed.

"What the fuck?" Destiny inquired, staring at the two men.

"Attack!" Pravus cried, rushing at the giant head.

"Idiots!" Destiny blurted out, forced to join the two in their charge. Chaos hesitated, then joined them, not wanting to be singled out. Even though his brain screamed to him that charging blindly into battle with a giant zombie head was a terrible idea, and that a more measured approach would've been far preferable. For in the end, it was human nature to follow the crowd rather than go one's own way. Even when the crowd was rushing to their tragic, untimely deaths, unfortunately.

Fallen smirked, folding his arms over his chest...and then the giant head's giant hand swung at them in a sweeping slap!

"Ha!" Pravus cried, being the nearest to the hand. He dropped to slide on his side in the pool of blood, slipping under the giant hand. Templeton did the same, while Destiny backpedaled out of range...and Chaos, luckily, having delayed his charge, was nowhere near the attack.

The giant hand slowed, then stopped...and promptly swung the opposite way, in a vicious backhand. But this time, it slid on the floor without a gap to slide under...and thus sent a wave of blood crashing toward them!

This wave struck Pravus and Templeton before the back of the hand could, softening the blow considerably...but carried them halfway across the room, sending them tumbling as the wave crashed in a foamy hiss. A bit of the wave reached Chaos, lapping at his knees, and he stumbled backward, thankfully managing to keep his balance.

Destiny had managed to keep out of range of the giant hand's second attack, and went to stand at Chaos's side.

"Re-glarb-group!" Pravus gasped, non-consensually swallowing some Fallen Blood in the process of scrambling to his feet. He and Templeton made their way toward the rightmost wall of the room, eyeing the giant hand nearby warily.

"You cannot win," Fallen declared, his voice booming across the temple.

"Succeed or fail, the glory is in the attempt!" Pravus shot back.

"Just so, sire!" Templeton concurred.

"Those two are going to get us killed," Destiny grumbled.

"What do we do?" Chaos asked.

"What would *you* do?" she shot back. Chaos paused, eyeing Fallen.

"Take out the brain and the body dies," he replied.

"Exactly."

"But Fallen's all the way up there," Chaos said, gesturing at the man. Who, being on top of the giant's mangled half-head, was still over a hundred feet up. "How are we gonna get up there?"

"Good question," Destiny replied.

The giant's hand curled into a fist, then lifted up on its arm made of countless zombie-limbs, moving until it was directly above Pravus and Templeton.

Then it slammed down upon them.

"No!" Chaos cried, rushing forward. Destiny did as well, cursing as she did so. But to Chaos's amazement, the giant hand seemed to have stopped a good six or so feet above the flooded floor. And there, standing with their arms raised overhead, holding the giant hand at bay, was none other than Pravus and Templeton, completely unharmed!

"Marvelous military press, sire!" Templeton exclaimed.

"Ngghh...thank you, Templeton!" Pravus grunt-replied. "It'll take more than a fisting to fell me, vile Fallen!" he added. And then bent his knees, squatting low...and then sprung upward to throw the hand aside.

Chaos slowed, as did Destiny, and they both stared at Pravus in awe.

"Wow," Destiny breathed. "He shouldn't have been able to do that."

"Even with Vita's Boundless Strength?" Chaos asked.

"Not unless he's incredibly strong," she answered. "It multiplies existing strength, so the stronger you are, the more it increases it."

Fallen stared at Pravus and Templeton, clearly surprised.

"Interesting," he stated, even as Pravus retrieved the greatsword he'd dropped into the pool, for the purposes of military pressing the fist. "This may be more entertaining than I thought."

"This is merely our warm-up!" Pravus shot back valiantly. "Have at you, villain!"

He and Templeton charged at the giant hand, or rather, the "arm" of countless fused limbs that attached it to the giant head. Pravus reached it first, near the "wrist" so to speak, and executed a vicious overhead chop, cutting a five-foot-deep gash into the thing. Blood spurted from the ends of the severed zombie limbs, spilling into the pool below.

"Ha!" Pravus cried, chopping again, then again, carving chunks out of the composite limb.

Fallen jerked the hand away from Pravus, hugging it close to the giant head. Then, as Chaos watched, the intact limbs that made up the "arm" around the severed sections detached from the wrist, using countless hands to grip the severed ends of their brethren and pull them together. Then Fallen rotated the hand so the damaged wrist was plunged into the pool of blood...and a moment later, lifted it back up to reveal that the damage had been completely healed!

"Oh crap," Chaos blurted out.

"He's going to keep doing that," Destiny warned. "We have to stop him from being able to heal!"

Chaos eyed the pool of blood, thinking back to the Great Flat. The only way to get rid of the pool – and thus Fallen's ability to heal – was to drain it. But that meant giving the blood a place to go. Unfortunately, the pool was already in the lowest portion of the room...and was continually fed by the Fallen Blood raining from the sky. Which meant, of course, that there had to be some way of draining it, otherwise the pool would've been higher.

Chaos wracked his brain for a solution...and then his eyes widened.

"When there's a problem, the answer is the Omen-63," he recited. Destiny blinked.

"What?"

"Cover me!" he commanded, turning his shovel around so it was aimed head-down. He thrust it through the blood-pool into the stone below, and sure enough, the silver shovel-head sank through the stone like a hot knife through butter. He scooped up the stone, picking the shovel up...and saw it was only holding a pool of blood. The stone, as before, had inexplicably vanished. He thrust his shovel down again and again, deepening the hole, until it was so deep he had to widen it to keep going. All while Pravus and Templeton conveniently kept Fallen's attention diverted, though that wasn't exactly their intention.

* * *

King Pravus stood at Templeton's side, eyeing the now-healed wrist of the giant head's giant arm.

"Heal all you want," Pravus told Fallen from his lofty perch atop the giant's head. "I can do this all day!"

"And I'll heal as fast as you cut," Fallen retorted haughtily. Templeton cleared his throat, and Pravus glanced at his gorgeous cousin, all wet and slippery and shiny with the Fallen Blood.

"Perhaps a bit of the old high-intensity interval training would fare better against our foe," Templeton suggested, giving Pravus a roguish smile. Pravus smiled back.

"Why, I think you're right," Pravus replied. "Shall we?"

"We shall!" Templeton replied with gusto. For when it came to derring-do, his dear cousin was filled to the gills with it, so to speak.

"Begin!" Pravus prompted, charging not at the giant hand or arm, but at the stump of a neck holding up the giant head. For while the giant's hand and arm could be easily maneuvered, and thus plunged into the healing blood, the neck was not so easily moved.

Fallen swung the hand at them again, and Pravus leapt forward, sheathing his sword in mid-air. Had he skipped leg day like so many unfortunate men did, he surely would've died of the coming slap. But such was the newfound strength of his already exquisitely developed quads and buttocks – and his bulging calves, stimulated six days a week, and no less – that he found himself launched so rapidly forward and upward that the hand missed him completely. He landed atop the thing's arm instead as it swung by, and unsheathed his sword, plunging it down into the pale flesh, holding on for dear life.

To Pravus's relief, Templeton landed behind him, then ran up, wrapping his arms around Pravus from behind and spooning him tightly. And oh! If only he hadn't been so distracted by being violently swung to the right atop a composite zombie arm, how Pravus would've cherished this moment!

"A false start, my liege!" Templeton cried as the arm finished its swing. "On your count?"

"One...two...three!" Pravus exclaimed, finishing right as the arm came to a halt. And then he tore his sword free, rushing up the arm as fast as he could, then leaping off toward the front of the giant's neck!

* * *

"Keep going," Destiny urged, standing in front of Chaos as he continued to dig through the floor, so as to hide him from Fallen's view. A futile attempt, given how high Fallen was perched, thus having a bird's-eye view. But it hardly mattered, given the spectacle

Pravus and Templeton were providing, a distraction of aristocratic proportions. Proportions as large as Pravus's, to be exact.

Chaos cursed, up to his waist in blood now, for he'd been forced to step into the rather wide hole he'd made. The floor of the Templeton was terribly thick, and he was starting to worry that he'd chosen a spot directly over a supporting column. But his fears were soon put to rest, for upon shoving his shovel down yet again, there was a sudden belch of air around him...and the pool of blood immediately began sinking.

Yes!

"Got it," he exclaimed, but not too loud.

"Good," Destiny replied. "Make another hole, so he can't just plug this with his hand."

"Right," Chaos stated. Because it was a *really* good plan. He moved to the left about fifty feet, then got to work again, all while Destiny stood in front to defend him. He heard gleeful repartee, evidence that Pravus and Templeton were still alive and fighting, and he couldn't help but smile at the strange duo. Though they sometimes displayed questionable judgement, there was no denying that they were quite possibly the bravest, most cheerfully valiant idiots Chaos had ever met. Who, when he glanced up from his work for a second, were busily hacking away at the front of the giant's neck.

Chaos continued his work, widening the hole he was making, then digging deeper...until he felt another *blurp* of air come up around him, and felt a sudden current pulling downward as his hole went all the way through the floor.

"Done!" he exclaimed, crawling out of the hole...just as Destiny cursed.

"Incoming!" she warned.

Chaos turned to face the center of the temple, and saw what the falling level of the blood pool had uncovered: hundreds of zombies, each connected to the base of the giant head's neck by what appeared to be fused-together lengths of intestine. Zombies that, when they stood, were revealed to have had their brains and the tops of their skulls removed. Which made perfect sense, considering that they were ultimately merely parts of the giant's body – and therefore Fallen's – and were controlled by Fallen's brain.

Which explained why the giant's brain had been removed, now that Chaos thought about it.

The zombie army turned to face Chaos and Destiny, then graarrrghed as a group, moving toward the two. Not slowly and pathetically like a proper zombie, but really *really* quickly.

"Oh *shit!*" Chaos swore, his heart leaping in his throat.

"Fight like your life depends on it!" Destiny cried, planting her feet wide, her mace at the ready. Chaos cursed, maintaining a good distance from her potential swing, readying his Omen-63.

Then the first of the zombies reached them, and one leapt at Chaos!

Chaos cursed, swinging the back of his shovel at the thing's head, connecting with a clang. It flew to the side…revealing another zombie right behind it. One that lunged at Chaos…who'd unfortunately overextended with his swing.

He backpedaled, swinging the shovel in the opposite direction…and saw a ball of white stone shoot out of the scoop of his shovel-head, smashing into the zombie's head and taking it right off.

"Holy!" he blurted out.

But more zombies were coming, another four converging on him. And Destiny couldn't very well help him, considering she was surrounded by plentiful enemies of her own.

You got this, he told himself, swinging his shovel again. This time not with the back of it, but using the front. Sure enough, another hunk of white stone flew out, slamming into one of the zombie's chests. Its rib cage caved it, and it flew backward, bowling over a few of its friends.

But ever-more came, far too many for him to take on. And in seconds, the wave of enemies overtook him!

* * *

King Pravus hacked away at the front of the giant's neck, his greatsword carving deep fissures in the pasty flesh. Blood spurted from the wounds, striking Pravus in the face, and spattering his pink-purple platemail in splotches of crimson. Pravus tolerated said assault with practiced ease, continuing to hack, even as Templeton did the same.

"Ha!" he exclaimed, his sword feeling as light as a feather as he swung it. Such that, despite having exercised his upper body for minutes straight at maximum effort, he still hadn't tired himself out. All thanks to Destiny's magic, no doubt.

Then he realized that something had changed, and looked down to see that the pool of blood he was standing in was receding. It revealed long, glistening tubes grafted to the giant's neck, which looked suspiciously like lengths of intestine.

Pravus grimaced at the sight, for while he found so much of human anatomy pleasing to the eye, the digestive tract was decidedly his least favorite. Save for the beginning and the end, of course, which he found quite delightful.

Then he paused in his exertions to follow a length of said intestine, finding it attached to the pale body of a previously-submerged zombie. In fact, there were *hundreds* of said zombies, all connected via undead digestion. To the giant's neck, which was exceedingly odd, and what's more, anatomically incorrect. Ish.

Then said zombies rose to their feet…and run toward Chaos and Destiny with shocking alacrity!

"Egads cousin!" Pravus exclaimed.

"I see them, sire!" Templeton stated. "Shall we endeavor to sever?"

"At once!" Pravus replied.

They got to work hacking at the intestines, which was most efficiently done close to where they connecting with the giant's neck. And upon cutting the cord, the zombie attached to it fell instantly, rendered as if dead. But when Pravus glanced Chaos and Destiny's way, he found far too many remained, and were rapidly closing in on the pair.

"Faster!" Pravus cried, doubling his efforts, Templeton doing the same. But as it turned out, it was too little, too late.

* * *

Chaos cried out as the horde of zombies closed in on him, the first wave leaping at him five at a time. He swung his Omen-63 as hard as he could, taking out two of them. But the others slammed into him, throwing him onto his back on the hard stone floor…and one of them crawled atop him, straddling his waist, and clawed at his face.

"Help!" Chaos shouted, grabbing the thing's wrists and shoving it back. But other hands grabbed his wrists, yanking them away and pinning them to the floor. He laid there, helpless, as the zombie astride him hissed…and then clawed at his face wildly.

He turned his head to the side, struggling against the hands that held him, feeling the awful creature's nails rake down the side of his face. A sudden, hot pain shot through his ear...and then, to his absolute horror, he felt it tear free from his head.

Chaos *shrieked*.

"Chaos!" he heard Destiny cry, and then his hearing went dull as blood filled his ear canal. He gasped in pain, feeling the horrid thing tearing at his scalp, clumps of hair and flesh ripping free.

In that moment, he had the sudden, mad urge to die. That his injuries had crossed a line.

Kill me, he pleaded silently. And it shocked him that going from desperately wanting to live to hoping to die could occur in the blink of an eye.

He heard the sound of metal scraping on stone, then looked straight up, seeing one of the zombies lifting something high in the air over him. A black-shafted shovel with a silver head.

It *hissed*, winding up...and then swung the Omen-63 in a vicious downward chop, embedding its edge into Chaos's skull.

Chapter 43

Destiny cursed as more and more zombies hurled themselves at her, no matter how many she felled with her mace. There were just too many of them, and she knew it.

We're not going to make it.

She closed her eyes, sending out a silent prayer...and felt Vita's warmth flow through her. A split second later, a dome of pure golden light expanded outward from her in all directions, slamming into the zombies and sending them flying.

The airborne zombies fell into their comrades, toppling over many in the process. But still the zombies came, surging over their fallen brethren as a mindless undead wave, coming right toward her.

"Help!" she heard Chaos shout from her left. She turned, seeing Chaos lying on his back on the floor, his arms and legs pinned to the ground by numerous zombies...while another zombie straddling him tore at his head with blood-covered fingers. Hunks of flesh and hair ripped off of Chaos's head, and Destiny felt a bolt of terror strike her.

"Chaos!" she cried, rushing to his aide...

...and then the giant zombie-hand smashed into her from behind, sending her flying over Chaos and the zombies, then tumbling to the floor.

Destiny gasped as her left hip *crunched* with the impact, pain shooting down her thigh and knee. She grit her teeth, and started closing her eyes in prayer to heal herself. But then she saw Chaos's shovel head gleaming silver above the heads of the zombies around Chaos, and realized that the zombie atop him was holding it.

Then she watched in horror as the zombie sent the shovel downward, striking Chaos right between the eyes.

"*No!*" she screamed, crawling toward him, her broken hip sending bursts of agony through her. She ignored the pain, screaming again as the zombie lifted the shovel up over its head to swing it again.

Then it went utterly limp, falling off of Chaos and dropping the shovel, which fell to the floor with a *clang*. And a moment later, all of the other zombies nearby went limp as well, falling to the floor in a heap.

Destiny turned her head, seeing Pravus and Templeton near the base of the giant's neck, hacking away at the lengths of intestine that connected the zombies to it.

Oh thank Vita, she thought, then grit her teeth, continuing her agonizing crawl up to Chaos. But as she reached his side, her heart sank.

"Oh no," she murmured. "No no no."

For Chaos lay on the floor, his eyes staring upward lifelessly, his left ear and the left side of his scalp missing, the flesh torn down to bone. And there, in the center of his forehead, was a horrible gash, one that'd penetrated through his skull and deep into his brain.

Blood welled up from the terrible wound, yellow-pink brain matter swelling and leaking from the gash.

"Oh Chaos," she mumbled, gritting her teeth. "You idiot."

She swallowed past a lump in her throat, hearing footsteps approach. It was Templeton, she realized.

"Are you...oh," the man blurted out, covering his mouth with his hand. "My deepest apologies," he stated. "We worked as fast as we could. I take full responsibility." He laid a hand on her shoulder then, in a hopeless attempt to console her.

Laid a hand.

Destiny glanced at the giant zombie-head, and Fallen standing atop it.

If you do this, you're done, she knew. There would be no more using Vita's grace, not for herself or anyone else.

Fuck it.

She closed her eyes, sending Vita one final prayer, and felt the goddess's warmth flow through her. She pressed both hands on Chaos's forehead then, feeling that warmth leave her. Golden light surged through Chaos, infusing every inch of his flesh. And before her eyes, his flesh knitted back together...until he was whole once again.

* * *

Chaos didn't know when the dream began.

One moment, existence didn't exist, and the next, he was lying in the grass by the shore of a great, sparkling lake. He heard laughter coming from nearby, and it made him smile. For he knew it was Fury, and as always, she'd discovered yet another reason to love her life.

He lay there, closing his eyes, feeling the sun baking his skin, the smell of grass and flowers delighting him. It was perfect here, in the dream. A place he never wanted to leave.

But then he felt himself shaking, his shoulders seizing of their own accord. He opened his eyes, and saw a great red eye appear in the middle of the bright blue sky, the eye of a demon gazing down at him.

"Rise," it commanded, and he resisted it instinctively. But somehow, of its own accord, his body did rise. Until he was sitting up, facing the lake. He saw Fury running up to him, and she sat before him, gazing at him in concern...

...and then her face *shifted*, and suddenly he was staring not at his sister, but at Destiny.

The lake faded away, replaced by a great big chamber whose floor was wet with blood. And all around him were the unmoving bodies of pale zombies...with a giant zombie-head rising over a hundred feet tall ahead.

"What...?" he blurted out, utterly confused.

"...dead," Destiny told him, shaking his shoulders. "Go!"

"What?" he repeated.

"We're dead," she repeated. "Get out of here. Now!"

He blinked, then turned forward...and spotted Templeton lying a few hundred feet to the left, his legs pinned beneath a giant hand. And directly ahead, King Pravus was trying to fight his way up to Templeton, carving his way through a literal army of zombies.

"*Templeton!*" Pravus screamed, beheading three zombies with a single swing of his blade. He charged through them, throwing them aside with his free arm, even as a train of zombies clung to his back, trying to bring him down.

And then Chaos's memories came rushing back to him, of everything that'd happened before now. Including the zombie cleaving his forehead in two with his own Omen-63.

247

"I said *go*," Destiny urged. Chaos got to his feet, feeling remarkably rested. As if he'd just had the best, most rejuvenating sleep of his life.

"Not without you," he countered. "And not without Templeton!"

"We're *dead*," she insisted, her tone cold. "Get out of here while you can, Chaos. Live your life."

"No," he protested. "I can't just leave you! He shook his head. "If I do that, I wouldn't be able to live with myself."

"Then we all die," she shot back.

And as Chaos watched, Pravus was taken down at last, and sank to his knees under the enormous weight of the zombies clinging to him. He roared, somehow managing to rise to his feet, but was taken down again.

"You cannot win," Fallen's voice boomed, the red-eyed zombie glaring down at them with arms crossed. "I warned you."

"He's right," Destiny muttered, tears welling up in her eyes. "I'm sorry I got you into this, Chaos."

"You didn't," he protested. "I came to help you, remember?"

"You were just following your destiny," she shot back.

"We can still fight!" he insisted. She gave a bitter laugh.

"What's the point?" she asked. "It would take a miracle to win now."

Chaos blinked, then turned to face Fallen and the giant head, even as Pravus rose to his feet a second time somehow. And in that moment, he knew that the king would do anything for Templeton. He would fight using every last bit of strength that he had, doing whatever it took to save the people he loved. Nothing would stop him until he was dead...and anything that tried to kill him would suffer greatly for it.

A miracle.

He took a deep breath in, then let it out, knowing what needed to be done. For the last nine years, he'd neglected himself, until the confidence he'd taken for granted as a toddler had been all but stripped away. By well-meaning parents, sure, but who'd done a disservice to him in the end. A love that'd ended up hugging him so tightly that it'd suffocated him.

Olivia's words came to him then, back before he'd opened the Gate to the magical kingdom of Pravus.

You'll need to face the dangers your father protected you from.

He lifted his gaze to the heaven's, to that bloody vortex in the sky.

Rediscover the magic that's been denied you.

Chaos broke out into a mischievous smile, a long-lost feeling coming over him. The complete, utter confidence that he was, in fact, a frickin' powerful-ass wizard, and everyone better watch the fuck out.

He focused on the Fallen Sky, then connected with the substance of the universe itself.

Surprise me, he told it.

And so it did.

He felt the universe *shift*, and a sudden wind tore at him. Then the bloody rain falling on them began to fly sideways instead…and then not down, but *up*. In a vortex that spiraled faster and faster, forming a giant cyclone that sucked everything upward…including the zombies atop Pravus, and every other zombie light enough to be carried upward. Chaos felt himself being pulled by the cyclone, and grabbed his Omen-63, shoving it into the floor and holding on tight.

"Hold on to it!" he urged Destiny, who did as she was told. She screamed as her legs lifted off the ground, gritting her teeth in pain.

"What did you do?!" Fallen cried, his voice rising over the howl of the wind.

"Without the rain and the pool, he's vulnerable," Chaos shouted over the storm. "We have to disconnect him from the giant's head and kill him!"

"Oh yeah?" Destiny shot back. "Who's gonna do that?"

And then they got their answer. Which was King Pravus, that's who.

* * *

Pravus cast off all the zombies clinging to him, but with the great weight of his armor and sword, not even the cyclone's power could lift him. And though every fiber of his being begged for him to go to sweet Templeton, he knew in his heart that he had to defeat Fallen first. So he tore his gaze away from his fallen cousin, fixing it on the creature atop the giant's head instead.

"FALLEN!" he bellowed, bending down into a squat, then leaping as high as he could.

With the power of Vita's Boundless Strength – and aided by the upward thrust of the cyclone – Pravus soared upward over a hundred feet, far above Fallen. Then he reached the apex of his flight, lifting his greatsword over his head, and fell right toward the vile enemy.

"No!" Fallen cried, tearing one foot free from the base of the giant's skull. And he was about to tear free the other when Pravus was upon him.

Pravus focused his energy, engaging his lats, posterior deltoids, and triceps in a singular symphony of muscular contractions. And with a great bellow, he brought his sword of justice upon Fallen's head, and verily did cleave the evil bastard in twain.

Pravus landed before Fallen, the impact shattering his ankles. He cried out in pain, but also triumph, watching as the two halves of Fallen fell to either side.

Then, far above, the Fallen Sky flashed with the brightest red light he'd ever seen…and the crimson faded, until the Fallen Sky was no more.

Chapter 44

Sunlight streamed down on the ancient city of Old Langsroth, its warm rays casting the white stone of the Temple of Langsroth in a gentle glow. And wherever it touched, the Fallen Blood dissolved. But instead of flying back up to the Fallen Sky, the blood vanished for good, the poor souls it'd trapped in this world freed at long last.

Chaos watched as the blood disappeared, unable to help smiling from ear to ear.

"Wow," he breathed, feeling practically giddy.

"Fuck," Destiny groaned, still lying on her side on the floor.

"What's wrong?" he asked, kneeling before her.

"Hip's broken," she told him. "It'll heal in a bit."

"But…you laid on hands, didn't you? I thought you couldn't use magic until you slept."

"Still have Vita's Dribbling Rejuvenation running," she reminded him. "Just like Pravus and Templeton."

"Sweet cousin, are you alright?" they heard Pravus cry from atop the giant's head.

"Down but not out!" Templeton replied with inexplicable cheer, though his legs were still being crushed by the giant hand.

"We are victorious!" Pravus declared, which was unnecessary because it was obvious.

"Well *done* sire!" Templeton replied. "A destiny fulfilled!"

"Only with your help!" Pravus shouted back. Which was a goddamn lie, because compared to Chaos and Destiny, Templeton hadn't done much of anything.

"Could use some help getting out from under this thing," Templeton confessed.

"I regret to say my ankles are currently broken," Pravus shouted down at him. "But they are healing gradually!"

"I fear you'll break them again on the way down," Templeton confessed.

"A worthwhile sacrifice, a temporary pain," Pravus declared. "A minor loss for a major gain!"

"He rhymed," Chaos noted, while Destiny shook her head at the two men. "Thought only wizards did that all the time."

"You just did," Destiny noted. He turned to smile at her.

"Told you I was a wizard."

"Never said you weren't," she replied. "Thanks for saving me, by the way."

"It's what heroes do," Chaos quipped. She rolled her eyes, which is exactly what he'd hoped for. "I'd better help Templeton," he stated, even as Pravus and Templeton continued to yell encouraging remarks at each other in the background. He walked up to Templeton, then used his Omen-63 to dig him out from under the giant hand. He dragged the man away a bit, then waited for him to heal. Which took quite a bit, unfortunately for Chaos and Destiny's ears.

But at length, the two men did heal, and Pravus climbed down the giant's head carefully, managing to make it to the floor unharmed. In the meantime, Chaos and Destiny strode to the open doorway leading out of the Temple of Langsroth.

Gazing out of the great arched entrance of the temple at the rest of the city, he witnessed every last trace of the Fallen Sky's curse vanish into thin air. What remained was a vast city no longer hidden in darkness, a stunning feat of ancient architecture, with nine stories of incredible sky bridges creating a place unlike any other.

And below, Chaos could see the surface of the water, no longer inky-black and glowing with a faint crimson light. No, it was perfectly clear now, and what's more, considerably less deep, the blood portion of it having dissolved into the ether. In fact, the water was so clear that he could see a good fifty feet or so below its surface. And what he saw was absolutely astonishing: a full other half of the city, with sky bridges and everything, extending downward as far as he could see.

"Beautiful, isn't it?" Destiny replied, stepping up to his side. He turned to smile at her. She looked utterly radiant in the sunlight, her golden hair glowing in it. He found himself struck with a sudden, mad urge to kiss her. Which he didn't, because he was a coward. And also because she had a strong tendency toward violence.

"Yeah," was all he could manage.

"Well done again Templeton!" Chaos heard King Pravus declare. He turned, seeing the pink-purple platemail-armored king standing triumphantly before the corpse of the giant's head. It occurred to him that the giant's head was almost certainly that of Harsgrof, the great giant who'd split a hill in half long ago. To think that the great giant had been defeated by the Fallen Sky, and then fused with Fallen, his hands used as weapons against them...

"Well done as well, my liege," Templeton replied cheerily. "Though I daresay that without Destiny and Chaos's help, we would never have won the day."

"Perhaps so," Pravus stated a bit grudgingly. Which was irritating, because it was clear to Chaos that he and Destiny had done the bulk of the work. "Thank you for helping us defeat this creature," Pravus added. "And thank you for helping to save my soul."

"Uh huh," Destiny replied.

"Sure," Chaos grumbled.

They all stood there for a moment, a bit awkwardly.

"Well then, shall we be off?" Templeton inquired.

"Indeed Templeton," Pravus declared authoritatively. "Kingdom to run and everything."

"They've been too long without us," Templeton noted.

"Quite," Pravus agreed. "Come, cousin!"

"A return on foot?" Templeton inquired. Pravus made a face.

"Gods no," he replied. "The adventure is done." Templeton broke out in a sly smile then.

"Fire dragon steed?"

"You read my mind, dearest Templeton!" Pravus replied. "Skylar!" he barked, crossing his arms over his massive chest. A moment later, there was a poof of choking smoke, and a bespeckled demon appeared.

"Yes?" the demon inquired.

"Summon the fire dragon," Pravus ordered. The demon just gazed at him. "Please," Pravus added, as if tearing the words from his throat.

"Already done," Skylar replied, bowing sarcastically. And then vanishing with another poof.

"I suppose this is goodbye then," Templeton told Destiny and Chaos. "Thank you again. You are truly heroes...and I would be honored to call you friends."

253

"Same here," Destiny replied, extending a hand. Templeton shook it, and then turned to Chaos, who couldn't help but smile at the cheery man.

"Friends," he agreed, shaking Templeton's hand.

* * *

After the fire dragon came to whisk King Pravus and Templeton away, Chaos and Destiny began the long journey to the ground floor of Old Langsroth. Which, now that the water level had receded a good two stories, was actually the third story of the city. In any case, they made it to the sky bridge leading to the wall, stepping over a truly massive number of bodies sprawled all over the place.

"Gonna start stinking real bad," Chaos noted, grimacing at the gruesome site as they neared the tunnel in the wall.

"It'll be better in a year," Destiny replied.

Chaos spotted one of the rocks he'd thrown earlier, and stepped over a group of dead bodies to retrieve it...which earned him a questioning look from Destiny.

"Memento," he explained. Which wasn't really an explanation, but she didn't push the matter. Probably because she didn't really care.

Back through the tunnel they went, and Chaos was surprised to find the current flowing in the opposite direction...toward the city rather than away from it. But with a moment's reflection, it was obvious why: with the city's water level having fallen below the level of the Great Flat, the Great Flat's water was pouring back into the city. Indeed, as they reached the propped-open portcullis, ducking underneath to exit the city, Chaos saw that the water level beyond was already significantly lower than before. Such that it barely covered the toes of his boots now. This of course revealed more bodies sprawled around the ruins of the town beyond the wall.

"Sure was a lot of zombies," Chaos noted.

"A whole city's worth," Destiny agreed. "Legend says that Old Langsroth was the largest and most advanced city in the world until it was cursed."

"Huh."

"I still wonder what it was all for," Destiny admitted. Chaos frowned.

"What do you mean?"

"Well, the necromancer wanted to get back at the Elders...the wizards who'd banished him from the city," she explained. "Cursing the entire city – millions of innocent people – seems...well, that's more than just revenge."

"Maybe he was just evil," Chaos replied. Destiny paused, then shook her head.

"No one is just evil," she countered. "People do things for a reason. He was hurt, so he lashed out at the people who hurt him." She paused. "I thought he'd cursed an Elder to make the Fallen Sky, but I guess he sacrificed himself."

"Huh," Chaos replied.

"But killing all those people – everyone in his hometown – well, there had to be another reason for it," Destiny continued. "I just can't figure out what it was."

"Have you asked Vita?"

"She doesn't know," Destiny said. "She's the goddess of life, not an all-knowing ultra-god."

"Oh."

They continued forward, splish-splashing as they went.

"Hey," Chaos blurted out. "Where's Gwendolyn?"

"Running free," Destiny answered. "Probably on dry land. I'll call her in a little bit."

"Oh."

They walked the rest of the way to dry land in silence, and by the time they'd reached the end of the Great Flat, the water level was barely puddle-deep. They stepped up onto dry land, and Destiny stopped, turning to face Chaos. Without speaking, which was weird.

"What?" he asked, feeling awkward.

"I know you wanted to kiss me back in the temple," she stated. Although to him, it definitely seemed like an accusation.

"No," he blurted out, terror gripping him. She folded her arms over her chest.

"Uh huh."

"I didn't," he insisted, which was a lie. But, having to pick between lying and never getting what he wanted, and telling the truth and risking a chance of being ashamed, he chose the former. Which was bad judgment, but also human nature, unfortunately. There was no end to the self-inflicted wounds one would endure to avoid humiliation, after all.

"Do it," Destiny ordered.

He blinked.

"What?"

"Kiss me," she commanded. "Now."

"Uh…"

He stood there, feeling quite terrified now. For, as should be quite obvious by now, kissing a girl was something he'd never done. Except his sister and his mother and Zora, which didn't count. Destiny rolled her eyes, lowering her arms to her sides.

"Fine," she grumbled. "I'll do it."

And with that, she did precisely as she'd threatened, stepping up to him and grabbing his head quite firmly, then planting a kiss. Like, right on the lips. But not at all firmly. Rather, she kissed him with surprising softness, and even gave a bit of tongue.

Which was…well, *fuck*.

She pulled away after a bit, giving him an approving look.

"Not bad," she told him. "First time?"

"Uh…"

"I'll take that as a yes," she replied. And then turned, continuing their walk. Chaos stood there dumbly, watching her go, while touching his lips with his fingers.

"Wo*wee*," he breathed.

"You coming?" she asked. Chaos blinked, then rushed to catch up with her, not knowing how to feel. His body felt all tingly, and light, as if he were walking on clouds. He found himself staring at her, still touching his lips.

"Why…uh?" he asked.

"I wanted to kiss you," she replied. "So I did. Because I'm not a coward."

Chaos blushed.

"Don't be scared of going after what you want," she advised. "Just remember to be polite."

"Okay," Chaos mumbled. While still staring at her, and definitely wanting to kiss her again. But not doing it, which of course was in direct opposition to what she'd advised. She glanced at him, then rolled her eyes again, stopping and yanking him up to her. Then came another kiss, which was amazing. Because as hard a person as Destiny was, when it came to kissing, she was anything but. On balance, however, any hardness she'd had was immediately transferred to Chaos, embarrassingly enough.

They separated, and Destiny continued walking as if nothing had happened.

"Why?" Chaos asked, walking beside her.

"Why what?"

"Why are you kissing me?" he clarified. She gave him a funny look.

"Because I want to?"

"Yeah, but...why do you want to?" he pressed. She gave him an even funnier look. A look as if she'd suddenly realized that, deep down inside, he was really, *really* stupid.

"Why did *you* want to?" she shot back. He blinked, then blushed. "Say it," she ordered.

"Because I...uh, thought you looked really...nice," he answered.

"And?"

"And it just came over me," he continued with a shrug.

"Right," she agreed. "There's your answer."

He frowned.

"You think I look nice?" he asked. Again, she gave him a look as if he was stupid. Which he was starting to think he might be.

"Duh."

Chaos considered this, feeling a bit stunned. For while he'd often marveled at the power that pretty girls had over him, he'd never once considered the possibility that *he* might have that power over someone else. It seemed ludicrous to him that anyone would be attracted to him, partially because he didn't have that power over himself. For perhaps the most common error of human nature was that each person assumed that everyone else thought like them. The second most common error was, of course, assuming that everyone else *should* think like oneself...with the third being trying to force them to.

Huh, he thought.

"So...does this mean we're ah, you know," he stammered.

"Say it."

"...going out?" he asked. "You know, like..."

"I'm not your girlfriend," she answered. Chaos blinked, then lowered his gaze.

"Oh."

"Is that what you want?" she asked.

"Um...no," he lied.

"Quit lying," she told him, shooting him a glare. "Just tell the truth."

He paused, then sighed.

"Yes, I want you to be my girlfriend," he confessed. "And I wanted to kiss you back there. And honestly, I want to do it again."

"Then do it," she replied, stopping and standing there. He stopped as well, eyeing her nervously.

"Like...now?"

"Now," she confirmed.

He paused, blushing furiously. And then stepped right up to her, blushing even more. He swallowed, then cleared his throat, and licked his lips. All while she stood there, waiting. At length, he leaned in, and by golly he *did* kiss her. On the *lips*. And to his delight, she kissed him right back instead of shoving him away.

So by gosh he *kept* kissing her, and she accepted this without complaint. Until he had to pull away for some air.

"Wo*wee*," he breathed, for the second time, staring at her with googly eyes.

"You're a good kisser," she told him.

"You too."

"Kinda got that," she quipped with a smirk. "No," she added, confusingly.

"What?"

"I'm not your girlfriend," she clarified. "Just your friend. For now."

"But...we kissed," he pointed out. Which to his mind meant they were going out. After all, every fairy tale he'd ever read had trained him to feel this way.

"So?"

"So...you like me, and I like you," he explained, feeling as if he shouldn't have to. Because it was obvious.

"And?"

"And we should go out," he concluded. Lamely.

"We'll see," she replied. "For now, we're friends having fun."

Chaos frowned, considering this. For again, he'd never imagined such a thing.

"Okay," he agreed, reluctantly.

Destiny stopped then, putting her fingers in her mouth and emitting a shrill whistle. One that carried across the land, echoing a bit before dying off. A moment later, Chaos spotted none other

258

than Gwendolyn far in the distance, breaking out into a gallop toward them. It didn't take long for the trusty mare to reach them, and Destiny mounted her, gesturing for Chaos to do the same. He did so with relative ease, in contrast to how difficult it'd proven the first time he'd tried it.

Then they were off, leaving Old Langsroth and the Great Flat far behind.

"So…what now?" Chaos asked.

"Hmm?"

"Well, you did what Vita wanted," he explained. "Old Langsroth is saved. So now what are you going to do?"

"I don't know," she admitted. "We'll see." She paused. "You?"

"Huh?"

"You completed Imperius's quest," she stated. "What now?"

"Honestly, I hadn't even thought that far ahead," he admitted.

"Me neither."

He paused, picking at his lower lip.

"So…have you ever been up north?" he asked.

"North of where?"

"You know, to the Kingdom of Pravus?"

She twisted in the saddle, giving him a look.

"I picked you up there, remember?"

"I mean, north of the Kingdom of Pravus," he corrected, blushing a bit. She continued looking at him.

"Are you offering to take me to Borrin, because you don't want to stop hanging out with me?" she accused. Which was awfully accurate. He paused.

"Yes," he confessed.

"Then ask me," she replied.

"Do you want to come with me to Borrin so we can keep hanging out?" he asked, feeling stupid doing so.

"Sure," she answered. Instantly. "That wasn't so bad, was it?"

"Actually no," he replied with a smile.

"Look, if you want us to work out, just speak your mind," she advised. "None of this beating around the bush crap."

"Okay," he replied. "I mean, I'll try."

"Keep practicing and you'll get better at it."

"Will do," he agreed. Then he frowned. "Wait, 'if we're going to work out?' I thought…"

"As friends," she interrupted rather quickly.

"Uh huh."

259

"Shut up," she grumbled, turning forward. And didn't say anything more. But Chaos couldn't help but smile.

"Thanks Destiny," he told her, feeling a burst of gratitude. "For everything."

"Thank you," she countered. "For helping me fulfill my destiny."

Chaos smiled again, struck by the strange twist of fate that had brought them to this moment. In searching for his destiny, he'd found his Destiny, and helped her fulfill her destiny. And now his Destiny was coming home with him, for whatever destiny now awaited him. A rather confusing string of events, which, considering his magic, was perfectly appropriate. Or rather, chaotically appropriate, as his magic had proven to be. Magic that, on reflection, had been working all along, just not in the way he'd expected it to. Which was again appropriate, considering his magic was to produce a surprise.

He wondered suddenly how much of his current situation he owed to his magic, and at the same time, knew that he'd never know for sure. His magic was anything but predictable or knowable, or it wouldn't be chaos. As such, he would have to make peace with whatever happened, and not try to think about it too hard. He was a wizard, and a powerful one at that. Not that it mattered to him so much anymore. His relationships mattered far more to him now. Not only with Dad and Mom and Fury – and Epic, he guessed – but also with Destiny…and most importantly, with himself. For he was on his way to becoming the kind of man he could be proud of.

If he did that – if he became a man he could be proud of – and did it consistently, then by golly, everything else would fall into place.

Chapter 45

After returning to Cumulus on the back of his fire dragon steed, King Pravus the Eighth found himself surprised at how happy he was to be home. For, having had quite the adventure, his lust for adventure was sated. As such, the relatively mundane life of a king seemed fine indeed.

So it was that, a few days after his and Templeton's return, Pravus found him back in the proverbial swing of things.

"What's next on the ol' docket, Desmond my man?" he inquired, eyeing his trusty old servant and part-time adviser.

"The envoy from Grissam," Desmond droned. Pravus made a face.

"I assumed they'd be gone by now," he grumbled. For as he recalled, Grissam had rudely sent a mere envoy to attend his celebration party. One that'd been postponed on account of Pravus's absence, to his dismay. He'd rather hoped it would've been canceled, but the Lords had refused, insisting that everyone suffer through it. For the people, naturally. Somehow.

"Apparently they were sent as a matter of utmost importance," Desmond explained. "That you dismissed."

"Destiny called, Desmond," Pravus chided, feeling snippy. "Should I have ignored the call of the great Imperius Fanning?"

"A meeting would have taken mere minutes," Desmond argued. Which was rude, considering that he was a mere servant, and Pravus was king.

"Go away Desmond," Pravus grumbled, waving his impudent servant away. Desmond was all-too-happy to comply. Or rather, less unhappy than he usually was. At length, the double doors to the throne room opened, admitting a woman, surprisingly enough. One who was barely five feet tall, but quite attractive, with bronze skin and long brown hair that contrasted nicely with her white shirt and pants. He supposed that she was the kind of woman that would turn men's heads, though not his, of course. For women did nothing to either of his heads. And never would.

She stopped a few yards from the throne, at the end of the royal red carpet, then curtsied, which was pleasant.

"Rise," he commanded. Which, being king, she did. "Your name?"

"Helena of Grissam," she answered. "Envoy to his Grace King Ernright the Third."

"Envoy?" he inquired. "I would've expected the ambassador…or King Ernright himself."

"They were…indisposed," Helena replied.

"Oh really." He paused. "My servant claims you've some disastrous news to give me."

"Unfortunately I do," Helena confirmed, her tone grave.

"Go on."

"A few months ago, we were alerted to some…unusual activity near the Dark Wood, a forest southwest of Tabula," she stated. "Reports of dark creatures coming out of the forest to steal chickens and dogs, and livestock and such."

"And?"

"At first the reports were few and far between," she continued. "But they became more and more frequent, until there were sightings every night…and reports of missing livestock, pets…and even people."

"Is there a point to this…?" Pravus snipped, feeling irritable after Desmond's accusatory exchange. Although his mood was far more likely due to his not having eaten yet. On occasion, he engaged in fasting, sometimes for half a day, and sometimes up to two days at a time. For, after extensive study, he'd determined that it might preserve one's health. With no risk of muscle loss, unless the fast extended past 72 hours.

"We sent search parties into the Dark Forest, and they never returned," she revealed, stubbornly refusing to start with the end. "So we sent larger search parties, and then soldiers."

"Let me guess…they never returned either?"

"Correct," Helena confirmed, her expression turning grim. "Our Lord Gaxon even led a small contingent of soldiers into the forest." She shook her head. "We haven't heard from him since."

Pravus leaned forward, curious despite himself. For there was nothing quite as mysterious as an unsolved mystery. Indeed, one of his favorite pastimes – other than going to the gym, of course – was to peruse the City Guard's roster of unsolved crimes…murders in particular. A pastime he shared with a rather surprising number of housewives in Cumulus, who met every Tuesday evening to discuss their findings.

"And?" he prompted, conveying interest rather than annoyance this time.

"The night after Lord Gaxon vanished into the Dark Forest..." she began...and then her voice broke. She swallowed visibly, her eyes growing moist, and lowered her gaze to the floor. And though Pravus was capable of immense heartlessness – a necessity to be king, or any other kind of upper management – such was her obvious dismay that he felt it tugging on his heartstrings. He did still have a soul, after all, thanks to Chaos and Destiny.

"Take your time," Pravus soothed. She nodded mutely, wiping away her tears. At length, she found the strength to lift her gaze to his. And to his dismay, her look was downright haunted.

"We call it The Dark Rising," she stated, her voice wavering a little. "The night after Gaxon's disappearance, the dead rose from their graves. In every cemetery near the Dark Forest. Even pets rose from shallow graves in their owners' backyards," she revealed. "They...came into the surrounding towns and cities, and..."

She shook her head, lowering her gaze again.

"I'm sorry," Pravus murmured. "And I apologize for being abrupt." Which was a rare admission, but in this case, appropriate. It was ever the case that the majority of issues brought before authority were petty, and would have easily been worked out by the parties involved, had either one of them had the maturity to do so. But give people government, and they inevitably outsourced the solutions to society's problems, expecting governmental Mommy and Daddy to fix everything without the people having to lift a metaphorical finger for themselves.

"I understand your annoyance," Helena stated, lifting her gaze. "Our people's problems are not your problems."

"Yet," Pravus corrected. "But I cannot stand idly by while your people suffer so," he added gallantly, feeling a rush of heroic resolve. "Please, finish your tale, but at your own pace."

"Yes your Highness," she murmured, bowing respectfully. "During The Dark Rising, many of Grissam's cities and towns fell to the undead hordes. And for every man and woman that died, another undead creature was added to their army. Entire towns evacuated, retreating to the nearest walled city, the city of Belfast," she continued. "A city that, every night since, has been under siege."

263

Pravus waited patiently, resting his chin on his fist.

"We fear that the undead will continue to multiply," she warned. "And sweep across Grissam, and might even reach our capitol in Tabula. If they do, it would only be a matter of time before they spread out, attacking neighboring countries."

"Including mine," Pravus noted. "This is disturbing indeed."

"Our ambassador would have preferred to attend your party," Helena stated apologetically. "But given the circumstances, we had to send representatives as quickly as possible to surrounding countries, to warn them of what was happening. Our ambassador went east, and I was sent north, to warn you."

"An act of courage I appreciate," he stated solemnly. He stood from his throne then. "I shall endeavor to help you Helena, and your people," he decided.

"But...how, your Highness?" she inquired. He put his hands on his waist, striking a perfectly heroic pose. The kind of pose that heroic people made, and at the same time, would make a man feel heroic, were he not otherwise inclined to feel that way.

"In the same way I saved..."

"*Helped* to save," Desmond corrected from the far left corner of the throne room. For while the man had gone away, as Pravus had ordered, he hadn't gone very far. Pravus grimaced.

"...the cursed city of Old Langsroth from the Fallen Sky," he declared. "With heroic resolve, and derring do, and such!"

"Wait, the curse of Old Langsroth has been lifted?" Helena gasped, clearly unable to believe it was true. Pravus eyed her with a steely, manly gaze.

"Indeed," he confirmed.

"It can't be," she breathed. Not in an argumentative sort of way, but in the spirit of hopeful doubt.

"Oh it is," Pravus confirmed. "Isn't it, Desmond?"

"So I've been told," Desmond droned. Which was true, because Pravus had been the one to tell him.

"So as you see, I have some experience in fighting the undead," Pravus concluded mightily.

"You'll truly help us?" she pressed, clearly daring to hope.

"By mine authority, the Kingdom of Pravus shall aid thee against the forces of evil!" Pravus declared resolutely. For in times of peak heroism, the use of the old tongue was only appropriate.

"Oh, thank you!" Helena blurted out. It was quite clear as she stood there that she desperately wanted to embrace him, so swept up in emotion was she. And, finding himself similarly swept on a wave of heroic resolve, he allowed it, opening his arms to her. Then, in a stunning breach of protocol, she ran to him, flinging herself at him and hugging him as tightly as she could. Which, on account of her poor muscular development, wasn't very tightly at all.

At length she pulled away, and Pravus held her at arms' length.

"I will send reinforcements to Grissam," he declared. "And bolster my kingdom's defenses to the south. Together, we will meet this new menace," he added. "And together, we will overcome."

Which was quite a nice sentiment, and would have been wonderful if fate had allowed it to happen. But as fate would have it, such a conclusion simply wasn't to be. For, in delaying his awareness of the threat posed by The Dark Rising – on account of blowing off Lord Ballister at the beginning of our tale, metaphorically, of course – King Pravus had set his kingdom on a collision course with tragedy. And while tragedy was a destination that wouldn't be reached in the immediate setting, it was only a matter of time before he met his doom.

Chapter 46

Having met his destiny by meeting Destiny, and having helped
her save the sorry souls of Old Langsroth – and King Pravus to
boot – Chaos found himself returning to his hometown of
Southwick feeling accomplished indeed. Such that, as he passed
through the massive silver double-doors of the Gate and into the
city, he felt like a completely different person than he'd been when
he'd gone through them roughly two weeks ago. He spotted the
guard who'd denied his passage and gave the man a curt nod,
earning a smile and a knowing nod in return. For the guard could
clearly sense the change in Chaos as well, and not just the change
in clothes.

He strode down the street toward the center of Southwick with
his head held high, his shoulders thrust back and his Omen-63
Tactical Shovel on his back...and beside him was none other than
Destiny. A fact that might've had something to do with the guard
showing respect. For there was nothing quite as deserving of
respect as a man who had the respect of a respectable woman.
Which Destiny very clearly was.

Chaos smiled at her as they walked, recalling the multiple
kissing sessions they'd enjoyed after having saved Old Langsroth.
A recollection that threatened to make it quite obvious what he
was thinking of. He suppressed said effects, shifting his
recollection to their time in Tabula, when they'd gone to the prison
to free his father. A trip that'd turned out to be in vain, for his
father had already escaped from prison somehow. After that,
they'd continued their journey at a leisurely pace, eventually
reaching the Gate.

"So this is where you grew up," Destiny mused, studying the
drab buildings and perfect grid of perpendicular streets. Everything
excessively orderly and secure, and not at all exciting, not in the
least.

"Yeah," he replied.

"Explains a lot," she stated, but not in an accusatory way, he knew now. She just said things as they were, without undue judgment. Which was quite rare, Chaos knew; only his mother seemed to do the same. Though Mom certainly loved to pretend to be judgmental, for the sake of initiating an argument.

"I'm better now," Chaos replied, still smiling. He'd learned from Destiny not to judge himself too harshly, though he still slipped up once and a while and got down on himself. But he'd also learned not to be too hard on himself about doing so, for inconsistency was perfectly human. Being consistent took practice, and it was practice he was more than willing to do. As long as it was on his own terms, of course, and not put upon him by those who claimed to have authority over him.

"Wanna see the shop?" Chaos asked. "It's the best place in town." Which was true, because it was the only magical place in town, save for the Gate they'd just come through. How appropriate that the best part about the Republic of Borrin was the way to get out of it.

"Sure," Destiny answered.

They made their way to the city center, marked by the large circle of grass that served as the city commons, with its rather battered statue of Archibald Merrick standing in the center. Chaos turned left toward the shop, eventually spotting its familiar sign:

And, despite his ill feelings for the shop over the last few years, Chaos found himself smiling at the sight of it.

"Come on," he urged, grabbing Destiny by the hand and speeding up a bit. To his surprise and delight, she didn't yank her hand away. Probably because, in this context, he was merely leading her instead of something more. But hey, he would take what he could get.

It wasn't long before they reached the front steps leading up to the door, and Chaos turned the knob, using his shoulder to pop the door open. It did so with a *dong*, and he was about to stride through when he remembered his manners and gestured for Destiny to go first.

"After you," he offered.

"Thanks," Destiny replied, striding through, Chaos following behind her.

"Pop-pop!" Mom cried from behind the counter, vaulting over it with remarkable athleticism, then rushing up to Chaos to give him a big hug. While picking him up in the process, despite the weight of his armor and his stuff.

"Rrrmmff," Chaos grunted, grimacing at the emasculating affection. But when he glanced at Destiny, she was smiling up at him rather than looking down at him.

"Brudder!" an adorable voice called out in glee, followed by a truly adorable girl rushing at him for a turn at getting a hug. It was Fury, naturally, and Chaos was all-too-happy to hug her. She gave him a squeeze so tight that he knew just how much she'd missed him. Which was, as it turned out, quite a lot. For Fury felt everything powerfully.

"Hey sis," he greeted, smiling from ear-to-ear.

"Who's this badass chick?" Mom asked, turning to Destiny. With an appreciative eye, Chaos noted. Destiny eyed Mom with similar appreciation. For though Chaos would never admit it, he knew damn well that Mom was the single most attractive woman alive. A fact that'd spurred on more than a few impromptu bath-time escapades. Which was a fact he would take to his frickin' grave.

"Mom, this is Destiny," Chaos introduced. "Destiny, this is Valtora, my mom, and my little sister Fury."

"Hi!" Fury blurted out, waving cheerfully. Destiny smiled.

"Hey," she greeted. She turned to Valtora. "You're gorgeous," she stated, for it was her habit to tell the truth.

"I know, right?" Mom replied, executing a perfect hair-toss. Time slowed, as it always did when she hair-tossed. As in, it actually slowed, for as a result of her magic of bedazzling, her hair had gained the power to alter time itself.

"Wow," Destiny breathed, having never seen it before.

"Wow," Chaos and Fury breathed, even though they'd seen it many times before. Because *damn*.

"So your name's Destiny, huh?" Mom asked. "That makes total sense."

"Really?" Chaos asked.

"Destiny," Mom recited. "Noun. The power or agency that determines the course of events."

"That's me," Destiny agreed.

"So…where's Dad?" Chaos asked. For he'd assumed Dad would be home, since he'd escaped prison in Tabula.

"He went to Addie's to uh…drop off some meat," Mom answered. Chaos frowned.

"I thought he *got* meat from Addie's store," he countered.

"Anyway, he'll be back soon," Mom promised.

Dong!

The door swung open behind them, but it wasn't Dad who entered the shop. It was a teenager a year older than Chaos, a tall, nerdy-looking boy named Dewey. One whose face – having been demolished by puberty – had seen far better days.

"Ehhh," Dewey blurted out, stopping in his tracks. For he clearly hadn't been expecting unexpected guests. His eyes locked on Destiny, performing an impromptu scan. And then stayed locked, to Chaos's dismay.

Destiny eyed Dewey, then stepped to the side, and Dewey's gaze tracked her.

"Hey," she called out, making Dewey blink. He recovered from his trance, glancing at Mom furtively, then rushing out the door with a rather awkward *dong*.

"Ooookay," Chaos said. "That wasn't weird at all."

"It wasn't," Destiny agreed. "He's just shy, like you were."

"*No*," Chaos retorted. Destiny didn't bother to reply, returning her gaze to Mom.

"So like, how'd you two meet 'n shit," Mom asked. Chaos grimaced, embarrassed by his mother's foul mouth. But Destiny hardly seemed to mind, to his relief.

"It was Chaos's destiny to meet me," Destiny answered. "I saved his life, taught him how to fight, and then he helped me defeat an undead city."

"Nice," Mom replied, eyeing Destiny approvingly. "I like her already," she told Chaos.

"I did stuff too," Chaos countered, blushing a bit. "I mean, by myself."

"You did," Destiny agreed. "Once you got your head out of your ass."

"He gets it from his father," Mom said. "Chauncy's far worse though. Every time he pulls his head out, he shoves it back in again." She paused. "Kind of like…"

"Anyway," Chaos interjected, blushing furiously. "I thought that Destiny could visit for a little while, and I could show her around."

"Sure, whatever," Mom replied.

"Problem is, uh, she doesn't exactly have a place to stay," Chaos added, blushing again.

"You wanna stay at our house?" Mom asked.

"Sure," Destiny answered.

"You'll have to sleep with Chaos," Mom stated, putting her hands on her hips. "We don't have any empty bedrooms."

"I was planning to," Destiny replied. To Chaos's horror. And she did it with a smirk, no less. Mom's eyebrows rose.

"You're…?"

"Not dating," Destiny answered before Chaos could think of a way to stop this train in its tracks. "Just sex. For now."

Chaos backed up a step, his breath catching in his throat. And if it were possible for a man to die of embarrassment, this would've been the time. To his dismay, he didn't die. Or even pass out, which he would've preferred.

"All *right*!" Mom exclaimed, clutching at her considerable bosom and hopping up and down.

"Sex!" Fury also exclaimed in a hopping sort of way, having absolutely no idea what it meant.

"You're…ah…happy?" Chaos blurted out incredulously, his cheeks on fire.

"Oh hell yeah," Mom replied. "You know what happens when a boy goes too long after puberty without *doing* it already."

"They start developing maladaptive sexual habits," Destiny replied.

"Wait, what?" Chaos asked.

"Like weird fantasies and compulsions 'n shit," Valtora agreed. "And the longer it goes on, the nastier and more specific the fantasies get."

"That's what Vita told me," Destiny confirmed. "And you'll be able to tell because they'll close their eyes during the act."

"So they can picture it in their heads," Valtora finished. "But they'll never be able to connect with who they're sexing while they're doing it."

"Yep," Destiny agreed. "Better to start early."

"Totally," Mom replied. "I sure as hell did."

This entire conversation occurred while Chaos stood there, trying his very best to disappear. Not only because his mother was talking to his not-girlfriend about sex, nor because she'd just lied about them having sex, which they most certainly had not. But because he'd already started employing said maladaptive habits. None of which he would ever, *ever* admit to, even at the threat of a painful death.

"You shouldn't wait either," Mom told Fury, turning to the little girl. Who just smiled adorably.

"I won't Mamma!" she promised, though she had no idea what she was agreeing to.

Just then, there was another *dong*, but this time it wasn't Dewey's. It was none other than Dad himself. He stopped short when he saw Chaos, and broke out into a smile.

"Son," he greeted.

"Dad," Chaos replied, unable to stop smiling himself. "Sorry about the whole 'leaving you in prison' thing."

"You did the right thing," Dad assured. "Did my magic help?"

Chaos blinked.

"Huh?"

"My magic," Dad repeated. "You know, that I gave to your shovel."

"Wait...you did that?" Chaos asked. "I thought it was just the Omen-63!"

"It is the top-of-the-line shovel," Dad conceded. "But it can't absorb and release earth. I mean, not without my magic."

Chaos slapped himself in the forehead. It was perfectly obvious now. Dad's magic was to make things absorb and release things...and that's exactly what his Omen-63 had done.

"How did I miss that?" he wondered, shaking his head.

"I figured if I couldn't be with you on your adventure, then I could at least help from afar," Dad stated. "I take it everything went okay?"

"We completed our mission," Destiny answered for Chaos.

"Let me guess...you're Destiny?" Dad asked.

"Yep."

271

"Nice to meet you," Dad stated, extending a hand to shake. Destiny gripped it. "Ooo-wow!" Dad blurted out, shaking out his hand. "You have a strong grip."

"She's a badass chick," Mom explained. Which was really all the explaining Dad needed. "And you're kinda weak," she added, adding insult to injury.

"How'd you get out of prison?" Chaos asked.

"I told a guard my wrist shackles were too tight," Dad replied. "He touched my magic hand, and…well, I let myself out."

"Magic hand?" Destiny inquired, arching an eyebrow at Chaos.

"He can switch bodies with people he touches with his left hand," Chaos explained.

"Interesting," Destiny murmured. "That could have many applications."

"*Oh* yeah," Mom replied, giving Destiny a significant look. One that was lost on Chaos, for which he assumed he should be grateful.

"Anyway, welcome and all that," Dad stated. "Feel free to look around, or have Chaos show you around the city."

"Right," Chaos replied, glancing at Destiny. "Shall we be off?"

"Where's your brother?" Destiny asked. Referring of course to Epic.

"Um…I dunno," Chaos answered.

"Me neither," Mom replied. "I just flew in from the Isle of Mundus a few hours ago."

"Huh," Chaos said. "Odd that he's not here."

"Everything about Epic is odd," Mom mused.

"Honey!" Dad protested.

"Pfft," Mom scoffed, crossing her arms under her bosom. "It's true and you know it."

"Not in front of the kids," Dad shot back.

"You think they don't know too?" she counter-shot. Chauncy glanced at Chaos, who smiled.

"He's good-weird," Fury declared, because everything was good according to her. Even the bad stuff.

"He's probably home with Zora," Mom guessed. "Why don't you meet him there?"

"Zora?" Destiny asked.

"Uh!" Chaos blurted out before Mom or Dad could reply. For it occurred to him – for the first time, like *right* now – that Destiny might not have a particularly positive reaction toward a zombie

272

living under their roof. Destiny turned to look at him questioningly. "Uh!" he repeated, because he really didn't know what else to say.

"Oh, she's Chauncy's mother-in-law," Mom explained. "Who I put in my old body, then murdered. I bedazzled her body so it couldn't rot, and then Chauncy turned her into a zombie using Zarzibar."

Destiny's eyebrows rose at this.

"Uh!" Chaos blurted out a third time.

"Zarzibar," Destiny stated, not as a question, but as a...well, a statement. As previously stated.

"Yeah," Mom confirmed. "He's a total badass lich. He keeps his spirit in Zora's crystal hand. He raised her from the dead, and Chauncy married her and had a baby with her, and that's how Epic was born."

Destiny stood there, staring at Mom with a suddenly stony expression.

"You're serious," she realized.

"I mean yeah," Mom replied blithely. "Why wouldn't I be?"

Destiny turned to face Chaos. Stonily.

"You failed to mention all of this," she noted, crossing her arms over her chest.

"Um," Chaos replied. "It kinda...uh...never came up?"

"Never came up," Destiny stated.

"...yeah," Chaos replied. Weakly.

"What's the problem?" Mom asked.

"Just that you've been harboring a zombie and the undying spirit of an evil necromancer in your house," Destiny replied. "And that you somehow had a child with the undead."

"Oh, Zarzibar's not evil," Dad countered, in the necromancer's defense. Destiny's eyebrows rose.

"Oh really," she replied.

"Really," Dad insisted.

"Actually, he's pretty bad," Mom piped in. "Evil as shit. Like *nasty* evil."

"But...uh...he treats us well," Dad stated in his defense. Which was really a quite weak defense, all things considered. But it was the truth, and it was unfortunately the only defense he had.

"So...Destiny is a paladin of Vita," Chaos announced, wringing his hands. "Her like, entire life is devoted to destroying the undead."

"Oh," Dad replied. Lamely.

"Riiiight," Mom said. "That makes total sense." She paused. "So this is awkward."

"Can you uh, make an exception?" Dad pleaded. Also lamely. "Just this one time?"

Destiny turned her stony gaze on each person present, except for Fury, of course. For the little girl was the only one who didn't deserve her fury, funnily enough.

"You have no clue, do you," Destiny declared.

"Um...about what?" Dad asked.

"Yeah, quit being all mysterious 'n shit," Mom complained. "Just tell us already."

"Yeah!" Fury exclaimed, in the spirit of joy. Inappropriately. Destiny faced them all, her hands on her hips.

"I've spent my entire life training to become strong enough to liberate Old Langsroth from the curse of the Fallen Sky," she proclaimed. "My whole purpose was to put an end to the curse placed on that city."

"And you did it, yay," Chaos interjected, instantly feeling as lame as his father after doing so.

"I did," Destiny agreed. "*We* did," she added, which was thoughtful. "And I thought that would be it."

"It is," Chaos insisted. Destiny gave him a look that told him he was dead wrong.

"Old Langsroth was cursed over two thousand years ago," she countered. "By a man who I thought was long dead."

"Right," Chaos replied. "That necromancer guy."

"And do you know what that necromancer guy's name was?" Destiny pressed.

"Um...no," Chaos admitted. "You never told me."

"Oh *fuck*," Mom blurted out.

"Crap," Dad swore, less explicitly.

"Crap!" Fury exclaimed excitedly.

"That's right," Destiny replied. "His name...was Zarzibar."

274

Chapter 47

Chauncy Little sighed as the last customer left the shop with a *dong*, locking the door and flipping the sign at the front window to "closed." Then he took the broom out of its closet, getting to work cleaning the floor. Or at least he started to.

"I can do it," Chaos offered.

"Oh," Chauncy replied, quite surprised. He handed his son the broom, and Chaos got to work cleaning the shop. Without complaining, which was something. And, he had to admit, doing a pretty darn good job. It was clear that, whatever Chaos had learned during his quest, it'd changed the boy for the better.

"My little *man*," Valtora gushed from behind the counter.

When Chaos was done, he put away the broom himself.

"Let's go home," he prompted. And promptly unlocked the door, opening it and gesturing for everyone to go through.

"Ooo," Valtora exclaimed, clearly impressed with this gentlemanly act. She went outside, stealing a kiss on Chaos's cheek in the process, and Fury was close behind. She kissed Chaos too, because she was Fury, and kissing and hugging and yay-ing formed the bulk of Fury's favorite activities. Dad followed behind, and Chaos closed up the shop, making sure to lock the door. Then he walked with his parents toward their home on the other side of Southwick center. Chauncy glanced at Chaos.

"You okay, son?"

"Yeah," Chaos answered. "Just...it's a lot."

"Tell me about it," Chauncy grumbled.

After revealing that the lich they'd been harboring was none other than the most hated necromancer in recorded history – a man who'd single-handedly cursed hundreds of thousands of people to suffer in undead agony (for millennia, no less) – Destiny had gone to the Little's home, everyone else in tow. All while Chaos had begged Destiny not to murder Zora, and Epic for that matter. Destiny had made no promises, but when she'd drawn near the house, her undead-sensing ability had made it clear that Zora wasn't there. And when they'd searched the house, they'd found that Epic wasn't there either.

Which was odd, because Epic never went anywhere by himself. At least not that Chauncy was aware of.

Oddly enough, Uncle Willard and Aunt Gretchen hadn't been home either, so perhaps they'd gone out for a day on the town. In any case, Destiny had retreated from the house, going into the woods behind it to sit down and pray to her goddess for advice. A process that she'd told Chaos would take hours, if not longer. So everyone had gone back to the shop, Chaos included. Chaos had of course insisted that Destiny not kill anyone until she discussed it with the family. To which she'd stared at Chaos as if he were an idiot, asking him if he thought she was stupid. He'd replied "no!" a bit too defensively for Chauncy's liking, and Destiny had saw fit to explain that no, she would not attempt to take on the most powerful lich in recorded history on her own, at least not without considerable preparation. Which, Chauncy had to admit, was admirable…and practical.

"She's something else, huh?" Chauncy told Valtora, grabbing her hand.

"The blonde chick?" Valtora guessed. Chauncy nodded. "Hell yeah," Valtora agreed. "Awesome as *fuck*." She smiled, ruffling Chaos's hair. "Good job pop-pop," she congratulated.

"Thanks Mom," Chaos replied.

"Was she, you know, good?" Valtora asked, waggling her eyebrows suggestively. Chaos blushed.

"*Mom*," he protested.

"Really don't want to know," Chauncy grumbled, to Chaos's obvious relief.

"Uh huh," Valtora shot back. "Sure you don't."

"Can we change the subject please?" Chaos begged.

"Fine," Valtora muttered. But she crossed her arms over her chest, glaring at Chaos. "You *will* tell me," she vowed. And Chauncy knew damn well that when Valtora vowed, she inevitably delivered. Chaos ignored her.

"I still don't think it's a great idea to have them sleep in the same room together," Chauncy said. Which was sort of changing the subject, but not really.

"Aww," Valtora replied, patting his cheek and giving him a cute pout. "No one cares what you think, honey."

Chauncy rolled his eyes at her.

"Piggy-back ride?" Fury interjected, giving Chauncy doe-eyes.

"Sure honey," Chauncy replied, picking her up. She threw her arms up into the air, then flapped them like a bird. "Zoom!" she exclaimed.

"Nice to see that some things never change," Chaos mused, eyeing his sister with a grin.

"And I hope she never does," Chauncy agreed.

"Keep dreaming," Valtora retorted. "I give her one more year before The Change."

"A year? No," Chauncy shot back. "That's way too young."

"Uh huh," Valtora replied. "We'll see about that."

"What's The Change?" Fury asked. Innocently.

"Valtora," Chauncy began, in an attempt to stop his wife from spilling the beans. An attempt that quickly failed.

"When you'll grow boobies and pit-hair and leg hair and start bleeding from your furry coochie," Valtora explained.

"Coochie!" Fury exclaimed happily, lowering her hands to point to said anatomy.

"Poopy-dooz!" Chauncy protested, blushing, then glaring at his wife. "We're in public!"

"And then your brain will go all crazy and you'll start hating me and wishing I was dead," Valtora continued cheerfully. "We'll like, fight all the time and I'll start hating you too, but I'll still love you anyways, just a lot less."

Fury frowned – actually frowned! – at this.

"Awww," she complained with a cute ol' pout.

"And I'll remember how you used to be, and wish you were like that, but it'll take like, *years* before you come back and admit how much of a goddamn shrewy bitch you were, and for things to back to somewhat normal," Valtora concluded. Also cheerfully, as if she was looking forward to said conflict. Which she probably was, considering how much she enjoyed a good verbal altercation. In fact, she was probably bursting at the seams at the thought of an argument lasting for years on-end; Chauncy had noticed that she'd been reading the dictionary even more frequently than usual, likely in preparation for this main event.

"There's something seriously wrong with you," he grumbled, to which Valtora only beamed a smile.

"Damn right," she agreed.

"So aren't any of you at all concerned about Destiny wanting to kill my mother-in-law?" Chaos blurted out incredulously.

"Nah," Valtora answered. "She tries it, I'll kill her before she can." She gave a swing of her diamond fist. "Hate to do it, but family comes first."

"Mom!"

"There's more fish in the sea," Valtora reassured him. Which clearly wasn't reassuring at all. "Handsome guy like you will be *drowning* in…"

"Okay!" Chauncy interjected, knowing her pension for rhyming. She *was* a wizard, after all. "Who wants Daddy horsey to gallop?"

"Me!" Fury answered gleefully.

Chauncy galloped forward down the sidewalk, as much to escape the conversation as to give Fury what she wanted.

"Weee!" Fury shouted.

At length Chauncy tired himself out, although at a much shorter length than he would've preferred, and he slowed to a walk, huffing and puffing. It wasn't long before Chaos and Valtora caught up with him, because again, he hadn't galloped very far.

"Daddy horsey can't gallop for shit," Valtora noted, shaking her head sadly. "Time for the glue factory."

Chaos laughed despite himself, and even Chauncy had to chuckle. Valtora cackled, because of course she did, while Fury laughed melodically. Not because she necessarily knew what was going on, the poor simple soul, but because she was happy that others were happy.

Which, while simple-minded, was a rather profound way to be.

It wasn't long before Chauncy spotted the Little residence ahead; there was, to his surprise, light coming from the windows. Which meant that someone was home.

"Uh oh," he warned. "This could be bad." For if Epic and Zora had come home, and met Destiny…

"Nah," Valtora replied. Chauncy frowned at her.

"How do you know?"

"No property damage," she explained, gesturing at the house. "No neighbors being nosy and looking out from their porches 'n shit." Which was, he had to admit, a darn good point.

"That's a good point," he admitted, because again, he had to.

They made it up to the front door, and found it unlocked. Chauncy glanced at Valtora, then took a deep breath in, lowering Fury to the porch. Then he twisted the knob, steeling himself for what was to come…and opened the door.

As it turned out, what was to come was the mouth-watering scent of delicious beef stew, made by none other than Destiny herself. For Chauncy found her standing at the kitchen stove, stirring a steaming pot of said supper.

"Oh," Chauncy mumbled, taken aback.

"Heya D," Valtora greeted, instantly giving Destiny a nickname. "Is that for us?"

"Yep," Destiny replied. "Come on in," she added. "No dead bodies here."

"Or undead?" Chaos asked.

"That too," Destiny confirmed.

"Oh come *in*," another voice insisted. One that Chauncy immediately recognized, for it was none other than Uncle Willard.

"Hey Uncle Willard," Chauncy greeted, finding the man seated at the table next to his long-suffering wife. "How'd it go?" he asked, for he'd just returned home, for the first time since his itty-bitty incarceration.

"Oh, you know," Willard replied, making a rather dismissive motion with one hand. Chauncy paused.

"No, I don't," he replied. "That's why I asked."

"Well, there were challenges," Willard confessed, transitioning to wringing his hands a bit. "Weren't there, dear?" he added, glancing at Gretchen. Who pointedly ignored the man, looking down at the tabletop with a thousand-yard stare.

"Like...?" Chauncy pressed.

"Oh, well, Fury did *just* fine," Willard replied. "Isn't she just a *darling*, honey?" he asked. But again, there was no reply.

"And Epic?" Chauncy pressed, sensing trouble.

"Hmm?" Willard replied, continuing to hand-wring.

"Epic," Chauncy repeated. "My son."

"What'd he do," Valtora interjected, crossing her arms over her chest.

"Oh, he was perfectly well behaved," Uncle Willard stated. "It's just, well..."

"Well what?" Valtora demanded.

"We're not quite sure where he's gone, are we darling," Willard answered, glancing nervously at his wife. Who remained in her zombie-like state.

"Wait, what?" Chauncy blurted out.

"Well, you see, he sort of stopped coming downstairs one day," Willard explained. "And we noticed that Zora didn't as well."

"When?" Chauncy pressed.

"Oh, I'd say what, a few days ago?" Willard asked, again shooting Gretchen a guilty glance.

"The morning after we came," she replied. Which, Chauncy realized, was the first time he'd ever heard her talk.

"Right," Uncle Willard mumbled, after which he refused to make eye contact with anyone.

"What the hell?" Valtora stated, putting her hands on her hips. "Did you notify the City Guard?"

"Oh yes," Willard replied. "They searched the whole city." He swallowed visibly. "They seemed quite motivated," he added. "On account of Valtora's, ah, history with them." Which was to say, she'd straight-out murdered one of the guards after being sort-of falsely accused of a crime.

"Well damn," Valtora grumbled. "Where the hell did they go?"

"They searched the surrounding towns as well," Uncle Willard revealed. He shook his head dejectedly.

"Well, Epic had to leave for a reason," Chauncy...well, reasoned. "He's a very logical child."

"That's for sure," Valtora agreed. "Frickin' weird-ass kid."

"Honey!" Chauncy protested.

"It's true," Valtora insisted. "How long have you known him?"

"Uh, for as long as he's been alive?" Chauncy replied.

"And how *well* do you know him?" she pressed. Chauncy paused, then lowered his gaze.

"Not at all," he admitted. But to be fair, no one did.

"Right," Valtora concluded, crossing her arms under her bosom triumphantly. Which was a win for both of them, really.

"We'd better start looking for him," Chauncy stated wearily, though the awful truth was that he really didn't feel like doing so. It'd been a long few days, after all.

"On it," Valtora replied. Her Inkling doppelganger peeled off of her back, then left the house, flying outside.

"I'll get my staff," Chauncy grumbled. But Valtora stopped him with an outstretched hand.

"Relax," she told him.

"My son is missing!" Chauncy protested. "And my w...friend!" he added, glancing at Willard nervously.

"The whole frickin' City Guard couldn't find him," Valtora pointed out. "After looking for days. You really think you'll do better? Getting real dark out, Chauncy."

Chauncy grimaced, then lowered his gaze.

"Besides," she continued, sensing weakness. Which to be fair, at least in Chauncy, was in abundant supply. "If Epic wanted to be found, he would've been found by now. Which means he's either dead, or he ran away from home. Because he *wanted* to."

Which was also a good point, Chauncy had to admit, but didn't, at least out loud.

"Now our guest spent all this time making stew for us," Valtora stated. "It would be rude not to stay and enjoy it."

So that's exactly what they did.

* * *

"Ohmygod," Valtora gushed, pushing her chair back from the table a bit and patting her belly. Which wasn't anywhere near big enough to justifying needing the extra space.

"I know, right?" Chauncy agreed, stuffing the last spoonful of his beef stew into his mouth, savoring the delicious taste and smell. Even the mouth-feel was perfect, not too mushy and not too firm. Just delightful, really. Easily the best meal he'd ever had…and he'd eaten at the court of King Pravus.

"It's amazing," Chaos declared, inclining his head at Destiny, who'd already polished her bowl off. "Thanks Destiny."

"You're welcome," Destiny replied. "I cook, you clean," she added, eyeing Chaos.

"Yes ma'am," Chaos stated, standing up and gathering everyone's bowls and spoons and such. Chauncy glanced at Valtora, smiling and shaking his head.

"I know, right?" she mouthed.

Chauncy chuckled, marveling as Chaos cleaned the dishes with nary a nasty word spoken or an evil eye given. And he did a damn good job, too, taking his sweet time. It was clear that he was focused on getting the actual job done – and done well – instead of going through the motions to just get it over with already. He was growing up, and far sooner than Chauncy had, he had to admit. Of course, Grandma Little had mothered him a bit too much growing up, in as grand a fashion as she could.

He could hardly blame her for her actions, as harmful as they'd been in the end. After his mother's apparent death and his father's disappearance, it'd been natural for Grandma to baby him. To protect him from the evils of the world, having experienced what she felt was quite enough already. But in protecting him from danger, she'd prevented him from having the opportunity to learn from it. And thus his development had been stunted...permanently, in some ways, though he was loathe to admit it.

And now, watching his son, Chauncy realized he'd nearly done the same to the boy, crafting a life so orderly and predictable – and thus secure – that Chaos had grown to hate it.

Imperius had been right, Chauncy realized. And, in allowing – at least eventually – his son to go on the adventure that he himself had been denied for so long, perhaps Chauncy had stopped the cycle of overprotection once and for all. For it was less likely that Chaos, having been allowed the opportunity to seek adventure as a boy, would force his children to suffer too great a dose of safety and security.

The cycle that Grandma Little had begun – or at least perpetuated – would end at last. But in Grandma's defense, the cycle of loving and caring, the focus on family, and safety and security she'd offered – in more appropriate proportions – would continue. Thus, what was good would remain, and what was not would die away.

Hopefully.

"*Well* then," Uncle Willard declared, pushing his chair back, then standing up. "I suppose we should be off, eh darling?"

His wife stood as well, pointedly not answering.

"So soon?" Chauncy asked, standing as well. Though to be honest, he was more than glad to see them going. One couldn't choose their family, so they said. But one *could* choose the dose. And when it came to Uncle Willard, a little went a long way.

"Get the fuck out," Valtora replied. With a big, cheerful grin that said she really didn't mean it in a mean way. But Chauncy knew that she meant it, otherwise she wouldn't have said it.

"Oh, aren't you *sassy*," Uncle Willard replied. "Isn't she *sassy* honey?" To no reply, of course.

"What do we owe you?" Chauncy inquired. Willard gave him a look as if hurt.

"You're family, Chauncy-boy," he replied.

"Still, you came all this way," Chauncy pressed. And left out the fact that he'd technically lost a child whilst babysitting.

"Well…we have been having a bit of a rough time, haven't we dear?" Willard confessed, giving her a guilty look. "Our floral shop…"

"*Your* floral shop," Gretchen interjected, to Chauncy's surprise.

"…went under," Willard continued, as if she hadn't even spoken. "No more peddling petals, I'm afraid," he joked. He made a pouty-face. "We lost the house."

"Oh no!" Chauncy exclaimed. "I'll get the checkbook."

"Oh, you don't have to…" Uncle Willard began, but his wife elbowed him in the ribs. Like really *really* hard. Willard made a sound then, one akin punting a chicken.

"I insist," Chauncy declared valiantly. He grabbed his checkbook, then wrote out an impressive sum. One which was a small fraction of his considerable fortune, but would still bring considerable fortune back into Willard's life. "That should be enough for a new house," he ventured, handing the check over.

Willard glanced at it, then stared, his eyes and mouth gaping open.

"Oh *my*," he breathed. Then he shook his head. "This is too much," he protested, while not making any attempt at handing the check over. In fact, he pressed it against his chest. "Usually that's what *you* say, isn't it darling?" he joked, nudging his wife. Who said nothing in response.

"Nonsense," Chauncy declared. "Happy to help."

"Well then," Uncle Willard stated, folding the check up. "I better put this somewhere my wife will never find it." And promptly stuffed it in inside the front of his pants. And not in a pocket, Chauncy noted with dismay.

"Okay bye," Valtora prompted, clearly done with it all.

"Toodles fam!" Uncle Willard said, blowing them kisses. And with that, the odd couple left, closing the door behind them.

"About time," Valtora grumbled.

"Be nice," Chauncy replied. Then he smiled. "But I agree."

At length, Chaos finished the dishes, then bade everyone goodnight. And to Chauncy's dismay, Destiny did the same, following his boy upstairs. Chauncy was suddenly struck with the overwhelming, paternalistic urge to intervene, and very well would have, if it hadn't been for Valtora's hand touching his shoulder.

"Let it be," she whispered.

He grimaced, then took a deep breath in, letting it out.

Let it be.

The operative word, of course, was *let*. An act of surrender, in a way. Of allowing things to work themselves out without attempting to interfere, or to force an outcome of some kind. It was very likely the hardest thing for a parent to do, Chauncy suspected. For not only did it mean allowing for the chance that something bad might happen, but it meant letting go of being a parent, if only a little bit.

And that, he knew, was a role he wasn't ready to give up. Not just yet, anyway.

A little bit at a time, he told himself, relaxing back into his chair. It was, in a way, like saying goodbye to his child. Bit by bit, piece by piece. An agonizingly long goodbye. And in the end, the child would be gone forever…and only an adult would remain.

The thought immediately depressed him, and he sighed, then stood, stretching his arms over his head.

"Ready for bed?" Valtora asked.

"Ready as I'll ever be," he replied.

"Well they'd better be quiet," Valtora stated, standing from her chair as well. "Otherwise we're not getting any sleep 'til they're done."

"*Really* don't want to think about it."

"Come on Chauncy-poo," Valtora prompted, grabbing his hand and leading him down the hallway toward the foyer, and the stairs. "If they're loud, we'll make it a competition."

"Poopy-dooz!" Chauncy complained.

"I hope to hell they're loud," Tip quipped, rising a bit at the thought.

"Shut up Tip," Chauncy grumbled, following Valtora upstairs.

His quip to Tip reminded him suddenly of Nettie and Harry, who he hadn't seen in quite a while. Which was odd, because they'd showed up for every other adventure in the last fifteen-odd years. He suddenly missed them terribly, and hoped he'd get to see them soon.

"Come on baby," Valtora cooed, coaxing him up the stairs. He followed her up, then went into their bedroom, unable to help keeping an ear out for Chaos and Destiny. But he heard nothing, to his relief. "Come to bed," Valtora growled, eyeing him hungrily. Whilst hardly giving him a choice in the matter, as she was pulling him quite forcefully onto the bed with her.

"Wait," he blurted out. "What about Fury?"

"Ugh," Valtora groaned, slapping her own forehead. "Totally forgot."

"I'll put her to bed," Chauncy said.

"Make it quick," Valtora urged. "Mama's feeling *frisky*."

"Reowr," Chauncy replied, even making as if to claw the air like a kitty-cat. Which was really *really* unsexy, at least traditionally. But to Valtora, it was just what she wanted.

"Hubba hubba," she replied. Also unsexily. But since she was immensely attractive, even saying unattractive things was immensely sexy. Less attractive people had it far harder, having to work for what attractive people took for granted.

Chauncy grinned, getting out of bed and going to Fury's room, which was the former guest room of the house. Sure enough, his sweet little girl was already lying in bed, waiting for him.

"Aww," he gushed, struck as always by just how frickin' adorable Fury was. Just the sweetest, kindest, most lovable human being ever.

"Daddy!" she exclaimed, thrusting her arms up for a hug. Which of course he couldn't help but give. She held him tightly enough that he knew beyond a shadow of a doubt that she loved him. A whole, frickin' lot. It was enough to bring tears to his eyes, so heartfelt was her embrace. At length, she let go, smiling angelically up at him.

"Goodnight Daddy," she murmured. He smiled back, running a hand through her brown, wavy hair and gazing into her adorable purple eyes.

"Goodnight Fury," he replied.

He went to stand up, but she grabbed his hand.

"Wait," she blurted out.

"What is it?"

"Do you think…" she began, then stopping, letting go of him to wring her hands.

"You can say it," he urged gently.

"Well, since Chaos went on an adventure, do you think…I could go on one too?" she asked hopefully. Chauncy did his darndest not to grimace, forcing himself to smile a fatherly smile.

"Sure honey," he replied. "When you're older."

Which in his mind, of course, was fifty. Not that she needed to know that.

"Yay!" she exclaimed, delighted with this response. Chauncy did stand then, blowing a kiss.

"Goodnight," he murmured.

"Night night," she replied, pulling up her blanket to cover everything but her face.

And that was that.

But if Chauncy had only known what fate had in store for his sweet daughter, he would've locked her inside her room and thrown away the key. For his adorable, sweet, simply wonderful daughter would – in a few short years – have a date with destiny. One that would change her, and the world, forever.

Now, dear reader, you may be wondering at something foreshadowed at the beginning of this tale. A certain promise that, having violated Imperius's order to not delay Chaos's quest, that someone he loved dearly would die. Something which, you might notice, has not happened. And this should naturally make you question the author of this tale, in light of dashed expectations.

But fear not, or rather, *do* fear, for while this tale is near its end, another will soon be told. And soon it will become all-too-clear what tragedy lies in store for our beloved Little family, and that what has been prophesized will most certainly occur.

Chapter 48

Chaos rested on his back in his bed, Destiny lying beside him. In her bedtime clothes, which of course she'd packed in her pack. Because Destiny thought of everything, and was thus prepared for anything. He was similarly dressed, but despite this, her presence nearby was still mildly terrifying. He could feel her warmth, and knew that her body was like, *right* there.

"Thanks again for making dinner," he offered. "And not murdering my family."

"Who says?" she shot back. He blinked.

"Huh?"

"I put poison in the stew," she explained, smiling inappropriately at this revelation. "Took a lot to hide the bitterness, but it worked."

He froze.

"Wait, *what?*" he blurted out.

"That's for lying to me about Zarzibar and Zora," she stated, her eyes turning hard. "Now your entire family is going to die."

Chaos stared at her in horror, feeling suddenly, enormously nauseous.

"Oh god!" he blurted out, making to leap out of bed and go to the bathroom to throw up. Destiny barred his way by putting a leg over his lap, pinning him in place.

"Kidding," she told him.

"What?"

"I'm kidding," she repeated. He hesitated, then relaxed.

"Really?"

"I ate the stew," she pointed out. "And I had seconds."

"Oh," he mumbled, relief coursing through him. He glared at her. "You suck at making jokes."

"That's not all," she shot back with a smirk. He blinked.

"Huh?"

"You wanna know what's better than my beef stew?" she asked.

"Um...kinda, yeah," he replied. And, getting the thrust of her conversation, he felt himself starting to rise. Which was terrifying, because despite Destiny's assertion that they'd...you know, *done* it...they actually hadn't. Not even close. To his horror, she definitely noticed his, uh, elevated mood, for unlike his father's, it was impossible to hide.

"Well that's a relief," she murmured.

"Huh?"

"Never mind," she replied.

"Hey, uh..."

"Yes?" she asked.

"Thanks for not killing my brother and my stepmother," Chaos told her.

"Yet," she corrected.

"Um...?"

"I'm sorry Chaos, but I *am* going to have to kill Zarzibar," she informed him. "And probably Zora."

"But..."

"Zombies suffer," she interjected. "They're soulless beings, forced to exist without...without really being wholly *them*." She sighed, putting a hand on his chest. While still having her leg draped over his legs, to his delight and terror. "Killing Zora would be a kindness, believe me."

"I don't know," he mumbled. "I mean, if you *knew* Zora..." He paused. "She's not like the other zombies we met."

"You're attached to her because you grew up with her," she argued gently.

"No, she really isn't," he insisted. "She's different. If you just spend some time with her, you'll see."

She didn't reply.

"Promise me you'll at least spend some time with her before making your decision," he pleaded. "She's never hurt anyone, I swear."

Destiny paused, then nodded.

"Okay," she replied. "I promise."

"Thanks," he murmured.

"And thanks for...you know, everything else you've done for me."

"Like save your life and train you and clothe you and give you lots of money that you blew on an Omen-63?" she asked.

"Um...yes," he answered, blushing a bit.

288

"Kidding," she reassured him. "You have good taste. The Omen-63 really is the best. Limited edition too," she added. "Probably got the last one in Grissam."

"That explains the cost," he mused. "In my defense," I didn't realize that the exchange rate was so…"

"It's fine," she interrupted. "I've got more money than I need, and I can always make more."

"I guess my family does too," Chaos admitted. All thanks to an old lady he'd never gotten to meet, since she'd died shortly after he'd been born. A kind old woman named Mrs. Thimblethorp, rest her incredibly loaded soul.

"Then we don't have to think about money," she concluded. "We can focus on what really matters."

"Like what?"

"Like things that are real…and alive," she answered, leaning in and kissing his cheek. "Like us."

Chaos swallowed in a suddenly dry throat, his heart thumping rapidly in his chest. Which Destiny most assuredly noticed, considering her hand on his breastbone. "Relax," she told him. "We're just going to make out."

"We…are?" he blurted out. He found himself rising to the occasion once again, this time far quicker, and more definitively.

"That's one vote 'yes,'" Destiny quipped with a smirk. She crawled on top of him then, leaning in and kissing him. On. The. Lips.

"Mmm," he murmured, freezing…and then promptly melting into it. She pulled away then, giving him a stern look.

"We're just making out, okay?" she told him. "Nothing more."

"Uh huh," he mumbled, feeling dazed.

"And we're not dating," she continued. "We're friends having fun."

"Yup," he replied. Which, at least in *his* heart, he knew was a damn lie.

"You can't *just* be friends with me, can you," she accused. Which was almost certainly true. But considering answering in the affirmative would jeopardize the making out session that was to come, Chaos decided to stay mum. She sighed. "Damn it, I was *really* hoping to just make out."

"You can," he insisted.

"And then what, break your heart?" she pressed.

"I mean, maybe," he answered. "But I'm willing to risk it."

She paused, eyeing him for a long moment. Then she sighed again.

"You look like a bad boy, but you really *really* aren't," she grumbled. He frowned.

"What?"

"You really have no idea how attractive you are, do you," she stated. He blinked.

"What?"

"Your parents really did shelter you," she mused, shaking her head. Then she eyed him critically. "Did your mother ever bedazzle you?"

"Huh? No," he replied. "I mean, I don't think so," he added. Because to be honest, he hadn't a clue.

"Doesn't matter," she decided. "You're pretty to look at."

"I'm not..."

"Shut up and kiss me," she interrupted. And then promptly forced the issue. He kissed her back, feeling all sorts of new and amazing "wowee" and "golly" and downright zingy sensations.

"Wowee," he breathed when the kiss was done. She rolled her eyes, but didn't seem *too* offended.

"You're totally falling for me, aren't you," she accused.

"Sorry?"

"Eh, worth it," she replied. And promptly continued their truly spectacular kissing session.

What happened next, dear reader, is none of your damn business. And as such, we'll have to close the door on this particular bedroom and leave Chaos alone with his Destiny. But suffice it to say, Chaos received more than adequate reward for helping his not-girlfriend save Old Langsroth. Without engaging in any age-inappropriate activities, of course. Mostly.

So it is, dear reader, that we find ourselves nearing the end of this particular tale. A tale quite different from the ones that'd come before. For as it turned out, Chaos had used his magic on several occasions throughout his quest, and while at the time it'd seemed to do nothing, his magic had most certainly changed the course of his adventure.

But as it turned out, while Chaos had spent most of his life prior to this point convinced he was destined to become a great and powerful wizard – with great and powerful magic – his ability to generate surprises only seemed less useful to him now. It was, rather, the power of discipline and ritual that enthralled him. For without this, surprises could hardly be appreciated for what they were: breaks from the usual routine, a zig when life had zagged many times before.

Still, his magic did have its place, as he'd demonstrated during the final battle with Fallen, in that it had forced a terrible fate from its tracks. Perhaps its function was to allow a life where the past didn't lock in the future. A life of possibilities instead of traps.

In any case, just as dessert was best served after a far less sweet meal, and eaten in small portions that made one crave for more, chaos was most powerful when it was occasional. This was the lesson of the Chaos Ring, which prevented order and chaos from overpowering each other. Thus, to become a great and powerful wizard of chaos, Chaos Little had to use a little chaos rather than a lot.

For as you know by now, dear reader, Little's do a lot...though they're often forced to do it with what little they've got.

Epilogue

Imperius Fanning stood at the edge of the Isle of Mundus, gazing at the massive, oceanic waterfall ahead of him. Levitating above a magical canyon formed in the middle of the ocean, the Isle of Mundus was a marvel of wizardly engineering, created countless millennia ago as the impenetrable home of the Order of Mundus. A fact that Imperius was well aware of, having borne witness to its construction.

He sighed, focusing inward though his gaze was outward, concentrating on his gut.

It was quiet, at least for now, but he knew very well that its peace would not last for long. The world was a massive and complex place, and danger was always rearing its head, in one form or another. This last episode – with Chaos Little, Destiny, and King Pravus and Templeton – had been only the latest in a string of crises so long that Imperius could scarcely remember some of them.

Imperius took a deep breath in, then let it out slowly, feeling some sort of way.

He sensed a presence then, of something that was a part of him, but apart from him. He turned to the left, seeing a shadow there…one that rose from the ground beside him to form a man. An older man in a black turtleneck, he was tall and slender, with thick, curly black hair and an impressive mustache and curly black beard. His skin was pale, and translucent, evidence of him not being all there. Not yet, anyway.

"The Dark One," Imperius greeted.

"Something wrong?" The Dark One inquired. Imperius paused, considering the question.

"I'm tired," Imperius confessed.

"You've been at this a long time," The Dark One pointed out. "When is the last time you took a sabbatical?"

"A century, give or take," Imperius answered.

"Too long," The Dark One opined. Imperius sighed, gazing at the waterfall that formed the wall of the oceanic canyon again.

"Danger is accelerating," he stated. "Both in frequency and magnitude."

"I'm aware," The Dark One replied with a smirk. Imperius smirked back.

"And how was your sabbatical?" he inquired. For, after being de-personalized by Chauncy Little, The Dark One had requested a vacation. One he'd taken up until now, it appeared, though Imperius's gut suspected the man had ended said vacation a couple of years ago, in secret.

"Refreshing," The Dark One answered. "I've more energy than I've had in centuries...and more focus, now that I no longer obsess over that woman."

And by that woman, The Dark One meant Valtora, whose personality had been so utterly magical that The Dark One had found himself uncharacteristically smitten. So much so that he'd allowed her to become the interim The Dark One, and had planned on having a child with her.

"You having focus doesn't exactly bode well for the world," Imperius noted, eyeing The Dark One warily. Indeed, he felt a stirring of his gut at the statement, an indication that his words were true. Which meant that the world was going to suffer The Dark One's return, though in what way, Imperius wasn't quite sure.

"I am a necessity," The Dark One countered.

"Indeed," Imperius agreed. "As are Chosen Ones to defeat you."

"As you say," The Dark One replied. "And so the dance continues."

They both stood there next to each other, gazing off at the waterfall. A cool breeze whipped through Imperius's blue cloak, giving him a chill. He felt another twinge from his gut, followed by a sudden sense of overwhelming dread. One so powerful that he suddenly had the urge to throw up.

"Something wrong?" The Dark One inquired, arching an eyebrow at Imperius. Imperius turned to the man, fixing the personification of evil with a glare.

"What have you got planned now?" he demanded. The Dark One raised his eyebrows in mock shock.

"Me?" he asked, far too innocently.

293

Imperius didn't deign to reply.

"Let's just say I find myself...filled with vim and vigor after my rest," The Dark One answered. "Having been depersonalized gave me plenty of time to think...and to ponder things from many perspectives."

"This is more than your usual antics," Imperius grumbled, his gut flip-flopping sickeningly. He grimaced, holding back a wave of bitter bile that welled up in the back of his throat. One that was even more bitter to swallow. "I would think twice of exceeding the boundaries we placed on you," he warned.

"Oh, don't worry," The Dark One replied with a too-sweet smile. "I have no intention of having to do such a thing."

"Then what are you up to?" Imperius pressed, knowing full well he wouldn't get a straight reply. The Dark One paused, as if considering his words carefully.

"I'm merely giving a little...push to something that's already well under way," he answered at last. "Nothing more, nothing less." He smiled then, putting a cold hand on Imperius's shoulder. One that sent another chill through him. "You really should take a sabbatical yourself," he advised. "You won't believe how refreshing it can be."

And with that, The Dark One sank back into the ground, a shadow once again. One that vanished as if banished by the sun casting its rays over the Isle of Mundus.

But as Imperius stood there, alone once again, the sun's rays could not seem to warm him, and his gut refused to quiet down entirely. He gripped his staff, its wood slick in his sweaty hand.

He lowered his gaze to his feet, feeling troubled indeed. And not only because his gut hadn't been this uneasy for centuries. For it'd also not escaped him that, during their entire exchange, he hadn't rhymed a single time...and rhyming was what wizards did. When they were feeling their magic the most, that was.

Something's wrong, he knew. Something terrible was going to happen...and it was going to happen soon. Perhaps not today, nor tomorrow, nor even in the next couple of years. But a day would surely come when the danger his stomach had prophesized would arrive.

And he hoped beyond hope that when it did, the forces of good – relatively speaking – would be ready for it.

www.ingramcontent.com/pod-product-compliance
Lightning Source LLC
Chambersburg PA
CBHW020254200626
46816CB00001BA/282